Anne Melville, daughter of the author and lecturer Bernard Newman, was born and brought up in Harrow, Middlesex. She read Modern History at Oxford as a scholar of St Hugh's College, and after graduating she taught and travelled in the Middle East. On returning to England, she edited a children's magazine for a few years, but now devotes all her working time to writing. She and her husband live in Oxford.

By the same author

The Lorimer Line
The Lorimer Legacy
Lorimers in Love
Last of the Lorimers
Lorimer Loyalties

ANNE MELVILLE

Lorimers at War

GRAFTON BOOKS

A Division of the Collins Publishing Group

LONDON GLASGOW
TORONTO SYDNEY AUCKLAND

Grafton Books
A Division of the Collins Publishing Group
8 Grafton Street, London W1X 3LA

Published by Grafton Books 1986

First published in Great Britain by
William Heinemann Ltd 1980

Copyright © Margaret Potter 1980

ISBN 0-586-06610-1

Printed and bound in Great Britain by
Collins, Glasgow

Set in Times

To the memory of my father
Bernard Newman

Contents

THE LORIMER LINE

Brinsley
William
John

Matthew — Samuel — Alexander

Rascal Mattison

Red

Luisa Reni (1852–86)

John Junius (1800–79) m. Georgiana Wells (1829–78)

William (1850–1909) m. Sophie Garratt (1853–1913)

Margaret (1857–) m. Charles Scott (1853–94)

Claudine (1859–)

Chelsea (1870–)

Ralph (1860–) m. Lydia Morton (1859–)

Aleza (1877–) m. Piers Glanville (1857–)

Frank Davidson (1886–1906)

Matthew (1873–)

Beatrice (1877–)

Arthur (1878–)

Robert (1894–)

Jean-Claude (1878–)

Marie (1908–)

Duke (1886–)

Harley (1913–)

Kate (1891–)

Brinsley (1893–)

Mary (1895–1902)

Alexander (1897–1902)

Grant (1905–)

Frisca (1907–)

Lucy (b&d 1911)

Pirry (1913–)

PART ONE
War

1914

1

The darkness of war had spread across Europe, but at Blaize, Lord Glanville's country house on the bank of the Thames, the chandeliers glittered as brightly as though the world for which they had been made could expect to endure for ever. Yet the ballroom they illuminated on this October evening was empty, and no sound disturbed the silence of the old house. It was the moment within the eye of a cyclone when the rushing wind suddenly holds its breath in an unnatural calm. The storm was just about to break.

For three days Kate Lorimer had looked on with admiration as the household bustled with activity, in preparation for the ball which would celebrate her brother Brinsley's twenty-first birthday at the home of their aunt and uncle, Lord and Lady Glanville. The idea that dancing and dining and drinking and flirting were unsuitable activities for a country at war was not one which was likely to occur to either the hosts or the guests tonight. England was fighting to preserve the values of a civilized society against the clumsy aggressions of a decaying Austrian empire, and a brash new German army and navy. Already young men were dying on the battlefields of France. It was necessary that gestures should be made, gestures of gaiety and defiance, to show that a way of life could not so easily be killed.

Amidst all the preparations of the past few days, only one small concession had been made to the fact that England was at war. The fragile silk curtains, intended to drape decoratively at the sides of the ballroom windows rather than to cover them, had been stored away. Their replacements were made of a heavier fabric which would prevent any light from being seen outside. It was unlikely that a Zeppelin would waste its explosive load on an isolated country house when the whole city of London, further down the Thames, offered so much more tempting a target. But it seemed sensible to remove even the slightest cause for unease.

Not until midnight would the party supper be served to the guests, so the members of the family who were staying at Blaize had assembled for a light meal earlier in the evening. Most of them now had retired to their rooms for a brief rest or last-minute adjustment of hair or gown. Kate was alone as, dressed for the ball, she wandered through the suddenly silent house. The heavy doors of the banqueting hall were closed. With the secret pleasure of a child opening her Christmas stocking too early, she let herself into the hall so that she could inspect the tables set for the buffet.

The sumptuous display represented the culmination of a month of planning and several days of feverish effort. A patisseur had been brought from London. Out of spun sugar he had fashioned exotic birds and butterflies, creating a feast as much for the eye as for the palate. The wives of Lord Glanville's tenants, tying their aprons and rolling up their sleeves, had augmented the normal kitchen staff in a heroic baking of breads and tarts and hams. A last-minute whipping of cream and the dextrous dressing of cutlets in paper collars had been preceded by two days of steaming endeavour in which the kitchen hobs and ovens were organized with military precision. Lobsters boiled in cauldrons, salmon simmered in fish kettles and sucking pigs turned on spits which, although rarely used, had been maintained in good order for three hundred years.

When it was cold, the food had been arranged on Jacobean banqueting dishes to be glazed and decorated.

Sixteenth-century refectory tables were covered with eighteenth-century lace cloths. Waterford glass sparkled with the light reflected off highly polished Queen Anne silver. Starched drawn-thread napkins were piled beside stacks of Waterloo plates, each hand-painted with a different scene from the Duke of Wellington's battles. It was a measure of the secure foundations of Lord Glanville's heritage, as well as the extent of his wealth, that although it had been necessary to transport a certain amount of china and glass to the country from Glanville House in Park Lane, there had been no need to hire a single piece.

By now all the preparations were complete. In less than an hour, as the first carriage or motor car drew up outside the door, the inhabitants of Blaize would begin to move in their appointed tracks like wound-up clockwork figures waiting only for a lever to be pressed. Lord and Lady Glanville would appear to greet their guests, footmen would step forward, maids would hurry along cold back corridors. But now the house was as quiet as though it were uninhabited. The housekeeper had come from her hall, the cook from her kitchens and the butler from his pantry, to inspect the ballroom and the buffet for the last time and, satisfied in their own spheres, had retreated downstairs again. Blaize was at peace.

Moving along the table, Kate reached forward to pick out a cherry from a huge punch bowl and caught sight of her own reflection in the gleaming silver. Even distorted by the curve of the vessel, the face it showed her was familiar – freckled and green-eyed, with wide, strong eyebrows and cheekbones and a generous mouth – but it seemed to be attached to the body of a stranger. In a way she felt herself at this moment to be as artificial a creation as the swan which had been made out of meringue or the miniature trees whose fruit, on close inspection, proved to be not apples but sweetmeats. With the help of her aunt's maid she had been laced into a corset which constricted her sturdy waist, and buttoned into a ball dress whose shot silk matched her sea-green eyes. She had refused to wear even the discreetest cosmetics, but had allowed the maid to pile her long, thick hair – the tawny colour of a lion's mane, and almost as unmanageable – elaborately high on her head. The strain of maintaining this edifice upright caused her to stand even straighter than usual.

This effect of stateliness was not one which came naturally to Kate. She had only recently qualified as a doctor, and her years of hard work as a medical student had allowed her little time for society entertainments of this kind. In any case, she had no taste for them as a rule. But she and her brother Brinsley were very close and she was anxious that he should not be ashamed of his sister's appearance in this celebration of his birthday.

Kate turned away from her study of the buffet tables, licking her fingers, and found that she herself had been under observation. Brinsley rose from the window-seat of one of the mullioned windows of the Tudor hall and stepped down to take her hands.

'You really do look absolutely ripping, Kate,' he said. 'I like the dress.'

'You should have said that before, when Aunt Alexa was listening. It's the one she gave me two years ago for my own twenty-first. It makes me feel a little like Cinderella – as though at midnight the clock will chime and all these trappings will disappear. But I must return the compliment. You look absolutely ripping yourself.'

Brinsley was wearing his new second lieutenant's uniform, still as smartly pressed as when the tailor first delivered it. But he had made no attempt to sleek down the exuberant curls of his golden hair in the approved military style, and his eyes sparkled with high spirits which were equally unsubdued.

'You approve, then?' he asked.

'Oh yes, very smart,' said Kate. 'How I wish that

Mother and Father could see you. You must have a photograph taken to send to them. They'll be thinking of you at this moment and wishing you were with them.'

'Could we take a walk?' asked Brinsley abruptly. 'Would you be too cold?'

'I'll fetch a wrap.' Kate was strong, and normally unmindful of the weather. But her ball dress was cut low at both back and front and she guessed she would feel the chill as soon as she moved away from the blazing log fires of the house.

She took Brinsley's arm as, a few minutes later, they made their way down the stone steps and strolled towards the river. Had the war not imposed a need for darkness, their Aunt Alexa would certainly have ordered the carriage drive to be illuminated with oil lamps, the front of the ancient house to be decorated with coloured lights, and spotlights to be fixed on the roof to pick out the twisting patterns of the sixteenth-century brick chimneys. As it was, a full moon provided a romantic substitute for all these. The woodland paths along which Kate and Brinsley wandered were dappled with the moving shadows of the trees, but were lit clearly enough for them to move without hesitation.

For a little while neither of them spoke. Kate guessed that Brinsley, like herself, would be thinking of their parents and of their childhood home in Jamaica. Hope Valley, the village community in which their mother worked as a doctor and their father, a Baptist missionary, as pastor, had been Brinsley's home until he was sent to England for his schooling. Kate had remained longer with her parents in the West Indies, but her wish to become a doctor like her mother had been so strong that when she was eighteen she too had been allowed to go to England to study.

The past five years had been satisfying ones for Kate, but she guessed that her parents must often have been lonely without their two elder children – for two of their other children had died in infancy and the youngest, still living at home, was a cripple. On this evening in particular they would be upset not to have Brinsley with them. Kate knew that her brother, coming down from Oxford in June without distinction but without disgrace, and then enjoying two leisurely months of playing county cricket, had planned to set sail for Jamaica in September, ready to celebrate his coming-of-age in his old home.

Two shots in a Sarajevo street were to change the lives of a whole generation. A birthday party in Jamaica was hardly a significant casualty. Brinsley had shown no interest in politics, and Kate felt sure that the rapid exchange of declarations of war across Europe must have taken him by surprise. Both at school and at university, however, he had been a member of the Officers' Training Corps, so he was one of the first to volunteer and to be commissioned. Now he was awaiting the summons to join his regiment, and it could not be very much longer delayed.

Their walk brought them to the bank of the River Thames. The moon, escaping from the net of the trees, was brighter here, reflecting in the broad band of water which scarcely rippled on this calm night as it swept steadily towards the sea. Peaceful and powerful at the same time, the movement hypnotized them into stillness at first. Then Kate surprised herself by laughing at an incongruous thought. Brinsley's questioning look made it necessary to explain.

'I was thinking, if we were in Hope Valley, we'd both have sat down on the bank of the stream without giving it a second thought.'

'When we lived in Hope Valley we were both shabby, all the time,' said Brinsley. 'No beautiful ball dress to be spoiled by mud or grass stains.'

'And no elegant uniform.' It was true that in Jamaica they had been allowed to run wild. Their mother had cared nothing for her own appearance and felt no need to dress her own children more smartly than those of her patients. In a tropical village, clothes were required for decency and not for either warmth or fashion. 'All the same, this birthday would have been a very special day for Mother and Father. They must be disappointed that you're so far away.'

'Yes. I'm sorry about that, of course.' Brinsley sighed, but almost at once Kate heard the regret in his voice giving way to excitement. 'But I don't really feel ready to settle down at home yet. I can't pretend that the prospect of acting as a kind of farm manager for the rest of my life is a very jolly one.'

Kate knew what he meant. Their father performed all the spiritual duties which his black congregation required of their pastor; but he was a man of great energy and ability, and early in his pastorate he had been so shocked by the poverty of the villagers that he had organized them into an agricultural labour force. Whipped on by his passionate oratory, they had reclaimed a derelict plantation next to the village, and now the efficient running of the estate had become Ralph Lorimer's chief enthusiasm. Since Brinsley had never shown any bent towards any other profession, it was taken for granted that he would return to help his father manage the plantation. Kate laughed affectionately now at her brother's lack of eagerness.

'What would you rather do instead?' she asked.

'Oh, nothing in particular. Anything that would leave me time to play a little cricket. I shall have to settle down to work sometime, I can see that – and I know I'm lucky to have a family business on offer. All the same, I'm in no hurry to start. A few months of adventure will be just the thing.'

Kate glanced across and saw that his eyes were alive with excitement at the prospect. For her own part, she had wanted to be a doctor for as long as she could remember. She had always known that years of hard work

17

would be needed to attain her ambition; and although her mother's generation had borne the brunt of the fight against prejudice and prohibition which had for so long made it impossible for women to become doctors at all, Kate had appreciated that determination as well as study would be required. Her social conscience and serious approach to life made her temperamentally the opposite of her brother, but her affection for him made it easy for her to sympathize with his light-hearted lack of ambition.

All the same, it was difficult not to wonder how 'jolly' he would find the next few months. Kate's own vocation was to heal, and she would have been appalled if she had ever found herself expected to take life instead of preserving it. Nor was she absolutely clear why it was so necessary for England to become involved in the war at all. Who were the Serbs, and why should the assassination of an Austrian archduke be of more than local importance? Brinsley had done his best to persuade her that now the war had started it ought to be won quickly; and the best way to win it quickly was to send as many soldiers as possible to fight in France, and with the greatest possible speed. It was certainly obvious to Kate that if the finest young men were required, Brinsley was one of them; but she could not help wondering whether Brinsley himself – although ready and indeed eager to fight – had recognized that at some moment he would have to kill.

The thought worried her, but it was not appropriate to this evening of celebration. Still holding Brinsley's arm, she turned away from the river.

'Time you were on parade at Blaize,' she suggested. 'They won't be able to start without the guest of honour.' They began to walk slowly up the hill towards the house.

'You really do look stunning, Kate.' Whatever Brinsley had been thinking about down by the river, it was clearly not the prospect of killing Germans. 'It's a pity I'm not older than you.'

'Why?'

'Because a lot of chaps like to marry other chaps' sisters.'

'It must be quite difficult to avoid doing so,' Kate laughed.

'Oh, come on, you know what I mean. The sisters of their friends. But of course all my friends are too young for you. You and I should have been born the other way around.'

'It's kind of you to offer me all your fellow-undergraduates and fellow-cricketers, even if you do promptly snatch the offer back again. But I haven't spent all these years training as a doctor just to give up without making use of my qualifications. I don't intend to marry anyone, whether older or younger.'

'There's nothing to say you'd have to stop being a doctor just because you got married,' Brinsley protested.

'How many of these friends of yours would allow their wives to work?' Kate asked him. 'And how many female doctors do you know who are married?'

'I only know three female doctors, full stop,' said Brinsley. 'One is you, and it's you I'm trying to persuade. One is my mother, and *she's* married.'

'Fortunately for our own reputations.' Kate was still laughing. 'But she's married to a missionary. Missionaries' wives are a special case.'

'And there's Aunt Margaret. She was married as well.'

'Aunt Margaret is another special case.' Kate was silent for a moment, thinking affectionately of their father's elder sister, who had provided a home for Brinsley and herself when they each in turn left Jamaica for England. Dr Margaret Scott was as dear to both the young Lorimers as their own mother, but no one could pretend that her life had followed the normal pattern of a Victorian woman.

'She didn't marry when she first qualified,' Kate pointed out now. 'She worked as a doctor until she was in

19

her mid-thirties. And when she did marry, she stopped working.'

'That was so that she could have a baby.'

'She stopped working,' repeated Kate. 'The only reason why she went back to being a doctor was because her husband died and she had to support the baby. She wasn't married for more than a few months out of the whole of her life. You can't argue from Aunt Margaret. And if I may say so, it's very *arrogant* of men to think that the only thing in life a woman wants is a husband.'

'It may be arrogant, but you have to admit that it's very often true.'

'Well, perhaps I can understand it being true of other women, because they can all long to get their hands on a gorgeous creature called Brinsley Lorimer. But since I'm disqualified from that privilege, I hope you'll allow me to get quietly on with my doctoring.'

They stepped out of the woodland as they spoke, and paused for a moment to stare in admiration at Blaize. The two wings which had been added to the old house in the reign of William and Mary provided the more comfortable rooms for normal living, but the Tudor structure in the centre of the mansion was the perfect setting for any grand occasion. As soon as it became clear that Brinsley would not be returning to Jamaica for his coming-of-age, Margaret Scott had offered him a party in her small London house; but his other aunt, Alexa, had swept the suggestion aside. She had never behaved as warmly as Margaret to her niece and nephew, but when it came to giving a dance, she would allow no one to consider any alternative to the Glanville country house. At this very moment, as the clock on the stable tower struck the hour for which the guests had been invited, the wide entrance doors were flung open and the carriage approach was flooded with a warm and welcoming light.

'How very thoughtful it was of Aunt Alexa to make sure

that the ballroom windows were blacked out!' exclaimed Kate. But there was no trace of anxiety in her laughing voice. In its peaceful country setting, Blaize could surely never be touched by the dangers of war.

'There'll be no Zeppelins tonight,' said Brinsley. 'It's my birthday, and everyone knows that I was born while Lady Luck was smiling. Only good things can happen on my birthday.'

They had been walking arm-in-arm, but now Kate moved her hand to rest lightly and formally on her brother's arm. They stepped forward into the light and progressed with dignity up the stone steps and into the house. But if they had hoped that the staff would be caught out by the arrival of an apparently over-punctual pair of guests, they were disappointed. Two lines of footmen wearing the Glanville livery stood ready to receive them, and the butler's silver tray awaited the first card which would tell him whom to announce. From the ballroom, a little way away, could be heard the last faint scrapings of sound as the orchestra tuned their instruments. There were a few seconds of silence and then, as though the ballroom were already crowded instead of completely deserted, the house was flooded with music as warmly as with light.

It was time for the ball to begin.

2

Even in portraiture the English nobility was not prepared to mix with trade. The Tudor long gallery on the highest floor of Blaize displayed a row of aristocrats with high foreheads and long noses. They were all descended from one of William the Conqueror's companions-at-arms, and they were all ancestors of Piers Glanville, the present holder of the title. But Alexa's father, who had once owned a shipping company and a bank in Bristol, had not been invited to join their company.

Instead, the portrait of John Junius Lorimer hung alone in the screened balcony above one end of the ballroom. The picture showed an old man, heavily built and dressed in sombre black. His long hair and beard and profuse side whiskers were white, but his bushy eyebrows had been painted bright chestnut. Margaret Scott, who climbed the steps to the balcony shortly before midnight, had once had hair as bright as those eyebrows; for, like Alexa, she was the daughter of John Junius Lorimer. But she was twenty years older than her half-sister and now, at the age of fifty-seven, the colour was fading and her forehead showed the lines of past sorrow and present responsibility.

In London, Margaret was a professional woman held in high esteem. Like her best friend Lydia, the mother of Kate and Brinsley, she had been a member of the first generation of women who had succeeded in qualifying as doctors in England, and now she was not only in charge of the gynaecological department of one of the great London teaching hospitals but was also responsible for the welfare of all the female students who trained there. But tonight her role was not that of a doctor but of an aunt and mother. This was a family occasion.

There were chairs in the balcony, but Margaret was a small woman and found that if she sat down she could not see above the solid lower section of the screen. Instead she stood, looking through the lattice at the picturesque scene below. Alexa, tonight's hostess, had been an opera singer in her youth, and when she married Piers Glanville he had encouraged her to convert a tithe barn on his estate into a small opera house. So she had the contacts to turn any party into a production if she chose, and the designer whose more usual responsibility was to create Count Almaviva's house or Don Giovanni's palace on the stage had been given a new challenge for

22

this special occasion. He had transformed the ballroom into a tropical forest, through which the women in their beautiful dresses dipped and swirled like exotic butterflies. Many of the young girls wore white, but Alexa had invited friends of her own generation as well as those on Brinsley's list, and above their rich silks and brocades sparkled the jewels of a wealthy and secure society.

The girls in their debutante season were pretty enough, but it seemed to Margaret that none of them could rival their hostess. Alexa Glanville at the age of thirty-seven was as beautiful as Alexa Lorimer had been at seventeen. Tall and slender, she brought elegance to any gown she wore, and to honour this evening's celebration her reddish-gold hair was coiled on her head like a crown in which delicate sprays of diamonds glittered, half-hidden.

Margaret looked for her son, Robert, and saw that he was partnering Kate. It was surprising how well they were dancing – for Robert did not attend many functions of this kind, while Kate's tall, sturdy body did not suggest that she would be graceful. But she had a musical ear, and her medical training had ensured that she was never clumsy. Certainly the two cousins seemed to be in perfect accord as they circled the floor – although Margaret noticed that Robert looked unusually thoughtful. Perhaps he was needing to concentrate on the steps, for there was no sign of the cheerful grin which had hardly changed since he was a little boy – although the carroty curls which he had inherited from his mother and grandfather had sprung up again from his attempts earlier in the evening to discipline them, and this tousled confusion made him look younger than his twenty years. Margaret felt her heart swelling with pride and love as she watched him. Robert was her only child, born after the death of his father, and her whole happiness was bound up in him.

The wooden treads of the stair to the balcony gave noisy warning that someone was coming to join her. Margaret turned away from the dancers and found that it was one of her many nephews. Arthur Lorimer was the son of Margaret's elder brother, who had died some years before. Although Arthur was a younger son, he had inherited his family's dock and shipping business, because his brother Matthew had abandoned the offices of the Lorimer Line to become an artist. Arthur himself, now in his thirties, found the world of business completely congenial and was never happier than when he was absorbed in his accounts. He lived in the Bristol mansion which had once belonged to John Junius Lorimer and devoted himself to making money. Although his business associates and competitors thought of him as a hard and cold-natured man, he had a strong family feeling, and had welcomed the invitation to join in Brinsley's celebrations.

They chatted now for a few moments, but Arthur's concentration was not on the conversation. 'Have you seen Kate?' he asked abruptly. 'She gave me the supper dance, but she seems to have disappeared.'

'She was dancing with Robert only a moment ago.' Margaret turned back to look over the screen, and found that the couple had left the floor, although the orchestra was still playing. 'Well, she's hardly likely to go without supper. And she's not the sort of girl who would stand you up.'

Arthur nodded his agreement. For a moment he seemed on the point of saying something else; but after looking down once more to check that Kate was not hidden anywhere in the jungle below he changed his mind and went down the steps without speaking.

Always observant, Margaret could not help noticing that he seemed to be under some kind of strain. She wondered, as she had wondered once or twice before, whether he wanted to marry Kate. She had noticed that ever since his cousin's arrival in England he had formed the habit of spending the night at Margaret's house whenever he had to come to London on business, although the return journey to Bristol was not a long one. He was not a man who found it easy to chat to young women or to spare the time from his business to indulge in the formal ritual of courtship. Nor could Margaret ever imagine him falling in love. But the relationship of one cousin with another was a relaxed one, and he had always seemed at ease with Kate.

There was another reason why Arthur – approaching the decision rationally, as he was certain to do – might have seen Kate as a possible wife. She was a doctor. This could make it easier for him to confess to her, as he had earlier done to Margaret herself, the consequences of the attack of mumps which he had suffered at the age of twenty-five. He might also hope that someone dedicated to her profession would be more willing than most ordinary women to embark on a marriage in the knowledge that her husband would never be able to give her children. Not many men allowed their wives to work; but it was a concession Arthur might be prepared to offer as a form of compensation. Whether Kate would allow herself to be bribed into matrimony was another matter.

Margaret tut-tutted to herself. Match-making, even when it was only in the imagination, was a temptation which ought to be resisted. The young people were perfectly capable of making their own plans. Of more immediate importance was Arthur's reminder that the next item on the programme would be the supper dance, for which she too was engaged. She turned to go down, and found herself facing the portrait of her father. His piercing eyes reminded her of the many occasions during her childhood when he had demanded an explanation of some misdeed. She had been frightened of him then, but now her chin lifted – not so much defiantly as in triumph. When John Junius Lorimer died he had left his family ruined and disgraced. If anything was required to prove how hard and how successfully his four children had worked to raise themselves out of that morass of dismay, it was tonight's ball, with its background of wealth and its strong ties of family affection. As she made her way back to the ballroom floor, the war was far from Margaret's thoughts, and she was happy.

3

Kate had been surprised when her cousin Robert interrupted their dance together to ask whether she would talk with him for a few moments. Usually teasing and carefree, he had become unexpectedly serious. They had both spent many holidays at Blaize, and knew their way around the old house. The library was not one of the rooms open to the generality of tonight's guests, so as she followed Robert there Kate guessed that they would not be interrupted.

'I need advice,' he said abruptly, closing the door behind him. 'I want to join up, like Brinsley. Or at least, I don't know whether I want to, but I think I ought to.'

'Robert! You can't do that. It would break Aunt Margaret's heart.'

'But everyone else is doing it. Of course no mother is going to *like* it, exactly, but other mothers are letting their sons go.'

'Other mothers may have other children, and husbands. Aunt Margaret has no one but you. She'd never have a moment's peace while you were away.'

'It would be hard for her, I know it would. But what am I to do, Kate? Have I got to spend the rest of my life wrapped in cotton wool because I'm the only son of a widow? There has to be a moment when I leave home and start living my own life.'

'Well, of course,' Kate agreed. 'And by any normal definition of leading your own life, I'm quite sure that Aung Margaret would want you to go. But this is different. You must see the difference.'

'What I see is that everyone else is going. What am I to say when my friends ask me why I'm still at home? "I can't leave my mother." I don't want to hurt her, Kate, but I feel this is my duty. I was hoping you could help.'

'If you want help, Uncle Piers is the best person to ask for it.' Kate knew that Lord Glanville had been Margaret's closest friend in England for almost twenty years. 'But if you're asking me for advice – '

'No.' Robert smiled, although it was only an imitation of his usual cheerful grin. 'I'm looking for someone whose advice will be to do what I already want to do. I can see you're not the right person. I mustn't make you late for your supper. Who's taking you in?'

Kate consulted the programme which, with its miniature pencil, swung from her wrist, and saw that Arthur had initialled the next dance.

'And he's a punctual man,' commented Robert when she told him. He held the door open for her. Kate hesitated, feeling that there must be something more she could say. But although Robert resembled her brother Brinsley in his laughing and apparently carefree attitude to life, there was a difference between the two cousins. Robert's light-heartedness, unlike Brinsley's, was not central to his character, but was the ripple on the surface of a pool of thoughtfulness. He laughed and he teased and he was always ready to play, but at heart he was serious. Brinsley might view with horror the thought of a settled future and a working career, but Robert was already in the middle of training to be a civil engineer. Kate saw that he had spoken the truth when he admitted that he was asking for support rather than advice. It meant, almost certainly, that he had already made up his mind.

Back in the ballroom, Arthur was looking for her with an impatience which contained a hint of anxiety. As Kate smiled, to show that she had not forgotten, she thought how well evening dress became him. Robert was too

27

young and somehow too rugged to look at ease in the shining, stiff-fronted shirt and long tail coat which were part of the black and white uniform worn by all the civilian men at the ball; while at the other extreme Lord Glanville, tall and silver-haired, looked distinguished whatever he wore. But Arthur's clothes changed him entirely for the better. By day his slightness made him appear insignificant; his face was too narrow to be handsome and his hair was already beginning to recede slightly, suggesting that he would be bald one day. Now, though, he appeared almost elegant.

Or perhaps, thought Kate, it was just that the whole atmosphere of the ball placed the dancers and the surroundings at one remove from reality. Just as a gauze might be dropped in Alexa's riverside opera house to blur the edges of the action behind it, changing it from drama – already far from real life – to fantasy, so now the romantic setting had transformed all those who enjoyed it, making all the men seem handsome and all the women beautiful. All except herself, of course – but even she felt herself walking taller, playing her part in the scene.

The doors of the banqueting hall were thrown open and there were gasps of admiration even from guests accustomed to such displays of tasteful extravagance. Kate and Arthur, as befitted members of the family, hung back for a little, accepting a glass of punch from one of the footmen as they waited. Kate was still conscious of some kind of tension in Arthur's manner, and searched for a subject of conversation to break their silence.

A group of Brinsley's friends, who had all volunteered at the same time as himself, led their partners to the buffet and gave her the chance to comment.

'How smart they all look in their new uniforms,' she said. 'Do you intend to volunteer, Arthur?'

'I'm thirty-six,' he said. 'Too old to learn to be a soldier. This is a young man's war. And even if that weren't the case, I can be more use to the country by remaining at work. We're not being told very much about the German submarines. I suppose the Government is anxious not to alarm the country. But there are certain to be losses at sea. Ships will be sunk, and they must be replaced quickly if the country isn't to starve. The Lorimer Line has had contracts with the same ship-building firm for a great many years. I bought that firm last week, and I intend to increase its output at once. I'd hoped to interest Brinsley in the new business, as a matter of fact – to keep as much as possible of its profit within the family. Naturally he couldn't do anything until the war is over, but after that I thought he might find a management position in Bristol more exciting than exile to Jamaica. But clearly he has too much to think about at the moment. He wasn't able to give the idea proper attention.'

Kate suspected that Brinsley had little interest in business of any kind, and even less aptitude for it. But her brother would have to settle down to some kind of work sooner or later, so she was careful not to spoil an opportunity by putting her thought into words. There was another objection, though. 'I imagine my father will want him to take over the work of the plantation eventually,' she said.

'It's my impression that your father has already found a capable assistant,' said Arthur. 'We have a good deal of business correspondence about the bananas which he consigns to my ships. I noticed two years ago that the letters which he signed were written in a different hand. And now his secretary, or whoever it may be, appears to have taken over all the office work. Besides being more efficient in keeping his accounts up to date, he's been quite awkwardly enterprising in looking for alternative markets and ships, which your father would never have done. I was forced to revise my quotations last year.' Arthur's thin lips curled in a smile of grudging admiration for the unknown Jamaican who had beaten him in his

29

own field. 'It seems to me that if your father needs a manager to succeed him, he already has one.'

'Do you know his name?' asked Kate.

'D. Mattison, he signs himself.'

'Duke!' exclaimed Kate, smiling with pleasure.

'You know him?'

'Very well. He was our best friend in Jamaica, Brinsley's and mine. He's older than we are – he must be almost twenty-eight by now. He used to play cricket with Brinsley. It's because Duke was such a good bowler that Brinsley became such a good batsman. And he always had a good head for figures. I suggested to Father before I left the island that he ought to take Duke into his office. I'm delighted that he's done so.'

'Duke is an unusual name to be christened,' said Arthur.

'Not for a Jamaican.'

'Are you telling me that he's black?'

'Well, brown, really. Quite a few of the islanders show signs of English blood, and Duke more than most.' Kate couldn't help smiling at the expression on her cousin's face. It was difficult to tell whether he was more shocked at the thought that he was doing business with a native or by the need to recognize that moral standards in the colonies had not always been as high as they should have been. Kate changed the subject quickly before Arthur should express some opinion with which she would be bound to disagree. 'Shall we find ourselves a seat for supper?' she suggested.

'There's no hurry,' said Arthur, and it was true that the space round the buffet tables was crowded. 'Will you come into the conservatory with me, Kate? It's very hot in here.'

Kate could not control a smile. She had heard from her friends so many accounts of proposals of marriage which had taken place in conservatories that the word had become a joke, as though such an extension of the house existed purely for this purpose, and not for the benefit of the plants which grew there. She was about to tease her partner – for although a few moments earlier she had felt herself enveloped in a romantic atmosphere, it had not touched her emotions – when it occurred to her that Arthur had not spoken in joke. He was displaying all the nervousness of a man planning to put the conservatory to this conventional use.

The idea came as a shock. Kate had been on friendly terms with Arthur ever since she arrived in England to start her medical training, but she had never thought of him as anything more than a cousin, and she did not wish to do so now. Instinctively she took a step backwards, searching for a reason to stay in the crowded hall.

The excuse which presented itself was not one which she would have chosen. While she had been talking to Arthur, Lord Glanville's butler had come into the hall, carrying the silver tray on which he was accustomed to present letters. But no ordinary letter would arrive at this time of night. What Brinsley was reading was a telegram.

His face flushed with excitement. He called to those of his friends who were in uniform and they hurried to read the words over his shoulder. They spoke briefly to their partners before moving in a little group towards their startled hostess. But Brinsley called them to a halt.

'One more dance!' he shouted. 'Lord Kitchener won't begrudge us a last waltz.' He dispatched the butler to call back the orchestra, who were taking their own break for refreshments, and led the way back into the ballroom. There was an eager chatter of voices as the other guests left their suppers and followed.

Arthur was saying something, but Kate did not hear the words. Too abruptly to be believed, the atmosphere of the ball had changed from a romantic dreaminess to a highly charged drama, and Kate's blood was cold with a sudden fear. Brinsley, without doubt, had received his summons to leave for France. His friends, commissioned at the same time, would in a few moments hurry to their homes to discover whether similar telegrams were waiting for them, but Kate's emotions were centred on her brother alone.

'How can he look so excited when he's going into such danger?' she exclaimed, appalled that the family should have admired Brinsley's enthusiasm without stopping to reflect that it was leading him somewhere where he would have to kill or be killed.

'How could he go into such danger if he were not excited?' Arthur countered. His arm was round her waist as though he feared that she might faint, but Kate was hardly aware of it.

'I can't let him go,' she cried, overwhelmed by the nearness of the parting; but as she tried to hurry into the ballroom, Arthur tightened his grip.

'You can't hold him,' he said. 'None of us can. We have no rights any more. He has to do whatever his country orders. And when he is happy to obey, it would be unkind of you to do anything but support him.'

Kate realized that her cousin was speaking the truth. It was unusual for her to reveal her emotions but her unhappiness now made some gesture necessary. She turned into Arthur's waiting arms, her head pressed against his chest, while she struggled to restrain her tears.

'Brinsley has an aura of good fortune,' Arthur said quietly. 'Can't you feel it as you look at him? Some people are lucky, against all reason, and he's always been one of them. He'll come back. They'll all come back. The war will be over by Christmas.' He paused for a moment. 'It's natural that you should be upset. Your parents are a long way away. You'll be lonely when Brinsley's gone. We could help each other, Kate. It's lonely for me as well now that Beatrice has decided she must work in London. You're losing a brother: I've already lost a sister. It's ridiculous for one man to live alone with so many servants in a great mansion like

Brinsley House. It would make me very happy if you'd agree to share it with me, Kate.'

Through the confusion of her anxiety Kate heard the words and – although not immediately – understood them. Appalled by her own weakness, she pulled herself away from Arthur and straightened her shoulders, steadying her body and her emotions at the same time.

'I shouldn't have allowed – I can't – I'm sorry, Arthur.'

She seemed unable to communicate and could see that he did not understand what it was that she was failing to say, for his puzzled frown gave place immediately to a sympathetic smile.

'I've chosen the wrong time to declare myself,' he said understandingly. 'How can I expect you to think of anyone but Brinsley at this moment? After he's left we'll talk again.'

'Excuse me,' said Kate. She knew that she was behaving badly in leaving him so abruptly but she could not bear to waste any more of the time which she might be spending with her brother. She hurried out of the banqueting hall and into the ballroom, arriving just as the waltz was ending.

'Have you been called to go?' she asked Brinsley.

'Yes, but not till morning,' he said reassuringly. 'The others will want to push off now so that they can pick up their things and say goodbye to their families. But everything I need is here. There's no reason why I shouldn't dance till dawn. Don't look so upset, Kate.'

'But of course I'm upset!' she exclaimed. 'It's only a few hours, isn't it, since I said I felt like Cinderella. And now midnight's struck, but it's not my dress that disappearing. It's – ' She was too near to tears to go on.

'It's what?'

'Everything.' Her gesture took in the whole of her surroundings, the jungle ballroom and the exotic display of food in the banqueting hall. 'You're all going. And the ball is ending too soon. It's as though the life we've known, everything about it, is coming to a close.'

'Nonsense,' said Brinsley. 'Why do you think I'm going, if not to make sure that everything will be able to go on as before? And why should the ball stop, when we're still here? Come on, Kate; keep your chin up. You've never let anything beat you before. Why don't we show them all what we can do?'

He spoke to the leader of the orchestra and then smiled at his sister as he took her in his arms, allowing her a moment to steady not only her body but her feelings after such an uncharacteristic display of emotion. Then they moved smoothly together in a rhythm which was unfamiliar to many of the guests, for the tango was still a novelty in England. Doubtless some of the young debutantes present would have learned the new steps, but in their eyes Kate knew that she was an oddity, dull and over-serious. They would certainly not expect to see her giving what was almost an exhibition dance. It would be yet another joke on the part of a young man who allowed nothing to subdue his spirits.

It was an odd side-effect of their childhood in Jamaica that Kate and Brinsley both had a strongly developed sense of rhythm. Neither of their parents was musical, but the two children had almost unconsciously absorbed the music in the Jamaican air. When the members of the Hope Valley congregation sang Baptist hymns, they transformed them into something powerful and thrilling. As they worked, they sang other songs, fitting the rhythms to the tasks; and in the evenings they sang and danced in a different way – a way disturbing in its intensity. Both the young Lorimers had learned to feel the throbbing of nonexistent drums through the stresses of the singers and the movements of their bodies. The rhythm of the tango was as different from Jamaican music as Jamaican from English, but Kate and Brinsley found no difficulty in moving with a graceful precision which brought applause from the older guests.

For a moment after the music had stopped they stood

close together. Neither of them had yet fallen in love, although Brinsley moved from one flirtation to another: their strongest emotional attachment was still to each other. Kate knew that this state of affairs could not survive for much longer, but for the moment she was bound by ties so tight that part of herself would go to France with her brother the next day. Even Brinsley, normally light-hearted to the point of frivolity, recognized this; and for a few seconds the gaiety of his smile faded into affectionate seriousness as he looked into her eyes.

'You're not to be frightened for me, Kate,' he said. 'I shall be all right. And it's only for a little while. It will all be over by Christmas.'

It was the second time within an hour that Kate had heard that phrase. She tried to make herself believe it and, with rather more success, forced herself to smile back into her brother's eyes.

4

In time of war, nothing makes such a fierce frontal assault on the emotions as military music. The sound of the drums was at first hardly more than a vibration, an almost imperceptible disturbance of the air, but it was enough to catch the attention of the excited, shouting, jostling crowds on the departure platform of Waterloo Station. Within a few seconds the full diapason of a regimental band could be heard, its bright brassiness piercing the air and lifting the spirits. Margaret tried to control the excitement which the music induced in her. A feeling of elation affected not only the soldiers who were waiting to board the train but also the civilians who had come to see them off. Although she reminded herself that a mass emotion of this kind was dangerous, warping the judgement, she was not proof against the contagion of patriotic pride.

Louder even than the band itself now was the tramp of well-drilled feet, and Margaret felt her eyes pricking with tears – of admiration rather than sadness – as a battalion of guardsmen marched the length of the platform and came to a stamping halt beside the carriages reserved for them at the front of the train.

The civilians cheered them as they passed and the men in uniform – most of them, like Brinsley, volunteer members of the British Expeditionary Force – watched their immaculate professionalism with envy. Then the chatter of farewells was resumed.

Six members of Brinsley's family had come to see him off. Alexa and Piers Glanville, Margaret and Robert and, of course, Kate, had all travelled with him from Blaize. Arthur had said his farewells there and had returned directly to Bristol; but his sister Beatrice had joined the party at the station.

In the years before the war, as it became clear that she would never marry, Beatrice had lived, as convention demanded of a spinster, in her brother's Bristol mansion. Fretting at her uselessness, she had allowed her temper to grow as sharp as her features, and had become the least popular member of the Lorimer family. But since the third day of the war she had been working full time in the London office of the National Union of Women's Suffrage Societies. Over a period of many years she had supported the movement in its efforts to win the vote for women, acting as its local secretary in Bristol. But now the organization had changed its immediate aim, and was assembling the staff and equipment of medical units to be sent to the front. Beatrice too had changed as she committed all her time to the cause instead of giving a few hours of voluntary work each week. Her resentment that she was still a spinster had been replaced by confidence in her own new-found efficiency and the knowledge that she was doing a worthwhile job. Almost overnight she had become friendlier and less prickly. Her absence from Brinsley's birthday celebrations had not been because of her admitted dislike of Alexa, but on account of an urgent need to pack up a consignment of drugs for France. Margaret could tell that her eldest niece was genuinely glad of the opportunity to join the family party, and anxious to assure Brinsley of her affection and support.

At the moment, though, it appeared that it was with Margaret herself that Brinsley wished to speak. She felt his hand on her arm as he led her a little way from the others. The platform was crowded, but each family group was intent only on its own leave-taking. Surrounded by strangers, it was possible to speak freely.

There was no time for any preamble. Knowing that he would be leaving at any moment, Brinsley came abruptly to the point.

'We'll be off soon,' he said. 'Aunt Margaret, you'll keep an eye on Kate for me, won't you?'

'I've never known a young woman better able to look after herself,' said Margaret. 'What foolishness do you anticipate?'

'She's turned down an offer of marriage from Arthur. I'm certainly not implying that's foolish. Arthur seems to me to be a cold man.' Brinsley laughed. 'Kate thinks he has his eyes on part of Father's estate as a marriage settlement.'

'Then Kate is uncharitable. I agree that Arthur doesn't appear likely to fall passionately in love with anyone, but he's been fond of Kate since she arrived in England. It would fit his nature to choose someone he knows well for a wife, rather than a strange young woman. Anyway, we may agree that Kate has made the right decision.'

'But for the right reason? She told me she'd be ashamed to devote herself to the comfort of one man when she should be using her skills to serve hundreds. I wouldn't like her to end up as an old maid like Beatrice.'

'One day she'll be swept off her feet by a dashing

young prince on a white charger and all her doubts will be forgotten. That's not really what's worrying you, is it, Brinsley?'

'I don't know what's worrying me,' he confessed. 'But she's planning something. She has that broody look. I'd like to feel that you'd discuss with her any ideas she may be considering.'

'Well, of course,' Margaret assured him. 'You know very well that Kate is almost a daughter to me, just as you are another son. Look after yourself, Brinsley.'

It was a foolish remark to make to a young man on his way to a battlefield. For a few seconds Brinsley's smile seemed a little less carefree than usual. As he kissed her goodbye, Margaret could feel the depth of his affection for her. He had never put it into words and he did not do so now, but it was true that for the past eight years their relationship had been almost that of mother and son. While she watched him make his farewells to Beatrice and Robert and Piers Glanville and Alexa, she felt a moment of sympathy for his mother, her dear friend Lydia, who had been deprived of so many years out of her elder children's lives.

Whistles were blowing. Brinsley had saved his last embrace for Kate and for a moment brother and sister clung together as though they feared that they might never see each other again. But the prevailing atmosphere was one of excitement, not sadness. Brinsley leaped on to the train and reappeared almost at once to smile from a window. Everyone was waving now: the platform fluttered with handkerchieves. With a blast from the steam whistle the engine began to hiss and puff. Very slowly, so that Margaret and Kate found it possible for a few seconds to keep pace with Brinsley as he leaned from the window, the train began to move. There was a last-minute rush of repeated messages; hands were clasped and reluctantly released. The engine picked up speed and the band started to play again.

They played 'It's a long way to Tipperary'. The soldiers leaning from the train sang it lustily and as their voices faded the civilians on the platform took up the chorus. They sang it through a second time, and a third, still waving at the blank end of the guard's van as it pulled away along the rails and curved out of sight.

The soldiers were not, of course, going to Tipperary but to Ypres. A dead weight of anti-climax stifled the excitement on the platform as the band ceased to play. The waving handkerchieves drooped and were put to a different use, dabbing at eyes unable any longer to smile. The little group of Lorimers lingered on the platform, reluctant to disperse – as though the parting need not be considered final until they as well as Brinsley had left the station. Even Margaret, who had taken time off from her hospital duties, could not bring herself to move at once. There was only one farewell which could have wrenched more cruelly at her heart – if it had been Robert, and not Brinsley, who had just been carried away. Sometimes she was frightened that such a moment might come; but then she reminded herself that Robert would not be twenty-one for another nine months, and surely the war would be over before then.

Even while she reassured herself, anxiety made her stretch out a hand to Robert for comfort. He took her hand, but failed to provide the comfort.

'I want to go as well, mother,' he said.

It was almost the first time in his life that Margaret had seen her mischievous, carrot-haired son looking so serious. She stared at him without at first understanding what he meant.

'Go where?'

'Into the army. The Royal Engineers. To go on with my engineering training but be of some use to the country at the same time.'

The shock was so great that Margaret still could not absorb it. She had prepared herself for the parting with

39

Brinsley but Robert, surely, was only a boy. Lord Glanville came up to stand beside him.

'Robert discussed this with me at Brinsley's party,' he said. 'He wanted to be sure that you wouldn't feel yourself alone while he was away. Naturally, I was able to promise that Alexa and I would always be at hand if you needed any kind of support.'

You mean, if Robert is killed, thought Margaret, but it was not a thought which could be put into words, though Robert and Piers must already have faced it. She had to struggle against a panic which closed her throat so that for a moment she was unable to speak.

'Well, we must think about it,' she said at last, trying to smile; but Robert's serious expression did not change.

'I went to the recruiting office this morning,' he said. 'It's done.'

'Robert, how could you! without even a word?'

'How could I expect you to debate a decision like that and be forced in the end to say that you agree? It must be easier, surely, for you to accept that it's settled.'

'You're not twenty-one yet,' she protested. 'I could – ' She checked herself. Whether or not Robert needed his mother's permission to enlist – and she was not sure what the legal position was – he had made a man's decision and she would never be able to treat him like a child again. They could discuss the decision, and if it proved that Margaret still had the power to annul it, she could try to persuade him to change his mind. What she could not do was simply to say No. She was forced to recognize that every mother must face the moment of realizing that her first-born has grown into an adult with a life of his own. But not many mothers were confronted in that moment with a choice which might be literally one of life or death. Was her whole life to consist of partings from the men she loved? Without making any pretence that she approved or even accepted his decision, she kissed Robert to reassure him of her love.

40

But the unexpectedness of his news had left her confused, almost dizzy. She heard her name called and
turned so sharply that she staggered, needing Robert's
arm to steady her.

Kate, who must have left the family group while Robert
was breaking his news, was running down the platform
towards them, her eyes wide with shock. Margaret held
her breath and waited to hear what new horrors this day
held in store.

5

Kate had left the family group as Brinsley's train finally
disappeared from sight, in order that no one should see
how close she was to tears. Sniffling vigorously and
rubbing her eyes, she was not at first conscious of her
surroundings. When at last she had brought her feelings
more or less under control, she was surprised to see a
row of ambulances drawing up in the station forecourt.
To take her mind off Brinsley she forced herself to be
curious and followed the men who hurried from each
vehicle as it came to a halt. They led her to the platform
furthest from that on which the band had been playing.

The platform was covered with stretchers, and more
were still being unloaded from an ambulance train which
must have arrived unobtrusively while everyone's attention was on the departing troop train. Kate stared unbelievingly at the rows of men who lay, too weak or too
shell-shocked to move, with grey faces and sunken eyes
which stared unblinkingly from black sockets. She began
to move amongst them, asking questions and occasionally
lifting a blanket to inspect the wound it covered. Then,
horrified, she ran as fast as she could to find Margaret.

'Come and see here, Aunt Margaret.' She seized her
aunt's hand and tugged her towards the other platform

while the rest of the family, startled, followed more slowly. For a moment the two women, both doctors, stood side by side, taking in the scene in silence. Then Kate led Margaret over to one of the wounded men with whom she had spoken a little earlier.

'Look at this,' she said quietly to Margaret. She raised the blanket which covered his leg. He was still wearing the khaki trousers of his uniform, covered in mud, and his blood-stained puttees: only the boot had been cut away. 'It's five days since he was wounded. I asked him. Five days to bring him from the front line to here with only a field dressing. Just look!'

Even in her state of horror Kate had enough tact not to describe what she had recognized. Perhaps the man had not yet realized that he would have to lose a leg. Margaret, staring at the slimy bandage and blackened, gangrenous toes, would not need to be told.

'Where are you taking them?' Margaret asked one of the ambulance men.

'Thirty to Charing Cross Hospital,' he said. 'The rest'll wait here till we find out where there's room.'

The rest of the party came up to join the two women and Kate repeated her indignant reaction to Lord Glanville. But Margaret gestured them to move away from the stretcher area so that they could talk without being overheard.

'The hospitals must be cleared to make room,' she said. 'I shall go back at once and stop admissions to my gynaecological ward. Given efficient transport, my patients can perfectly well be cared for in the country. These men need surgeons and skilled nurses, and they need them at once. All the London teaching hospitals ought to make all their beds available to these emergency cases while the crisis lasts.'

Kate, who had only recently qualified as a doctor, had none of her aunt's power to take decisions like this. While the members of the older generation discussed what should be done, she stood back in silence.

Margaret had spoken with the authority of a professional woman and Lord Glanville, even more accustomed to taking decisions at a high level, was considering the situation with equal gravity. Kate knew that he had been personally responsible, fifteen years earlier, for persuading Margaret to leave her country practice and supervise the women students of the hospital of which he was a benefactor and governor. So although he had no medical experience, he was familiar with hospital administration.

'These men are surgical cases, I take it,' he said to Margaret. 'They'll need operations without delay and surgical nursing for some time afterwards – and then what? A less intensive standard of nursing for what could be a considerable period while their wounds heal?'

'If they're lucky, yes,' said Margaret. 'If they arrive at the operating theatre in time.'

'And during this healing period they'll be occupying beds which may be needed by the next trainload of wounded, and the next.'

'But this can't go on indefinitely!' exclaimed Alexa – though like her husband she kept her voice low. 'Obviously there has been a major battle. Something must have been decided by it. And I understood from the newspapers that the war is almost over, that we are on the point of victory.'

'The newspapers are telling us what we hope to hear,' said Piers. 'It was true a few weeks ago that the Germans were in retreat. But when they became too tired to retreat any further they dug trenches to protect themselves for a breathing space and found – as each of the men on this platform has found – that a row of concealed machine guns can be remarkably effective in keeping an army at bay. I suspect that there will be many more injuries of this kind. It seems to me a matter of some urgency that the surgical wards in London should be kept available for acute cases; and that means that convalescent soldiers

43

must be moved out as fast as emergencies move in. No doubt the hospitals are making their own plans. What I have in mind is a specific proposal.' He turned towards Alexa. 'Your opera house at Blaize is not due to open for its next season until the summer,' he suggested. 'It would not take too much reorganization to convert it into a long ward for men who require rest and some care, but not the most skilled nursing. There would be room in the main house for the doctors and nurses to stay. It must be your decision, of course. What do you think?'

'But rehearsals are due to start – ' Alexa's first reaction was a selfish one. Before she could express even a single objection, however, her gaze returned to the rows of stretchers and the men who lay on them, too weak even to groan. She put a hand apologetically on her husband's arm. 'You're quite right, Piers,' she said. 'How ought we to arrange it? We should need medical advice if the conversion is to be efficient.'

'The best plan would be to attach Blaize to one of the London hospitals as its country branch,' suggested Margaret.

'And since I'm already a governor of yours, there's no need to waste any time in choosing between them all,' said Piers. 'I hope you won't mind if I put forward your name, Margaret, to be medical administrator of the country branch, since we shall all have to live and work together so closely.' He thought for a moment. 'I'll take Alexa back to Park Lane now and then come straight to the hospital to see what arrangements can be made.'

'It's too late!' Kate cried, watching as Piers and Alexa hurried off. Robert went with them, perhaps still fearing an emotional outburst from his mother if he stayed. But it seemed that Margaret had for the moment succeeded in pushing her personal distress to the back of her mind.

'Too late for these men, perhaps,' she agreed. 'But Piers's plan will help others. And all his colleagues in the House of Lords have large country houses. If a first experimental scheme can be seen to work successfully – '

44

'I don't mean that,' interrupted Kate. 'I mean that it will be too late for the next batch of wounded as well as for these if they are always to be sent back to England. How many lives are being lost by this kind of delay, do you think? The men should be treated as soon as they are wounded; and that means within a short distance of the battlefield.'

'Well, obviously there must be dressing stations and field hospitals,' Margaret began; but again Kate interrupted her.

'And obviously there are not enough. Or else they are not adequately equipped. Or else there are not enough doctors. Aunt Margaret, I must go to France as well.'

'You may think you see a need, Kate.' Beatrice – Arthur's elder sister – had taken no part in the earlier conversation and she spoke now with the the cold edge of sarcasm which came naturally to her voice. But Kate could tell that she had been as deeply affected as any of the others by the contrast between the strong young men who had set off from Waterloo that morning and the broken bodies of those who had returned. 'I can promise you, though, that the War Office will not think any emergency great enough to warrant the recruitment of women doctors. In the suffragists' office we have fought this battle twice and lost on each occasion. Since the generals are finding the Germans more difficult to defeat than they had expected, they console themselves by putting women to rout instead.'

'What's happened, then?' demanded Kate.

'The French have accepted us. Dr Louisa Garrett Anderson and Dr Flora Murray are already in France. They are the leaders of a Women's Hospital Corps which has been entirely paid for by private subscription. And the Scottish Federation has raised enough funds to equip two complete units. The first of them will be leaving for France within the next two weeks, if all goes well.'

'I want to go with it,' said Kate. She was overwhelmed by the strength of her need to become involved.

'It's fully staffed.' Beatrice spoke with a firmness as great as her cousin's. But her brusque comment did not prevent her from looking thoughtfully at Kate as though to estimate how far she had spoken only out of impulse. 'But there's still a vacancy in the second unit. We expect that to be ready in January.'

'Will you accept me?'

'You haven't had much experience yet,' Beatrice pointed out. 'But it's not for me to say yes or no. The surgeon who'll be in charge of the unit has already been appointed. You'd have to convince her that you could make yourself useful. I'm expecting her to call at the office this afternoon with the list of equipment she wants me to provide. If you'd like to come at two o'clock – '

'I'll be there,' said Kate. 'Thank you, Beatrice.'

The change in Beatrice did not go so far as to make her smile easily. She nodded as Kate in acceptance of the arrangement and advanced her lips towards Margaret's cheek without actually touching it. Then, businesslike and matter of fact, she strode away.

'Don't rush into a decision like this, Kate,' Margaret said, putting a hand on her niece's arm as though that would be enough to hold her back. 'It's too important to be settled all in a minute. And I promised Brinsley I'd look after you. He's fighting in order that the people he loves shall be safe. He wouldn't want you to put yourself in such danger. Besides, you've seen for yourself how great is the need for doctors here.'

'One doctor in France could save the work of ten in London,' Kate argued. 'Suppose Brinsley were to be wounded, Aunt Margaret. One of the men I spoke to had lain for three days at Boulogne waiting for a ship. No one even changed his dressings. Could you bear to think of something like that happening to Brinsley when I might be able to prevent it? Or if not for him, for some of the others like him.' She saw Margaret shiver and guessed that her aunt was imagining not Brinsley, but

Robert lying on a stretcher in a railway shed. 'When you know, absolutely know, that something is the right thing to do, no amount of thinking about it is going to change the rightness. It isn't exactly that I *want* to go, Aunt Margaret. I don't see it as Brinsley does, as a kind of adventure. But the need is there. I have to go. There's no choice.'

'I'm frightened, Kate,' said Margaret. 'It's only a few hours since we were all dancing at Blaize. And now the place is to be filled with wounded men and Brinsley has gone and you and Robert will follow him. Where is it all going to end?'

'God knows. Do you think the Germans are as convinced that God is on their side as we are that he's on ours?'

She tried to make the question sound light-hearted, almost a joke, but in her heart she too was frightened. Everyone in the family – everyone in England – was having to make plans for an emergency which stretched into an indefinite and unpredictable future. Only one thing must be reckoned as certain. The war would not, after all, be over by Christmas.

6

Two days after her interview in Beatrice's office, Kate learned that her offer to serve as one of the two doctors in the next women's medical unit had been accepted. Perhaps her cousin, knowing her to be hard-working and conscientious, had recommended her, or perhaps she owed her success to her youth and strength and energy. Certainly Kate herself was as well aware as anyone else that although she was fully qualified she had not had a great deal of unsupervised experience of dealing with emergencies – and in work of this kind, most of the casualties brought to her were likely to be emergencies.

Since it would be ten weeks before the unit was ready to leave, she took steps to improve her usefulness by volunteering for temporary hospital work. Doctors and surgeons were working round the clock to accept the flood of wounded soldiers sent back from France, and Kate was welcomed as a member of a team which inspected each man as he arrived, supervised the cleaning of wounds, made a detailed observation of the damage, performed the more straightforward operations or those which were necessary to prepare for major surgery, and kept a close watch for a few days afterwards to guard against complications. She worked four twelve-hour duties each week, and this allowed her the opportunity also to play her part in the upheaval which was taking place at Blaize.

On her first visit she found Margaret already installed there. Lord Glanville had wasted no time in making his property available and pressing both the hospital governors and the army to accept his sister-in-law as its commandant. Alexa had cleared a corner room in the east wing to act as an office, and by the time Kate arrived, it had already taken on the appearance of an operations room at the front line. Plans of the various buildings on the estate were pinned to the wall and every piece of furniture was covered with papers listing equipment required or actions to be taken. Kate had already learned from Lord Glanville that Robert had had to report for training within two days of volunteering. The leisurely process which had carried Brinsley to the front was a thing of the past, and it did not require very much sensitivity to recognize the worry behind Margaret's frown of concentration.

Kate found it curious to walk through the house which she knew so well from holiday visits and to consider its amenities now in such a different light.

'The family will keep the whole of the west wing,' Margaret told her. 'That's where the nursery suite is, and we don't want to disturb Frisca and little Pirry. Most of the east wing will be made available for the medical staff. That means Alexa loses her drawing room and morning room, I'm afraid. They're going to use the library as a drawing room instead. As for the Tudor part of the house, there are problems in converting it. We've had a surveyor in to look at the long gallery up at the top. It's the perfect shape and size for a ward, but apparently the floor wouldn't take the weight. There would be trouble with stretchers on the stairs as well. The ballroom is more promising, and reasonably straightforward because it's empty. The decisions still to be made are about the opera house.'

They walked together through the wood. The path down towards the river was not too steep, but rain the previous night had left it muddy and slippery. Lifting her skirt to keep the hem clean, Kate paused to look back.

'Do you expect to transfer any of the patients from the theatre to the house?' she asked. 'It may not be an easy journey. And if doctors are coming and going all day, the mud will get much worse.'

Margaret nodded and made a note in the notebook which was tied by string to her belt.

'So we shall need a path with a firm surface and a gentler slope,' she agreed. 'Gradual enough to push a wheelchair up, in fact. Now then, give me your ideas on this.'

They had arrived at a very long brick building, older even than the house. Once upon a time it had been a tithe barn, built right on the bank of the Thames so that tenants of the Glanville estate could bring that part of their harvest which they owed to the church to a convenient place of storage – especially convenient in view of the fact that the Glanvilles had the patronage of the living, and could usually find a member of the family to accept it. During the last century, though, the tithe barn had been allowed to fall into disuse and decay, and only in the past few years, since Lord Glanville's marriage to Alexa, had it been repaired and converted to an opera house.

Even Kate, who was so strongly aware of the need, felt a moment's sadness to see the building which had been Alexa's pride stripped so unceremoniously of its trappings. Already the seats had been taken out, and at this very moment workmen were taking up the raked floor. There would be no need for any of the hospital beds to have a better view of the stage than the rest.

At this moment, however, the stage proved to be in use. A little girl in a white dress was dancing to music which issued from the huge horn of a gramophone. So intently was she concentrating on her energetic but graceful movements, that she did not notice the two new arrivals. This was Frisca, Alexa's daughter, made fatherless even before she was born by an earthquake in San Francisco and adopted by Lord Glanville when he married her mother.

The record came to an end and Frisca curtsied to the workmen before running to wind the machine up again.

'You ought not to be here, Frisca,' said Margaret, stepping on to the stage. 'You're distracting the men.'

'They like it.' Frisca pirouetted as she spoke. Her dimpled smile was infectious. It was impossible to feel gloomy in Frisca's presence – and equally impossible to be strict. Everyone knew that the seven-year-old, angelically blonde, was spoiled, but no one could bring himself to be the brute who would dim the radiance in those wide blue eyes. Kate watched with amusement as Margaret did her best to be severe.

'Yes, I'm sure they like it, but they should be getting on with their work instead of watching you. Off you go.'

Frisca's pretty face clouded. 'Everywhere I go today people tell me to go somewhere else. All the rooms are

50

different and everyone's busy and I can't do anything I want to.'

'You should be in the schoolroom, surely,' suggested Kate.

'Miss Brampton's saying goodbye to her cousin. He's going to be a soldier like Robert, and she's been crying all morning. She gave me some sweets to keep out of the way for half an hour.'

'By the time you get back to the house, the half-hour will be up. Run along.'

Pouting, the little girl made her way off the stage and out of the theatre, dawdling at first but unable to restrain herself from skipping happily before she was out of sight. Kate continued to smile.

'I've never seen such a child for dancing,' she said. 'One of these days I'm sure she's going to become as famous as her mother – but as a prima ballerina, not a prima donna. Now then, tell me what you're going to do with all this.'

There were so many details to be discussed and so many decisions to be made that Kate was filled with admiration for her aunt's appreciation of each problem and the firmness with which she made up her mind. They discussed catering, and accommodation for nurses. They considered how the actors' dressing rooms could best be used, and whether there was a need for an operating theatre.

On this last point the two women held different views.

'We can hardly hope to equip Blaize as a complete hospital,' Margaret pointed out. 'I see it only as a place for recuperation and convalescence. Surely it would be a mistake to attempt anything more ambitious. We've set ourselves a limited objective: to free other beds and services for the men in most urgent need by accepting those who need only time and care for their recovery.'

'I know that was what Uncle Piers suggested,' Kate agreed. 'But when I came off duty this morning the corridors of the hospital were lined with beds. These were the men who had been moved out of the acute wards, and these are the cases who will be sent to a place like Blaize if the present rate of casualties continues. They've had their main operations, certainly. But there's gas gangrene in almost every wound. At a guess, I would think that one in ten may need further surgery. I agree that those cases ought not to be sent here. But I suspect very strongly that in fact they will arrive.'

Margaret's face paled, and Kate guessed that she was thinking about Robert. She continued to talk quickly, forcing her aunt to concentrate on the matter in hand. more notes were taken, more measurements made. It was a relief, back at the house, to see the calmness with which Lord Glanville accepted the day's new sheets of requirements. He had made himself responsible for obtaining everything Margaret wanted, whether it was equipment such as beds and blankets or labour for the necessary tasks of conversion. His authority, and his many friends in the world of affairs, cut through the red tape of War Office inefficiency and smoothed away difficulties which would have been daunting to a mere doctor. Kate watched and admired.

For eight weeks she lived a double life. Her work in London would once have been considered full time, but she travelled regularly to the country to undertake what was in effect a second week's work. At first it was only administrative: but even before Blaize could be considered ready to receive its first patients, the ambulances began to arrive, and Kate took turns with Margaret in assisting the hard-pressed admissions doctor. There were times when she could have wept with tiredness, times when she would have paid any price for a full night's sleep. But the survivors of the Battle of Ypres lay in such stoical silence as they waited their turn for attention that Kate found it impossible to turn away as long as there was still work to be done. She had never been a frivolous young woman, but these first months of her working life matured her with remarkable speed. She never ceased to be appalled by the injuries she saw, but with every day that passed she was able to deal with them more competently.

When Christmas came she allowed herself a single day of rest. By now Margaret had closed her London home and it was tacitly accepted that Blaize would be the family centre for as long as the war lasted.

Already, though, the family was scattering. Brinsley was still in France and Robert too had left for the front. Even to Kate it seemed that his period of training had been very short, and she could see the same anxiety in Margaret's unhappy eyes. But he had assured his mother that his role would be to lay the tracks of light railways for the movement of supplies, and this would be done behind the line. Kate could feel no such consolation when she thought about Brinsley.

So it was a small and not very merry group of people who assembled in the library at Blaize to celebrate Christmas – the Christmas which had once been expected to mark a return to peace. Nor were Kate's spirits raised by a piece of news which came from Beatrice. A date had been fixed – two weeks ahead – on which the second women's unit would leave England. But it was not going to France.

Kate knew that there had been great difficulties in getting women doctors admitted to the war zones. The British War Office had remained adamant in its refusal to accept the offer of skilled workers and modern equipment, while the French had proved unable to use the first unit to good advantage. All the same, it was a specific desire to help British soldiers on the Western Front which had prompted Kate to volunteer. It was with dismay that she learned that her unit would be going to Serbia.

Six months earlier she would not even have known where Serbia was. Even now she found it difficult to care greatly about the fervent nationalists whose hatred of Austria had started the war. She sat in silence for a little while, wondering whether to withdraw her application. No one could say that the work she was doing in England was not a valuable contribution to the war effort.

Lord Glanville noticed her silence and guessed at its cause, although Kate was ashamed to admit that her own form of nationalism was making her reluctant to care for anyone but her own fellow-countrymen. It had always been a joke in the family that the Glanville library contained every book, on however unexpected a subject, that anyone could need. Now its owner not only produced a map, but proved himself to be the unlikely owner of a Serbo-Croat dictionary, brought back to England by an ancestor whose Grand Tour had once taken in Diocletian's palace. Kate accepted the gift without enthusiasm and continued to consider her future.

But there was no real choice. It would be disgraceful to withdraw from her commitment so late in the day, leaving Beatrice less than a fortnight to find a substitute. And certainly if she did withdraw, she would never be offered a place in any other unit and so would lose her only chance of working in a front-line hospital. It was not so long since she had been convinced that it was there, in the places where men were actually being wounded, that she could be most useful, and that conviction had not changed. Perhaps after a little while she would be allowed to transfer to a different theatre of war. But soldiers could not choose where they would serve. Why should she expect different treatment for herself?

Kate allowed herself one long sigh of disappointment and resignation. Then, as the others looked at her in curious sympathy, she forced herself to smile. After only a few seconds the smile ceased to be a pretence as the warmth of her feelings for her family made themselves felt. When she had so little time left in England, she must fill every moment with happiness. Who could tell, after all, when she would be able to spend Christmas at Blaize again?

1915

1

On the Western Front the enemy was the German; in the Dardanelles it was the Turk; in Serbia it was the louse. Its killing power took Kate by surprise, and the battle against this unexpected adversary began almost from the first moment of her arrival in Serbia.

The journey across a continent disrupted by war had been long and uncomfortable. Kate and her fellow-doctor applied themselves to the Serbo-Croat dictionary and by the end of the journey had at least mastered the difficulties of the Cyrillic alphabet. But this achievement proved to be of only limited use. Now they could read and pronounce words in the unfamiliar letters, but they had yet to learn what the words meant.

Communication was the first problem to confront them when at last the party of doctors and nurses stepped off the train at Kragujevatz. They had been invited to come here and they were expected – a reception committee was waiting for them at the station. But their first impression, gained from an interpreter whose English was almost as incomprehensible as the Serbo-Croat of his companions, was that the British team were not wanted in the town. Women in the medical world were so often under-valued that it was easy to see slights even perhaps where none was intended; but to Kate, tired after the journey and still disappointed that she had not been sent to France, the impression that they were being turned away came as a last straw. To keep her temper under control she supervised the unloading of the expedition's stores while the senior doctor, Dr Muriel Forbes, established that she and the Serbs could converse, after a fashion, in German.

'The reason why they're suggesting we should establish ourselves away from the town is that the arsenal is here in Kragujevatz and there are regular bombing raids by Taube aircraft,' Dr Forbes reported when the situation had been explained to her. 'It doesn't mean that they don't need or want us. Far from it! Twenty-one of their own doctors have died in the past five weeks.'

'From the bombs?' asked Kate incredulously.

'No. From typhus. There's an epidemic raging. They've had four thousand civilian deaths in this town alone and nobody knows how many are dying in the villages. As well as the regular military hospital here, there's an emergency building filled with men wounded in the campaign. That's where they'd expected us to work, but the typhus is spreading through there as well.'

'If we split into two teams, could they give us orderlies?' Kate asked.

Muriel's smile showed that she had been thinking along the same lines. 'Yes. I asked that question, and the answer was that with the greatest of ease and pleasure we could be provided with as many Austrian prisoners of war as we needed.'

'Is that safe? I mean, would they have to be under military guard all the time?'

'I gather that they're only Austrians in the sense that they were conscripted into the Austrian Army because they lived in land under Austrian occupation. They're Serbs by race – Bosnians – and delighted to have been captured – in fact, it sounds as though most of them deserted. They'd work as volunteers.'

'Then we ought to establish a separate hospital for the typhus victims,' said Kate. 'Under tents, if possible, and a little way out of town.'

The two women were so closely in agreement that there was not even any need to discuss where each of them should go. Muriel, the elder, was a surgeon and volunteered at once to care for the wounded soldiers who could not be housed in the main military hospital.

Three days later Kate's tented hospital received its first patients. Those of the British team who stayed with her had been allocated their own spheres of responsibility – for nursing, the kitchen, the dispensary and the stores – and had set to work at once to train the Serbo-Austrian orderlies allotted to them. Kate herself had grasped the greatest nettle of all, that of sanitation and disinfestation. She was only twenty-four years old and all her training had been done in teaching hospitals run with an almost military discipline along lines laid down many years earlier – establishments whose methods of organization could not even be queried by a junior doctor, much less completely re-thought. But her recent work at Blaize had provided useful experience of organizing a hospital almost from scratch, and from her father she had inherited the ability to be definite, taking responsibility and giving firm orders even when she lacked the experience to be sure that the effects would be as she hoped. From her mother, too, she had from childhood absorbed the principles of community hygiene. Lydia's battle in Jamaica had been against the mosquitoes which carried malaria and yellow fever and against the the insanitary habits which made dysentery endemic. With the same singlemindedness Kate declared war on the lice which carried typhus and on the polluted water which spread the equally dangerous typhoid fever.

To save the wounded soldiers in the town from further infection, Muriel would direct typhus patients to the tented hospital at once. Even though she expected this, Kate was not prepared for what she saw as she stepped out of the staff tent at six in the morning. A row of carts stretched from the perimeter of the camp back along the road until it disappeared behind the brow of a hill. There were ox wagons and donkey carts and occasionally a smaller vehicle – hardly more than a platform on two wheels, pulled between the shafts by the mother of the child who lay on it. Old men carried babies in their arms;

58

exhausted women slept on the verge. There was no noise, no jostling for position; the line of sufferers waited patiently until someone was ready to help them.

Kate was already dressed in the costume which she had designed for everyone concerned in the reception of new patients. It was not beautiful, and only time would tell whether it was effective. She had rubbed her body all over with paraffin and was now wearing a one-piece garment tightly strapped round her neck, ankles and wrists. One of her first actions when she realized the dangers had been to cut off most of her thick tawny hair so that the short crop which remained could be easily contained inside a rubber cap. Long boots and rubber gloves completed the outfit.

Careless of the impression she must make, she called for stretcher bearers and hurried to the head of the queue. A tall man with only one arm jumped down from the front of the first ox wagon and led her round to the back. He pulled the canvas aside to reveal more than a dozen children. All were between the ages of three and ten and all were either asleep or unconscious. Their hair was dirty and their clothes ragged, but that was of no importance. What made Kate stare in dismay was the state of the little girl nearest to the light. Her leg rested on a pad of folded sacks but there was no flesh on the bone of the foot and the gangrene was spreading above the knee. Several weeks must have passed since she survived the first onslaught of the typhus and it was clear that in all that time she had received no medical attention.

The one-armed man was saying something, presumably in Serbo-Croat. Kate shook her head to indicate that she did not understand and he made a second attempt in a language equally unfamiliar to her. She put up a finger to silence him as she made a quick count of the children. Three were in need of immediate surgery, five were in the semi-comatose stage of typhus which suggested that they were approaching the point of crisis, two others –

59

awake now and moaning for water – showed the brown blotches on their skins which were the earlier signs of infection, and three were already dead. Only one little girl appeared to be free of typhus and her state was the most serious of all, for it was clear that she was suffering from diphtheria and that an immediate tracheotomy was essential.

Kate pointed out this child and two of the gangrene cases to be the first to go to the special admission tents, where they would undergo a routine of cleansing and disinfecting before being admitted to the ward tents. As she turned away, realizing that all the reception arrangements must be multiplied, she had to fight down a sense of panic. In the weeks of waiting she had done her best to fill the gaps in her experience, but even then she had been part of a team and had never been required to attempt the most dangerous operations. She had had some surgical experience as a medical student, but she was not a qualified surgeon. Beatrice, allowing her to join the unit, had expected her to act only as Muriel's assisstant in this field. But to put a child who was already almost dead from diphtheria back on to a jolting wagon in order that she could be entrusted to Muriel's safer hands would be a risk too great to take. From now on, Kate realized, everything she did would be a question of life or death for someone. This was the moment in which the sentimental disappointment she had felt in being unable to work with British soldiers fell away from her mind and never returned. The need for a doctor here was as great as it could be anywhere else in the world. Within a short time she would have a little girl's life in her hands, and it was a life just as important as that of a soldier in Flanders. To be a doctor, nationality must never be of any importance.

The one-armed man made a third attempt to communicate with her and this time he spoke in French. Kate had learned the language only from books, but she had a natural talent for languages and could both understand what he said and answer him. Recognizing the anxiety in his voice, she paused for a moment to answer although there was so much to do.

'Can they be saved?' he asked.

'Three are already dead. We will do our best for the others. But the gangrene is very serious. Why were they neglected for so long?

'They are not my children,' said the tall man. 'They are orphans. All of them: no mother, no father. I am a Russian. My name is Sergei Fedorovich Gorbatov. A woman gave me shelter on her farm. When she died, there was no one left alive on the farm except her son there.' He pointed to a three-year-old whom Kate had already marked out as the most likely survivor of the wagonload. 'I heard of your hospital and set out to bring him here. All these others I have found on the road as I came, or they have been brought out of their houses by neighbours. Their fathers killed in the army, their mothers dead of disease. Who will look after them?'

Kate was already sufficiently dismayed by the enormity of the medical task which she faced. This was no time for her to consider how a ruined social order should rebuild itself. She repeated her promise to do her best before turning away more decisively to make the necessary new arrangements.

'May I give you help?' Sergei was at her side as she crossed the field. He made a gesture towards the empty sleeve of his shabby military coat. 'I'm no use to any army now, praise be to God. But I can work as a nurse or a messenger. As your orderly, I could help with any problem of language, between French and Serbo-Croat or German. If you will teach me a little English as well, you will find I learn quickly.'

Kate had been too greatly concerned with the children to pay much attention to their escort. Now she looked at him more closely. His tangled beard had given the

61

impression of an older man, but he might not be more than thirty. His eyes, unnaturally bright, glittered out of a face which was too pale, almost grey. His clothes were ragged and he himself was dirty. Nevertheless it was immediately clear that he was not a peasant, but an intelligent and perhaps even an educated man.

His offer was tempting. Kate had known even before she arrived that she would not be able to communicate in Serbo-Croat, but she had not realized what a disadvantage her lack of German would be. So many of the Serbs had lived under Austrian rule that this was their second or even their first language. Without Muriel, problems of interpretation could arise with an irritating frequency. Kate's knowledge of the political situation in the Balkans was too vague to explain why a Russian should be here. Perhaps he had deserted and now saw the hospital as a kind of shelter. But it was true that his amputated arm must have turned him into a non-combatant, and he had shown compassion by accepting responsibility for so many sick children. It was time to make another quick decision.

'You may stay as long as the children you have brought are patients here,' she said. 'First you must move your wagon from the road. Then present yourself at the admission tent. Your beard must be shaved. You will have to be stripped and bathed and rubbed with paraffin and given new clothes before you may go near the other tents and if you leave the compound at any time after that, you may not come back.'

Had she spoken in such a way to an Englishman he would not have been able to believe his ears, but Sergei saluted her now in a manner which was not a correct military gesture but was clearly intended to be admiring rather than mocking. The small incident was reassuring, re-emphasizing her discovery that if she was decisive enough about giving orders, even men would obey promptly.

Sergei made himself so useful that there was no further

mention of the suggestion that he should leave with the children. During the next four months at least a hundred thousand Serbs died in the typhus epidemic, and in the whole of the country fewer than a hundred doctors remained alive. Some deaths took place in Kate's hospital, for many patients arrived too ill to be saved. But her sanitary barriers proved effective and there were no cases of cross-infection. Even dysentery was kept at bay in spite of the lack of plumbing. She also found time to organize dispensary teams to go out to the villages so that when a second epidemic began – this time of diphtheria – its victims could be treated with serum in their own homes.

Kate had been taught that typhus was a cold-weather disease and as the summer sun grew hotter it did indeed seem that the plague was coming to an end. Fewer new patients were brought to the hospital and, now that the sides of the tents could be tied up to let the breeze blow through, those who remained made a faster recovery. For the first time since her arrival there were moments – even half-hours – when Kate could feel herself off-duty. Sergei, quick to pick up a little English, insisted on teaching her Russian in return. Kate protested laughingly that of all the languages in the world Russian was the one least likely ever to be of use to her, but was disarmed by his sweeping assertion that to acquire useless knowledge was the mark of the civilized person. Her good ear for both languages and music enabled her quickly to acquire a conversational vocabulary. Learning to read and write was more difficult, but there was an attraction in finding a use for her previous study of the Cyrillic alphabet, and the unavailability of any other books gave her an incentive to master those which formed Sergei's only luggage. Welcoming the necessity to clear her mind of medical problems for an hour or so, she enjoyed her lessons and made good progress. Like a dutiful schoolgirl she studied grammar and was rewarded by poetry.

Sergei still acted as her orderly but by September had become a friend. So when a message arrived to say that Muriel was ill, Kate took him with her as she hurried to the town. Muriel had already diagnosed her own symptoms.

'It's typhoid, not typhus,' she murmured. 'I don't understand it. We've been boiling everything. All the milk, all the water, everything. And I was inoculated in England.'

'You'll be all right,' said Kate, although she was alarmed by her colleague's appearance.

'Yes,' said Muriel. 'That's only a matter of nursing. I didn't send for you for that. It's the hospital.'

'Leave that to me,' Kate said. The organization of the tented camp was running so smoothly that the rest of her team could continue without her for a while. Putting Muriel in the care of a Scottish nurse, she set out to inspect her new territory.

The building horrified her. She could see that efforts had been made to clean it and keep it clean, but the size and rough condition of the converted barracks made sterile conditions impossible. Typhus, which was dying out elsewhere, still lingered here, fastening on soldiers who at the time of their arrival had been wounded but not infected. She set to work with all the energy she had shown on her first arrival in the country, but as the days passed she found herself more and more tired. Then she could hardly drag herself out of bed in the morning, and merely to move about the hospital became an unbearable effort. Yet in spite of the tiredness her head ached so much that she was unable to sleep. Even before the night when she found herself sweating in bed, her body glowing and almost bubbling with heat, even before that she recognized the symptoms. Typhus! She took her own temperature and was just able to read that it was 105° before she collapsed.

Returning to consciousness, she found Sergei's forearm

pressing down on her chest. Her lungs were bursting and there was an almost unbearable pain in her heart. She seemed to have forgotten how to breathe, but Sergei's pressure continued until the pain became too great to endure. She screamed, and at once the tensions in her chest snapped and relaxed. Her lungs emptied and filled again, emptied and filled. Sergei slid down to the floor and sat there for a moment, apparently as exhausted as herself.

When he stood up again he was smiling. He began to sponge her – not only her face but her whole body. She ought to have felt shocked, but somewhere in her memory was the realization that this had happened before when she was almost but not quite unconscious. Like an expert nurse he rolled her first to one side of the bed and then to the other so that he could change the sheets. She was clean, she was cool and – although still too weak to move – she was better.

'In these three weeks you have died twice,' Sergei said. 'No heartbeat, no breathing. Even Christ was content with one resurrection. You have always been a most demanding mistress. Keep still and I will find you a proper nurse.'

Nurse Cameron arrived within a few moments. She took Kate's temperature and gave an unprofessional sigh of relief.

'Crisis over?' asked Kate. Her body was so weak that she could only whisper, but her mind was as clear as though she had never been ill.

'We'll be needing to feed you up, Doctor. But it should be plain sailing from now on.'

'And Dr Forbes?'

'I hoped you wouldn't ask that so soon.'

'You mean – she died of the typhoid?'

'I'm afraid so.'

Kate was silent for a few moments, but her responsibility for the hospital overcame her sadness.

'Who's in charge now?'

'The army sent us an officer. Major Dragovitch. He's seen to the general administration while I've done my best to look after the medical side.'

'So who's been caring for me?'

'The Russki,' said Nurse Cameron. 'He's spent three weeks in this room with you. Nursing and talking. Whenever you were at your lowest he'd talk non-stop, almost as though he thought you'd be too polite to die in the middle of a conversation. How he expected you to understand his foreign lingo I can't imagine. I'm not saying a word against him, though. The reason you didn't die is because he wouldn't let you.'

He came back an hour later and looked critically at his patient.

'You're not to think that you're better,' he said. 'There must be at least three weeks of convalescence. As much of it as possible in the sunshine. I shall arrange for you to go back to the tented hospital so that you can lie in a bed outside all day.'

'Yes, Doctor,' said Kate. 'And Sergei – thank you.'

They smiled at each other. In this unexpected life, Kate realized that Sergei had become her closest friend. It was an unlikely enough fate which had brought Kate herself to Kragujevatz. She had often wondered what equally surprising story might explain Sergei's exile from his own country, but had never before liked to enquire. But now weakness and gratitude combined to make her feel that there were no questions she could not ask.

'Why did you leave Russia, Sergei?' she asked.

Sergei sat down on the wooden chair beside her bed. 'Do you know what happened in St Petersburg in 1905?' he asked.

Kate shook her head and he tutted sadly. 'The British are interested in nothing but the problems of their own empire,' he said.

'If that were true, we should hardly be fighting a war

on behalf of Belgium. In any case, in 1905 I was a child living in Jamaica.'

'So you've never heard of Bloody Sunday? That's where I lost my arm. You may have thought I was fighting valiantly against the Germans when I was wounded. It's an impression I don't trouble to correct. But I was just a student, marching peacefully with thousands of others to deliver a petition to the Tsar, when the Cossacks charged into us. The Cossacks have a very special kind of whip. Long and strong, and at the end dividing into two thongs with a thin strip of lead between them. It's not intended for use on their horses, you understand. I was one of the lucky ones. At least I was alive when at last the horses galloped away. But while I was lying there in the snow I realized that it would be useless ever again to appeal to the Tsar against the incompetence and cruelty of his own agents. The people must take power into their own hands.'

'So you became a revolutionary?'

'All I did was to travel round the docks and factories, suggesting to the workers that they should form committees and consider the possibility of strikes. In October of that year there was a general strike and it was successful. The Tsar granted us a constitution. But within a week everyone who had been concerned with the strike was either under arrest or in hiding. Once again I was fortunate. I was able to escape. But I can never go back to Russia. There have been sad years.' He paused for a little while as though to remember them. 'Now the roads of Europe are filled with refugees, owning only what they can carry on their backs. I have become merely one of millions. You remember the children I brought to the hospital? The orphans?'

'Of course.'

'I arrange for those who recovered to go to a monastery in the north. There's someone there who will never turn away anyone in need, as I found for myself. This morning

I received a letter from him to say that a new offensive has started. The Germans and Austrians have launched a combined attack along the whole length of the northern front. The monastery is under shellfire and he has had to send the children south for their own safety. So they're on the road again with nowhere to go – no homes, no families. What hope have they for the future, these little ones? Who will feed them? Who will care for them?' He sighed. 'Well, we must give thanks for each extra day of existence that is granted to us. If we can survive to the end of this trouble, perhaps it will be possible to build up a new life somewhere. As for you, you must build up your strength as fast as possible, before we have to go.'

'Go where?' asked Kate.

'You've seen the Serbian Army. Brave men, but peasants. They have good discipline but no equipment, and there are too few of them. How long do you think they can hold back the armies of two military nations? For a little while, perhaps, because they know the terrain and they have the support of the people. But unless the Allies can spare men from the Western Front to strengthen them, this hospital will be in the hands of the invaders before November. The Germans and the Austrians are civilized enough. At least they obey their officers. But as soon as they win their first victory, the Bulgars will take the opportunity to invade from the south, picking the bones of Serbia like vultures. And I can tell you, the Bulgars are animals. They violate children, they cut off women's breasts. I haven't kept you alive for the enjoyment of devils like these. Before the town is captured, you will have to take your hospital away.'

In the village where Kate Lorimer had spent her child-hood, her father lay ill in bed. The secret of Jamaica's luxuriant vegetation lay in the generous proportion of tropical rain to tropical heat, but the same combination produced a humidity oppressive to a sick man. Soaked in his own sweat, Ralph Lorimer listened to the pounding of the rain as it hurled itself against the roof. He shivered with cold even while his body burned with fever. A dozen times an hour he flung off his bed coverings, but on each occasion was forced to grope for them again almost immediately. This was the most severe attack he could remember since the first bout of malaria had taken him by surprise nearly thirty years before.

Lydia would come as soon as she could. It would be humiliating to send a messenger for her merely in order that he might be made more comfortable. As a general rule Ralph was proud of the dedication with which his wife devoted herself to the medical care of his congre-gation. He knew how childish it was to wish that for once she would neglect her surgery in the interest of her husband. He knew, too, that his illness was not danger-ous. It would burn itself out, as it always had before – and any of the village women would have been proud to come to the pastor's house and nurse the head of their community. It was Ralph's own choice that only Lydia should care for him, and the price he paid for it was her absence whenever anyone else was ill.

As abruptly as it had begun three hours earlier, the drumming of the rain stopped, although for some time longer he could hear the splash of water dripping from the roof on to the edge of the verandah. The wet season was coming to an end. Soon the December days of unbroken sunshine would be here and Ralph, fit and strong once again, would be able to stride as usual across the land of the Bristow plantation which had been reclaimed from jungle under his inspiration. Violent changes of weather were part of the Jamaican pattern. It was normal that November should bring rain and just as normal that the rain would stop. The only difference between the routines of 1915 and those of previous years was the fear which nagged perpetually at Ralph's mind: the fear that some harm would come to Kate or Brinsley. To Lydia he never spoke of the dangers – there was no need to, for she knew them well enough and shared his anxiety. And sometimes he was able to persuade himself that they were groundless. Kate was not in Flanders; whilst Brinsley, who had spent more than a year at the battlefront, appeared to bear a charmed life. So many of his fellow-volunteers had been killed that he had already been promoted to captain, but so far he had not been even slightly wounded.

In the comparative silence which followed the rain-storm, Ralph could hear Lydia approaching. She came very slowly, her progress tracked by the cheerful shouts of the villagers she passed and her own quieter, breathless responses. The village was built on a double slope: the land fell from the mountains of the interior towards the flat coastal plains and was also cut almost into a gorge by the stream which crashed down in a waterfall before tumbling towards the sea. That might have been enough to explain Lydia's frequent need to pause and rest – but Ralph knew that there was another reason. His resent-ment of it rose even before she came into the room.

She carried his medicine in one hand and, although everything about her face and body proclaimed her tired-ness, she smiled at him with an attempt at her old liveliness. Her other hand supported her ten-year-old child as he straddled her hip. Grant was reluctant to release his clutch of her neck as she set him gently down in a corner of the room and Ralph found himself grinding his teeth in a vain attempt to control his anger.

'Lydia, it will have to stop!' he exclaimed. 'You're not strong enough to carry Grant around like this.'

'I can manage for a little longer,' she said. She gave him the medicine and with cool water and clean sheets applied herself to making him comfortable. But although Ralph was tempted to relax in the ease she provided, he could not control the irritation caused by his son's presence.

'Could you carry me?' he demanded. 'If I asked you to lift me out of bed, could you do it? Of course you couldn't. And no more will be be able to carry Grant as he grows. The moment must come when he'll no longer be able to depend on you in such a way, and you're doing him no service to prolong the dependence.'

'It's very difficult for him when the paths are so wet and slippery. I don't think you realize. His lameness – '

'I know all about his lameness,' Ralph interrupted. 'But I also know that he is ten years old. He's not a baby to be pampered and petted, and you're not strong enough to treat him as though he were. He must find some way to move about by himself. I had a crutch made for him, and he ought to use it. Otherwise his other muscles will waste away as well for lack of exercise.'

'You ought not to talk like this in front of him,' said Lydia uneasily.

'Then he is the one who should go. This is my room and I'll say what I please in it. Go to your own room, Grant.' He waited a moment but his son did not move. 'I said, get out. Did you hear me? Get out of here.'

Naked and very tall, he must have appeared like a giant to the frightened boy as he left his bed and staggered across the room, dizzy with the effects of fever. At the last moment, the fair-haired boy twisted away from his father and half rolled, half slithered out of the room.

'You see!' exclaimed Ralph. 'He can move well enough

when he wants to. It's our duty, yours and mine together, to teach him the best way to use what strength he has. But how can I expect him to succeed when you always go behind my back to spoil him?'

Exhausted by the effort, he flung himself back into bed, hoping that Lydia would smooth the sheet and make him comfortable again. But instead she followed Grant out on to the verandah, her lips tight with anger.

Ralph groaned to himself as he lay back on the pillow. Lydia had been the best wife that any man could hope for until the birth of that last, unwanted child; but these days there seemed to be as much quarrelling as love between them. He tossed restlessly from side to side until weakness combined with the humidity to exhaust him. For a little while he slept, and awoke to find Duke sitting beside the bed.

The sight of his assistant never failed to cheer Ralph. Perhaps it was Duke's own smile which worked the miracle. At least three of the young man's ancestors had been white men, so that his skin was lighter than that of most of the islanders, but his flashing white teeth and ready grin were typical of Jamaica. Sometimes when Ralph was angry with Lydia, and sickened by the sight of Grant, he longed to proclaim that Brinsley was not the only son of whom he could feel proud, that Duke was a Lorimer as well. But that was a secret which had been kept for twenty-eight years and he recognized how hurtful it would be to reveal the truth now.

'I brought the accounts,' Duke said. 'But if you too tired, next week good enough.'

'No, I'll look at them now.' Ralph struggled to sit up, with Duke's help. 'Bring me something to drink.'

The water from the covered pitcher was too warm to be refreshing. Ralph drank it thirstily but without enjoyment. Half apologetically, Duke took a small bottle from the pouch on his belt.

'Put that away!' Ralph ordered. 'If you came more

often to chapel, you'd know how strongly I feel about total abstinence.'

'A little rum in the water helps fight the fever,' said Duke. 'Strong medicine, not drink.'

He poured it as he spoke, and held it out. Ralph shook his head and then looked in irritation towards the open door as he heard from outside the familiar sound of Grant calling for his mother. He would have gone out to whip the whining child if he had been strong enough, for suddenly he felt that he could bear Grant's petulance no longer. Perhaps that was why he abandoned the principles of a lifetime and in an angry gesture drained the gourd which Duke was holding to his lips.

The rum was not watered at all. Ralph gasped as the spirit burned his throat. For a moment he dared not move or even speak; then his whole body flushed with warmth, balancing the heat of the fever so that for a little while he ceased to shiver and could relax in comfort.

'Mother! Mother!' Outside, Grant was still shouting, more loudly now and with a trace of desperation. 'Mother!'

It sounded as though Lydia for once was not near enough to come running to the boy's call. Perhaps, thought Ralph hopefully, she had at last taken some notice of her husband's opinion and had left Grant to look after himself. His anger faded into a feeling of well-being. It might be as well after all to leave the accounts until next week. He was just sliding back into a sleeping position when Grant called again. 'Father! Father!'

'Come here if you want me!' Ralph shouted back. The response was automatic and yet even as he expressed his annoyance he was uneasy. It was surprising that Grant should call for someone he knew to be angry with him. And there were other sounds outside by now: a scrambling of bare feet, a murmuring of low voices. Ralph gestured at Duke to go and see what was happening.

'And tell that child to stop shouting,' he said. While he

73

tried to keep a normal irritation in his voice, fear was growing in his heart. He stayed in bed as Duke went out, so that for a few moments longer he could pretend that nothing was wrong, but the effects of the rum had worn off already and his body was rigid with cold.

When Duke returned he was carrying Grant. He stood in the doorway for a moment, almost as near to tears as the sobbing ten-year-old. Then he moved out of the way, and four of the villagers carried Lydia inside.

3

The building of Brinsley House at the end of the eighteenth century had been a gesture indicating a change of status. From that time onwards the Lorimers ceased to be merely one out of many shipping families of Bristol and were acknowledged as merchant princes. Magnificently dominating the Avon Gorge, the house was designed to be filled with large numbers of children, servants and guests. It was in Brinsley House that John Junius Lorimer had brought up his three legitimate children: William, Margaret and Ralph; and it was to this same house that Margaret had brought her half-sister Alexa, orphaned at the age of nine. From the ruins of the family fortune after the bank crash of 1878, William Lorimer had managed to salvage his father's mansion, and had in turn brought up his own three children there. But William was dead; and his elder son, Matthew, had quarrelled with his parents in 1895 and, turning his back on any possible inheritance, had left Bristol for Paris, never since returning. As the end of 1915 approached, Arthur Lorimer lived alone in the mansion, attended only by a few servants who were too young or too old for war work. It was not a style of existence which suited the old house and, at the moment when one of the Lorimer Line's banana boats was

74

approaching the Portishead docks with letters from Ralph Lorimer on board, as well as produce from the Bristow plantation, Arthur had evolved a plan to bring the place briefly back to life.

'I've been thinking about Christmas,' he said to his sister Beatrice, who had travelled from London for a weekend free from the fear of Zeppelin raids. 'You'll spend it at Brinsley House, I hope. Mrs Shaw asked yesterday whether she should arrange for the usual decorations to be put in place. At first I thought it unnecessary to go to such trouble when only the two of us will be here. But then I had second thoughts. It seems a pity to abandon old customs. So I told her that I should want a tree to be decorated as usual, and holly and candles to be arranged in the galleries. And with that picture in my mind, I've decided to hold a children's party. Or even more than one.'

He was amused by the expression of horror on her face. Beatrice had no interest in children and no liking for them. 'Whose children?' she demanded.

'First of all the children of my employees. But in addition to them, there are a good many boys and girls in Bristol whose fathers are at the front and whose mothers have trouble enough to provide even the most necessary food. They're not likely to receive many of the presents which you and I could always expect in our childhood. We could give them here, I thought, an afternoon to remember, a little brightness in the gloom. It wouldn't be too difficult to arrange. A few games to play, perhaps a conjuror to amuse them, a really good tea and a parcel to take home. I hope such a prospect wouldn't frighten you away, Beatrice. I should need your advice. And your help too, on the day.'

He knew that he could rely on it. Beatrice's talent for organization had been increased rather than completely satisfied by her office work in London. She acted as a kind of remote quarter-master for all the women's units sent abroad by the suffrage movement and took pride in obtaining and dispatching all the supplies for which she was asked, although their safe arrival was not always within her power to secure. As he had expected, she gave the quick nod which meant that she accepted his proposal in spite of its unexpectedness.

'I'll buy the gifts for you and wrap them, if you like,' she offered. 'Tell me how much you want to spend on each, how many girls you expect and how many boys. And of what ages.'

'Thank you very much. But Beatrice, don't choose presents that are too sensible.'

'What do you mean?'

'I've no doubt the mothers would like to see a warm garment or a pair of shoes come out of each parcel. But I want to see the children smile with pleasure rather than gratitude. They should have toys. Something to play with. Something that their parents might consider a waste of money.'

'You surprise me more and more, Arthur, but very well. I'll buy skipping ropes and dolls and footballs and tin soldiers.'

Arthur was not ashamed that she should think him sentimental. He had never tried to hide the pleasure he took in the sight of children. The smallness of their neat, slim bodies, the animal energy of their movements, their unrestrained pleasure in making a noise: all these things won his approval. Perhaps he envied them a freedom of movement which he had never been able to indulge – the precision of his mind as he marshalled the figures which kept his business prosperous was reflected in his tight, unhurried walk and quiet voice.

'Would Aunt Margaret care to come to your party, do you think?' asked Beatrice. 'I remember how very much she enjoyed playing with us when we were small.'

'I should think she'll have enough to do as commandant of the hospital at Blaize,' Arthur replied. 'But I'll invite

76

her, of course. And Frisca would be the same age as many of the young guests. She might like to come as well.'

While he was considering his idea for the party he had needed to remind himself that not all children were like Frisca. It was true that he liked little girls in general, but Frisca was almost an idealization of childhood made flesh. Blonde, blue-eyed, beautiful and irrepressibly energetic, she aroused in him a longing to own her so that he could buy pretty clothes for her and show her off and feel proud of her. But the children of his employees were more likely to be shy and badly dressed.

Enough time had been spent on frivolities. Even on a Saturday evening Arthur was not sorry to be interrupted by a messenger from his dockside office. A ship was just in from Jamaica and a lengthy detour made necessary by the danger of submarine attack had put part of her cargo at risk of spoiling.

'I'll come at once,' Arthur said. He glanced at the letters which the messenger had brought from the ship. Two of them were from his Uncle Ralph – one addressed to himself and one to be put in the post for Margaret. But they, like the rest, could wait until he returned.

'We could ask Matthew,' said Beatrice suddenly.

Puzzled, Arthur paused in the doorway. He had already dismissed the subject of the party from his mind and did not take his sister's meaning at once.

'For Christmas,' explained Beatrice. 'His quarrel was never with us but only with our parents. Now that they are both dead, we could all be friends again.'

It was not a suggestion to be adopted too impulsively. Arthur knew how attached Beatrice had always been to the elder of her two brothers, and how much it had upset her when he ran away from home to become an artist. But it was necessary for Arthur to consider his own position.

There was no danger, he decided. Their father's will –

in which William recognized that it was his younger son who deserved to inherit the Lorimer business interests and who had the talent to manage them – had been watertight. And if Matthew had wished to challenge it, or even to appeal for generosity, he would have done so long ago. As Beatrice said, there was nothing to prevent them from resuming a friendly relationship.

Except, it occurred to him, for one practical difficulty.

'I agree with you in principle,' he said. 'It would be a good gesture. But how are we to get in touch with him? I've no idea whereabouts in the world he is at this moment.'

4

Young men were swept into the army by dreams of glory, by the shame of being presented with white feathers, or by the prospect of a regular weekly wage. None of these considerations affected Matthew Lorimer and if anyone had asked him why he had enlisted, he would have been hard put to find a sensible answer. There was no conscription as yet and his forty-second birthday even excluded him from the voluntary scheme under which men attested their willingness to serve when they were needed. He felt no hatred for the Germans, although it was true that his years in Paris had given him a love for France and a wish to see its soil free once again from the devastation of battle. Nor was he in any sense a combatant. He had joined the army only because that was a necessary first step towards secondment as an official war artist.

Nobody had compelled or even invited him to spend his time sketching the shell-shocked landscape of craters and barbed wire, with wounded men propped against sandbags and stretcher bearers ducking low as they dashed from the dubious shelter of one hedge to another – in fact, his realistic pictures of soldiers hardly recognizable as human beings beneath their coverings of mud and blood were not always to War Office taste. He could have continued to prosper as a painter of portraits. There were still plenty of rich women in England. They looked a little more tired than in the previous year and their eyes could not always conceal the sadness of bereavement as their sons or brothers, husbands of fiancés, were lost to them in the Flanders trenches or on the Gallipoli beaches. But their commissions for portraits could have kept Matthew alive, if he had chosen to make his living in that way; and in addition a new market had opened as the war news grew grimmer and frightened mothers commissioned paintings of sons who might never return from France.

Only restlessness could explain why Matthew should have turned his back on all that. He had been restless all his life, but at first there had been a purpose to his sudden movements. When he left England as a young man, it was not solely because he was bored with accounts and shipping statistics: more positively, he had set his heart on a painting career. And when, ten years later, he abandoned his life in Paris, it was not out of dissatisfaction but because of his projected marriage to Alexa. The discovery that Alexa was his aunt – a relationship for many years concealed by her adoption and by the closeness of their ages – had left him in a state of shock. Recognizing that he could never marry her, he was unable to prevent himself from continuing to love her. Jealous and unhappy, he had watched from the back of the admiring crowd as she emerged from her wedding at St Margaret's, Westminster, on the arm of Lord Glanville. Secretly he hoped that she had chosen to acquire a title and a fortune by marriage only as a compensation – because by an absurd accident of birth she was separated from the man she really loved. At some point, he knew, he would have to accept in his heart what his reason had already recognized as an inevitable and permanent separation; but until that point came he drifted without purpose, using the war as an excuse for physical insecurity in order that he need no longer come to terms with the deeper purposelessness of his life.

In the last month of 1915, Matthew was back in England. The Battle of Loos seemed to have existed in a different world from that of his quiet Chelsea studio, but as he worked his sketches up into a large painting of the battlefield at night all its sounds came back to haunt him: the boom of cannons, the spitting of machine guns, the erratic stabs of rifle fire, the deafening explosions of shells and grenades and, above all, the screams of the wounded. He slept badly, continually waking in a nightmare conviction that he had been blinded and would never paint again. In an effort to tire himself out, he stayed at the easel until the small hours of every morning. So when his doorbell rang late on a December evening, his strained eyes failed to focus immediately on the young woman who stood outside.

She was a working girl whose shabby clothes were too thin to prevent her from shivering in the winter air. After allowing him a few seconds to study her, she gave a resigned laugh.

'You don't recognize me.'

Her voice, with its Midland accent, stirred Matthew's memory and he stared harder at the strong-boned face.

'Of course I do.' Matthew had abandoned the snobbish class judgements of his parents on the day he left Brinsley House. Even if he had not had a particular reason for kindness in this case, he would never have begrudged politeness to someone whom his mother would have regarded only as a possible applicant for a post as kitchen maid. 'It took me a moment to move my mind from the picture I'm working on, that's all. Come upstairs.'

She looked curiously at the huge painting as she followed him into the studio and allowed him to take her coat.

'Is that what it's like, then?'

'No. I can't find any way to paint the noise. This is a safe and silent version of Hell. The reality is rather different.'

'Bit of a change from when you were painting me.'

'It's all connected, though. These explosions of light are caused by the shells which you help to make. Well, perhaps these are shells filled by some German Peggy, but yours will be having the same effect on the other side of the line.'

She was intelligent enough to be amused at the way in which he let her know that he had remembered her name.

'What happened to the picture you did of me?' she asked.

'The munitions factory one went to be turned into a poster. One of a series to persuade women to take up essential war work. The other one's here somewhere. Sit down, and I'll find it.'

Earlier in the year he had been asked to make a portfolio on the Home Front and chose to concentrate on the contribution which women were making to the war. Everywhere he went he found women doing men's jobs, from farm labourers and gamekeepers in the country, to bus conductors and policewomen in the towns. Particularly in the factories, as the men moved out the women moved in. Peggy had been making fuses in a munitions factory when he first sketched her three months ago. She worked long hours in conditions which he privately regarded as criminally dangerous, and was faced at the end of the day with a long walk to the poor lodgings which were all she could afford. She was not by birth a town girl, and yet not exactly a country girl either. Her father was a coal miner and her home in Leicestershire was a mining village. There had been no openings for girls there, she had told him and, although she could have found employment on a farm nearer to home, she had some talent for sewing and was reluctant to expose her hands to such rough work in all weathers.

Matthew had found the firm boldness of her features intriguing, marking her out from the other girls in the fuse-room. He offered her money to spend a few hours sitting for him in his studio, but her exhaustion when she came was such that she fell asleep while he was painting her. The canvas which he now pulled out of the rack depicted her in just that state – a young woman completely worn out by her work.

She stared at it critically for a few moments; then sighed.

'I should've stayed asleep a bit longer,' she said. 'I've fallen.'

The phrase was unfamiliar to Matthew and she realized that he was puzzled. 'A baby,' she explained. 'I'll be having a baby, come June.'

Inwardly Matthew groaned, but he did not allow any dismay to show on his face. 'Is it mine?' he asked. There was no denying that he had taken advantage of her in every sense, at a moment when she was only half awake; and there had been other meetings in the month which followed, before he left for France. But she had not been a virgin.

'Oh yes,' she said: 'The first time, it were with a lad from our village. More nor a year ago. I were going to marry him. He never came back from Ypres. That were the reason I took this munition work. To get my own back, so to speak. There were no one after him, till you.'

'I'll give you some money,' said Matthew. 'You can go home to your parents, I suppose.'

'Not in this state, I can't. I could go home as a wife. Or even as a widow, if it came to that. But I'll not show my face there with a bastard. Me Dad would kill me. And me Mam's dead.'

'I can't marry you, if that's what you're after,' said Matthew. He chose the words carefully. They meant only that if he could not marry Alexa he was not prepared to marry anyone at all, but with luck they would suggest that he was married already. If necessary he would tell the full lie, but he still hoped that the matter could be settled without a quarrel.

'But you live alone here.'

'That doesn't mean that I'm free.'

'It means I could move in,' she said. 'You'd find it cheaper to support me and the child here than in lodgings. You could do with a bit of housekeeping, by the look of it. And a baby ought to have a father.'

'You're asking too much,' said Matthew; and some of the spirit which had first attracted his attention flashed angrily into her eyes.

'*You* asked enough, didn't you? You expect me to walk out of here with a pound or two in my pocket and to feed your child on it for fourteen years or so, until he's big enough to earn?'

'Of course not. I'll send you something every week. It won't be a lot, though. I'm not much better off than you are.'

Peggy laughed her disbelief. 'It won't do,' she said. 'If you can't marry then I must do without the marriage, but there's no reason why you shouldn't pretend. If I live here with you me Dad'll think all's right and proper. And if it turns out later that you've got a wife tucked away somewhere he'll be sorry for me, perhaps, instead of spitting at me on the doorstep.' The anger faded from her face and was replaced by a look of mischievous invitation. 'The baby won't be here for getting on six months,' she pointed out. 'We could have a bit of fun before that. And if I keep on working for a while longer, with no lodgings to pay, I can save enough for clothes to start him off. It wouldn't be so bad, you know.'

She stood on tip-toe to kiss him. Even while he returned her embrace, Matthew considered the proposal. He had been lucky so far, he supposed – because she was certainly not the only one of his models over the years who had been persuaded to stay for the night when a sitting was over. It had been a mistake, in retrospect, to expect that Peggy would behave like a professional, accepting any accident as the luck of the game; but since he had made the mistake he must pay for it. And although he had no very strong family feeling, Matthew recognized his responsibility to the unborn child. It could not be right that his son should be brought up in the kind of poverty to which Peggy would soon descend if she were left unsupported.

There was not even any reason why he should not allow her the marriage certificate which would make her respectable in the eyes of her family. That was not a decision to be taken on impulse now, but it was something to be considered. Peggy was a decent enough girl, clean and hard-working. He might even find himself emerging at last from the squalor in which he had lived for the past twenty years. Certainly, as she reminded him, he could take pleasure in her company. The collapse of his hopes of marriage to Alexa had left him emotionally shattered and his experience of war in the past year – even as a spectator – made him profoundly pessimistic. His ambition to be a great artist one day had already faded and now he no longer expected to obtain any great satisfaction from life. There were no plans which would be endangered merely because he found himself encumbered with Peggy.

And perhaps, he thought as he kissed her again with more enthusiasm, responding to her invitation, perhaps a permanent relationship of this kind, and the family life which the birth of a child would bring, might have one positive effect. Alexa's marriage to Lord Glanville had not succeeded in stifling his obsession with her. But a new way of life and a woman of his own – surely now at last, if he really made the effort, he could force himself to forget Alexa.

5

The guests who enjoyed the hospitality of Blaize at the end of 1915 wore uniforms of hospital blue instead of the clothes appropriate to weekend house party guests. And they stayed longer. But the mistress of the house continued to regard herself as a hostess. The change from country house to hospital, originally planned to meet a temporary emergency, had by now taken on a permanent air. The old tithe barn which Alexa had earlier converted to a riverside theatre had been filled with hospital beds, and was used as a single long ward for soldiers who had survived operations in France or London but were still seriously ill. A scattering of ugly huts around it housed nurses and orderlies and could provide an isolation ward in case of infectious disease. As the men became convalescent, they moved up to the house. The orangery was a ward for wheelchair cases. The ballroom was divided into cubicles for men who were learning to walk on crutches. And the east wing was occupied by doctors and a dozen patients, mainly blind, who were unable to manage the stairs.

With thoughts similar to Arthur's in Brinsley House, Alexa had been making plans to entertain her many guests for Christmas. In the office which had once been a smoking room she expounded them now to Margaret.

'Each of the men will find two stockings on their beds on Christmas morning,' she said. 'Khaki ones, of course. All the women in the village have been knitting frantically to get enough finished. And Piers has been collecting little things to put inside. Tin trumpets, false noses, bags of sweets.'

'You're treating them like children,' said Margaret, laughing.

'They must feel like children, lying there helpless. If they didn't, how would they ever be able to tolerate all the business of bedpans and being washed by nurses? But there'll be adult things as well. Plenty of cigarettes, of course; and we've been offered two hundred copies of St Matthew's Gospel in a pocket size. Anyway, we shall see to it that the stockings are filled. And I shall provide a Christmas meal. Everything will come from our own resources, the home farm with the help of one or two of the tenants, so you won't need to go through all this ridiculous War Office requisition business. I've already been promised turkeys, sausages, bacon, beer, potatoes and sprouts; and the plum puddings were made here a month ago. Piers will look out some port wine to drink the King's health.'

'Are you leaving me anything to do at all?' asked Margaret.

'We need some crackers,' said Alexa, consulting her list. 'The children in the village school are making paper chains and streamers and painting nativity pictures to be hung up. We must make the wards look really cheerful. There's plenty of holly and mistletoe in the grounds.'

'Just stop for a moment,' Margaret pleaded. 'Who's going to put up all these decorations?'

'The VADs could do that in their spare moments, surely,' Alexa suggested.

'You'll need to check that with Matron. They aren't allowed to have many spare moments, poor girls. Whatever you ask them to do will be extra to their nursing duties.'

'They'll want to do it, all the same,' Alexa said confidently. 'We'll have carol-singing in the ballroom on Christmas Day, and I'll form a little choir to sing in the Theatre Ward.'

'The VADs again?'

'Well, we ought to have a few women's voices. I should think there'll be plenty of volunteers. And on Boxing

Day you've already agreed that we can put on an entertainment.'

Alexa had made it her contribution to the war effort not only to sing to the troops herself, but to assemble a concert party which would provide a programme of varied entertainment. Naturally she had reserved the Christmas booking for her home ground.

'Ah now, I have a point to raise on the subject of the entertainment,' said Margaret. She searched her over-crowded desk for a letter and read it out with a solemn expression on her face. '"Dear Commandant Aunt, Mamma is going to give a concert at Christmas and there will be a lot of singing and playing the piano and making jokes but no dancing. I wish to offer my services as a dancer and I shall be very good. Yours faithfully with love and kisses, Frisca." I take it she's already approached you on the subject?'

'Yes,' said Alexa. 'I've never included dancing in the programme because so many of these men will never be able to dance again. And because often they can't *see* the concert very well, if they aren't able to sit up, but they can hear it. In any case, Frisca's too young for this sort of thing.'

'How old were you when you first sang in public?' asked Margaret.

'My mother was dying. I needed the money.' But Alexa had not needed the reminder that she was only nine years old when she made her first public appearance – in a music hall, not an opera house, but to just as much applause as she was to attract later on. She was willing to be persuaded if Margaret felt strongly enough to press the point.

'Some of these men have babies they've never seen,' Margaret said. 'A good many of them must have won-dered whether their children would grow up without knowing what their fathers looked like. They've spent more than a year, most of them, living with death and

87

with other men in a world which hardly seems to include children at all. I think the sight of Frisca might well make some of them cry. But if she's prepared to face this rather special kind of audience, it can do nothing but good to remind them that they can hope to return to the sort of normal domestic life in which little girls smile and show off.'

'Whatever you command shall be done,' Alexa conceded. 'And now I can see that you'd like to be left to your paperwork.' She smiled at her sister as she went out, but before the door closed behind her she saw that Margaret was about to be interrupted again and stepped back into the office to give warning. 'There's someone else waiting to see you. One of the VADs. And by the look of her, you're going to need a spare handkerchief.'

6

The young women who joined the Voluntary Aid Detachment as their contribution to the war effort were conscientious and willingly hard-working. But most of them were girls of good family, brought up in homes run entirely by servants, so that even the simplest chores had to be explained to them. It was easy for Matron and the charge-sisters to become impatient when, out of anxiety to please, the VADs spent longer on some routine duty than a professional nurse would have done. It was tempting, as well, to allocate all the most unpleasant tasks to them on the grounds that they were still only semi-skilled.

Margaret sympathized with both sides in the frequent disputes which arose. But she regarded herself mainly as the protector of the girls who were young, inexperienced and overworked, and who in most cases had never lived away from home before. Matron was well able to look after herself.

For this reason she was careful not to show any sign of impatience as Nurse Jennifer Blakeney came in, although the weekly roll of patients required by the War Office still lay uncompleted on the desk.

'Good morning, Nurse,' she said. She kept her voice cheerful, although Jennifer's unhappiness was plain enough. 'What's the problem?'

'Matron told me to report to you,' said Jennifer, and was then apparently unable to go on.

'Yes?'

'She said I ought to consider with you whether I was suited to my work.'

'That's a fairly large matter to consider,' Margaret said. 'Sit down, Nurse. Have I had a chitty from Matron about you?' She began to search through the papers on her desk to see whether there was some complaint that she had overlooked.

'No, Dr Scott. It's only just happened.'

'What has just happened?'

As carefully as though Matron herself were presenting the case for the prosecution, Jennifer recited a list of her offences, culminating in Sister's discovery that she had poured out twenty mugs of tea, left them standing on a tray for half an hour, and had then poured the tea away and washed up the mugs.

'So you're not concentrating properly on your work,' said Margaret. 'But I've had good reports of you before. I take it that something has happened.' She recognized the silence which followed as that of someone who knows that if she tries to speak she will burst into tears. Alexa's quick summing-up of the situation had been correct. 'Have you had some bad news?' she enquired.

It was not a question which required very much intuition on her part. There was hardly a family in England which had not by now been given cause for grief. Margaret herself, with her son and her nephew still unhurt, knew that she was luckier than most people.

Jennifer nodded and the tears began to run down her cheeks. 'My brother,' she said.

'Killed?'

Jennifer nodded again, doing her best to stem the flow with much rubbing of her handkerchief.

'I'm very sorry, my dear.'

'But it's not just that,' said Jennifer. Now that the main fact was established, the words came tumbling out. 'It was my father who wrote to tell me. He's quite old. My mother died six years ago and now that Geoffrey's dead – well, he's upset, of course, as I am, but more than that.' She looked up, red-eyed. 'He wants me to go home.'

'To give up your work, you mean?'

'Yes. To look after him. Or just to live with him. He's lonely. He didn't mind too much while he could think that Geoffrey and I would both come back in the end, but now he's frightened.'

'You're only a volunteer, of course,' Margaret said carefully. 'Not an enlisted soldier. You have the right to resign if you wish.'

'But I don't want – Dr Scott, I don't know what I ought to do. I've done my training, I think I'm some use here – I know I've been careless this last week, but I could stop that. I'm sure it's my duty to go on nursing, and yet there's my duty to my father as well, and no one else can do that for me.' The tears welled into her eyes again and she buried her head in her hands.

Margaret allowed her a moment to bring herself under control. She was a slight girl, probably not more than twenty, with fair hair and a pale, pretty face spoiled only by anxious eyes. It was tempting to be purely sympathetic, and certainly the child needed comfort. But Margaret had spent many years acting as the supervisor and friend-in-need of young women who were training to be doctors, and knew that there were times when firmness was more helpful than kindness.

'So you're doing one of your duties badly because you can't choose which of the two you ought to accept,' she said as Jennifer's sniffs came to an end at last. 'I know how tempting it is for parents of my generation to believe that they have a right to their daughters' company and I can see that your love for your father makes this a very difficult choice for you. It's not for me to say what you should decide. There's no right or wrong about it. What is certain is that you must make a decision and when you've made it you must hold to it without regrets. Sometimes, I think, it's better to be definite than to be right.' She paused for a moment to consider. 'Did you tell Matron about your brother's death?'

'No, Doctor.'

'I'll have a word with her. As far as this past week is concerned, I'm sure we can all forget about it and you'll make sure that there's no further cause for complaint. But with regard to the future – I'll give you a week's compassionate leave. A visit to your father will be a comfort to you both, and while you're at home you will take your decision.' She opened the leave book which Matron had brought for her approval that morning. All the VADs hoped that they might be allowed home for Christmas, but Jennifer's case seemed stronger than most. 'I'll present you with another choice at once. If you think it will mean more to your father, I'll change the rota so that you may have Christmas leave. Or else you may go home at once and come back before Christmas Eve.'

It seemed that Jennifer had learned her lesson, for she made her choice without hesitation.

'I wouldn't want to spoil anyone else's hopes for Christmas,' she said. 'I very much appreciate your offer of leave now, and I'd like to accept it.'

Even after Jennifer had left, Margaret was not allowed long without interruption. But the arrival of the post was always welcome and she smiled to see a letter from her brother.

Her smile was quick to fade. Ralph's letter was long and rambling, incoherent almost to the point of incomprehensibility. But although he did not state in so many words that Lydia was dead, there could be no other possible interpretation of the grief and anger and loneliness which he had poured out on paper.

For a long time Margaret stared blankly at the wall in front of her. Lydia had been her friend for fifty years. They were playmates as children in Bristol, and as medical students in London had lived and worked together for the hardest and happiest years of their lives. It was as a direct result of Margaret's match-making that her brother had married Lydia and taken her off to Jamaica. And now her dear friend was dead. It was to be expected at her age, she supposed, that she must lose one by one everyone whom she had loved when she was young, until now only Ralph himself remained, but this particular bereavement made her feel that her youth itself had disappeared. There would be no one now with whom she could exchange memories of bicycle rides and theatres and examinations and all the struggles that had been necessary before the two of them were accepted in a profession dominated by men. Lydia, dear ugly Lydia, had always been so merry, laughing away the tiredness of nights on duty and the drudgery of each new subject which had to be studied.

How merry had Lydia been in the last years of her life, Margaret wondered. She had never complained at the need for her two elder children to spend so much time away from home for the sake of their education, but it must have come as a bitter blow when the war prevented their return just as hopes of a reunion were highest. Brinsley and Kate were such handsome children, sturdy both in body and in the independence of their character. Grant could hardly have provided a satisfactory compensation for their absence. If Ralph's letter were to be believed it was Grant – crippled and clinging – who had been responsible for the final strain on his mother's heart.

Margaret was not a woman who succumbed easily to grief, but the months of war had taken their toll of her nerves. It added an extra dimension to her sadness that a chapter of the past should so finally close at a time when the present was grey and uncertain and when it was not possible to look into the future at all without terror. If a woman surrounded by love on a peaceful tropical island could die, what hope was there for a young man on a battlefield designed for killing? The sense of desolation which overcame her embraced everyone she loved and clouded the future, as well as the past. She mourned for Lydia. And at the same time she feared for Robert.

7

The gales of late December had whipped the Channel into a fury almost as spiteful as that of the Western Front, and the troop trains in both France and England were slow as well as over-crowded. By the time Robert arrived at Paddington Station on his first home leave he was exhausted by forty hours of travel. The train which was already pulling away from the barrier was the last of the day, his only hope of sleeping in a comfortable bed at Blaize and waking up to Christmas Day amongst his family. He forced himself to make one last effort and began to sprint as though the widening gap between himself and the end of the train were exposed to machine gun fire. Still running, he fumbled with the handle of the last carriage and fell rather than stepped inside.

As his panting subsided and he looked around, he saw that the only other occupant of the compartment was a fair-haired young woman wearing the uniform of a VAD. She looked startled, even a little apprehensive. Robert glanced at the window and saw the diamond-shaped label which reserved the compartment for Ladies Only.

'Sorry,' he said. 'I'll move at the next stop.'

'It doesn't matter.' Her voice was shy and attractively soft. She hesitated as though she were either wondering whether it would be proper for her to continue the conversation or else was doubtful about the particular question she wanted to ask. In the end, however, she was unable to restrain it. 'Where have you come from?'

Robert was reluctant to answer. He had promised himself that for the next ten days he would forget the canal and the bridge, pretend that Loos had never existed and that he would never return to Hédauville. In any case he had been warned by friends who had been on leave before him that civilians were not genuinely interested in the details of battles. They made polite enquiries but rarely listened to the answers. Perhaps they lacked the imagination necessary to envisage the horror of life in the trenches; or perhaps, imagining it too well, they were embarrassed to discuss it amidst the comforts of England with someone who was enduring it on their behalf.

'What sector of the front, I mean?' She hesitated again. 'My brother was killed – '

Now Robert saw what she wanted – the description of some landscape which would furnish her attempts to reconstruct the scene; and, most of all, some kind of reassurance that the death had been necessary, a means of understanding why it had happened.

It was not a reassurance which he could give. There was nothing deliberate about his evasion of her question. It was more than three weeks since he had last enjoyed an undisturbed night and he had not slept at all for the past forty-eight hours. As though the catching of the train represented the last positive effort of which he was capable, he gave one deep sigh and felt himself toppling sideways. From what seemed to be a deep sleep he was conscious of the girl shaking him by the shoulders. She was worried, perhaps, about his sudden collapse, because her finger was pressing his wrist to feel the pulse. He managed to grunt as an indication that he was still alive and the focus of her anxiety changed.

'What station do you want? Where are you going?'

'Blaize,' he murmured, and fell weightlessly through the darkness into sleep again.

He awoke in a mid-morning light to find Frisca sitting beside his bed, staring intently at him. He had just time to consider that this must be the first occasion on which his young cousin had ever managed to keep still for more than two seconds at a time when she flung her arms round his neck.

'Steady, steady!' he protested, laughing. 'I'm still asleep.'

'No, you're not.' She hugged him again. 'You're scratchy, though.'

'Let that be a lesson to you. You should never come into a gentleman's bedroom until he's had time to shave.'

'Aunt Margaret said I could sit here. She said no one was to wake you until you were ready, but she wanted to know when you did wake.'

'Off you go and tell her, then.'

Frisca must have had difficulty in finding his mother, for he had time to bathe before he heard her footsteps hurrying along the corridor. He opened the door so that she could run straight into his arms and for a moment they stood close together without speaking. They would both have been embarrassed, though, to say what they were feeling. Margaret's voice was light and smiling as she sat down on his bedroom chair.

'You're just in time to help with the carving of all the turkeys.'

'What an exhausting business it is, coming on leave,' Robert laughed. 'But I can hardly believe that I'm here at all, so a little strenuous carving may help to persuade me that it isn't a dream.'

'If it hadn't been for Nurse Blakeney, you *wouldn't*

have been here at all – you'd still have been asleep on the train when it arrived at Bristol.'

'Is she one of your nurses? I must thank her.'

He found the opportunity to do so later in the day, when he met Alexa leading a group of a dozen VADs and convalescents out of the house towards the Theatre Ward.

'Come carol-singing with us, Robert,' she called.

He had been on his way to find Frisca in the stables so that she could show him the puppy she had been given for Christmas, too young yet to leave its mother. But they had fixed no definite time. He joined the group without admitting that the attraction lay in one member of it, the fair-haired girl who turned when Alexa called. She smiled at him, first in a nervous, tentative manner, and then again with pleasure as she saw that he intended to come. It was easy for him to catch up with her as the party walked down the gently winding path which had been built to connect the original tithe barn with the house at a gradient more suitable for wheelchairs than the old woodland walk.

'I'm jolly grateful to you,' he said. 'Not many people on that train would have known which station I needed for Blaize. I hope you didn't have too much trouble getting me off it.'

'The station master helped,' she said, smiling again. 'And he knew who you were. It was a relief to discover that you lived here and were on leave. I was afraid at first that you'd been told to make your own way to the hospital for convalescence after some kind of injury or illness, and that perhaps you were having a relapse which I ought to be able to recognize.'

'No. Just uncomplicated tiredness. We'd been having a fairly noisy show. You asked me a question in the train, Nurse Blakeney. I don't remember whether I had time to answer it before I flopped.'

She shook her head. 'No. But I shouldn't have asked.

Of course you don't want to think about that when you're on leave.'

'It's all right. I don't expect I'll know much about your brother's sector. But I'd be happy to answer any questions that I can, if it would stop you worrying.'

'It's not worry, exactly,' she said. 'I mean, he's dead now. There's nothing to be done. But we were always very close. It seems terrible that he should go into a world that I don't know anything about and simply disappear for ever.'

He could see her eyes filling with tears and was tempted to take her hand and comfort her, but the occasion was too public.

'This isn't the moment,' he said, referring to her question. 'What are your working hours tomorrow?'

'I start at seven in the morning and come off duty at eight in the evening. But we usually have two hours off sometime in the afternoon.'

He fixed a rendezvous and then, anxious not to draw attention to himself and the girl, increased his walking pace to catch up with Alexa. Only then did he wonder whether his promise was a wise one. To describe the mud and stench of the trenches, to list all the stupid, useless ways in which her brother might have been killed, could be of no possible benefit to Nurse Blakeney. The truth was that he wanted after all to talk about it for his own sake, to build some kind of bridge, if only of words, between the year he had spent in Flanders and these few days in Blaize. His mother, surrounded by the casualties of the fighting, must have some idea of its fierceness, but in no circumstances could he tell her – when she was already so anxious about his safety – how much worse the conditions were than anything she could imagine.

The patients in the hospital had been given their Christmas meal at noon, but it was not until the evening that the family, fully occupied throughout the day with their efforts to make the festival a joyful one, sat down to

Christmas dinner. Alexa and Margaret had dressed for the occasion and Piers brought up some of his best wine; while Frisca, over-excited, was allowed to stay up late for once. For a little while they all relaxed as though the evening and the kind of normal domestic life it represented would last for ever. But sadness was not far away even from the peaceful candlelit table on which glass and silver gleamed and glittered with a brilliance undimmed by war. When Piers rose to propose the toast of Absent Friends, Robert noticed at once that a name was missing from the list. He made no comment at that moment; but later, as they moved towards the library which was now used as a drawing room, he held his mother back for a moment.

'Aunt Lydia?' he asked.

'I didn't want to spoil your return home with bad news,' Margaret said. 'She died in November, although the news only reached us here ten days ago.'

'I'm very sorry.' Robert had had little opportunity to become acquainted with his aunt, but he knew her to have been his mother's best friend. 'Do Kate and Brinsley know?'

'Ralph asked me to write to them. He can never feel sure that the addresses he has aren't out of date. Brinsley probably will have heard from me by now. Hardly the most welcome kind of letter to receive at Christmas time. But then, I suppose no one can expect to have a very merry Christmas in the trenches.'

'Oh, I don't know.' Robert realized that it was his duty to cheer his mother up. He sat down on the floor in front of the log fire and allowed Frisca, sleepy now, to snuggle up to him. 'Last Christmas was quite a jolly affair. I remember it very well.'

'Tell us,' said Frisca.

'Well, I hadn't been at the front long enough to know what was normal and what wasn't, but the first thing that seemed odd on Christmas Day was the birds.'

'Birds?' Margaret laughed in surprise. 'You never told me in your letters.'

'I hadn't seen a bird since I arrived in France. They had more sense than to hang about the front line. But on Christmas Day, there they were, perching on the barbed wire. That was what first made us realize that the firing had stopped. And the rain had stopped as well. A crisp frosty dawn, and sparrows sitting still.'

'Did you feed them?' asked Frisca.

'Yes, we did. We scattered crumbs all over the place And while they were pecking away we saw four Germans walking across No Man's Land. They were jolly nervous, I can tell you that. One of our officers went out to talk to them and within an hour there were fifty of us out there, swapping cigarettes and looking at family photographs. Mind you, for every ten men above ground there was probably one tunnelling away below, laying mines to blow up our trenches. But we didn't think of that at the time.'

'I remember the newspapers said that soldiers had been singing across to each other from the two sets of trenches,' Margaret said.

'That's right. Auld Lang Syne and Good King Wenceslas and Stille Nacht. But that was only part of it. I remember there was a field of cabbages between the two lines. Someone had sown them and was never able to get back for the harvest. By Christmas they were all slimy, even though the ground was frozen. We started half a dozen hares in that field, and coursed them.'

'You mean you and the Huns together?' asked Frisca.

'They didn't seem like Huns that day. Just ordinary chaps who didn't want to fight any more than we did.' Unusually serious, he looked at his mother. 'It was an important day for me,' he said. 'I'd been frightened when I first arrived at the front. And then to stop myself being frightened I'd had to concentrate on killing and hating. But suddenly, just for one day, I was able to feel like a decent human being again.'

'Did you catch any of the hares?' Frisca asked.

'Yes. We got two of them for the pot, and Fritz bagged one as well. The cook didn't quite rise to the Blaize standard of jugged hare, but it was an improvement on bully beef, I can tell you that. I can imagine Brinsley's Christmas well enough. But not Kate's. Where is she now?'

'The last we heard for certain was that she was somewhere in Serbia. I don't expect the name Kragujevatz means any more to you than it did to me at first.' Margaret stood up and looked along the lowest of the library shelves until she found a large leather-bound atlas, so heavy that Robert hurried to take the weight. He laid it on the desk and she searched the index for the Balkans. 'The national frontier lines in this are probably a century or two out of date; but then, no frontier can be guaranteed for more than a week nowadays.' She frowned over the small print before stubbing her finger down. 'Here we are, south of Belgrade. But it's three months since I last heard from her, and even that letter was written in July. I've no idea whether any normal postal service gets through. Beatrice was in charge of keeping the hospital supplied, at least until the invasion, so I sent my letter to her and asked her to include it with any stores that she was able to send out. I haven't really much hope of it reaching her, though.'

'What invasion?' asked Robert. The war to him was a matter of a few yards of muddy ground gained or lost. Although he knew about the Dardanelles, nothing but the Western Front was real. Serbia, small and remote, had been responsible for the start of the war, but seemed to have no further importance.

'The Germans and Austrians and Bulgarians launched a joint attack on Serbia two months ago,' Margaret told him. 'Kragujevatz is behind the enemy lines now.'

'And Kate?'

Robert had noticed as the evening passed how his

mother's face had lost its expression of strained tiredness as she was able to relax in an evening off duty, knowing that her son was safe. Now the lines round her eyes tightened again in anxiety.

'My only news comes from Beatrice and even she isn't sure what's happened. Some of the nurses stayed behind in the hospital to care for the Serbian soldiers who were too badly wounded to move. They're in Austrian hands now, though since they're civilians Beatrice is hoping that they'll be repatriated. The others decided to move as many of the men as they could, hoping to establish another hospital further south. Kate was the only doctor in the unit who was still alive in October, and she took charge of that group. But nobody knows what has happened to the convoy which retreated, or where it is. And the most terrible stories are coming out of Serbia, Robert. It's not just the sick who are trying to get away. The whole Serbian Army is in retreat. And all the civilians are escaping as well, if they can. Those who stay are starving and those who take to the road are dying of exhaustion. I haven't dared to tell Ralph any of this, when he's already distraught over Lydia's death. But I'm very frightened for Kate.'

8

Time had changed its nature: there was a difference in kind between living and surviving. No longer did each day present itself to Kate to be lived through, moment following moment – not necessarily to be enjoyed, but at least to be taken for granted. Instead, as the retreat continued, she had to fight for every second of the future, and each pace forward was a triumph of determination.

More than two months had passed since the Germans and Austrians invaded Serbia from the north. Kate had evacuated the patients from the military hospital in Kragu-jevatz only a few days before the building was destroyed by bombs and the town was occupied. Ever since then they had been retreating southwards as the enemy advanced, and they were not alone. The whole country was on the move, trying desperately to escape before the enemy caught up. With so many of her charges sick, Kate could not hope to cover the ground fast, but as the end of the year approached they had crossed the Serbian frontier into Albania.

There was no comfort to be found there. The sea might promise safety, but between Kate and the sea lay brigands and mountains – high, cruel mountains, covered with snow. It was difficult to believe that the retreat would ever end. As she trudged on towards the top of yet another mountain pass, her mind mechanically repeated the same phrase over and over again: one more step, one more, one more.

Her shoes had long ago worn out, but she had bound her feet and legs with long strips of hide from one of the dead oxen, and had replaced her tattered clothes from the bundles of possessions dropped by the roadside by refugees too weak to carry them any further. There was no element of theft or looting in this. Anything left behind would be snatched by the enemy. Serbia was represented only by whatever could be carried over the Albanian mountains. So by now Kate wore trousers and a military greatcoat as well as a thick layer of dirt. It was three weeks since she had last been able to wash more than her face, hands and feet and she had been sleeping in her clothes ever since the retreat began. Her head was swathed in scarves, whitened by the snow, leaving only a slit through which her eyes peered down at the path immediately ahead.

In a way the desperate nature of her situation reduced the anxiety she felt. At the beginning of the evacuation she had been almost overwhelmed by her responsibilities.

No longer then was it merely her business to keep wounded men alive. She had to provide wagons to transport them, and that meant that every night corn or hay must be found for the oxen or horses. The nurses and orderlies and patients and men of the military escort must be fed and there was no system which provided food or even ensured that it existed. Billets or camp sites had seemed necessary for night halts, and again it was nobody's business to arrange these for her. By now, of course, after weeks of enduring freezing temperatures in the open, she had almost forgotten how essential it had seemed at the beginning that everyone in the column should have at least a tent over his head for the night.

And then, each morning, there had been the strain of insinuating her own small unit into the unending stream of people and wagons which blocked all the roads south. It had been necessary to shout and bully, allowing artillery units to pass but forcing a way into the line in front of the pathetic groups of villagers who hauled their own carts, laden with children and possessions, at a pace even slower than that of the oxen. And all the time the sound of the guns had boomed through the air to remind the refugees that the Germans were only eight hours behind them, and the Bulgars advancing from the side – in each case held up for what could only be a limited time by the remnants of the Serbian Army, brave but under-equipped. There had been hopes at first that the British and French might send help, but by now this was a subject which no one mentioned in Kate's presence.

Ten weeks had passed since the retreat began, and one after another her responsibilities had slipped away. All that was left was a determination at the beginning of each day to keep the survivors of her party alive until they reached the sea; but by each evening it seemed that it would be enough if she could drag her own exhausted body across the mountains. The Austro-German invasion, which forced the Serbian Army and the royal family to evacuate Kragujevatz, had begun while she was still convalescent after her attack of typhus, and at the beginning of the trek she had had a horse to carry her south across the Serbian plains. But as the hospital column reached the foot of the Albanian mountain ranges and began to climb, there had been no more roads but only narrow paths marked out by goats and goatherds. There was no difficulty in finding the way, for every route which led towards the sea and safety was lined with the bodies of men and horses, but the tracks had proved too narrow for the ox wagons which had carried the wounded soldiers from the hospital. In the foothills it had been possible to transfer the patients to small forage carts for a few days, but by now they were strapped to all the available horses in litters, and anyone with two sound legs was expected to carry his own weight.

As comfort and even hope disappeared Kate felt increasingly surprised that the men of the military escort did not desert. Almost all of them had wives and children whose homes would by now be occupied by the Germans, and the temptation to protect their families must have been strong. But somewhere in these mountain passes the point of no return had been reached. The soldiers would perhaps starve if they went on, but they would certainly starve if they attempted to return. They might die of exposure in the mountains but they would be at the mercy of the Bulgars if they turned back to the plains. Probably, too, those of them who had been born in Austrian territory and who had willingly allowed themselves to be taken prisoner by men of their own race would be shot as deserters if they fell into Austrian hands again.

There was one form of desertion, of course, which was amenable neither to discipline nor to the reasonable balancing of alternative dangers, and her party's numbers shrank every day. They could protect each other against the wolves which howled in the darkness and against the

Albanian bandits who attacked stragglers for the sake of their clothes; but there was no protection against the increasing weakness of their own bodies. Even able-bodied soldiers were by now collapsing into the snow, unable to go any further, so it was not surprising that the wounded should succumb.

They were nearing the highest point of the pass. In terms of the total journey, that meant nothing. There had been high passes before and no doubt there were more still ahead. But on the southern side of the peak, the wind would perhaps bite less fiercely and there would be a better chance of finding a sheltered spot in which to sleep. Kate bent her head lower and forced her feet to keep moving. One more step, one more, one more.

Four hours later she wrapped her blanket tightly around her shoulders and leaned back against the black rock of the mountain, staring up at the sky. The blizzard had ended and the moon was full, reflecting off the snow and frost as clearly as though it were day. Ready to sleep, she felt completely at peace: the peace of someone too exhausted to care whether or not she would wake in the morning.

Sergei came to sit beside her. He pressed close against her side, not in any flirtatious way but in order that whatever body heat they retained might be shared.

'I have brought you your Christmas feast,' he said, setting down a plate of beans and stale bread and a tin mug filled with water from snow melted over the camp fires.

'Is it Christmas, truly?'

'Truly.'

It seemed incredible that she should not have known, that Christmas Day should not somehow have had a character of its own, impinging itself on her consciousness. Kate dipped the bread into the water without comment. For the first weeks of the retreat there had been few problems with food, for the invasion had begun

105

before all the harvest could be brought in and the peasants who fled from their farms left plums on the trees and grapes on the vines and maize still standing in the fields. But since crossing the frontier it had been necessary to avoid inhabited areas, because the Albanians were unfriendly and fierce. By now their rations were almost exhausted. There were still horses which could be killed for food, but then the wounded men they carried would die, for it would be hard to find stretcher bearers still strong enough to carry any load along the steep and slippery paths.

From further down the mountain came the plaintive sound of a gusle as someone began to draw his bow across the single string. The sound was tuneless and very sad – Kate had never heard a guslar play a gay melody. Even when the instrument was used to accompany the kolo, the dancers required only a firm dignity of rhythm: light-heartedness was not demanded. But no one would have the strength to dance tonight, Christmas or no.

The men were not too tired to sing, though. The sound began as a kind of humming, which swelled as more and more of them joined in until at last it exploded into a cry of anguish. Kate did not need to understand the words to know that the soldiers were singing about their homeland, Serbia, which they had left perhaps for ever, and about the wives and children they might never see again. The emotion was infectious, almost unbearable. Kate felt her own heart breaking with sympathy for the singers.

'At home,' said Sergei. 'What would you be doing now at home?'

Home was Jamaica; and the Jamaicans, like the Serbs, celebrated Christmas with song. Kate remembered the hymns and carols which her father had taught to his congregation and the poignant harmonies with which the people of Hope Valley sang them on Christmas Day. When the Jamaicans sang about death they swung their shoulders and clapped their hands and shouted to the skies in a kind of exultation. But when it was time to celebrate the birth of a baby their voices dropped to a whisper and the sadness of their singing had often moved Kate, as a little girl, to tears. At the time she had been unable to understand their attitude; but by now it was easier to sympathize with the feeling that a newly-born child was condemned to a life of hardship on earth while a dying man might hope for happiness in heaven.

But Jamaica was too far away. Kate had been cold for so long that she could hardly remember how delightful it had felt to be enveloped in the balmy warmth of a tropical island. Instead, as she gazed at the line of camp fires which flickered along the line of the track, she remembered the log fires which burned throughout the winter at Blaize. She had sat in front of one a year ago with Margaret and Alexa and Piers. At the time she had believed that she would never be so tired again as after the weeks of effort needed to equip and staff Blaize as a temporary hospital. Now, of course, she had learned what true tiredness was.

'My uncle will be opening a bottle of champagne now,' she said. 'If I were with him, I should be drinking a toast to Absent Friends. As it is, he'll be drinking the toast to me. And we can respond.'

She lifted the mug of water to her lips, but Sergei put a hand on her wrist to stop her. He pulled a bottle from his pocket.

'I'd been keeping this to celebrate the new year,' he said. 'But who knows where we shall be on New Year's Eve.'

'Still on this mountain, I should think,' Kate said. But Sergei shook his head.

'The reconnaissance party has returned. Journey's end is in sight. This is the last high pass. And there are ships waiting at Durazzo to take any members of the Serbian Army to Salonika. Before the old year is over, you and I will have to say goodbye.'

'Why, Sergei?' Kate was startled and upset.

'You will return to England, surely. It will be possible, and if I were your doctor I would order you to do so. You need rest, good food.'

In a long silence Kate allowed herself to day-dream. She imagined herself eating meals, hot, satisfying meals. But even the thought of delicious food was not as tempting as the prospect of sleep. To lie in the comfort of a bed, to be warm, to sink into sleep and to awake in the morning rested and still warm! She sighed at the thought, savouring the prospect but not really expecting to enjoy it again.

It was reasonable that she should return to England. A year away from home, in almost constant danger, must surely qualify her for a short period of leave. And then she would be justified in asking Beatrice to send her to France for her next tour of duty. That was where she had wanted to work, and by now she must have deserved the right to choose.

It should have been simple to decide, and yet it was not. Round the camp fire the men were singing again, their inadequate meal quickly eaten. There was no sense in which she could feel them less deserving of care than the British soldiers in France. And there was Sergei. The thought that she would have to sail away from Sergei stabbed at her heart with an unexpected pain.

She glanced at her companion and could not resist a smile. Like herself he was dressed in many layers of ill-fitting garments picked up from the roadside, crowned by a woollen hat which he had pulled down over his ears. He had sewn up the empty sleeve of his greatcoat and used it to carry the paper-bound books which he would not abandon even in this emergency. Shaving had been one of the first luxuries to be abandoned by all the men and Sergei's beard, like his hair, was long and untrimmed. Its raven blackness made his face appear even paler than normal, and his eyes had sunk more deeply into their dark sockets, although they still flashed with the fire

108

which had impressed Kate at their first meeting. If she had come face to face with such a man a year ago, in the civilized surroundings of Blaize, she would have gasped and hurried away. But now Sergei was her closest friend.

Language, which had once been the barrier between them, had in the end drawn them together. In the relaxed days of the almost-forgotten summer, Sergei had begun to teach her Russian and later, in a curious way, she had absorbed much of what he was saying to her during the course of her illness, while she was only half conscious. Since then, she had used the intellectual effort needed to understand him as a way of taking her mind off physical problems. She and Sergei conversed sometimes still in French, but more often in Russian; and it was during these conversations that she felt closest to him. For his part, there was no one else to whom he could talk in his own language, and he showed in his smile how much it meant to him. They were speaking Russian now, and Kate was not at all sure that she could bear to part from him.

'Where will the men be going after we reach the coast?' she asked.

'There's talk of a Serbian Division which will be assembled in Salonika and sent to fight on the Eastern Front.'

'And you? Will you go with them?'

Sergei sighed, shaking his head sadly. 'No. The Serbs can no longer fight as an independent army. They will come under Russian command. And I can tell you that the first Russian officer to set eyes on me would have me shot. Whether you go to England or not, we shan't see each other again.' He filled her mug from his bottle. 'So we'll drink first to the absent friends of this Christmas. And afterwards to those who will be absent friends next Christmas but for a little while longer are present comrades.' He filled his own mug and they clinked them together.

He had found the slivovitza, no doubt, in the cellar of one of the abandoned farms they had passed, distilled by the farmer from his own plums. More cautiously than Sergei, Kate allowed it to make its fiery way down her throat. The warmth it brought to her body was comforting, but she could not prevent her eyes from filling with tears.

'I seem to spend my life saying goodbye to everyone I love.' By now her knowledge of Russian was good enough for her to choose precisely the word for love which expressed her feeling of affection and respect and friendship. There was no romantic attachment on either side, but that did not make her any less unhappy.

'You must tell yourself that if a parting is sad, it's because the comradeship which went before was good. And perhaps after all we shall meet again one day. I shall return to Russia when the revolution comes.'

'Are you so sure that it will?'

'You've seen all these people on the road, half alive or half dead, driven from their homes for some reason which they will never understand. What we've endured isn't only the retreat of an army: it's the flight of a nation. And what's happening in Serbia is happening all over Europe. There are French refugees, and Belgians, and Russians. Do you think they will endure such suffering for ever? There will come a moment – it *must* come – when they will turn on their rulers and say "We have had enough." It may not be in Russia. If the Germans are defeated, it will come in Germany. It could happen in England if the Germans win and your people understand how their generals have sacrificed a generation of young men through their stupidity. If the Tsar's army defeats Germany and Austria, he will survive for a little while, no doubt. But his ministers are incompetent and his wife is German and gives him good advice under the influence of a drunken hypnotist. No. Russia will be defeated and then the voice of the people will be heard. We shall build a new society.'

'There would be no place for me in it,' said Kate. 'And Russia is so large that I would never find you even if I were there. So it will be a final parting. What will you do, Sergei?'

'I shall go back to look for the orphans. Not just the few I brought to your hospital. A quarter of a million people have died in South Serbia, and who knows how many more must have been caught behind the enemy lines in the north. There must be children wandering all over the country with no one to help them. I shall see how many of them I can keep alive. We will drink another toast. To the children of Europe!'

Brought up in a teetotal household, Kate was unused to drinking spirits and the second mugful of slivovitza had an immediate effect on her tired and undernourished body. She could feel her head swimming and this was followed by a delightful sensation as though she were floating, warm and peaceful, high above the snowy pass. If this is being drunk, I like it, she thought, and fell asleep.

Sergei had been right when he promised that the end was in sight. Within three days the depleted party which had left the hospital ten weeks earlier made its way wearily down the last steep track and arrived at the coast. After so much hardship it was almost bewildering to be welcomed by an Italian relief unit with hot water and fresh clothes. There was a generous ration of bully beef and flour, as well as a token issue of such almost forgotten luxuries as coffee and sugar. The refugees ate and then, with one accord, lay down to sleep.

Warm and well-fed at last, Kate made a list of her surviving patients. The most seriously wounded had died during the retreat and those who were still alive now could hope to recover. But they still needed medical care. With increasing disquiet Kate tried to discover who would give it to them. Many of the doctors in the Serbian Army had died in the typhus epidemic at the beginning of the

111

year, and others had been killed at the Battle of Kossovo. Of all the soldiers who had embarked on the retreat across the mountains, a hundred thousand had died on the road, and that number included many medical officers. There were no qualified doctors available to sail on the ship which was soon to leave; nor were any known to be waiting in Salonika.

Had Sergei been intending to travel with the Serbs, Kate might have decided what to do on personal grounds. But he had made it clear how impossible that was, so there was no weight of friendship to put in the balance against the prospect of seeing her family again. For the whole of one morning she paced up and down beside the grey winter waters of the Adriatic. She longed to go home, but more and more clearly she realized that her duty lay in a different direction. No real choice existed. She must stay with her patients.

Two days later she watched the last of the sick and wounded men being carried up the gangplank of the ship which would take them from Durazzo to Salonika – if it was able to thread its way successfully through the minefields. Sergei had been standing beside her, checking off the name of each man who went past. As the last of them disappeared down the companionway, he handed her the list.

'Goodbye then, my brave, foolish Katya,' he said.

A feeling of desolation robbed Kate of speech. She stared at him in silence for a moment. Then Sergei put his one arm round her shoulders and kissed her, Russian style, three times. Still without speaking, Kate watched as he strode away.

Darkness fell as the ship moved away from the port. She stood for a long time on the deck, watching the dark silhouettes of the mountains gradually merging with the blackness of the sky and wondering whether she had indeed been foolish. Her spirits were low. This was New Year's Eve and there was no one with whom she could

112

drink a toast to a happy new year. Her surviving nurses had accepted with relief the offer of a passage home, so that of the original team which had come from Britain Kate was the only one who would be staying with her patients. At the time when she made the decision she had been sure that she was right; but this was a lonelier moment. She was sailing towards 1916 with no friends or close companions at hand and no hopes that the year could bring anything more than new tragedies.

Major Dragovitch, her colleague from the hospital, appeared at the top of the companionway. The ship was blacked out for fear of submarines, so she did not recognize him until he was close.

'We dance the kolo now for the new year,' he said, bowing and offering his arm. The small gesture cheered Kate at once. It was an accident of administration which had cast her lot with the Serbian Army rather than with the British or French. But by refusing the chance to return to England she had demonstrated to the Serbs that she regarded herself as one of them, and now they were making a gesture in return,' accepting her as a well-tried companion. She let the major lead the way below into a large cabin which had been set aside for the use of officers. There she took her place in the circle of dancers, moving her feet rhythmically to the sound of a flute and a violin.

After each dance she was offered drinks – for all the officers, it seemed, had made good use of their two days in the port. It was a party after all, and as for the second time in her life she became a little drunk, she pushed the sadness from her mind.

As midnight approached, the music stopped while every glass was refilled. There was a moment's pause until a blast of the ship's siren marked the time. The single melancholy note, dispersed by the wind into a mournful diminuendo, was enough to introduce a new mood. A second earlier they had all been determinedly cheerful.

Now the same thought entered the mind of each of them – that they might never see Serbia again. They had been holding their glasses ready, but the toast which emerged was not what had been expected. They drank to their homeland and the day of their return to it.

Kate's homeland was not theirs – indeed, she hardly knew where it was. Was it Jamaica, in which she had been a child? Or England, where she had lived as a student? She had left Hope Valley behind her without putting down roots anywhere else. The Lorimer mansion perched above the Avon at Bristol: Margaret's friendly house in Queen Anne's Gate, closed now for the duration of the war: Blaize, rich and peaceful before the war and now crowded and businesslike – all these had welcomed her, but none was her home. Not from choice, she had become a wanderer.

It was not important. People mattered more than places. She was amongst friends, and that must be enough. And suddenly her companions were cheerful again, with the abrupt change of mood which she had learned to expect from the Serbs. Their gaiety, unfounded but determined, was infectious. To the sound of shouted good wishes for the new year, and the smashing of glasses after the toast had been drunk, Kate sailed into 1916.

1916

1

On the last day of June 1916, Robert Scott began to write a letter to Margaret. He was not the only man to be writing to his mother at this moment and to judge by the tense quietness of his companions and the uneasy chewing of fountain pens, he was not alone in finding the letter difficult to phrase. For some days now they had all guessed that a big new offensive was imminent. No one was anxious to put his suspicions into words in case they should be confirmed, but Robert had drawn his own conclusions from the number of Decauville railway tracks which he and his section had laid in the past three weeks and the weight of ammunition which had been hauled along them. The tramp of men moving forward along newly surfaced roads had told its own story. So too had the piles of wooden crosses waiting ready in the villages behind the lines and only partly concealed by coverings of torn tarpaulin.

That afternoon the orders which they had all been expecting had come at last. After almost two years of war, officers and men alike knew the odds against them. Robert calculated that his cousin, Brinsley Lorimer, who was in the front line and would be one of the first to go over the top, had less than one chance in four of surviving the next day and only one chance in three of emerging from it unhurt. Robert's own odds were less daunting, for the sappers would not take part in the first wave of the attack. It would be their task to move rapidly forward after the first line of German trenches had been taken, to repair the damage done to them by the British guns during the attack and to build a road capable of carrying guns and supplies across the shell-pocked surface of what at the moment was No-Man's-Land. But they would be working under fire.

So this letter home could not be composed without thought. If it should turn out to be the last letter his mother ever received from him, she would keep it for the rest of her life. It was an occasion for writing something memorable, some statement of a personal philosophy which would serve as his memorial: or something especially loving, an expression of thanks for all the happy years of his youth.

What was so appalling was that he simply couldn't do it. Strong and healthy and twenty-one years old, Robert was incapable of stretching his imagination to envisage the possibility that within twenty-four hours he might be dead. And if his mother were to receive a solemn letter from him, different from his usual matter-of-fact style, she would be frightened, possibly without reason. With a sigh he bent his head nearer to the lamp and began to write.

'Dearest Mother, Guess who I saw two days ago. Brinsley, no less – for the first time since I waved him goodbye on Waterloo Station. I was sent up to the front line to take a good look at the terrain and check my maps, and I noticed a lot of chaps wearing his regimental flash, so I asked whether Captain Lorimer was around and finished up by having a meal in his dug-out. Not much difference in the menu from my own mess. Same old powdered soup, same old tins of meat and peas and potatoes. But someone had brought some quite decent wine back from his last rest period, so we made a party of it. Thanks to a near miss from a howitzer a couple of days ago, Brinsley is down to his last gramophone record so we all had to listen to "If You Were The Only Girl In The World" about twenty times during the evening. He seems to have had a jolly good time on his last leave, and taken in all the shows.

'I could hardly believe it at first, but Brinsley does actually seem to be enjoying the war. As though it were some kind of game, just a bit more exciting than cricket. A lot of fellows put on that sort of act, of course, but in Brinsley's case it seems to be genuine. I won't pretend that I share the feeling – or even understand it. But his men practically worship him for it. Some of them helped me to find my way back afterwards and we chatted for ten minutes while we waited for a break in the barrage. He's had so many narrow squeaks – and has come through them all without a scratch – that they reckon he has the devil's own luck, and they'll follow him anywhere because they feel safest when they're close to him.

'There's going to be a big push tomorrow. I can say that because by the time this reaches you, you'll know all about it. Brinsley's looking forward to it. And perhaps I am in a way as well, but a different way. We can't go on like this for ever, thousands of men sitting in holes and shooting at each other, but obviously things have got to be worse for a while before they can be better. So let's hope that this one is going to be the decider, and that we'll be in Berlin before Christmas.

'I send my love to all the family at Blaize. But most of all, of course, dearest Mother, to you. Your loving son, Robert.'

He read the letter through carefully to check that the last sentence was not too sloppy and that the rest contained no information – details of his position or the name of Brinsley's regiment – that would infringe the censorship regulations. Then, although it was still early, he lay down to rest. He did not expect to sleep.

At half past four the next morning he went to rouse the two men he had chosen to act as his runners. They had not slept either and seemed almost grateful for the opportunity to move. Together they made their way in silence along the communication trench. Then there were thirty yards of open ground to be covered before they could reach the shelter of their observation post.

117

The front line curved at this point in front of a small hill which had once been heavily wooded. By now only the stumps remained, with a few bare spikes to indicate the original height of the trunks. Once shellfire had destroyed the trees, the debris had quickly been appropriated for firewood, so the observation post was a dug-out. Robert had always been good with his hands and eighteen months of war service had provided good practice for his ingenuity. He had made and installed three large periscopes and had also made sure that the post was concealed from air observation by camouflage.

It was not possible to see the German trenches from the British line, nor even from Robert's position on the hill, for the ground of No-Man's-Land rose to a ridge which divided the two armies. The ground was a mess of craters and hummocks bounded by formidable lines of tangled barbed wire and peopled now only by the decomposing bodies of men who had taken part in earlier attacks. In a few hours Brinsley and his fellow-officers would be leading their men up the slope towards the German machine guns. Although he would not be amongst them, Robert found himself shivering with fear on their behalf. It seemed impossible that they could break through – and even if the main attack succeeded, how many of those in the first wave could expect to arrive at the further side?

In the hour of waiting there seemed no alternative to such thoughts as these. Over and over again Robert looked down at his map, checking it with the actual contours of the land, making preliminary choices of the best line for laying a supply route. The final decision could only be made after the attack had succeeded, if it did succeed, and when it was possible to assess which section of the area had been least devastated by shellfire.

Gradually the sky lightened, cloudless and clear, bearing all the promise of a perfect summer day. Robert found himself suddenly thinking of his cousin Frisca.

Probably it was because he was trying to visualize summer in England, to conjure up a mental picture of girls in white frocks playing croquet on smooth green lawns or eating strawberries in the shade of cedar trees. Blaize in peacetime seemed to sum up everything he was fighting for, but Blaize had changed as unexpectedly as his own life, although less dangerously. He did not want at this moment to visualize his mother sitting in her office and signing death certificates or drug requisitions, nor to think of Alexa endeavouring with all the skill of a professional actress to conceal the heartache she felt at the sight of her beloved theatre converted into a hospital ward. Nine-year-old Frisca, alone amongst his family, had not changed at all. She was still dancing through life, her golden curls bobbing, her bright blue eyes flashing with gaiety. He remembered how he had awoken from an exhausted sleep on the first morning of his last leave to find his cousin sitting at his bedside, and how the expression on her young face had changed from almost maternal solicitude to delight that he was ready to be talked to at last. With a rush of emotion that was almost a physical desire he wished that he could hug little Frisca now and tell her that there was nothing to worry about.

He thought of Jennifer as well, whom he had wanted to kiss at the end of that leave. Her shyness had restrained him on the last occasion when they had been alone together, and their final goodbye had been said with his mother watching. Although there was nothing to suggest that she disapproved of their deepening friendship, her presence had proved inhibiting to them both. But Jennifer had written to him regularly during the past six months, and he had replied to each letter. The correspondence was important to him. To his mother he wrote only in reassurance. He told her about his rest periods, his billets, the pleasures of buying an occasional meal or cup of good coffee. His letters to Jennifer were quite different. As though it were necessary to tell the truth to somebody, he described to her with complete honesty his moments of fear and nausea, disgust and shame. Perhaps he hoped that the moment would come when she would tell him that she could not bear to hear any more, so that he would have reason to hope that she was beginning to care for him; but until that time he poured out his feelings about the war without reserve.

She, like himself, might be awake at this moment, approaching the end of night duty in a ward full of men who in their time had awaited the dawn with as much apprehension as Robert felt now. He tried to force himself into her mind, so that his own mind should be distracted. Robert suspected that Jennifer was not a particularly good nurse. She had none of the controlled compassion which enabled his mother to recognize a need and alleviate it as far as she could with all the sympathy and skill she possessed but without allowing any kind of emotional involvement to distort her judgement. Jennifer was too young and too highly-strung to remain detached. She suffered with her suffering patients, deliberately indulging her own feelings, whether of anger with those who had inflicted the injuries she tended, of anguish with those who endured them, or of desolation with the bereaved. She had confessed to Robert that she chose to work as a nurse deliberately to ensure that she should not be happy when so many people were frightened or unhappy. It was an attitude wholly to her credit; yet in these moments of waiting it proved not to be the memory of Jennifer which brought most comfort to Robert, but that of Frisca. He felt almost that Jennifer had a need to suffer and did not want to be spared anything; whereas it seemed important that Frisca should be protected, that nothing should ever happen to sadden those sparkling blue eyes. Dear little Frisca, he thought affectionately. And then suddenly it was not possible to think about England any longer.

The barrage which began at six o'clock was more

intense than any he had heard before. As though a conductor had signalled with the sharp double tap of his baton, a symphony of gunfire began with a single ear-splitting chord. With a rolling reverberation it developed through all its different movements: of surprise, range-finding, concentration, obliteration, deterrent – all leading up to what must be the finale: the creeping curtain barrage of attack. There could be no crescendo, because the fortissimo was sustained from first to last; and after the first few moments it was impossible even to distinguish the notes of the different instruments: the smacking percussion of field guns, the rasping of the medium artillery, the drumming boom of the biggest guns and the high-pitched scream of shells. The orchestra became a double one as the reports of guns firing behind him were echoed in sinister fugue by the explosions of the shells out of sight in front. These in turn were joined by another band of instruments altogether when the distinctive notes of the German howitzers began to punctuate the score, their crashing chords coming nearer and nearer as they probed behind the lines for the British guns.

Beneath Robert's feet the ground was shuddering. His ears were battered not only by sound but by the vibrating pressure of the air. His whole body became tense, as though by drawing in on himself, holding every nerve-end under tight control, he could give himself immunity from death's flying splinters. An hour passed, and more, but still there was no pause in the relentless battering on his ear drums. The noise hung over him like a cloud, a huge umbrella, filling the atmosphere almost visibly, with no chink or break in its intensity. Nothing but noise existed: nothing but noise was real. Robert felt himself beginning to tremble, his self-control stretching towards snapping point. Only the presence of his two equally dazed companions prevented him from crying.

In the firing trench at the foot of the hill the rising sun glinted on a row of bayonets. Robert reminded himself that, unlike the men who held them, he was not just about to walk towards a line of machine guns. A sudden conviction that he would never see Brinsley again made him angry with himself. He had said goodbye to his cousin too casually, wishing him good luck with nothing more than a smiling nod of the head. Just as he ought to have told his mother how much he loved and admired her, so he ought to have touched Brinsley on the arm, shaking him by the hand, even embraced him. How ridiculous it was that it should be so difficult to demonstrate affection even where affection so genuinely existed. Well, it was too late for regrets. He could think only of himself, and by now the tension had become unbearable. How much longer would the barrage continue? When would the attack begin?

In the trenches, no doubt, whistles were blowing. To Robert, who could not hear them, there was something uncanny about the manner in which an unbroken line of men, stretching away as far as he could see, began to move. They scrambled out of the shelter of the trench, paused, steadied and then advanced, with rifles held at the port and heads down so that their steel helmets would provide some kind of shield. The solidity of the line and the slowness of its pace was almost unbearable to watch. Robert knew well enough that the speed of the advance was determined by the movement of the curtain barrage, that if the men moved too quickly they would run into shellfire from their own supporting guns; but he felt sure nevertheless that if he had been amongst them he would have found the temptation to run and zig-zag overwhelming.

For the first thirty yards the slope of the ridge gave the attackers some protection. But as they approached the top they were greeted with a savage burst of machine gun fire. Within seconds more than half the men within Robert's viewpoint were flat on the ground. Some of them might have flung themselves down in self-protection, but as he searched the nearest part of the ridge through his binoculars he could tell that many would never rise again.

A second wave followed twenty yards behind and received the same welcome – although rather more of these, bending low, broke into a run as they reached the dangerous point of exposure and pressed on towards the German lines. A third wave moved at first much faster than the other two: the artillery barrage was well ahead of them by now. But as they approached the top of the ridge they began to falter. Robert knew from his own experience how great a mental effort was needed to step over or upon a man's body, even when it was quite certain that he was dead.

As they hesitated, they were rallied by an officer who straightened himself ahead of them and turned, gesturing them to follow him at a run. It was not possible for Robert to hear what he shouted, but the effect was immediate. The third wave charged forward, the officer at their head. He was running in front of them, moving diagonally to avoid a large crater, when he was hit. Even without binoculars Robert could see all too clearly what happened. The man's head jerked backwards, either as a direct result of the impact of shrapnel or bullet or because the strap of his steel helmet, dislodged, tightened across his neck. For a moment or two his legs continued their running movement, but his arms were thrown upward and his shoulders forced back. Losing his balance, he fell into the shellhole which he had been trying to avoid. But there was time, as he staggered on the edge, for Robert to see, beneath the displaced helmet, the officer's curly golden hair. So distinctive; so familiar. Surely it couldn't, mustn't be Brinsley.

Yet as he raised his binoculars to his eyes and adjusted the focus with fingers trembling with shock, Robert had no doubt that it was his cousin's face he would see. He had to wait a moment for the smoke of the battlefield to clear briefly. Then his fears were confirmed. Brinsley had not fallen to the bottom of the crater – a huge hole, big enough to stable a team of horses or store an ammunition wagon – but was clinging with one arm to its side. He was writhing with pain, his legs from time to time jerking convulsively. Robert felt every spasm as though his own body were suffering. With a feeling of panic which increased as every moment passed he waited for someone to carry Brinsley back to the British lines. But Brinsley's own men had by now surged forward, beyond him, and although the stretcher bearers had begun to make their quick dashes out of cover to pick up the wounded, they were bringing the nearest in first. With so many fallen men in need of them, it was hardly surprising that they should leave until last those who lay on the top of the ridge, within the range of the German machine guns.

Robert handed the binoculars to one of his runners. His trembling had stopped and he felt both very calm and very much afraid. 'Wait here,' he said to the men, though there was little enough danger that they would follow him unbidden into the smoke and chaos below.

He dashed first for the shelter of the communication trench and used that to lead him into the section of the firing trench from which Brinsley had led his men. If one of his own senior officers had seen him, he could well have been court-martialled for leaving his post, but he had only one thought in his head: that Brinsley was still alive and must be brought in. As he climbed out of the trench he automatically crouched low, head down. The ground was littered with men and equipment and made rough by shellholes and mounds of soft earth, but he ran as straight as he could over the first uphill stretch, only beginning to zig-zag as he approached the brow of the hill. The noise here was perhaps no louder than it had been in the observation post, but it was more confusing, and punctuated with the shouts of the assault troops as well as the cries of the wounded. All the craters which could be seen through the smoke looked much alike, and others were visible only when he reached the very edge. It was difficult to preserve any sense of direction. Twice he thought he had arrived at the right place and twice was disappointed. He paused briefly and saw across a stretch of exposed ground a shellhole which was large enough to be his goal.

Again he began to run. Then, without warning, there was no more noise. He was floating in the air, turning slowly over and over in a state of bliss. Or at least, part of him was, for it seemed that he had left his body behind on the ground. He could see it, but he was not inside it.

The silence seemed timeless but ended with a crash. Now he was back inside his body, and his body was lying inside the crater he had been hoping to reach. Earth at first trickled and then rushed down its side as though from an erupting volcano. It covered his face as he lay prone. He lifted his head for a second to escape from it, and put up a hand and arm for protection. That was something – that there was nothing wrong with his head or his arms. But he found himself unable to sit or stand or move his legs. He tried to work out where he was injured, but there was no pain to guide him, only numbness as he pressed whatever he could reach and tried in vain to flex the muscles of his lower limbs.

Raising his head again and propping himself up on his elbows, he looked around for Brinsley. But even if this was the right crater, the new shell-burst had destroyed its shape, throwing out or burying any previous occupants. Robert lay there alone as the battle raged around him. His mind, still in some curious way detached from his physical state, was unable to make itself care.

In the course of the day he received company. A grey-haired man, too old for war, weeping uncontrollably and unable to advance any further. An injured stretcher-bearer, flinging himself in for shelter as a mortar exploded

125

nearby. Two dead men and a third who died within an hour. And a blood-showering rain of arms and legs which arrived after a shell-burst that made the ground tremble as though an earthquake were beginning. Robert observed what happened, but felt no reaction to it. He supposed that he was dying, but the fact did not seem to be of any importance. He tried to remember his mother, and to feel sorry for the grief she would experience, but he was unable to visualize her face. His imagination refused to move outside the confines of the crater. He lay without moving, waiting without knowing what he was waiting for or what he hoped would happen.

The noise around him continued throughout the whole of the long day and so dense was the smoke at the top of the crater that it was impossible to tell for certain when night was falling. But at some point in the early evening the numbness of Robert's wounds began to recede. Uncertainly at first, his mind re-established its link with his body. He became frightened for himself and angry at the chain of events which had brought him where he lay. But these feelings did not survive for long, for they were driven out by a pain so overwhelming that he could not even begin to control his reaction to it. It first attacked his hips and then spread downwards through his legs. Finally, as though carried in his bloodstream, it moved upwards, towards his heart, into his head, agonizing and unendurable. Robert began to scream: uncontrollably, on and on and on.

2

On the morning of 1 July Margaret heard from Kate at last. The letter – the first to arrive since the brief message which had announced her niece's escape from Serbia and decision to remain with the Serbian Army – was a cheerful one. She was on the Romanian Front, Kate told her aunt, and had established a hospital with a hundred beds at Medjidia. The remnants of the Serbian Army were now under Russian command, so she was finding it very useful that a Russian friend's tuition had made her fluent in the language some months ago. She had to spend half her time arguing with Russian transport officers and quartermasters. The inefficiency of the Russian Army was almost unbelievable, and she was glad that her medical supplies came directly from Beatrice's office.

The situation she described sounded appalling to Margaret, who was accustomed to discipline and efficiency in hospital management, but the letter contained no hint of complaint. During the long retreat across the mountains Kate had obviously been depressed, facing problems far outside the ability of a single doctor to solve. At least now she was in a position to be of real help to those in need of medical care.

Margaret was glad on her behalf and looked forward to passing on the news. Alexa had been spending the week at Glanville House in Park Lane, taking her concert party to perform in the London hospitals. When the time came for her return in the evening Piers went to the station to meet her train. Glancing from the window of her office at the sound of the returning motor car, Margaret noticed how serious they both looked as they went into the house. The observation worried her and after a little while she went to look for them.

She found them in the nursery, beside their sleeping son. The day had been one of the hottest of the year and little Pirry had thrown off all his bed coverings. His soft and seemingly boneless body sprawled in total relaxation on the mattress. One hand stretched above his head; the thumb of the other was in his mouth. The door was open, but Margaret felt it would be an intrusion on the family group to go in. She paused in the doorway and the two adults, speaking quietly to each other while looking at the sleeping child, were not aware of her presence behind them.

'A vigorous offensive!' said Piers. He glanced down at the newspaper he was gripping. 'Such an easy phrase to write, but what does it imply? Last week, Alexa, when the House rose, I went out on to the terrace and found myself standing next to Lord Falmouth. His two elder sons were both in the army and both killed in the first months of the war. He'd heard that morning that he'd lost his youngest son as well. The last. He hadn't been able to face his wife with the news. I think he told me just to see whether he was capable of speaking the words without breaking down. The boy was only nineteen. He'd been in France for five months. That made him fortunate in terms of statistics. Did you know, Alexa, that the average expectation of life of a nineteen-year-old second lieutenant is twelve weeks from the day he arrives at the front. How long can we go on like this? But how can we stop? I never thought I'd live to bless the fact that my son was born when I was already an old man. All my friends of my own age are either in mourning already or expecting the worst. I feel almost guilty that I'm so fortunate.'

He turned to embrace Alexa and caught sight of Margaret. There was no reason why Margaret should have felt guilty about her accidental eavesdropping, but equally there was no doubt from her brother-in-law's expression that he had not intended what he had been saying to be heard by her – as though she were not as well aware as he of the risks that faced her son. To reassure him, she smiled as though she had only just arrived.

'Is there anything new in the paper?' she asked.

Piers handed her the copy of *The Star* which Alexa had brought from London. Underneath the black headlines which announced the opening of a British offensive came the brief official communiqué. 'At half past seven this morning a vigorous offensive was launched by the British

Army. The front extends over twenty miles north of the Somme. The assault was preceded by a bombardment, lasting about an hour and a half.'

'I heard the guns,' said Alexa. They moved away from the nursery, closing the door behind them. 'I woke up at six o'clock this morning. There was no one about in Park Lane: no traffic. The air was very still. And I heard the guns.'

'All the way from France? It's not possible, surely.'

'I wouldn't have expected so. I can only tell you that it happened. And I wasn't the only one. From time to time throughout the day I've seen people standing motionless in the middle of London, not doing anything, just straining their ears. Everyone's been snappy and uneasy today. Partly because of the heat perhaps. But it's as though we've been having knowledge forced on us when we would have preferred not to know. And if we can hear the sound in England, what must it be like to be only a few yards away from the guns?'

'Brinsley is somewhere near the Somme,' said Margaret. Both her son and her nephew were careful not to give anything away in their letters, but Brinsley had recently been on leave and had mentioned the names of villages near to the base town of Albert. Margaret had looked them up later on the *Daily Mail* map which hung in the library, and knew that she had reason to feel anxious. But to talk about her fear would do no good. The day was over now. If Brinsley and Robert were safe, there was nothing to worry about. If they had come to harm, it had happened already. Her own anguish could do nothing to help them and she had long ago ceased to believe in the power of prayer. She was frightened, but determined not to show it. In an attempt to talk of something more cheerful she asked Alexa how London was looking.

'Drab and dowdy,' Alexa told her. 'There are no flowers in the parks, no water in the lakes, no lights in the buildings at night, no street lamps lit either, for fear of Zeppelin raids. The soldiers on leave are lively enough and there seem to be plenty of over-painted young women ready to go with them to the theatre or music hall. But there's no feeling of style any more. Hardly anyone wears evening dress to the theatre now, and a gentleman in a tall hat is almost a curiosity. To tell you the truth, there's hardly anyone I know left in London. The museums and galleries are closed, and the shops are so under-staffed and under-stocked that anyone who owns a house in the country has retired to live in it and to buy food from the nearest farm. If I didn't believe that our concert party brought a little glamour to men who deserve to be cheered up, I'd never stir from Blaize. As it is, I think we shall have to close Glanville House. It's becoming impossible to replace the servants as they leave to join up. Even the maids are going to work in factories. It doesn't seem to worry them that their skin will turn yellow from the munitions or that they may even blow themselves up. The last kitchen maid I employed had never been outside her own village before last Christmas and now she's gone off to sell tickets to omnibus passengers.'

Once Alexa embarked on the subject of servants there would be no stopping her for the next ten minutes. Margaret withdrew her attention, trying to calculate when she could expect to hear any personal news, and what value it would have – since a letter received today would only mean that the writer had been safe five days earlier.

In the event, she did not have to wait long. Piers was always the first to read the daily paper. He marked anything in it which he thought might be of special interest to his wife or sister-in-law, but when Margaret arrived for her own later breakfast after an hour spent in her office reading the nurses' overnight reports she always looked through the casualty lists for herself. They might contain names recognized by her but not known to Piers.

130

On Tuesday, however, there was a name which Piers neither overlooked nor marked. He brought the paper to her office and silently handed her the page which announced that Captain Brinsley Lorimer had been killed in action.

Margaret wept. Her life had not always been a happy one, but for almost the whole of her fifty-nine years she had been able to accept its setbacks without tears. Only within the last few months had each new blow seemed less supportable than the one before. And Brinsley, light-hearted and life-loving, had been a second son to her for ten years – ever since her brother had sent him to her in England at the age of thirteen for his education. She felt Piers' arm round her shoulder, but each of them knew as well as the other that there were no words which could bring comfort.

A long time passed before she was able to control herself. Then she looked again at the page. Her swollen eyes refused to focus on the tiny type, but she could see that the list of names continued for column after column. 'Robert?' she asked.

'I've been right through,' Piers said. 'Not just the Royal Engineers but every single name, to make sure. He's not there.'

That was a comfort only in the sense that she could not have endured a double blow. She thanked Piers for staying with her, promised that she would be all right now, and was left with the task of writing to Kate and to Ralph. Brinsley's father would have had the official telegram of notification and so would know already of his son's death.

The morning post brought a letter from Robert. It had been written on Friday, before the battle began, so that the mere fact of its arrival gave no reassurance. And its casual mention of an unusual social occasion brought a new chill to Margaret's heart. If Robert had been near enough to Brinsley to share a meal with him, then Robert

131

was on the same section of the front. Her face was pale as she went out to do her morning round.

Pale enough, presumably, to be noticeable. In the long ward which had been converted from Alexa's little opera house, Margaret was aware of one of the VADs staring at her with an intensity which merited a reprimand. With some difficulty she focused her eyes and attention on the nervy face and recognized the young woman who had helped to get Robert off the train at the beginning of his last leave. Nurse Blakeney, wasn't it? The girl approached her, visibly summoning all her courage. A VAD was not expected to speak unless she was spoken to.

'Dr Scott. Please forgive me – I know I shouldn't – but I have to ask. Doctor, have you had bad news?'

'Yes,' said Margaret. She was aware that she spoke brusquely – it was because her tears were still not wholly under her control. Only after she had answered did she understand the question. This girl was not a friend of Brinsley's. She might have glimpsed him on his last leave, but she could have no real interest in his safety. It was Robert's welfare which concerned her. 'Not about my son, though,' she said. 'As far as I know, he's all right.'

The girl's relief showed on her face. 'I had a letter yesterday,' she said. 'But of course it was written last week, before he went into action. So I was afraid – I'm sorry, Doctor.'

Margaret remembered now that Robert had seen something of Jennifer Blakeney during that leave earlier in the year, but she had not realized that they were corresponding. Well, that was none of her business. She felt no need to stand on her dignity when it was possible to be kind.

'That's all right, Nurse,' she said. 'When I hear anything more up-to-date, I'll let you know.'

She moved on, forcing herself to keep her attention on her work. But it was impossible not to be edgy, not to feel frightened whenever she caught the sound of bicycle wheels on the gravel path in case it should prove to be the telegraph boy and not some unimportant domestic delivery. Each morning the casualty lists were longer and more delayed, making it clear that the offensive had developed into a continuing full-scale battle and that the death roll was running into thousands. She had no interest in the communiqués which claimed that a few yards of ground had been won, but spent every free moment obsessively re-reading the lists of names. On Thursday she learned that Robert had been wounded.

This time Piers did attempt to comfort her. 'It's a terrible thing to say, but a wound may prove to be the best way of saving his life,' he pointed out. 'He'll be out of the battle. With any luck, he'll have been sent home.'

'The Blighty one!' said Margaret. Every patient in the hospital at Blaize had had his own Blighty wound and it was true enough that some of them were grateful for the small hurt which had removed them from the scene of greater danger. But for many the price was a larger one than they could ever have wished to pay. Margaret could not afford to stop feeling frightened until she learned the details of Robert's injury. 'There are too many wounds,' she said. 'I've been warned to expect fifty acute surgical cases in the next two days. They know we haven't got the facilities, that we're only equipped for recuperative nursing and convalescence, but apparently there simply aren't enough hospital beds in England and France to cope with the numbers. Some of the men have been moved around for up to five days with nothing more than a bit of emergency attention. Five days! And there's gas gangrene in every wound!'

She realized that she was in danger of becoming hysterical and was not surprised at the firmness with which Piers addressed her.

'I'm going to London to find him,' he said. 'You concentrate on your job here, keeping other people's sons alive. I'll get on to the War Office and track him down. When I find him, do you want him here?'

The need to answer had a steadying effect, as no doubt he intended. Neither of them wasted words on the hypocrisy of pretending that they would hesitate to pull any official strings necessary to obtain special treatment for Robert.

'If he's in need of major surgery, he must go somewhere equipped to do it,' Margaret said. 'I'll give you the telephone number of someone who could advise you on the best specialist units. But as soon as he only needs nursing, yes, I want him here.'

3

Robert had no recollection of being carried from the crater. At the regimental aid post he had recovered consciousness briefly. His groan – whether of pain or merely despair that he was still alive after what had seemed to be the peace of dying – brought a nurse to his side. He felt the stab and pressure of an injection, the firm marking of a cross on his forehead. His eyes closed again.

When he was next able to look around him he was in a casualty clearing station, lying on a stretcher at the side of a tent. His hips were bandaged, but that part of his uniform which had not been cut away was stiff with dirt and blood. It was night, although presumably not the same night, and he could see a surgeon, his white smock soaked in blood, bending over a trestle table by the light of an acetylene lamp. It was the beginning of a new nightmare.

He had become nothing but a helpless body, conscious now, but to be moved or forgotten in accordance with some plan which he could not understand or control. His stretcher was stacked into a bunk in a railway truck, was swung on to the deck of a ship by a crane, was carried off to another train. From time to time he was offered a drink, a cigarette, or another injection of morphine, but he had no clear idea of how time was passing, except that the smell which he carried round with him grew more nauseous with every hour. No one had time to talk. Doctors and nurses, orderlies and stretcher bearers were all overworked, silent and grey from lack of sleep. It was as though he were on a conveyor belt so badly overloaded that it could only be kept moving if everyone concerned winched it by hand, knowing that if they were to stop for a moment the weight would be too great for any movement to start it again.

The recurrent injections muddled his mind while keeping the pain of his body more or less under control, but it was in a moment of comparative clarity that he found himself lying on the platform of a railway station. There was nothing to tell him where it was. He could only hope that he had reached London at last, that the apparently interminable journey was in fact near its end. Without warning he remembered a day almost two years earlier. He had broken the news of his enlistment to his mother on a station platform just like this one, and almost as crowded with stretchers. It was the day that Brinsley had left for France – and with the memory of that moment Robert recollected for the first time since the explosion of the shell what it was that he had been doing when he was hit. The horror of what he had seen had sealed the picture off from his mind, but now he saw Brinsley running through the smoke, saw his bright yellow curls spring up as they were freed from the flattening weight of the dislodged steel helmet, saw the jerk of his arms and shoulders as the bullet stopped him in his tracks. Remembering, too, the agonized twitching which had continued after his cousin fell to the ground, Robert began to vomit.

The feeling that he had been abandoned was so strong that it seemed a small miracle when he felt his face being

135

sponged. The woman who was bending over him was shabbily dressed and undernourished, but her eyes were full of sympathy. He muttered his thanks as soon as he could speak again and in return she told him that her own son had died of wounds. She met every hospital train now to give to strangers the kind of care which might have eased his pain.

'Where am I? Is this London?' Even talking was an effort, but he did his best to speak clearly.

'That's right, dear, London. Live in London, do you?'

'I want someone to know where I am,' he told her. 'Will you get in touch with my mother? Or my uncle. Anyone. Tell them where I'm being taken.'

She bent again to read the label which had been tied to his tunic, giving his destination as though he were a parcel. 'Where shall I find them?' she asked.

'What day of the week is it?'

'Friday, dear. Friday morning.'

The battle, he remembered, had begun on a Saturday. But there was no time to wonder what had happened to the missing days. Painfully he groped for the linen bag which had been tied round his shoulder and which contained his papers and valuables. There was some money there. He pressed it all into her hand.

'Take a cab to Glanville House in Park Lane,' he said. 'Even if there are only servants there, they'll know where to telephone my mother in the country. Speak to her yourself if you can. But tell someone where I am. Robert Scott.'

'Robert Scott,' she repeated. 'All right, dear.' She sponged his face once more and left him.

A little at a time Robert's body, which had for so long been tensed against pain, began to relax. He had been taken from the battlefield where he was in danger of his life; he had survived the nightmare journey; and he had come to the country where strangers were friends. Very soon now he would see his mother again and then everything would be all right. She would tighten her lips when she saw how dirty he was; she would bathe him and be gentle with him and heal his broken body and hold him tightly and warmly close to herself for the rest of his life. 'Mother!' he murmured, closing his eyes in an attempt to prevent the tears from forcing their way out. 'Mother! Mother!' Half delirious, he was still calling aloud for her when Lord Glanville arrived.

4

Robert's plaster was due to be cut away on the first Monday in December. He longed to escape from the heavy cast which had imprisoned him for so many months, and yet was a little frightened of what his release might reveal. On the Sunday morning he held his mother back for a moment when she stood up to leave after her usual breakfast-time chat.

'Mother, am I going to be all right?'

'You're almost all right already.' But Margaret recognized his anxiety and came back to sit beside the bed for a moment longer.

'Normal, I mean. Back to what I was before. Nobody's ever told me exactly what damage was done, you know.'

'The damage was to the bone.' With the professional air of a qualified doctor, Margaret touched her own hip and thigh to indicate the areas which had needed repair. 'Obviously, the flesh was badly torn as well, and the surgeon had to get out all the shell splinters and broken bits of bone before he could set what was left and allow the healing process to begin. The reason why he's kept you still for so long is to give the breaks the best possible chance to knit. He thinks, and so do I, that yes, you'll be back to normal. One leg perhaps fractionally shorter than the other, but hardly enough to notice. An extra half-inch on the sole of your left shoe and you won't even limp. We caught you in time, thank God, to prevent the gangrene from getting a hold. You're bound to be very stiff and weak at first, though, Robert. You must be prepared for that. You won't simply be able to stand up and walk tomorrow. You'll have to take things slowly. Do exercises. As a matter of fact, I'm going to experiment on you.'

Startled, he looked to see whether she was joking, and was not entirely reassured when she laughed.

'*You're* going to be all right, but we've had a lot of men through our hands who aren't. They're alive, but not whole. And very depressed, as you can imagine. I mean, suppose you're used to earning your living as a train driver and suddenly you're blind. What do you do?'

'Alexa has a blind piano tuner,' Robert remembered.

'There aren't enough pianos in England to keep the new generation of blind men busy,' said Margaret. 'I've been trying to think of new possibilities. It started as a search for some sort of therapy – to keep the men occupied while they were still here, to take their minds off the future. And then I thought, it ought to be therapy for the future as well. I've had a friend down here who's helped me work something out. He specializes in muscular diseases. He has evolved a training. Half a dozen of our long-stay patients have gone through it already, and now they're teaching the next batch. To massage muscles which have gone out of use for a while, or have been strained or injured.' Robert felt her firm fingers kneading his arm for a moment as she demonstrated what she meant. It invariably surprised him that his mother, who had always been small and by now was young no longer, should have such strong hands. 'As soon as you're out of this suit of armour, I shall send one of them in to pummel you until you're ready to go riding with Frisca again. She can't wait to get you out of bed,

138

you know. You won't have a moment's peace after tomorrow.'

'I'm afraid I'm just about to give her a nasty shock,' Robert told her. His mother had so often teased him about the devotion which his lively little cousin felt for him that he knew she would understand at once. And she did: he could feel the sudden tension in the atmosphere as she waited for him to speak the words. 'I have actually become quite fond of Jennifer,' he said.

It could hardly come as a great surprise to her. When he had first been brought to Blaize after a series of operations in London, it was Jennifer who had made it possible for him to find a place in the overcrowded hospital by giving up her leave to nurse him in his own room for the first two critical weeks; and since then she had spent almost all her free time caring for him. Robert knew that his mother would have noticed. He did not expect her to pretend surprise, but had hoped that she might look pleased. Instead, the thoughtful expression with which she received the news came as a disappointment. 'You don't mind, do you?' he asked.

'I'm a little anxious, perhaps,' Margaret said. 'Jennifer only knows you as a soldier and you only know her as a nurse. But those are temporary roles for each of you. When the war is over – '

'Will the war ever be over?' demanded Robert. 'And shall I still be alive when it is? I can't stretch my mind to think of the future, Mother, not when it's as far away as that. I can imagine tomorrow. I can just about believe in next month. That's all. I want to be happy now, not one day. I could be happy with Jennifer.'

'Yes,' agreed his mother. 'Yes, of course, I'm sorry if I sounded doubtful, darling. The mothers of only sons are notorious for being possessive. But that was nothing to do with Jennifer. She's a very gentle, conscientious, loving girl. She worries too much, but the best cure for that is happiness, and I'm sure you'll be able to find it together. Have you asked her yet?'

Robert shook his head. 'I wanted to tell you first. And to be sure that – that I'd be all right. After tomorrow, you know. But I think she guesses. And I think I know what she'll say.'

There were no doubts in his mind at all, in fact. Only a determination not to allow Jennifer to sacrifice her life to someone who might prove to be a cripple, or worse, had restrained him. But he had kissed her, and she had come close enough for him to kiss her again. He knew enough about her shyness and the careful way in which she had been brought up to be sure that she would not have allowed that unless she intended to accept his offer as soon as he made it. He was sorry that his mother had felt unable to show more enthusiasm, but he loved her enough to be charitable. She had given the reason herself. She was a widow, and he was her only son. She would realize soon enough that she would be gaining an affectionate daughter by the marriage. He smiled up at her and was rewarded by her kiss, and the familiar feeling of her fingers riffling through his hair. Then – even on a Sunday – it was time for her to return to her duties.

5

As Margaret left her son's bedroom she was angry with herself for allowing her feelings to show. Robert had been right to guess that she felt little enthusiasm for the thought of Nurse Jennifer Blakeney as a daughter-in-law. Everything she had said about the girl's good qualities was true enough, but it was also true that Jennifer was too tense and anxious, seeming to live on the edge of her nerves and to be easily unbalanced by the need to make choices. It was not the recipe for the sort of carefree married life which two young people ought to be able to enjoy – but then, who could be carefree nowadays? To be free of anxiety in 1916 was to be callous or simply unintelligent. Margaret reprimanded herself for falling into the same trap that she had seen waiting for Robert. Jennifer had not settled easily to the strain of a nursing life, but it was a temporary life. In her own home, with her own loving husband and children, she would be a different person, calm and contented. And Robert would be happy. They were all agreed on that, that Robert should be happy.

She was intending to spend an hour in her office before making her round of the wards, but was caught on the way by one of the village girls who seemed nowadays to have taken the place of the under-footmen.

'If you please, Doctor, her ladyship asked me to tell you that Mr Lorimer of Bristol is waiting to see you in the library!'

Margaret went there at once, wondering what could have brought her nephew to Blaize without even a warning by telephone. For a moment, as she hurried along the corridors, she was frightened lest something should have happened to her brother Ralph. Arthur, whose ships still plied – although less regularly now – between Jamaica and Bristol, might well have been the first to hear of any accident.

But the emotion which was causing Arthur to pace up and down the room was one of irritation, not mourning, whilst Alexa looked merely perplexed as she waited for information. Ralph was, however, at the root of the trouble. Arthur was hardly able to go through the politenesses of greeting his aunt before he thrust a letter into her hands.

'This is from Uncle Ralph!' he exclaimed. 'Without a word of warning! Without it apparently occurring to him for a moment that we in England have far greater duties than anything he can imagine out there. How can he expect any of us to shoulder his responsibilities for him at a moment's notice? Really, it's too inconsiderate. Read it, Aunt Margaret. See what it says.'

Alexa came to stand beside Margaret as she frowned over the almost illegible scrawl. Remembering how neat her brother's tiny handwriting used to be, Margaret could hardly believe that he was responsible for this.

'He was drunk when he wrote it,' said a voice from beside the door. Margaret looked up in astonishment. She had not realized that anyone else was in the room. An eleven-year-old boy was sitting on the floor with one leg in front of him, the other at an awkward angle. He had been tugging at the threads of Lord Glanville's Turkish carpet and now, as a spider scurried away towards the corner of the room, he slapped his hand over it and began to pull off each leg in turn with an expressionless face. Instinctively Margaret moved to stop him. But then, disentangling her mind from the puzzle of the unreadable letter and the brusqueness of the boy's comment, she realized who he was.

'You must be Grant, then.' She left the letter to Alexa and opened her arms to welcome the youngest child of Lydia, her best friend and Ralph, her favourite brother. 'And I'm your Aunt Margaret. We haven't seen each other since you were about six weeks old. I don't expect you remember that.'

She smiled at him and was disconcerted by the scowl with which he responded, making no effort to stand or even to lift his arms to return her embrace. He was an unattractive child, pale-faced, podgy and shabbily dressed. His hair, long and straight and with the appearance of having been roughly chopped with scissors, was so fair as to appear almost white, and his blue eyes were hard. Margaret had spent a great part of her professional life looking after children and took her ability to establish an immediate rapport with them almost for granted. For a moment, faced with this cold sulkiness, she was taken aback. But perhaps the letter would offer some explanation of her youngest nephew's mood as well as of his presence.

142

'I'll tell you what it says.' Arthur was too impatient to wait for the two women to puzzle out the words. 'Uncle Ralph has sent us his youngest son. He's not capable of caring for the boy any longer, now that Aunt Lydia is dead, so he expects us to do it for him. Without bothering to ask in advance. Obviously it was a mistake on our part to behave so generously to the others – to Kate and Brinsley. He takes it for granted that we'll look after as many children as he cares to ship to England with the rest of his merchandise.'

'You forget yourself,' Alexa rebuked him. She turned to the boy. 'I'm your Aunt Alexa, Grant, and this is my house. I have a little girl almost the same age as you – just a year or so younger. Come with me and we'll find her. You can play with some of her toys while we prepare a meal for you.'

'I don't play with toys,' said Grant.

'All the same, I'd like you to meet Frisca.' Alexa opened the door, expecting Grant to follow her, but the boy did not move.

'He has to be carried everywhere.' Arthur was still too outraged by the imposition to accept Alexa's hint that it should not be discussed in the boy's presence. 'That's another problem. It may have been possible in Jamaica, but which of us can carry that sort of burden?'

'Stand up, Grant,' said Margaret gently, while Alexa rang for a servant. Half helping, half pulling, she steadied the unwilling boy on his good leg. 'Oh, we can soon find a way to deal with this. We've got a whole store room full of crutches. We'll cut one down to size and you'll soon be running around on your own.'

'I don't want to,' said Grant, but Margaret took no notice.

'This is a hospital as well as a house,' she said. 'Anyone who isn't able to look after himself has to do what the doctors tell him; and I'm the doctor.' She was still smiling, but made no attempt to conceal the firmness in her voice. 'Off you go now to meet Frisca.'

143

The footman who had answered the bell picked Grant up in answer to her gesture, and Alexa went with them to introduce the two children to each other. At last Margaret had the chance to read her brother's letter.

'This is written in grief, not drunkenness,' she said. 'At the very moment when he'd just learned of Brinsley's death in France. I suppose it was too much for him to bear, that the deformed child should survive when he had lost his golden boy.'

'I'm not concerned with Uncle Ralph's reasons. Only with his actions. What he asks is impossible. Quite impossible.'

'There's plenty of room in Brinsley House, Arthur.'

It seemed to Margaret that Ralph was not the only one behaving selfishly. Her nephew was one of the few people in England who was doing well out of the war. He had no personal attachments and so did not share the strain endured by all those whose loved ones were at risk on the battlefield. The family shipping line and the shipbuilding firm which he had bought more recently were both profiting from large government contracts, and even before the war started he had been a wealthy man. He could keep Grant in a corner of his mansion in Bristol, with a tutor and a nurse if necessary, and hardly even know that he was there. 'And I thought you liked children,' she chided him.

'Children like Frisca, perhaps. But not a boy like this. Spoiled. Sulky. Ugly. Raging every time he fails to get his own way. He's been at Brinsley House for three days already, because I couldn't get away sooner, and I can tell you that I've had enough. I'm not surprised that Uncle Ralph wants to be rid of him. I must repeat that I recognize no responsibility in the matter at all. If you can't take him, then I'll send him back to Jamaica on the next available ship.'

'*I* take him?' Strained as she was with lack of sleep, overwork and anxiety about Robert, Margaret hardly knew whether to laugh or cry. How could Arthur imagine for a moment that she could carry this load as well?

'Or Alexa, of course. I realize that she doesn't have your feeling for children. But she has servants. And as she said herself, there can't be more than eighteen months difference in age between Grant and Frisca. They could share the same governess.'

Alexa's first words, when she returned to the library, were sufficient to throw doubt on that suggestion even before it was put to her.

'I'm afraid there's going to be trouble there,' she said. 'It's difficult for someone as lively as Frisca to know what to do with a boy who can't or won't move. I suppose I shouldn't say this in front of a doctor, but one wonders sometimes whether it wouldn't be kinder if babies with such disabilities weren't allowed to survive the moment of their birth.'

The casual remark had an effect on Margaret which Alexa could not have anticipated, for it was Margaret who had cared for Lydia during her last pregnancy, Margaret herself who had delivered the baby in that steaming West Indian village. She still remembered the moment in which she too had wondered, staring down at the new-born child, whether if he had the choice he would prefer never to draw his first breath. It had been a moment of temptation made stronger by the knowledge that the pregnancy was an accidental one and that the baby was unwanted by either parent. She had resisted the temptation and in so doing had condemned the child to a life in which his father resented him and his mother was weakened by his demands. Unlike Arthur, it was not possible for Margaret to say that she had no responsibility at all.

In any case, the boy was a Lorimer, descended – like each of the three adults in the room – from John Junius Lorimer of Bristol. He was a member of the family, and what was a family for if not to deal with emergencies like this? Inside a family, the question of whether someone had an attractive or unattractive personality was irrelevant. Whether or not Margaret could make herself like Grant, she had a duty to help him.

'When does your next ship sail for Jamaica?' she asked Arthur abruptly.

'Not for some time. The number of German submarines operating in the Atlantic makes the risk not worth taking too often, and that route is one of the government's lower priorities.'

'Give me good warning as soon as you know a date, if you please. Alexa, may Grant stay here until then? We will speak of it only as a holiday, so that he won't feel too greatly rejected when we send him back. It's natural that Ralph should have been distraught by the news of Brinsley's death. We must give him time to recover. In the meantime, this is a hospital and poor Grant is in need of treatment. Arthur may be right in saying that he has been spoiled, but it's equally clear that he has been neglected. There are surgeons performing miracles every day in England now. We must see if there's anything to be done for the boy. If there isn't, we must teach him how to live with his own body. I'm too old to bring up another child. But at least for a limited time, I think we should all recognize our family responsibilities even if we take no pleasure in them. If Arthur will contribute towards the cost of any medical treatment and Alexa will allow Grant to live here with Frisca, I will do my best to find some course of treatment which will benefit both his body and his mind.'

The decisiveness with which she spoke made it difficult for the others to demur. Alexa no doubt realized that her frequent absences from Blaize and a continuing sufficiency of servants meant that an extra guest would cause her little personal inconvenience. And although Arthur's interest in making money was almost obsessional, he had never been mean about spending it in a cause which

146

touched his pride. Their realization that Margaret was accepting the responsibility for sending Grant home as well as for keeping him for the time being made it easier for them both to accept her decision. Arthur gave the quick nod with which, like Beatrice, he was accustomed to approve a new proposal. Alexa, as befitted a chatelaine and prima donna, murmured something which could be taken as a gracious acceptance.

'That's settled, then,' said Margaret briskly. 'As a temporary arrangement at least. But that still leaves us Ralph to worry about. Do you think Grant was telling the truth when he said that his father drank? Ralph has been a total abstainer all his life. As a boy he never drank spirits because of his enthusiasm for games, and as a Baptist minister he was determined to set a good example. I can hardly believe that he would abandon his principles.'

'I'm afraid it may be so,' Arthur said. 'We must make allowances for the fact that Grant and Ralph are clearly on bad terms, but there's evidence to support what the boy says. Most of the business letters which have reached me recently from Hope Valley have been written by Duke Mattison, Ralph's assistant – because, he explains, the pastor is ill. The nature of the illness is never defined, but it may well be – '

'Then perhaps Kate should come home to look after her father,' Margaret said. 'She's only a volunteer, after all. Even a conscripted doctor would have been entitled to leave after two years. I'll write and suggest that just at this moment Ralph may be more in need of his daughter's care than the patients in her hospital are of a doctor. And in the meantime we shall all do our best to help Grant, shall we not?'

Her smile met little enthusiasm. Grant had managed to alienate his relatives in England in record time. But neither Alexa nor Arthur made any further objection. The war had ushered in a new world, but some of the old values survived. Even when scattered all over the globe, the Lorimers remained a united family.

6

Everything about England came as a bewilderment to Grant. To begin with, he had not expected it to be so cold. He was accustomed to rainy days, but in Jamaica it was warm even while the rain was falling and as soon as it stopped the sun came out, making the air steamy with heat. He had been given no new clothes since his mother died and now he found that in this chill December weather everything he was wearing was too thin as well as too small.

He was astounded, too, by the size of the houses. There was not a single building in Hope Valley which had more than one floor – most of the village homes contained only one room. Brinsley House, his cousin Arthur's house in Bristol, had seemed like a palace, and yet Brinsley House was quite small compared with Blaize. Did everyone in England, he wondered, live in such a grand style?

The immediate problem here was one of stairs. Although Grant was careful to conceal the fact as much as possible, he had become quite adept at moving around on level ground, but he had never before been faced with so many flights of stairs and his difficulty in coping with them was genuine – even if he could not make anyone believe this.

It came as no surprise to realize that he was not wanted: he was used to that. He had not been wanted in Jamaica, either, since his mother's death. But it had been an unpleasant shock to discover that he was not even expected, that the letter which his father had scrawled had travelled on the same boat and had been delivered, so to speak, by the same post as himself.

It was Miss Mattison, the village schoolmistress, who had really been responsible for his journey. On the day when the telegram arrived from the War Office to announce that Captain Brinsley Lorimer had been killed in action, the whole community had watched in horror as their pastor raged across the length and breadth of the valley, and the Bristow Estate which adjoined it, and even climbed the rocky path to the Baptist Hole, roaring his grief aloud and feeding it with forbidden rum.

Grant had spoken the truth when he claimed that his father had been drunk. His father's flock had accepted their shepherd's lapse more tolerantly than the frightened boy, for they would have behaved in the same way themselves. Most of them had kept out of the way until the fury of his mourning had spent itself. But Duke, on whom he depended, had made it his business to follow the pastor unobtrusively and make sure that he did himself no harm. And Duke's mother, Miss Mattison, had equally unobtrusively arranged for Grant to be carried to the schoolhouse. She kept him out of the way there for several weeks, in case his father's frenzy should vent itself on his unloved youngest child, and it was she who suggested, when she thought the time was ripe, that the boy should go to England. She knew from what Duke had told her, and what rumour in the Valley confirmed, that Arthur Lorimer, master of Brinsley Great House in Bristol, was a very rich man.

But when Miss Mattison's plan had been put into effect and Grant found himself unloaded at Avonmouth with a consignment of bananas, Arthur had made no pretence of a welcome. Grant found that easy enough to understand. What was more bewildering now was the attitude of his two aunts. They had agreed, apparently, that he should stay at Blaize, and yet they seemed to have no interest in him. Aunt Alexa had simply disappeared into another part of the huge house, while Aunt Margaret was always busy, always hurrying on her way to somewhere else, always tired, always worried.

'She's anxious about Robert, don't you see?' Frisca told him when he commented on this. Of all the surprises which England had in store for him, Frisca was the most astounding. In Hope Valley everyone was black – except for his own family, of course, and the Mattisons, who were a light shade of brown. He had known that in England everyone would be white, but Frisca had a brightness about her which was different again. Her golden ringlets were shiny as the sun, her eyes were alight with liveliness, her clothes sparkled with cleanliness, and her whole body somehow had a bouncing brightness of energy. Grant had spent the whole of his life pretending to himself that as long as he had his mother he didn't care whether or not anyone else in the world cared a fig for him. But now his mother was dead. He pined for someone else to like him. Could he persuade Frisca to do so?

'Who's Robert?' he asked, looking up at her.

'Aunt Margaret's son. My cousin. Your cousin, too. He's a hero. He was wounded in the war. Tomorrow he's going to have his plaster cut off and then everyone will find out whether he's going to be able to walk properly again. That's why Aunt Margaret's worried. In case he can't. Would you like to meet him? Come along. I'll take you.'

She jumped up and led the way out of the schoolroom, skipping along the corridor. Grant scrambled to keep up. His crawl was ungainly, and he was defeated when she disappeared too fast down a narrow flight of stairs. He managed to bump himself down them in a sitting position, but at the bottom he had no idea where to go. He was stamping and almost crying with vexation when his Aunt Margaret appeared.

'I'm looking for Robert's room,' he pouted. 'Frisca was

150

taking me, but she's gone too quickly and I don't know the way.'

'I'll show you,' said his aunt, turning back. She was still looking anxious, but she smiled at him kindly. 'Are you warm enough in those clothes, Grant?'

'No.' His voice expressed his resentful misery.

'I thought not. We must do something about that.' She watched as he pulled himself along. 'Your crutch will be ready tomorrow. That will make things much easier for you.'

Grant had always refused to use the crutch which his father had made for him in Jamaica. He would have liked to refuse this one too, but already he had realized that although his aunt was small and tired and quite old, she was used to people doing what she said. She made no attempt to help him now, but walked slowly enough for him to keep up.

'Another visitor for you, Robert,' she announced as she opened a door for Grant. 'Turn them both out as soon as you feel tired.'

The young man propped up in bed had bright red hair. He grinned at Grant in a friendly way and persuaded Frisca, who was hanging round his neck, to let go for a moment so that he could greet his new cousin properly.

'Hello, young Grant. Glad to meet you. You're just the chap I've been waiting for.'

'Why?' asked Grant, still snivelling.

'Are you good with trains?' Robert asked him.

The expression on Grant's face turned to bewilderment, and Robert laughed.

'Perhaps there are different kinds of toys in Jamaica. What do you play with mainly?'

'I never had any toys,' said Grant. 'Only books.'

'Then I'll have to show you what to do. I ought to have grown out of such things at my age, but I still like playing with trains. I make my own nowadays. And I've had an idea for a new sort of points system – you know, for

151

making the engine go along one track rather than another. I can see you don't know what I'm talking about. I'll ask someone to bring the box in, and then we'll see if you can do a lay-out for me. I can't get down on the ground, you see, with all this plaster.'

'I could do it for you,' said Frisca indignantly. 'You never asked me.'

'It's a man's job,' Robert said. 'Girls are meant for looking pretty and dancing about and cheering up their sick cousins. Trains are serious business, and something tells me that Grant's going to be very good at them.'

Apart from Miss Mattison, who had once remarked that he was clever, no one had ever told Grant before that he might be good at something. It was a new astonishment, that this cousin who hardly knew him was prepared to be friendly. A few minutes earlier Grant had been anxious to attract Frisca's interest, to establish some special claim on her. But although Frisca was polite, even kind, he could tell already that she would never want to slow down to the pace of someone like himself. Robert was different. At least for the time being, Robert was even less able to move around than Grant. He needed help, and the cheerful grin with which he asked for it was so friendly as to be irresistible. Within the space of a few minutes Grant had banished his sulky expression, changed his allegiance, and given his devotion to his cousin Robert.

7

For four days after the removal of his plaster Robert would not allow his nurse, Jennifer, or any members of his family to visit him when he was out of bed. He was appalled by his own weakness. His left leg seemed as useless as if it had been shot away. Even his arms, after

152

such a long period of inactivity, were hardly strong enough to control the heavy crutches which had been brought him. Every day he practised walking up and down his room, brushing aside the help of the orderly who came to make sure that there was no accident. But after only a short spell he was forced to fall back on the bed, exhausted by even such a small effort.

On the fifth day, however, he waited until he heard Jennifer's knock on the door and then stood up, steadying himself on the crutches before he called her to come in. She clapped her hands with pleasure as she paused in the doorway, her pale face flushed with happiness.

'That's no way to congratulate a fellow on being vertical again,' said Robert. 'I hoped you'd fling yourself into my arms and smother me with kisses.'

'I was afraid of knocking you off balance,' Jennifer answered in a whisper. Her shyness revealed itself in her face as well, but she came towards him in spite of it.

'Knocked off balance is what I want to be.' He could only spare one arm to hold her as she kissed him, but when his head began to swim again it was with excitement, not weakness.

'Darling Jennifer!' he exclaimed. 'But perhaps, having made my little gesture, I'd better sit down again. And you can give me a demonstration of your bedside manner.'

'I'm so glad for you, Robert. It's marvellous to see you up after such a long time.'

'I'd begun to think it would never happen. But now I really do feel that it's only a matter of time before I'm trotting round normally again.'

'Of course it is,' she agreed. 'And not very much time, either.'

'So there's no reason any longer why I shouldn't ask the most beautiful girl in the world whether she'd consider marrying me.'

There was a moment's silence, but it was not a pause which caused him any anxiety, for he could feel the pressure of Jennifer's hand on his own. She was savouring a few seconds of joy, that was all.

'There never was any reason, Robert,' she said softly.

'Oh yes there was. That standard plot about the beautiful nurse who devotes her life to her crippled patient is fine and romantic in stories, but highly unsatisfactory in real life.'

'That would have been for the nurse to decide. But I'm delighted for your sake that it will never be necessary.'

'You haven't actually answered me yet.'

'You haven't actually asked me yet,' she replied. But her head was on his shoulder and her arm round his waist. 'Will it be all right with your mother, do you think?'

'Mother will be delighted.' Robert spoke with certainty, knowing that whatever his mother's reservations might have been at first, she would welcome Jennifer into the family whole-heartedly once the engagement was a firm one. 'I've dropped a hint to her already, as a matter of fact. Made it clear, of course, that it all depended on you and I was only telling her what *I* wanted. But any mother thinks that her son must be irresistible, doesn't she, so I don't believe the announcement will come as much of a surprise. What about your father?'

'Daddy's sixty-four,' said Jennifer. She flushed slightly. 'Ever since my brother was killed, he's only got one ambition left in life: to have a grandson. Each time I go home I'm put through a great inquisition to find out whether I'm – what's his phrase? – "interested in anyone". He's desperate for me to be married. I can promise that he'll welcome you with open arms.'

'Mother would love a grandchild as well,' said Robert. 'Well, I've no objection to making the old folks happy, have you?' He laughed affectionately to see how Jennifer flushed again. It made her look prettier than ever. 'So the sooner we get on with the wedding, the better. All the same, I need to get a few more muscles back into use. January, d'you think? Let's tell everyone the middle of January.'

He kissed her again, his happiness so complete that he could think of nothing but the present moment. It was impossible to plan for the future, disagreeable to wonder whether he would have to return to the front, unreal to visualize a peacetime job and a married life in a home of his own. Too many things were beyond his control. The only certainty was that he loved Jennifer and she loved him. His mind clung to those two facts as tightly as his arms gripped her body – a body which looked so slim and fragile but felt surprisingly solid and reassuring.

When the time came for her to go on duty he felt a need to share his happiness with someone to whom he need not explain it.

'Could you find young Grant on your way out and tell him I need company?' he asked. As he expected, it was some time before the boy appeared. He was still dragging himself along the ground, Robert noticed with a frown.

'Where's your crutch?' he demanded.

'I can't manage it. It's too heavy and it won't go where I want it to go.'

'I know the feeling,' Robert sympathized. 'All the same, it's a battle which has to be won. Let's declare war together on old Kaiser Crutch. I'm just getting the hang of mine. It comes suddenly, if you practise. From now on you and I are going to have a session together every day until we've got it licked.'

He was as good as his word. At first, because he himself tired so easily, all they could do was to walk in turn up and down his room, but as Robert's strength returned, so did his adventurousness. By the time Christmas came, the two of them were climbing the stairs every day to the Long Gallery in which the Glanville ancestral portraits hung and playing complicated games of football and crutchball with a soft woolly ball stolen from little Pirry's nursery.

155

'It's not fair really,' Grant complained as Robert scored his third goal one morning. 'You've got two crutches and I've only got one.'

'But you've got one perfectly good leg. You can stand steady even without a crutch. I've only got two weak and feeble legs. If you take *my* crutches away, I shall simply collapse on to the floor.'

'You'll be all right soon, though,' said Grant. 'I'm going to be like this always.'

'All the more reason to make the best of it.' But Robert looked consideringly at his young cousin even as he spoke, and later that day he brought up the subject with his mother.

'Can anything be done about Grant?' he asked. 'This chap who's pummelling me about every morning, for example. Could he do any good?'

Margaret shook her head. 'No. He can help to strengthen muscles. But he can't alter the shape of a bone.'

'Suppose Grant had been standing next to me when the shell burst,' Robert suggested. 'Suppose his hip had been smashed up like mine. The doctors could have set it into the position in which it *ought* to be, couldn't they, instead of back where it was before?'

'Sending a boy of eleven out to a battlefield in order that he shall be blown up is rather a drastic solution.'

'Of course. But I mean – I can only put it crudely. Wouldn't it be possible for someone to hit Grant with a hammer – scientifically, of course, and under anaesthetic – and break whichever bit of bone is causing the trouble? And then put him in plaster, like me, until it mends, but in a better position. Or wouldn't his leg be long enough to reach the ground even if it were straight?'

'No, it wouldn't,' said Margaret. 'But that could probably be remedied. He could wear a surgical boot. You're quite right to prod me, Robert. These past few months, with such a never-ending stream of casualties to cope

156

with, it's been difficult to think of anything but the hospital. But it's wrong of me to neglect the family. Before the war there wouldn't have been anything to be done in a case like Grant's, but doctors who've been treating a wide range of casualties are working miracles nowadays. There are all sorts of new operations and techniques. I'll make it my New Year Resolution: to find someone who can help Grant.'

1917

1

Margaret stared at the sulky face in front of her and sighed. She had gone to a good deal of trouble to have Grant examined by a specialist. The verdict was a hopeful one. The boy's body could never be perfect, but a considerable degree of improvement was possible. An operation which might have been thought chancy in 1913 had become routine by the beginning of 1917. Margaret had felt pleased and enthusiastic as she explained to her nephew what would be involved, but his reaction was all too familiar.

'I don't want to,' he said.

'Is it because you're frightened of being hurt?' Margaret asked. 'You don't feel anything at all in an operation, you know. The doctor puts a mask over your face, with ether on it. Before you know what's happening you're in a deep sleep, and when you wake up it's all over.'

'I don't want to,' said Grant again.

'Come with me,' said Margaret. She found it continually necessary to fight against irritation in her dealings with her uninvited guest. Grant was no longer quite as unattractive in appearance as on the day of his arrival. Piers had taken him to a tailor to be equipped with clothes which were not only warm enough for an English winter but were also cut to accommodate his distorted limb without looking too ungainly. His hair had been neatly cut and the exercise of moving about on his crutch had helped him to lose a little of the podginess developed in a childhood spent mainly sitting on the ground. But although Robert seemed to have the knack of cheering up his young cousin, Margaret herself was offered nothing but sulkiness in response to her efforts to be helpful.

She led the way now to a large room which had once been the main dining room at Blaize. Half a dozen empty Bath chairs stood against the walls. The men who had arrived there in them were standing in the middle of the room, each helped by an orderly to come to terms with a pair of crutches, just as Robert had been forced to do once. But Robert was now as fit as he had ever been, able to ride or walk as well as any other member of the family. Each of these men, in their suits of bright hospital blue, had one empty trouser leg.

'Take a good look,' Margaret said. She did not intend to discuss her plans for Grant in front of the disabled men – but the boy had no such inhibitions.

'Is that what you're going to do to me?' he demanded. 'Are you going to cut my leg off?'

'Of course not.' More roughly than usual, Margaret pulled him out of the room and into what had once been a serving pantry. It was time, she decided, to stop trying to be kind and to see whether a little bullying would have a better effect. 'I brought you here to show you that it's time you stopped being sorry for yourself. You've got a bit of trouble in one leg; just a little bit, and you think that entitles you to spend the rest of your life sulking. All the men you've seen in that room have had to get used to the idea that they've got to live the rest of their lives with only one leg. They'll never be able to run anywhere again, never be able to ride a bicycle; some of them will never be able to work. And it's painful, having only the stump of a leg – did you know that? The part that isn't there seems to go on aching, and there's nothing any doctor can do about it. They've got to get used to that as well. If I offered any one of these men the chance to have a simple operation which would leave him with two good legs, he'd jump at it. He wouldn't be frightened.'

'I'm not frightened,' said Grant.

'Yes, you are. I don't know whether you're frightened of the operation or whether you're frightened of suddenly finding yourself the same as any other boy, with no more excuses for all these sulks, but you're certainly frightened of something. Well, it's time you stopped. Do you think your brother Brinsley was frightened when he led that attack?'

'It's easy being killed,' said Grant.

Margaret stared at her nephew, horrified to hear such a remark on the lips of an eleven-year-old. 'Listen to me, Grant,' she said. 'When you were born, I was the doctor who looked after you and your mother. Quite often a new baby needs a little help before it can take its first breath. No one would ever have known if I'd allowed you to die before you'd even begun to live. But you wouldn't have wanted me to do that, would you?'

'Yes, of course I would!' exclaimed Grant without a moment's hesitation. 'I'd never have known, anyway. But nobody wanted me to be born. My parents didn't. It was all a mistake. My father told me that.'

'Oh, Grant!' Overcome by compassion for the unhappy boy, Margaret opened her arms to him. And suddenly he was crying – not with the tears of petulance and frustration to which she had become accustomed, but from a deep misery of spirit. Margaret found that she was crying as well. Her grip tightened, and she was conscious of the boy's stiff body relaxing as he came close to her for comfort instead of holding himself aloof.

After a little while she found her handkerchief and dabbed dry both her own eyes and Grant's. '*I* wanted you,' she said. 'I wanted you to be alive then, and I want you to be alive – and happy – now. And your mother loved you: you know that. As for your father, I realize that you and he have found it hard to be friends, but you must make allowances for his unhappiness at your mother's death, and then Brinsley's. I remember him saying, when you were born, that God must have some special purpose for you. When you grow up, you must make him as proud of you as he was of Brinsley. And the first thing is to get you strong and fit. You came to Blaize at an awkward time, Grant. We were all unhappy, and too busy to welcome you properly. I'm sorry about that. Everything's going to be different from now on. You're part of the Lorimer family and we all love you. Now that Robert's married, I need to have someone else to care for specially. I want you to trust me to arrange what is best for you. Will you do that?'

He nodded. Margaret was relieved – but anxious at the same time. She had already recognized in Grant the all-or-nothing emotions of the fanatic. Until now, it seemed, he had found more people to hate than love. But if he attached himself to her, she would have a responsibility to accept his devotion without disappointing him. To send him back to Jamaica, for example, unless he asked to go, would surely be a rejection too great for him to bear.

It was difficult for Margaret not to feel a little weary at the prospect of adding to her family responsibilities at a time when she was within a few days of her sixtieth birthday. But she had never been able to resist the appeal of a child in need, and Grant's need was greater than most. It was necessary to look on the bright side. 1916 had been a terrible year. There were no indications that 1917 would be any better as far as the war was concerned, but she could make it her business to see that the family at least was kept as happy as possible.

It was a resolution which came under strain. Robert and Jennifer had been married early in January and Margaret had watched her son's firm stride down the aisle with a proud happiness. When she remembered the shattered body which had been returned to England it seemed miraculous that he should have made such a complete recovery. Foolishly, it did not occur to her that his state of health would be of interest to the army too.

She did not expect him actually to be discharged, but had imagined that rather than being returned to active service at the front he would be found some convalescent post such as that of an instructor at a training camp. So it came as a bolt from the blue when one day in February Jennifer burst into her office in a state of hysteria.

'What's happened?' Margaret's first thought, as she jumped to her feet, was that Robert must have had some kind of accident.

'He's got to go back. They say he's fit enough. They're going to send him over to France again. You've got to stop it. Please don't let them.'

Margaret sank back into her chair, just as upset as her daughter-in-law, but corseted against shock by her age. Until that moment she had not fully realized how great a relief it had been to have Robert in England. Even at the beginning, when his condition was still a grave one, he had at least been surrounded by people who were trying to save his life, not take it. There was little she could say to comfort Jennifer.

'I hoped, like you – ' she began; but to finish the sentence was unnecessary. 'There's nothing we can do, I'm afraid. He's a soldier. He has to do what he's told.'

'You're a doctor. You could say that he isn't fit. All they did was look at him and make him walk about and take deep breaths. That's not a proper medical examination. You could tell them that he isn't ready yet.'

'I can't say that if it isn't true. In any case, they'd hardly believe his mother, doctor or not. And think how humiliating it would be for Robert. What does he say about it?'

'He takes it for granted that there's no choice. But it *would* be true that he isn't ready yet. He has nightmares, terrible nightmares, every night. About walking over dead bodies – ' Jennifer was weeping again by now – 'and arms and legs falling off when he touches them. And when he wakes up, he's shivering. He trembles for hours sometimes. He'd never admit it, but he's frightened. Deeply, deeply frightened.'

'If no one were ever frightened, there'd be no such thing as courage,' said Margaret. 'He's already proved that he's a hero, trying to save his cousin's life. You should be proud that he's prepared to go back in spite of his experiences.'

'I don't want to be proud. I want to be married. He's never told you how terrible it is out there. The mud and the smells and the noise and the danger. He never wanted you to be worried. But he wrote to me. He told me all about it.'

'Get a grip on yourself, Jennifer. I've spent two years caring for the victims of the battlefield. Do you think I supposed that people were throwing grenades and gas shells at them during some peaceful country walk? You could give me credit for a little imagination. I didn't need to be *told*. Oh, I'm sorry, dear.' She stood up again and put her arm round the girl's shoulders. 'It's as much of a shock to me as it is to you. But I'm afraid there's nothing we can do. If there are any choices at all, we must leave them to Robert.'

'Then he'll go,' said Jennifer flatly.

'Yes.' Margaret kissed her daughter-in-law. 'Give him as happy a time as you can until then, my dear. Don't let him see you crying.'

In obeying that instruction Jennifer proved more successful than Margaret might have expected. But when the day of parting came at last and she returned alone from London, it seemed that the effort had exhausted her. Twice during March she fainted in the ward, and Margaret began to receive complaints – cautiously worded, in view of the family relationship – about Nurse Scott's tendency to weep and dream. Before long it became necessary to have an official interview.

'I can think of an explanation for what's been happening,' Margaret said. 'I'm hoping you're going to tell me that I've guessed right.'

She was rewarded for the gentleness of her approach by seeing the shy flush which had won Robert's heart. Jennifer nodded.

'You're expecting a baby?'

'Yes. In November.'

All problems of discipline forgotten, the two women hugged each other. Then Margaret, her eyes shining, prepared to exercise her authority as a prospective grandmother as well as the administrator of the hospital.

'This feeling of weakness may not last for more than a month or two,' she said. 'But all the same, I'm going to suggest that you go home to Norfolk. There's too much heavy lifting in your work here. It's not good for you or for the baby. I know how much your father has longed to have you back with him, and this is the time when you'd be justified in indulging him. Country air and country food and plenty of rest. It's the best recipe. Do you agree?'

'Yes, Mother. Thank you very much.'

Margaret was touched by the girl's first use of the word which Robert had from the beginning urged her to adopt. In the first weeks of the marriage the dual relationship had apparently made it impossible for Jennifer to decide whether she was talking to her commandant or her mother-in-law. From now on, Margaret was sure, their relationship would be a much easier one. Her happiness at the news was such that for a little while she was able to stop worrying about Robert. She did not even feel any great uneasiness at first when Piers came into her office a day or two later and enquired whether she had an address for Kate.

'Yes. A new one has just arrived. It's somewhere in the south of Russia.' She handed her address book across the desk. 'I'm not sure how much one can count on letters reaching her, though. She obviously never received my message about Brinsley's death. You look worried, Piers. Has something happened?'

'Yes,' Piers told her. 'It may not be important, but she's a long way from Moscow and Petrograd and news may take quite a time to travel. By the time she hears from there, it could be too late for her to get out of the country. And in my opinion she ought to leave. There's some very disquieting news coming through from Russia. Very disquieting indeed.'

2

Every day Kate allowed herself two minutes of rage against Russian inefficiency. It acted as a safety valve, making it easier – a little easier – for her to cultivate during the rest of the day a Russian quality of resignation.

There was nothing wrong with the postal arrangements. What was left of the Serbian Division was now under Russian command, and if the youngest and most useless of the Russian officers sent a message to his family in Moscow or Petrograd requesting the dispatch of a new pair of gloves or some favourite item of food, the parcel would arrive in the minimum time needed for the courier to make the double journey by train. But none of Kate's letters to the Minister of War or any of the committees which had recently been set up to deal with supplies or transport or hospitals was even acknowledged.

No one, it appeared, was willing to authorize the release and dispatch of the crates of medical stores which were waiting uselessly in some warehouse or other. In vain did Kate argue that the consignment was private property, sent from London specifically to re-equip the volunteer hospital which the suffragist movement had re-established after the Serbian retreat, this time on the Romanian Front. Somewhere in the tortuous bureaucratic process through which even the simplest transaction had to travel, some stamp or signature must be lacking.

Before she learned better, Kate would have expected that in an autocracy decisions could be made simply and speedily. But in practice she found that no one in any sphere was willing to take responsibility for anything – not even the Autocrat himself.

At first it had been possible to make excuses. Almost before she had recovered from the hardships of the Serbian retreat, Kate – along with the new staff of English and Scottish nurses who had joined her in Medjidia – had found herself retreating again, this time across the Dobrudja plain. It was reasonable that her supplies should be stored securely until the hospital had been re-established in a position which could be considered temporarily safe from capture. But by January 1917 the situation was stable and still the supplies did not come.

It was not only the hospital which was under-equipped. The soldiers – Serbs and Russians alike – were short of ammunition. There were not enough rifles for each man to have his own; someone leaving the front line for a day's rest had to hand his weapon over to his relief, together with a ration of cartridges which would be quite inadequate in any full-scale battle. For the time being everything was relatively quiet along the frozen front, but there was talk of a spring offensive. Kate knew little enough about the strategy and mechanics of war, but it was plain to her that if an attack by either side began before the Russians had supplied their men – including the Serbs – with rifles and machine guns, cannons and ammunition, there would be a massacre. And if there were a massacre – or even nothing more than the normal run of casualties after a battle – Kate and her staff, lacking even the most basic drugs and bandages, would be unable to cope with it. Throughout January she waited with mounting frustration.

But the beginning of February brought a possible explanation of the delay. She had asked one of the Russian officers to take the matter up for her while he was on leave. It came as no surprise when he returned empty-handed, for she had already realized that more perseverance would be required than he was likely to display; but it was of some value that he could tell her what the obstacle was. Beatrice – far away in London and aware of the chaos which had surrounded the hospital unit in the second retreat – had consigned the stores to Dr Kate Lorimer by name, presumably as a precaution against misuse. 'You will have to go personally to Petrograd to sign the papers and accept delivery,' the officer told her.

'And will that be enough?'

'Who knows? Have you friends? In such matters, it is always as well to have friends.'

Kate knew no one in Petrograd and for a day or two longer she hesitated. But her life since leaving England had matured her far beyond her years. She was not yet twenty-six years old, but responsibility and the habit of command had given her the authority of an older woman. The knowledge afforded her little pleasure: she would have liked to be young for a while longer. But it meant that she did not lack confidence. And there would be no language problem. Her lessons in Russian from Sergei had enabled her to converse with the Russian officers right from the start, and constant practice had by now made her fluent. It did not take her long to decide that she must make the journey.

She was still in the process of arranging for her duties to be covered during an absence which might extend itself beyond her expectation when a bundle of letters arrived from home. She had written to England with a new address, and here were the answers, more promptly than she could have dared to hope. Had she judged only by their dates, in fact, the speed would have seemed nothing less than a miracle. But she knew that Russia – unlike the rest of Europe – had never adopted the Gregorian calendar and was by now thirteen days behind everywhere else. It was a small matter, but one which she found typical of the backwardness of the country.

Guessing that it would be the dullest, she opened her cousin Beatrice's letter first. As she had expected, it was devoted to the business of the hospital unit. With typical efficiency Beatrice enclosed a copy of the stores inventory in case the first notification had been lost during the Dobrudja retreat. The supplies had reached Petrograd in the late autumn, just before the port was closed by ice. The ship had already returned to England to confirm the delivery.

Kate sighed as she read the businesslike communication, but it told her nothing that she did not already know. By contrast, Alexa's letter was gossipy and casually organized, hopping from one subject to another. Just as the typed list reflected Beatrice's character, so it was in keeping with Alexa's interests that she should enthuse about the musical life of Russia – the excellence of the bass singers, the grace of the ballet dancers, the taste and discrimination of the aristocratic audiences who were as likely to throw jewels as flowers at the feet of their favourite artists. Kate could not help laughing to herself, so different was the Russia in which she was living now from the Russia which had fêted Alexa during her opera season in St Petersburg, eight long years ago.

'And if you find yourself in Petrograd, as I believe they call it now,' Alexa continued, 'you must on no account fail to visit my very dear friend Prince Aminov. Prince *Paul* Aminov, I should perhaps say, because you will have discovered by now that even younger sons in Russia take their father's title, so there are probably half a dozen Prince Aminovs scattered around the family estates. Paul is a great patron of the opera. In one of his palaces, at Tsarskoe Selo, he has a private theatre. It was when I sang there for him that I became determined to have my own little opera house one day. He'll be interested to hear from you that I did at least manage a season or two before this terrible war interrupted all our lives. He had a younger brother – I forget his name, but he played the piano so well that in England he could have been a professional concert soloist. In Russia, of course, it would be unthinkable for a nobleman to stoop to earning his living in such a way. Paul is officially an admiral, and his brother was something in the army – but I doubt whether he saw much more of his regiment than Paul did of his fleet. I'm writing to Paul by this same post to tell him that my niece is a guest of his country. So I can promise you a welcome if you should ever go north. They have a palace in the city itself, of course.'

Of course, agreed Kate, and for a second time she laughed aloud. No doubt it was true enough in peacetime that admirals could amuse themselves with their private theatres and their favourite singers; but in war even the least military-minded officer must recognize where his duty lay. Whether he was competent to discharge it was a quite different matter. However, Alexa's promise of an introduction strengthened her confidence in the success of the journey she planned. The requirement of her personal signature made the visit necessary: the name of a powerful family increased the hope that it might be successful. The warning that she might need friends had not surprised her and, although her claim on the Aminovs was so tenuous, it still might be enough. The Russian officers with whom she messed were all members of the nobility, and she had had time to learn that they were as generous as they were unpredictable when favours were asked.

She was still thinking about her journey when she opened Margaret's letter, but within a few seconds all thought of medical stores had vanished from her mind. She stared at the words with incredulous horror.

Brinsley was dead. Brinsley had been dead for more than six months. Margaret, it seemed, had made two attempts already to break the news, but realized from the cheerful note in Kate's last letter that they must have gone astray. She gave some details of the battle, of the letter which his commanding officer had written praising his gallantry, of his posthumous DSO. Kate found it impossible to believe any of this. There had been a moment, as she said goodbye to her brother on the platform of Waterloo Station, when she had been frightened lest she should never see him again, but beneath the fear had lain a belief that someone so young and full of life could not possibly die. Brinsley – his mouth curling with mischief – had claimed to be lucky, and Kate had believed him.

Still shocked, she allowed her eyes to run over the rest of the letter without taking much of it in. Robert had been wounded but was recovering well. Her father, though, was showing signs of breakdown as a result of Brinsley's death. Duke Mattison was writing alarming reports of his increasing irrationality, and there were hints that he was drinking too much. Margaret asked Kate to consider seriously whether her duty now might not lie at home in Jamaica. If she decided to return, Beatrice could find another doctor to replace her.

Kate set the letter aside and began to pace up and down. Almost as though she were sleepwalking she made her way to one of the hospital wards. The night sister looked up in surprise, since it was not the doctor's hour for a round, but Kate did not explain her presence. There was an immediate cry for water from the men at one end of the ward; whenever anyone new came in they renewed their pathetic requests for a drink. Neither doctor nor nurses could ever persuade soldiers whose stomachs had been shot away that a sip of water could kill them as certainly as a glass of poison.

What was it all for, Kate asked herself as she looked at the faces of the injured men. One of her early grievances had been that the Russian command had proved readier to risk the lives of their Serbian allies in battle than those

170

of their own army. As a result, few of the Serbian Division survived: most of the patients now in the hospital were Russian. Sixteen-year-old boys, grey-haired fathers of families, uncomprehending peasants who had probably never travelled more than ten versts from their villages before the recruiting officer arrived. What were they fighting for? What were they dying for? For these men, at this moment, it was possible to say that they were fighting to defend their own country; but that had not been the case at the beginning of the war. And what had a complicated network of treaties and guarantees and invasions ever had to do with Brinsley, except to make him their victim? How much longer could it go on? How long would women see their sons and husbands taken from them without protest? How long would the men themselves continue to obey officers who might have to order them to advance against machine guns whilst armed with nothing more than pitchforks? Kate knew that such a thing was happening already and would happen even more frequently in future. Some of the patients in her hospital had arrived with wounds to their feet or fingers which Kate knew to be self-inflicted. If despair had already reached that pitch, the time must be near when the men would simply turn and run away.

The thought increased her sadness. It should have been possible to think of Brinsley's death as glorious. No doubt he had acted heroically in the moment of battle. But was it worthwhile? He had not survived to ask the question, so Kate put it to herself instead. The answer came easily. No, it was not worthwhile. There was nothing that any politician or general had ever told her which would justify the death of one young man like Brinsley, much less millions. Kate suspected that the war continued only because no one knew how to stop it.

The only clear fact was that she was doing some good where she was. Armies would continue to kill each other whether she was in Europe or Jamaica, but every single doctor at the front line saved lives every day simply by being on the spot. It didn't matter whether the lives saved were Serbian or Russian or even Austrian or German. Her responsibility as a doctor was wider than her responsibility as a daughter. She loved her father deeply, but in the middle of a war she could not devote herself to the care of a single man. As a doctor herself, Margaret would surely understand.

All that night Kate wept for her dead brother, but grief served only to stiffen her resolve to stay and do her job properly. That meant that she must have the right equipment. The very next day, grim with determination, she set out on the long journey to the city which had once been Alexa's glittering St Petersburg – the Russian Paris, the Venice of the North – and was now, simply, Petrograd.

3

The Astoria Hotel was full. Or, at least, not necessarily full, but reserved for accredited members of military missions. Kate was startled and depressed by the rebuff. Tiring and uncomfortable, the journey had been unexpectedly protracted, for the train had twice been halted for several hours by a lack of coal, and on a third occasion had been forced to wait for the removal of an engine which blocked the line after its boiler burst in the extreme cold. She had been looking forward to a comfortable bed and perhaps even a bath.

Disappointed, she paused in the lobby to consider what she would do. All foreigners visiting Petrograd were accustomed to stay at the Astoria as a matter of course. It was the only hotel in the city with international standards of service and language comprehension. Because Kate spoke Russian she could search for the kind of accommodation which ordinary Russians used, but after so many crowded days of travelling she felt desperate for rest and welcome. Even more to the point, she was not adequately dressed to endure the biting wind which came straight off the frozen Gulf of Finland. The south of Russia had been cold enough, but here the temperature was so low that without a scarf across her mouth and nose it was painful even to breathe. She returned to the droshky which had brought her from the station and gave the driver the address of the Aminov town house.

There she used her own language to ask whether Prince Aminov was at home. Even if they did not completely understand, the servants could be expected to get the gist of the request and it seemed a good idea to make it clear from the start that she was a foreign visitor. The prince himself would certainly speak English, although French would be his first tongue. Russian was the language of the peasants.

The numerous servants in the hall were formally dressed in livery, but informal in behaviour. Kate discovered at once that Prince Paul was not in Petrograd; and her attempt to learn the whereabouts of his brother – whose name Alexa had omitted to mention – was greeted wtih a real or pretended lack of comprehension. They did not realize that she could understand the discussion which they proceeded to hold amongst themselves. From it she learned that Prince Vladimir had arrived home on leave that day but had given orders that he was not to be disturbed. Different opinions were expressed as to whether the arrival of the foreign lady would justify the overriding of these instructions.

Kate's tiredness, subduing her sense of polite behaviour, drove her to interrupt a discussion which seemed set to continue interminably. She demanded to be taken to Prince Vladimir, and by the firmness with which she turned towards the staircase made it clear that she would find her own way if no one was prepared to escort her.

Her knowledge of the Russian character was accurate enough. Confronted by determination, the servants shrugged their shoulders and accepted her wishes. Two of the footmen went up the wide marble staircase in front of her to lead the way.

The grandeur of the rooms on the first floor almost took Kate's breath away. She had visited Brinsley House and had lived for several months in Blaize, so she was not unfamiliar with the life of the rich. But this house was built and furnished on an unimaginable scale of opulence. Alexa had not been exaggerating when she talked of palaces – and even then she had been describing one of the family's country homes, giving the impression that what was maintained in the town was merely a pied-à-terre. Kate's eyes widened as she followed the footmen through huge rooms decorated largely, it seemed, with gold leaf. Crystal chandeliers hung from the high ceilings. Carpets of luxurious thickness or of delicate Chinese colours covered the floor. Vases and urns of green malachite stood on Boule commodes. And small ornamental objects, of gold or jade or crystal decorated with jewels, were set out on Louis XV tables as casually as though each of them were not worth a fortune.

Someone was playing a piano, and as they came nearer to the sound, the footmen fell back. The intrusive foreigner, it seemed, should be left alone to face their master's anger at being disturbed. Ready to do so, Kate opened a door and found the pianist. But at first she could not bring herself to look at him, so overwhelmed was she by the room. It was a hall rather than a mere room – perhaps actually intended as a private concert hall, since there was a raised platform at the far end: or perhaps as a ballroom, with provision for an orchestra. Except for the grand piano on the platform and fifty or so gilded chairs arranged against the wall, it was unfurnished: but the proportions were so perfect that it did not appear bare, and the materials of its construction so beautiful that it did not need decoration. The walls were of a pale pink marble into which had been set, as a pattern, panels of other marbles in a range of colours which seemed too fragile to be stone: pale blue and delicate mauve, the sea shades of green, clear yellow, misty grey. It was an aristocratic room in its own right; a fit setting for an aristocrat.

Kate had been an enthusiastic concert-goer in her student days and recognized the work she was hearing as the piano part of an early Beethoven concerto. But the piece was interrupted by the pianist's awareness of her presence. He was a fair-haired man in his early thirties, wearing the style of moustache currently sported by the dashing young officers of the cavalry regiments. But instead of wearing uniform he was casually dressed, with a scarf loosely knotted inside his open-necked silk shirt. And although a moment earlier he had been hunched over the keyboard, projecting an impression of great physical power and control through the crashing chords and rapid trills of his performance, in repose he gave the impression of softness, as though there were no bones in the wide, long-fingered hands which rested on his knees as he looked at her. He would have had the right to be impatient or indignant or aggressive, but instead his brown eyes watched her passively as she walked towards the platform.

'I'm trespassing in your palace and disturbing your practice,' she said as she approached. 'I must apologize. But the servants – '

'Oh, the servants!' He interrupted her with a shrug of his shoulders. She had spoken in English and, as she expected, he answered her fluently in the same language. 'What can I do for you?'

'I'm Dr Kate Lorimer, from England,' said Kate. 'I have an introduction from my aunt, Lady Glanville, to Prince Aminov – Prince Paul Aminov.'

He stood up and bowed over her hand in languid

acknowledgement of the introduction. 'I fear your journey is not ended, Dr Lorimer,' he said. 'As an admiral, my brother feels obliged to be at least within sight of the water while the war continues. He is at Murmansk. And my sisters and their children have retired to one of our country estates to avoid the food shortages in the city. I regret that I am the only member of the family here to welcome you. But I can see that you are fatigued. I shall not allow you to continue in search of my brother until you have dined with me and enjoyed a good night's rest. And if your business is not with him personally, I hope you will allow me the pleasure of representing him.'

'I should certainly be most grateful – '

Again she was interrupted, this time by a clap of the hands. The two footmen hurried in with a promptness which made it clear that they had been listening to the exchange. Kate heard them ordered to take her and her luggage to a room. Then the prince turned to her again and for a second time formally kissed her hand.

'When you are rested, we will meet again for dinner,' he said. 'It will be an unexpected attraction of my leave to enjoy such charming company.'

To Kate, knowing herself to be tired and dirty and crumpled, the remark sounded like a joke. But during the past winter she had spent enough time with aristocratic officers of the Imperial Army to know that the compliments which would have signified insincerity in England were only normal politeness with them. In any case, she had come in search of hospitality and did not intend to let pride rob her of it. With so many rooms and servants, her presence was not likely to inconvenience her host – and the speed with which he resumed his piano playing as she withdrew suggested that he would not allow it to do so. She had been received and temporarily dismissed.

How could she discover at what hour she would be expected to appear for dinner? Her enquiry to the maid received the courteous answer, 'It is as you wish, Madame.' So the problem was solved by sleep, which overcame her as soon as she lay down on the huge four-poster bed, intending only to rest for a moment or two. By the time she awoke, the short northern day had long since ended and the maid was standing in the doorway, awaiting instructions.

Over dinner Kate felt it her duty to give more information about herself, especially to a host who clearly thought it rude to ask questions. The first matter to be established was that of Alexa's name. Prince Aminov had never heard of Lady Glanville, but as soon as Kate remembered that Alexa's visit to St Petersburg had taken place before her marriage, and mentioned Alexa Reni, there was a very different reaction.

'The beautiful Alexa! Oh, but most certainly I remember her visit. I thought her the most ravishing creature I had ever seen. And her voice was as perfect as her face. I dreamed of composing an opera for her. My brother, alas, took care that she should not notice me. I half expected her to become my sister-in-law, but it seemed that Paul was not quite persuasive enough.'

'From what my aunt told me, I had the impression that he was offering a little less than marriage.' Kate spoke mischievously. At the first moment of meeting she had been tired and uncertain of her welcome and her host had been patiently suffering an interruption: no wonder they had behaved stiffly to each other. Now that they were both relaxed, she found him easy company. Her professional acquaintance with the Russian officer class had led her to divide it into two categories: one containing drunken boors and the other delightful but often idle dilettantes with the charming manners of international society. Prince Aminov, it seemed to her – although only a dilettante in the sense that his talent for music was not exercised for money – fell into the second group. Already he was flirting with her in the manner of a man who knows he will not be taken seriously, and for this one evening of relaxation Kate was prepared to match his mood.

'You are probably right,' he laughed. 'When Paul did marry, two years after your aunt left Russia, he chose a Grand Duchess from the imperial family for his bride – with highly advantageous effects on both his fortune and his career. We are close in age, but he was an admiral before he was thirty, while I, as a bachelor, have to endure the more usual intervals between promotions.'

'I hope your brother's marriage has proved as happy as my aunt's.'

'Ah, well,' he sighed. 'Unfortunately my sister-in-law died in childbed last year – and the baby died as well. So you'll find my brother unencumbered. Perhaps you'll have more success than the lovely Alexa in persuading him to take an English wife.'

Kate flushed. Too unsophisticated to make a joke of his teasing, she could counter it only with her true reason for coming to Petrograd, although the effect was to make it clear that she was using the Aminov palace as a hotel. Fortunately her host took it for granted that she should have done this, and insisted that she must stay as long as might prove necessary. He listened with a frown to the details of what she needed.

'I can tell you where to go and whom to see,' he said. 'But the difficulties you face will be no less here than they were at a distance. The inefficiency of the ministries is almost unbelievable. The armies lack ammunition because the trains lack coal, and yet there is plenty of coal in the country. The city bakeries can bake only a tenth of the bread which is required because they are short of flour, and yet the granaries in the east are full. Every department is ruled by incompetence.' He sighed. 'There must be some efficient officials somewhere, but they are all afraid to act on their own initiative and are strangled by bureaucracy if they attempt to use the system laid down for them. It is my duty as an officer of His Majesty's Regiment of the Imperial Guard to protect the Tsar's life with my own, but I would be doing him a better service if I could persuade him to dismiss his present ministers and committees and give direct power to one or two men who know what the army needs and would cut through every knot to provide it. We are losing the war. You, on the front, must know that as well as I do. There are too many Russians who are ready to give in, to make a treaty. The rest of us, those who remember Japan and are not prepared to be humiliated again, have only one defence against such defeatism – we must win.' He smiled apologetically. 'Well, I mustn't start delivering political lectures. What difference does it make to an Englishwoman whether we win or lose?'

'If Russia were to surrender, the German and Austrian armies could turn their whole force against the French and British,' said Kate; but even as she spoke she realized that a Russian could not be expected to care greatly about that. Tactfully she tried to rouse the prince from his mood of depression. Would he play to her, she asked him, and the charm of his smile showed at once how much the suggestion pleased him.

It was as well that the evening finished on a restful note, for the next day tried Kate's patience to the limit. To sit in a hospital hundreds of miles away and fume because letters were never answered had been hard enough. Far worse, she discovered, was to wait in a government building and see that her request for an appointment was not even conveyed from the reception area to the office of someone who might conceivably deal with it.

On that first day she tried to cultivate the patience shown by her fellow-petitioners. It did not come naturally to her, and she wondered whether the Russians themselves were not being pressed close to the edge of tolerance. Surely in such conditions even they might abandon the fatalism which had endured for so many centuries. On her way back to the palace on that first evening she noticed the long line of women queueing for bread and realized that they would have to wait all night in the bitter cold for whatever might be available the next morning. Twenty-four hours later, as Prince Aminov's sleigh was carrying her back from a second wasted day, she saw the lines break. The windows of the bakery she was passing were broken by stones and the crowd rushed inside to seize what they could. So great was the crush that the sleigh was brought to a halt. It was able to continue only when the clatter of horses' hooves on the frozen ground alerted the looters to the fact that the Cossacks were coming.

'One thing surprised me,' said Kate when she was describing the incident to her host later that evening. 'A friend once described to me the whips which the Cossacks carry.'

'Yes?' Prince Aminov showed no interest in whips. 'What of it?'

'They were not carrying them today.'

It had seemed significant to Kate, but the prince merely shrugged his shoulders. 'The crowd was mainly of women, I imagine. It is when students riot or soldiers mutiny that the Cossacks need to establish their authority. Now then, I have an invitation which I hope that you will accept. On Sunday evening Princess Radziwill is giving a gala ball. She has heard that you are my guest here and insists that I bring you as my partner.'

Kate considered the offer doubtfully. A society dance would not have attracted her even in England. Here she would find it even more difficult to converse – in French – with the kind of wit and intelligence which would be expected.

'I'm afraid I came to Petrograd prepared only to petition ministers,' she said. 'My clothes are more than unsuitable – it would be an insult to a hostess if I appeared in them.'

Prince Aminov waved away her objection. 'My sister-in-law's wardrobe is still hanging in her dressing room. Paul has not been back here since she died. He will never want to see them again. Please take your choice. No one will be hurt or offended, and each of the ball dresses will have been worn only once. You will make me very unhappy if you refuse.'

Kate hesitated still. She found it easy to converse with her host, but less easy to know what he was thinking. Except when he was playing the piano, his eyes held a dreamy, far-away look, as though nothing were of any great importance to him. She realized that out of politeness he would have been bound to pass on the invitation to her, but she was unable to guess whether the corresponding politeness on her part would be to accept or to persist in her refusal.

Prince Aminov took her hand and bowed to kiss it as though they had only just been introduced.

'You are too serious,' he said. 'It is good that you should be so greatly concerned for your patients and I admire your perseverance in battering your poor head against the doors of our bureaucracy, fighting your own private war. But you are too young to be angry all the time. There is nothing you can do for your hospital by staying here in the evening. And a good deal that you might achieve by coming.'

'What do you mean, Excellency?'

'I mean that this may prove the way to unlock the warehouse which holds your goods. I shall introduce you to the right people – the highest people, who are never likely to grant an audience to someone who comes without appointment to their waiting room. You will meet them on their own ground, as an equal. Together we shall approach the little difficulty with delicacy. They will realize that you are a friend of mine. Then they will understand that the customary procedures will be observed, and the difficulties you have faced will disappear.'

'Are you trying to tell me that they are corrupt – that they need to be bribed?' Kate demanded.

The prince gave an amused smile. 'Is it corruption to operate a system which is generally known and accepted? It would certainly be corrupt if they allowed your property to go to someone else for a consideration, but I'm sure they would never dream of doing that. All they expect is a little present – a fee, you could call it. And I only use this argument to show you that you will be serving the interests of your patients in going to the ball, because I could not bear to be disappointed of your company. The evening is a time for pleasure – and how could I enjoy myself if I knew that you were here alone, fuming with rage? You will come, please? For my sake.'

His smile was curiously sweet, banishing the dreaminess from his eyes and replacing it with a pleading warmth. Kate was not easily charmed and was well aware that any claim that he would be miserable without her was only a pretence. Nevertheless, she found the mixture of formality and persuasiveness in his manner to be irresistible.

'Thank you, Excellency,' she said, half laughing at herself for the weakness of her capitulation. 'I shall be most honoured to be your partner.'

4

Early on Sunday morning Kate stared out of her bedroom window across the frozen water of the Neva. At this time of day the ice was a pale green, as delicate in shade as the panels of the marble hall. Later, if the sun shone, it would glint with gold for an hour or two before sunset turned it a rosy pink. On the further side of the river the spire of the Peter and Paul fortress, too slim to show the snow, was golden as well: a beautiful sight but a symbol of ugliness. The contrast was too acute to be believed –

on this side of the river, the pampered comfort of the prince in his palace; and on the other, the hardship and oblivion to which political prisoners were condemned.

There was no bureaucracy to be besieged today – its officials would replace obstructiveness by absence. The Aminov palace was equally silent. Kate was growing familiar with the timetable of the Russian nobility, whose day – Sunday and weekday alike – hardly began before nightfall. Still governed by the habit of hospital routine, she herself woke early, but never saw her host at breakfast.

If the prince had known that she intended to go out and explore the city – and unescorted into the bargain – he would certainly have prevented her. There had been a series of strikes on the previous day. No trams or trains had run, and crowds carrying red banners paraded through the streets demanding the resignation of the Cabinet and expulsion of the German Tsarina. The army had been called out and some of the demonstrators were killed. But it was rumoured that many of the soldiers had disobeyed the order to fire.

Kate was well aware that the streets of the city were becoming unsafe. Being Kate Lorimer, however, she was not prepared to make any concessions to the fact. After almost a week spent in ministerial ante-rooms, she felt the need to treat her frustration with a dose of fresh air and exercise.

For more than two hours she tramped over the frozen snow in the boots which the army cobbler had made for her. In spite of the blackness of her mood and the heavy greyness of the sky, from which new snow was falling, the beauty of this most un-Russian city took hold of her. Already she had admired the magnificence of the Winter Palace, and she was able to appreciate the classical elegance of the pale yellow buildings which curved round the facing side of the palace square even though they housed the General Staff offices she hated. The elaborate ceremonial arch in the centre of the curve and the picture-book array of noble palaces, like the Aminovs', which stretched along the river bank, were all part of the same splendid architectural centrepiece with which she had become familiar. But now for the first time she wandered further afield, exploring the network of canals, admiring the decorative bridges which ran so elegantly across them, and the handsomely painted mansions on either side.

It was as easy here as in Prince Aminov's marble hall or golden drawing room to forget the other aspects of the city: the slum tenements with their insanitary courtyards, the poverty of the people on the streets, the deep puddles which formed when the sun shone warmly enough for an hour or two to melt the snow. From the first moment of her arrival in Petrograd she had been appalled by the contrast between the luxuries of her temporary home and the world of pain and misery on the battlefront which she had been attempting to describe to the indifferent bureaucrats of the General Staff. Only that morning she had become aware of another contrast, with the world of the political prisoner. And now she realized that the extremes of luxury and sordid discomfort were to be found inside the central living area of the city. How long could such a state of affairs be tolerated, she asked herself. Her step became firmer and even less ladylike than before as her anger rose.

The sound of singing drew her towards the Cathedral of St Nicholas. Reminding herself that it was Sunday, she went inside. It was a long time since she had last been able to attend a Baptist service, and it was likely to be an equally long time in the future before she had any contact with the faith which her father preached so eloquently in Jamaica. But although the form of the Russian Orthodox service was so different from that of a Nonconformist chapel, the same God presumably listened to prayers in all languages, and Kate was in need of comfort.

On the ground floor a funeral service was in progress.

A crowd of women, fat and dowdy in their winter coats and headscarves, wandered, weeping, in and out. But the singing came from a higher floor. Kate climbed the stairs and found herself in a treasure house. The light of many hundreds of candles was reflected off jewelled icons and golden mosaics. Even here, it seemed, she could not escape from the contrast between great wealth and great poverty. Gorgeously attired in yet more gold, a black-bearded priest was reading from the Bible to his crowded congregation. Almost imperceptibly his reading voice changed to chanting and the chanting to an operatic style of bass singing. All her life Kate had been susceptible to the influence of music, whether soothing or stimulating. She made no attempt now to listen to the words, but allowed her troubled spirit to be comforted by the beauty of the sound.

The voice of the single singer was joined by a choir in the gallery above. The new sound filled the building, swelling and diminishing, harsh and even discordant at times, its harmonies changing abruptly from major to minor key with that especial Slavonic characteristic which was so difficult to analyse but so easy to recognize. Kate tried to pray but found the atmosphere uncongenial. Her Baptist upbringing had given her a positive attitude to religion and life. She was not prepared – as the Russian Orthodox worshippers were – merely to prostrate herself on the ground and await events. Her father, in his services, was accustomed to converse aloud with God – to put forward problems, and to receive solutions which owed a good deal to the pastor's own conclusions. Kate knew that prayers were not always answered – but that could be the fault of the petitioner: it remained important to continue the dialogue. But above all it was necessary to take whatever action might be necessary to achieve God's revealed wishes, to walk firmly down the path illuminated by His will.

Such an attitude was out of tune with the mood of this

congregation. Already in the hospital Kate had learned to recognize what appeared to be a peculiarly Russian aptitude for suffering – an ability to accept separation, hunger, pain and even death without a murmur of complaint against whatever inexplicable fate had brought all these things to pass. The women in this congregation – for there were few men – seemed to display the same passivity: whatever was God's will was to be accepted.

No doubt the obstructive behaviour of Russian officials was encouraged by this attitude. Their procrastinations or outright refusals to take action would all too often be accepted without complaint: or, if that was too much to hope for, the petitioner would continue to wait patiently for something to happen which might change the situation. More than once in the past few days Kate had longed to leap to her feet in some crowded waiting room, allowing her rage to explode. She had persuaded herself that restraint would be wiser, but now she wondered whether she was right or whether the time had come to protest. In this cathedral, too, she would have liked to shout out, interrupting the service to tell these submissive women that life ought to be good, that it was not necessary to be always unhappy and – most of all – that to accept the blows of fate or government without complaint was to invite further tribulation. Oh, for the throbbing vitality of Hope Valley!

She held her indignation under control now, just as she had controlled it during the search for the right rubber stamp; but the intensity of her feelings, raised to a higher pitch by the melancholy music of the choir, drew her into a state of exaltation – a trance-like ecstasy, illuminated by a visionary flash. There is no God, she thought, and at once everything was explained.

Her father had preached in the name of God, but it was his own hard work as an administrator which brought happiness to his people, and she suspected that he had always known this himself. For the past two years she had done her best to reconcile the death and suffering she saw with the faith of her childhood, the belief in a loving God who ordered everything for the best. She had failed in the attempt. How could a loving God have wanted Brinsley to die? But if God instead were angry or uncaring, why should He be worshipped? The reconciliation of faith and fact had proved to be impossible. Now she knew that the effort had never been necessary: there was no God.

So there was no excuse for passivity. The world might be destroying itself, but the destruction was not inevitable. There was no God. Men who were the victims of other men must save themselves by their own exertions and build a new society out of love for their fellow-men, not from hatred or fear. It was all so obvious that she could not understand why she had taken so long to comprehend it. She even remembered that Sergei had tried to convince her of the need for a change in society. Revolution was the word he had used, and she had been alarmed by it, thinking in terms of the French terror. But a spiritual revolution would be as effective as a political one. All that was needed was a change of attitude, a determination to be positive.

Kate Lorimer's vision was the opposite of Saul's, but Petrograd was on her road to Damascus. 'There is no God,' she repeated to herself. 'No God. Only men, who must love one another.'

Around her the service continued, but it had nothing more to offer. Kate pushed her way out of the crowded cathedral and began to walk back towards the Neva. The day was lighter now: the sky seemed to have lifted. Was it only the excitement of her vision which made her want to run and shout? Was it only her imagination which made her see the people in the streets in a light very different from that of the early morning? They were holding their heads higher, surely – were walking with a more purposeful air. Her excitement increased, as though

187

the change in her faith had imperceptibly attuned her to the mood of the city. Her own anger made her sensitive to the anger around her. The Russian people were ready at last to break through the shell of their old passivity and she, Kate Lorimer, felt herself spiritually to be a Russian.

Within sight of the river she paused in surprise. It had not all been her imagination, then. Crowds of people were approaching on foot across the bridge. There was nothing threatening about their pace or attitude: only their number made it clear that this was no ordinary Sunday promenade. And if she had had any doubts, a disturbance behind her would have dispelled them. A line of soldiers, their footsteps quietened by the snow, was marching down the Nevsky Prospekt towards the Admiralty building, leaving a few of their number in a group at each street corner. Hardly more than boys, they looked uneasy in their ill-fitting uniforms. But they were armed.

There was no confrontation. The crowd filled the heart of the city but did not threaten it. The demeanour of the soldiers made it so clear that they did not wish to use their weapons that their officers, equally uneasy, showed no disposition to test their authority by giving the order to clear the area. Nevertheless, the steady increase in the size of the crowd and the silence which was as sinister as it was surprising, brought Kate down to earth again. In any kind of battle it was important to be recognizably on one side or the other: the man in the middle was too often the target of both. Prudently she made her way by back streets to the Aminov palace.

5

The moment of revelation inside the cathedral had changed Kate's whole attitude to life. She was aware that she would never look at society in the same way again – and yet the knowledge did not affect her actions immediately. She was still the same punctual and efficient woman who kept promises once she had made them. When Prince Aminov had first asked her to go to the Radziwill ball she had felt doubtful. But the possibility that the occasion might prove of practical value had persuaded her to accept, and the mere fact that her doubts about going to a party had deepened did not seem a good enough reason now to disappoint her host. As the maid came into her room that evening with a heavy weight of creamy satin over her arm, Kate's gasp was not one of rejection but merely of incredulity. She had been promised the choice of a gown and had intended to look for the simplest, but it appeared that the maid had taken the decision out of her hands.

'It's unlucky to put on clothes which have been worn by someone who is dead,' the girl explained. 'But this dress was ordered by the princess to be ready for her after the birth of her baby. She never even saw it.'

'It's too rich for me!' Kate exclaimed, for the low-cut sleeveless bodice and the hem of the skirt were both patterned in hundreds of tiny pearls.

'The others will be too tight,' said the maid. Not for the first time, Kate was amused by the frankness of Russian servants. And this one, no doubt, was telling the truth. Kate's experiences during the past two years had hardly allowed her to grow fat through overeating; but she was sturdily built and it was unlikely that even the most vigorous attempt at tight lacing would reduce her waist to a fashionable smallness. If for this one gown the dressmaker had guessed at a slight increase in size on the part of a new mother and had allowed her a little looseness even on top of that, the maid's choice might indeed prove to be the best. Laughing, Kate allowed herself to be taken over. Only when she was ready, with her hair veiled and ornamented, her shoes buckled, her necklace fastened, her long gloves smoothed up to the elbow, was she allowed to look at herself in the glass.

Her first reaction was one of amusement. The maid had turned her into a princess. Kate was tall enough to give the impression of elegance when, as now, the cut of her clothes imposed it. No doubt she would destroy the illusion as soon as she moved, for she had never been able to subdue an unladylike stride. But as long as she stood still, straight-backed and with her head held high, she recognized that Prince Aminov would not need to be ashamed of his partner at the ball.

For a moment she felt all the ordinary feminine excitement of a young woman who sees herself to be attractive. Her complexion was freckled instead of fashionably white and her auburn eyebrows were too thick. But her wide-set green eyes were clear and bright and her smooth forehead, strong cheekbones and generous mouth combined to give an impression of freshness and candour. Half ashamed of her moment of conceit, she admitted to herself nevertheless that she was not too bad-looking after all. She lifted her heavy skirt off the ground and walked slowly downstairs.

Two footmen were waiting to throw open the doors of the drawing room. As Kate paused, just inside the doorway, Prince Aminov rose from a Louis XV sofa to greet her, but it seemed that for a moment he could neither move nor speak. He stared as though he could hardly believe what he saw, and Kate was conscious that she was staring back in very much the same way. The uniform which he was wearing for the evening was too elaborate even to be mess dress. The profusion of gold braid and the jewelled Order on its blue diagonal ribbon must surely have been designed for attendance on the Tsar. Kate, who despised ostentation and was accustomed to judge men by their behaviour and not by their clothes, told herself that she ought to laugh, or at least not to notice. But instead she was overcome by the dignity of his presence. Seeing the prince in his informal day clothes she had already realized that his appearance was attractive, but now she had to admit that he was outstandingly handsome.

It was an artificial effect, of course. Unmarried though she might be, Kate had seen so many men naked that she was able mentally to strip Prince Aminov of all his trappings, and deliberately now she did that. It was the tightness of his high collar, she reminded herself, which made him hold his head so proudly erect, when his shoulders more naturally hunched themselves over the piano keyboard. It was the thickness and embellishment of his jacket which gave the impression of a strong chest, when really his figure was slight and unathletic. It was his tailor who had cut trousers of such elegant slimness, his valet who had polished hand-made shoes of such smartness. She was looking at a production, not a person, but the very fact of recognizing this made her see the man more clearly, and what she saw had an effect which she could not have anticipated. Both as a medical student and as a doctor working amongst soldiers Kate had counted a good many men as her friends, but she had never fallen in love with any of them. To be attacked by first love at the age of twenty-five was so overwhelming an experience that she was silenced by the pain of it.

She tried to fight against the realization of what had happened, but Prince Aminov did nothing to help her. She could feel his hand trembling as he raised her own to his lips; and although only his eyes told her how much he admired her appearance, they spoke so eloquently that she knew she was not mistaken. Neither of them spoke as, in answer to his pull at the bell, a footman appeared with a full-length sable cape to protect Kate from the bitter cold of the evening.

Even during the journey to the Radziwill palace – short in distance but lengthened by the need to take their place in the long line of equipages which were bringing the guests to this gala occasion – they made no attempt to converse. Kate could think of nothing but the strong, smooth hand which was holding her own beneath the fur of the cape. Only when at last they stepped inside the reception area, dazzlingly lit by scores of chandeliers, did Prince Aminov laugh in what seemed a deliberate attempt to break the spell and to bring to a glittering social evening only the gaiety it deserved. They were surrounded by warmth and light and music and champagne. As soon as Kate had been presented to Princess Radziwill, and curiously but graciously received, the prince led her into the first of a series of reception rooms. A gypsy orchestra was playing, almost drowned by the noise of conversation. Kate accepted a glass of champagne and switched her thoughts into French and her expression into the vivacity required to accept meaningless compliments from the strangers to whom she was bewilderingly introduced.

The ostentatious display of wealth took her breath away. Kate had often heard Alexa describe how the women of the Russian nobility wore their dresses cut almost indecently low in order to adorn the décolletage with the maximum number of diamonds; but she had been talking about the early years of the century. It had not occurred to Kate that the same fashion would still prevail at a time when Russia had endured two and a half years of war and was on the verge of defeat. She thought of the bewildered Russian peasants who lay wounded in her hospital and found that she could not pretend to smile any longer. Even the champagne seemed less sparkling, although all around her the effervescent chatter continued unabated.

Prince Aminov was sensitive to her change of mood, although not prepared to indulge it.

'I've just seen the Grand Duke Boris disappear into the card room,' he said. 'To continue, no doubt, his conspiracy against his cousin Nicholas. My own belief is that it's safer to do one's plotting in public. So I am going to present you now to someone whom you must charm. You may think him stupid, as indeed he is, but you must use his stupidity to make him believe that he would have a conquest if only I were not here to guard you.'

Flirtation was not Kate's style, and to pretend to flirt was even more degrading. She was about to demand an explanation and was ready to behave coldly if she did not receive one. But Prince Aminov gave her no time to ask questions before introducing a white-haired gentleman of distinguished appearance, conspicuous even in this company by the number of medals he wore. His name caught her attention at once for this was the titular head of the Committee of War Materials which was so stubbornly refusing to hear her case. Kate knew as well as his staff that he rarely went near his office. But she also knew that without his authority no one would ever take action.

That she should attempt to flatter a man whose criminal inefficiency was responsible for so much suffering made Kate feel sick with disgust. But as long as she had the power to relieve that suffering by any action of her own, it would be equally criminal to let pride hold her back. Like any simpering ninny she forced herself to smile at his jokes and blush at his compliments. Whether she could have brought herself to ask him a favour she did not need to discover, for Prince Aminov was doing it for her.

'Bandages? Medicines? Of course she must have them. Who is the idiot who has been holding them up? Well, it will be Lev Ilyich Kharsov. He must be shown where his duty lies. Tomorrow, my dear young lady, you must take tea in my office. At four o'clock. Or five. I shall expect you. Everything will be arranged. And in the evening you must join me in my box at the ballet. The whole of St Petersburg is in a state of civil war, disputing who is the greatest dancer. Is it Pavlova, or Kschessinska? Or even Karsavina? You must form your own opinion, so that you can argue with the same heat as the rest. Till tomorrow, then.'

Kate's face was pale with anger as someone else claimed his attention. Prince Aminov misunderstood her expression.

'Don't worry. He won't try to seduce you. There will be secretaries in and out of his office all the time. He'll want them to see that he's still irresistible to beautiful young women, but that's all. You must go, in order that Kharsov, whoever he may be, understands that you are a friend of his master. By tomorrow evening, all your difficulties will have disappeared. And now that our business is over, we may give ourselves up to pleasure. Will you dance?'

Still too disturbed to object, Kate allowed him to lead her through a series of imposing rooms, each crowded with guests. In the first two chambers the white walls and ceilings had been covered with a filigree of gold, so delicate that it might have been spun by a spider. But the walls of the ballroom, and the surfaces of the pillars which supported its high roof, were covered with sheets of mirror, each set at a very slight angle so that the light of the chandeliers was dazzlingly reflected and magnified. Another orchestra was playing here. As Prince Aminov turned to face Kate with a formal bow, she slipped her finger through the loop on her skirt to lift the hem from the floor, and was ready to dance.

Her French conversation had not disgraced him, and neither did her waltzing. The disquiet she felt stiffened her back and increased the dignity of her bearing, but did not distract her feet from their rhythmic movement. As though she were watching from outside, she was conscious of herself moving around the ballroom with as much grace as any other of this aristocratic company. From time to time she glimpsed her own reflection in the mirrored wall, but hardly recognized it. She, just as much as Prince Aminov, had become a clothes horse and not a person. What she saw had no connection with the way she felt.

The prince, delighting in the dance, was holding her more tightly than he ought. Only an hour or two ago his closeness would have given her pleasure, but now she resisted it, refusing to remember the flash of desire she had felt as her host rose to greet her. Her mind had established control over her body again, and all the pride she had felt in Prince Aminov's admiration, all the excitement of her own reaction, had been devoured by an anger which left her at once hot and cold. When the dance came to an end she stood for a moment without moving before raising her head to look steadily at her partner.

'I'm very sorry, Excellency,' she said. 'I can't stay here. I must ask you to be good enough – '

He interrupted her anxiously. 'Are you not well?'

'I will say that I'm not well, because I don't wish to disgrace you by letting anyone guess any other reason. But really I am perfectly well. I ought not to have come here tonight, that's all.'

'You must explain more than that.' The orchestra began to play again and he led her out of the ballroom, opening a door at random so that they could talk in private. Surrounded by their host's collection of musical clocks, Prince Aminov waited to hear what she had to say.

'I can't give you a good explanation. It's just that I feel this occasion isn't a suitable one for the times. When there's so much poverty in the city and so much suffering and death all over Europe.'

'If princesses never gave balls, the poverty in the city would be far greater,' Prince Aminov pointed out. 'Because Princess Radziwill entertains her friends today, there will be money tomorrow in the pockets of servants, grooms, florists, jewellers, dressmakers, caterers, musicians.'

Kate was tempted to voice her suspicion that princesses took a good deal longer than a single day to pay their bills, but she had no wish to quarrel. Instead, she tried as sincerely as possible to make him understand a little of what she had felt earlier that day.

'I was walking in the city this morning, Excellency,' she said. 'You must know far more than I do about what is happening here. But it seems to me that there is an inexorable division – a chasm – opening between the sort of people who are here in this palace tonight, and all the others.'

'The division has always been there,' he pointed out.

'Then I suppose it must always have been accepted. Until now. I don't believe it's going to be accepted any longer. And I have to make it clear which side I'm on.'

'I would like you to be on my side,' he said.

'You don't need me. And there are so many others who do. I can't in honesty say that I'm on your side, because that would mean supporting everything which has helped to create that hell out there on the battlefield. I thought perhaps I could forget that just for one evening, when it seemed that to come here might be of practical use, but – '

'But we have talked of bandages and drugs, and you have remembered.' His voice was still soft, but it had lost the languid drawl which sometimes gave the impression of insincerity. It seemed to Kate that he was sympathetic, but she did not dare to accept sympathy. Just because she had found him so attractive earlier in the evening she needed now to distance herself from him.

'I'm ashamed,' she said. 'Ashamed that I came here in

the first place, and ashamed of asking you to take me away. I know I'm behaving unpardonably. Enjoying your hospitality, wearing your sister-in-law's dress, your family jewels. A complete stranger, and you've been so generous to me! I'm more grateful than I can say, but all the same – ' She sighed, angry with herself and with the whole situation.

'But all the time you have a headache and I have insisted that you should let me take you home. Come, then.'

They made their way back through the golden rooms, thronged with people who were now not entirely sober. Nor, Kate suspected, was the Aminov coachman, who had not been expecting a call so soon; but fortunately the horses knew their way home. Back in the Aminov palace the prince himself took the sable cape from Kate's bare shoulders and smiled at her.

'May I ask you an impertinent question? How old are you, Dr Lorimer?'

'Twenty-five.' Kate had promised herself she would never be the sort of woman who was ashamed to admit her age.

'When I first saw you, you looked older; did you know that? But tonight, for three hours, you have looked twenty-five – or even younger. If I tell you that you ought to wear satins and jewels always I suppose I shall make you angry. But beauty deserves to be adorned. I hope you will stay young for a little while yet, Dr Lorimer.'

Kate wasted no time in protesting that she was not beautiful, although she did repeat once more her apologies for her behaviour. But when she returned to her room she could not resist the temptation to stand in front of the glass for a second time that evening – for if anything in her life was certain, it was that she would never look like this again. She made an attempt to rebuke herself for vanity, but instead she found herself flushing with pleasure because Prince Aminov had called her beautiful.

What of it, she demanded, working her self-criticism into indignation. Not to flirt with a young woman was by the standards of his class to be uncivil. It didn't mean anything. She didn't want it to mean anything. Even in England Kate had held strong views about the social obligations of the aristocracy – but most British land-owners, when compared with the Russian nobility, might be considered impoverished and full of social concern. Although more fortunate than others, they were members of a community, not merely of a social caste, isolated by its wealth from the rest of society, as was the case in Russia.

In other circumstances, perhaps, she could have enjoyed a friendship with Prince Aminov, for she found his company congenial and his conversation excitingly different from anything she had enjoyed since she said goodbye to Sergei. In other circumstances, indeed, she could have fallen in love with him. Even as she formulated the thought, she knew that she was being dishonest with herself. She had already fallen in love – but if she could continue to pretend indifference on her own part and attribute insincerity to him, perhaps she could cure herself of the affliction. Circumstances were what they were. The prince was a representative of a privileged class of which Kate could not bring herself to approve. It was unfortunate, but it was final. Slowly she unfastened the tiny buttons at her waist and slipped the low-cut bodice off her shoulders, stepping out of the gown as it fell heavily to the floor.

That night there was shooting on the Nevsky Prospekt. But the soldiers who fired on the workers during the hours of darkness streamed out of their barracks the next morning, killing the officers who tried to stop them. They joined the demonstration and by their own desertion turned it into a revolution. When the hour arrived at which Kate might have seen her papers stamped at last beside a samovar of tea, her prospective host was already a prisoner of the Duma. In the Tauride Palace, Kerensky took into his hands the power which the Imperial Cabinet had abandoned, and did his best to prevent a massacre. But in the city outside ministries were burned, police stations besieged, and the streets were crowded with students, workers and soldiers, destroying every trace of the old regime.

Only thirty hours after Kate had stared across the frozen Neva at the beautiful golden spire of the Peter and Paul fortress, she watched again as it fell to the forces of the revolution, and saw the political prisoners and their military guards streaming together across the bridges. Her instinct had been a true one. She herself would never look like a princess again, and nor would anyone else in the country for very much longer. The face of Russia, too, had changed for ever.

6

The Tsar had abdicated but the liberal Provisional Government, sharing power and premises uneasily with the Petrograd Soviet of Workers' and Soldiers' Deputies, was no more willing to interest itself in Kate's medical supplies than the old regime had been. While the struggle for authority continued, no one would spare the time to take a decision about such a trifle, although it would have taken only a moment for someone to stamp a paper of release – freeing himself with a single thump of the nuisance of Kate's daily attendance at the supplies office.

Prince Aminov had returned hastily to duty as soon as the troubles began, telling her before he left that she must stay as long as she needed. It was with increasing anxiety on his behalf that Kate read the various proclamations which issued from the Soviet, for their intention and effect was to destroy discipline in the army, robbing officers of any power to enforce their orders and encouraging mutiny and desertion by the abolition of the death penalty. One of these orders provided that local soviets of soldiers or sailors should in future control all arms and equipment. Kate saw how she could use this to suit her own purposes. It would need a good deal of courage, but in the interests of her patients she steeled herself to be brave.

She went as usual the next day to the offices of the General Staff, and as usual found them swarming with petitioners like herself. Also as usual nowadays was the presence of the troops who lounged in the huge entrance hall with red ribbons tied round their arms, content to show themselves without posing any great threat to anyone. There was a junior officer ostensibly in charge of them. Kate had had plenty of time during the past few days to study his increasing nervousness and the care he took to give no direct orders which might lead to trouble.

She began by making a fuss at the desk of the man who had so often before told her to wait. He did so again, but this time she did not move far. Instead she climbed on to the desk and made a speech.

Even in Russian the words came fluently, fuelled by the frustrating weeks in which she had had time to rehearse them. Her appeal was made directly to the soldiers. She was speaking on behalf of their comrades at the front, she told them, men who were dying for lack of the drugs withheld by these other men who had been careful to keep themselves at the greatest possible distance from danger. The property *belonged* to the soldiers in the hospital. It had been refused them by ministers and generals but now it was true, was it not, that generals no longer had any right to obstruct the needs of the people. She herself knew where the goods were held. If they could not be extracted by the production of the right piece of paper, they could be taken without permission, by force. Kate promised that they would be handed over to those who needed them and were entitled to have them. She appealed for help. Looking straight at the young officer, she asked him to lend her a section of his men.

As she had calculated, he hesitated and her point was won. Ten men were instantly ready to follow her. Anxious not to delay, lest the impetus of her vehemence should be lost, Kate nevertheless needed to press further demands on the officer. When she returned, an official permit for the transport of the goods must be ready, she told him, and an escort to help load and guard them. She expected the necessary papers to be prepared within the hour.

They would be ready: she felt no doubt of that. The men were anxious to exercise their new powers over officers, and the officers would wait for more important issues than this one on which to make a stand. Striding out victoriously, Kate led the way to the warehouse.

Three hours later she returned to the Aminov palace to collect her bags. Was it only the triumph of her achievement which made her feel that spring was on the way at last? After weeks of bitter cold, the sky was filled with pale sunshine; the snow was melting and it was possible to fill her lungs with air which seemed almost warm. She was singing aloud with happiness as she approached the palace door.

It was open. That was unusual enough, but the scene inside was more unusual still. The floor of the entrance hall was awash with wine and half a dozen of the servants were sprawled around in a manner which made it clear that what had not been spilt had been drunk. From their quarters behind closed doors came the sound of singing and shouting. Kate found herself tip-toeing through the confusion and up the stairs, uneasy lest some obstacle might arise at the very moment when success was in sight.

Still quietly, she opened the door of her bedroom and

then was alarmed into silence. Prince Aminov, standing in the middle of the room, was pointing his revolver at her.

He put the weapon away as soon as he saw who it was, and apologized for frightening her.

'I needed to speak to you, and there was no other room in the palace where I could feel safe from discovery while I waited. Even this room will not be safe for long. You must leave Russia at once, Dr Lorimer. I have come to warn you, in case you are not aware how dangerous the situation has become. You should go immediately to the British Embassy and arrange for your government to get you away. It may be that these people have no good reason to attack foreigners but they have ceased to be ruled by reason.'

'What has happened, Excellency?' Kate asked. She could see that he was shocked and upset, and at first she assumed that it had been caused by some event on the battlefield.

'Mutiny has happened,' he said. 'Murder has happened. My brother has been killed – on his own ship, by his own men! And the Imperial Guard itself has proved disloyal. Who could have believed it? I was ordered back from the front to command the garrison at Tsarskoe Selo, but when I arrived I was greeted by a disorderly mob who first of all demanded that I should join them and wear the red cockade. And then they recognized me as a member of the nobility. I was lucky to escape with my life. And when I return here, thinking that at least I can rely on the loyalty of my own people to protect me, I find – I find – '

'They're drunk, Excellency. This isn't their normal behaviour. It's not the expression of their true feelings.'

He shook his head in disagreement. 'There are different kinds of drunkenness. If all they wanted was their own pleasure, they would have drunk only vodka. They don't like wine. They are consuming it only to show that I am no longer master in my own house. The same thing has happened in our theatre palace at Tsarskoe Selo – it has been completely sacked. Not looted. Spoiled. The chandeliers cut to the ground, the pictures slashed, the panelling defaced. Now I shall never be able to show you the theatre where Alexa sang. But what does all that matter beside my brother's murder? You must understand that he was not like me. I am a reluctant officer, serving because it is my duty. But he – his ship was his whole life. What has happened to loyalty?' He buried his head in his hands for a moment. 'But for you now the important thing is that you should go. Go back to England. That was why I waited, in case you did not understand how grave the position is.'

'No!' Kate cried. 'It's impossible. I have my supplies at last. After waiting so long, I can't leave now. I must take them to the hospital. It is you who should leave the country.'

'There is no way of doing so. The British and French will send ships to take away their own people as soon as the ice breaks, but they will not use precious space to save Russians from each other.'

'Then where will you go?'

He threw out his hands in a gesture of helplessness. 'There is nowhere. Yesterday I owned three estates. Today, after my brother's death – ' his voice faltered again – 'I own seven. But it seems that the places where I am known are the most dangerous. Ever since our father died we have cared for our people, Paul and I. I truly believed that they loved us. But now – '

He sat down on the edge of the four-poster bed and for a second time buried his head in his hands. It was not fear which made him tremble, Kate realized – although he had good cause to be afraid – but the shock of his brother's death and the servants' disloyalty. Like the ice on the Neva, the established order had cracked and there was nowhere he could feel safe.

Kate took a little time to consider the question seriously before she spoke. This was not an occasion for impulsive gestures. She must be sincere, and practical in regard to details. It proved not to be too difficult. Only a little time had passed since she had regretted the way in which circumstances made it impossible for herself and the prince to develop a true friendship. But circumstances had changed with a vengeance. No longer over-privileged, he lacked at this moment even the precarious security of every other class of society. Yet there were no crimes for which he could be held personally responsible.

'You could come with me,' she offered. 'For a while, at least, until this first violence subsides. For all we know, the revolution may not yet have spread outside Petrograd. In any case, as you've already recognized, you'll be safer where you aren't known. Come south with me. I can arrange it. The train leaves in two hours.'

'You don't know what you're proposing. For a woman – and especially a foreign woman – to travel across a country in a state of anarchy is foolish enough. As your companion, I should double the danger. It's out of the question.'

'Listen to me, Excellency,' Kate pleaded. 'I arrived here unknown, uninvited, tired and not even very clean. You've made me welcome. You've treated me like a princess. It's not just that you provided me with the first taste of comfort that I've had for two years. I've been spoiled by your kindness, your conversation, your music. Was it presumptuous of me to hope that we might become friends?'

'Of course we are friends,' he said. 'And for that very reason – '

Kate wouldn't allow him to finish. 'As your guest, I have an obligation to give you a present as an expression of thanks for your hospitality. It's an English custom. And as my friend, you have an obligation to accept whatever I choose to give you.' She forced herself to laugh, trying to deflate the solemnity with which she had spoken. 'Although it may prove in the end that I have nothing to offer except words. But I can try, and you must let me try.'

They were discussing what might well be a matter of life and death – and yet it seemed to Kate, as she gazed steadily into Prince Aminov's eyes, that he was not really listening. She waited for his answer, and it did not come directly.

'I remember – it can be only a short time ago, but it seems to have been in a different lifetime – how I danced with you at Princess Radziwill's ball,' he said. 'You were wearing my sister-in-law's ball dress, and you were magnificent. Magnificent! I had never seen a woman looking beautiful in quite that way before. Not a Russian way, not a fashionable way. It was your eyes, I think, so green, so full of fire. Of course, I could not understand at once what it was that made you hold your head so high. I would have liked to kiss you, but before I could do it you were telling me that society was divided and that you and I were on different sides. And now again I would like to kiss you: but today the division is a real one, not a theory, and I must keep in my own place if I am not to drag you down.'

'This is not the time to speak of kissing,' said Kate severely. 'And as for the rest, you're talking nonsense. If we were both on the same side there would be no need of help and no opportunity to offer it. But if we waste any more time in argument, the opportunity will be talked away. Is it that you don't trust me?'

His eyes showed that she had hurt him, and he gripped her hands fiercely with his own, as though that were an answer.

'Well then,' she pointed out, 'the division isn't as great as it seems. I'm on the side of the Revolution because even in such a short time I've seen a whole nation being pushed to its doom by stupidity and greed and

205

inefficiency. I don't pretend to understand the causes: I only know that the system has to be changed. But I've also seen that you share most of my feelings – of compassion and a wish to help poorer people, to protect your dependants. It's only your birth which puts you on the other side. You can't change that, but I'm not going to let you suffer for it if I can help it. I shan't speak to you in English again. From now on we must talk in Russian. Nor shall I address you again as Excellency. You are my comrade – Comrade Vladimir – and you are going to work in my hospital.'

Her forcefulness was enough to bring the sentimental moment to an end. He even forgot his family grief for long enough to laugh wryly at her, and himself. 'That a woman should speak to me so!' he exclaimed, shaking his head unbelievingly. Yet there was no sign of resentment. If anything, Kate suspected that he admired her most when she was at her most determined. From his nursery days he would have been accustomed to give orders and expect them to be obeyed. The necessity for command and discipline must be so much a part of his character that rather than flounder in a chaos of equality he was prepared to obey someone else's equally arbitrary instructions.

'Well then, Comrade Katya,' he said – speaking, as she had ordered, in the language which was almost as foreign to him as to her. 'I am your friend, so I accept whatever you have to offer. I am your slave, so I obey. What would you have me do?'

'Get out of that uniform,' she said. 'Take some clothes from the servants. They're too drunk to notice. Shabby clothes, but warm. Then make your way to the station. I'll meet you there in about an hour. Will you bring my bag for me?'

Unexpectedly she remembered Sergei, whom she had ordered about in exactly the same way at their first meeting. That meeting had been the start of an affectionate friendship – no, more than that: they had loved each other, in a way. Was she becoming one of those bossy women who only liked men they could bully? Later on she would need to consider that and be careful. But for the moment she must not allow the impetus of her determination to slacken.

'You speak Russian very well,' the prince said. 'Not just fluently, but with the right amount of passion. No Russian who didn't know you would recognize you for a foreigner. He might think you came from a different province from his own, with a dialect which he couldn't quite place, but that would be the only question in his mind.'

'I feel almost as though I *am* Russian,' Kate said, turning briefly back from the doorway. 'I'm sorry, truly sorry, about your brother's death, Vladimir. It wasn't right and I don't believe it was necessary. I don't like to think of anyone being in fear of his life. But I can't help being excited. To be in this country, at this moment! For more than two years Europe has been destroying itself, and now at last a new society is being built, and I'm here. I intend to be part of it, to help.'

'The fire has returned to your eyes,' said Prince Aminov softly. 'And the beauty to your face. And all because you feel so passionately about people who are strangers to you.'

He was about to kiss her. Kate wanted him to do so. She had wanted it once before, and had been able to control her feelings only because she had recognized the barriers of class and idealism which separated her from Prince Aminov. Now that those barriers were broken down, there was nothing to hold her back – and indeed she found his new vulnerability even more attractive than his earlier kindness and glamorous appearance. What made her at this moment long to step forward into his arms, to press her body close to his and to comfort him in his distress was the lost look in his eyes. His whole way of life, from the moment of his birth, had been supported by the service of other people, and all those supports – except hers – had been abruptly withdrawn. He had believed himself to be loved and respected, and found himself hated instead. He must have expected that his wealth would cushion him for the whole of his life and even now it would be possible for him to fill his pockets with jewellery or Fabergé trifles which alone would represent more wealth than a Russian worker would see in the whole of his lifetime: but such riches, if they were discovered, would betray rather than sustain him. He had never needed to earn a living, but now he must step out into the ordinary world. It was a tribute to his courage that he showed no sign of fear, for the prospect must certainly be alarming. Even if he escaped physical harm, he was so badly equipped to adapt his life to the demands of a new society that he was bound to suffer. Kate saw all this, and felt her heart swelling with the wish to protect him.

But this was not the time to confess her feelings. Far more important was the need to maintain her earlier mood of excitement and determination. The same forcefulness which she had used to appeal for help and to demand authorization must be maintained at its highest pitch if she was to be of any help to Vladimir. Keeping her voice brisk, she repeated the arrangements for their meeting and hurried from the room.

The papers which awaited her appeared to cover all the checks and emergencies which might arise on the journey, authorizing the movement of the supplies as well as of herself and a soldier who had been left on guard at the station. It was this young Estonian, Vassily Petrovich Belinsky, who was an important part of Kate's plan to smuggle Prince Aminov out of the capital. He had enjoyed helping to break open the warehouse door and carry out the crates; but his pleasure had turned to sulkiness when he found himself appointed as the escort. Clearly he had no wish to exchange his lazy life in Petrograd for the long and uncomfortable journey south.

Kate set to work on him as soon as she had congratulated him on defending the reserved wagon containing the crates of supplies. The train was so overcrowded that this was a considerable achievement, even allowing for the fact that civilian passengers were accustomed to observe military priorities.

'You are in luck, Vassily Petrovich. There is no need for you to make the journey. I have a volunteer to accompany me.'

'Why should anyone wish to do that?'

'He has a son, five months old, whom he has never seen: and two weeks' leave but no money or permit to travel. He will gladly take your place for the sake of a day or two with his wife. All he asks is that you should keep away from your officers and comrades for two weeks, so that they believe you to be obeying instructions. And he has sent this basket in order that the two weeks need not be too dull.'

As she left the palace she had picked up some of the bottles of wine which littered the floor. Prince Aminov had been right to suggest that vodka would always be welcome, but in these days of shortages no sort of drink was likely to be rejected. It required little persuasion to show the young soldier that he could enjoy a fortnight's leave. If he remembered that he had left his identity papers at the office, in order that his details might be entered on the travel permit, he presumably thought that they were still there, instead of folded inside Kate's money belt. It would be two weeks before he discovered the truth and then he would find it safer to claim that he had lost them in the confusion of the journey than to confess the truth. Kate allowed him no time to think about them, but hurried him on his way as soon as she saw approaching a shabby, rather furtive peasant figure whom she recognized as the prince.

'Your name is Vassily Petrovich Belinsky,' she told her former host as he climbed into the wagon. 'It's hard that

I have to learn to call you Vassily when I've only just become used to calling you Vladimir.'

It was partly relief which made her chatter on, but in addition she was excited by the adventure. By her own efforts she had achieved what she came to Petrograd to do and had a good chance of taking her friend to safety at the same time. But the prince looked dazed, and as the train pulled out of the station on its long journey she noticed how sadly he looked back at the city which had been his home. Whilst she looked forward, seeing little good in the old regime and eager to take part in the building of a new way of life, he was conscious only of what he was losing. For him, the future promised only danger and hardship.

Her sympathy silenced her. She gazed at her companion as he leaned a little way out of the wagon, still watching the receding city. There had been a moment once before when she had been forced to admit to herself how attractive she found him. On that occasion she had controlled her admiration first of all by mentally stripping away the uniform which made him look so handsome. Then, as she realized that it was the man himself, unadorned, who excited her, she had in a manner of speaking dressed him again in order that the gold braid and jewelled Order should act as a barrier between them, reminding her that the two of them lived in different worlds.

Now the splendid trappings of nobility had disappeared. Beneath the shabby overcoat was not a prince but a man. But Kate, assuming authority, had changed in the opposite direction, so that in a sense she was not a woman but a doctor. Would that, she wondered, be any protection during the long journey? Did she want to be protected?

The train picked up speed. Vladimir pulled the heavy wagon door across until it clanged into place. He gave a single deep sigh, a groan of loneliness and misery and insecurity. Then he turned towards Kate and, still without speaking, took her into his arms. She did her best to comfort him, and found that it was no longer possible to control the love she had felt and concealed since the night of the Radziwill ball.

In the days and nights which followed, Kate should have been worrying about her patients and nurses, for the journey across Russia would have been complicated enough even for a passenger who had only himself to move from one train to another. When it was a complete wagon which had to be uncoupled and then attached to another engine, the difficulties at times seemed insuperable. As one obstacle succeeded another, Kate would in normal circumstances have become indignant. But the new experience of love made her for a little while unusually passive. It was easy to live from moment to moment, accepting each delay as it came, because she was so completely overwhelmed by the happiness of her honeymoon.

This was not the sort of honeymoon which might have been envisaged either by the daughter of a missionary or by a Russian prince. But Kate felt no qualms about the fact that she lacked a marriage certificate; nor did Vladimir complain about a honeymoon suite which consisted of a nest of blankets, extracted from one of the hospital crates, in a corner of the goods wagon. To the nurses who greeted her when at last they reached the Romanian Front, Kate announced that she was married, because that was how she felt.

7

Born in a spring of despair and hope, the Revolution stumbled through a summer of chaos towards a winter of defeat. From her field hospital on the Romanian Front,

Kate watched with dismay the disintegration of the Russian Army. The orders and decrees which flowed from the capital effectively sapped all discipline, and the Germans and Austrians were quick to take advantage of the fact that their opponents no longer had any firm chain of command. Their summer offensive found Kate's medical unit well enough equipped to deal with the casualties, but lacking any military protection. Those of the Tsarist officers who had been born into the nobility had been killed when the first news of the Revolution arrived. Most of the others had fled; and the few who remained were well aware that if they ordered a counter-attack or tried to impose any punishment, the rifles of their men were as likely to be turned on themselves as on the enemy. What followed was not a mutiny in any active sense, for most of the Russian soldiers simply slipped away to their villages, knowing that they could no longer be shot for desertion. The Serbs remained in the line, because they had nowhere to go – but of the men who had sailed with Kate for Salonica in 1916 only a handful were still alive.

Without Vladimir at her side Kate might well have despaired, overwhelmed by the responsibility for the safety of her nursing team and her patients as the enemy advanced. At first his support was only that of a lover, for he had few practical skills. But in order to establish him as one of the medical team she taught him how to administer anaesthetics: he had the strong hands necessary to hold the mask down over the face of a struggling patient and, although he never overcame his distaste for watching an operation in progress, he did not allow his squeamishness to distract him from checking the patient's breathing. In addition, he was recognized as Kate's personal assistant, and if at times he seemed quiet and withdrawn and uncertain of himself, this was assumed to result from the natural reluctance of a man to obey the orders of a woman, of a husband to run errands for his wife. Kate, not daring by any word or gesture to hint at the difficulties which he faced as a result of his birth and upbringing, watched with loving anxiety as he gradually learned to get the necessary tasks accomplished not by giving orders but by taking part in the work.

Even though she no longer felt alone, she was still left to take many decisions with which no one else could help. In the disorganized conditions which now prevailed she realized that there could be no possibility of further support from Beatrice and the suffragists' movement. She alone had to decide, as the Germans advanced, when it was necessary to pack up the unit and retreat; and with increasing clarity she saw that she would have to recognize the moment when the nurses on her staff had done as much as could reasonably be expected of them.

The moment came on a night in the autumn of 1917. For the third time since the beginning of summer they were retreating. So many Russian soldiers were taking the same direction, whether as deserters or as the ragged remnants of an army, that it was difficult to find billets for the night. The peasants in the villages were suspicious, and unwilling to part with any of the food they had hidden, for they saw that the coming winter would be a hard one. For this night, Vladimir had found a riverside site and had supervised the erection of tents, and Kate had already made her evening round of the wounded. She knew that after a day of jolting over rough roads in carts with wooden wheels, their best treatment was to sleep in peace. So she had no duties to disturb her enjoyment of the night, and for a little while it was enough to be alone with Vladimir in the small tent which they shared.

Later, though, she lay awake in the darkness, listening to the noises of the night – the croaking of frogs, the rustling of the wind in the reeds, the gentle tapping of the willow trees against the canvas, the rippling of the river over the stones near the bank. How much longer, she asked herself, would her nurses be safe? Behind them was an advancing enemy army and in front of them was a country in anarchy. The hand-to-mouth existence they had been leading during the past three months had been only just tolerable in summer: how could they hope to survive a Russian winter in such conditions? There was talk of famine, and Kate believed this to be well-founded.

All the nurses had been serving abroad for more than a year. They deserved to have leave, but they would know as well as she did that if they went back to England it would not be merely for a holiday: they would never return. In those circumstances many of them no doubt would be willing to stay on a little longer, but as Kate considered the situation it seemed to her that a choice which might exist now would very soon disappear. At the moment the sea route from the Crimea was still open, and foreign nationals were being taken out of the country, although no Russians were allowed to leave. But the unit was being pressed steadily further north. Very soon it might become impossible to reach Odessa or Sevastopol: very soon there might be no more ships.

What disturbed Kate most was the unexpected change in attitude of the Russians towards the nurses. Always before, their profession by itself had been enough to earn them respect, quite apart from the fact that they were women. But in the last few weeks she had been aware of a change. Deserters would rob anyone they met unprotected on the road, and serving soldiers showed no chivalry in grabbing for food or shelter. If their uniforms no longer protected the women, it was difficult to see how else they could be made safe.

The nurses were not, of course, Kate's only responsibility. She must think of her patients as well. But during this evening's round she had counted that out of forty-three Russian patients, thirty-seven had self-inflicted wounds. They had chosen with some care where to shoot themselves, so none of the wounds was likely to prove dangerous. Kate had given them the treatment they needed and in the circumstances it seemed reasonable that they should be handed back to the care of the Russian Army. Her own unit, after all, had been directed specifically to the care of the Serbs. There were so few of these left that she could take care of their wounded alone, and could count on the protection of the fit survivors.

All this time, she realized, she was taking it for granted that she herself would stay. The assumption was an important one, and she forced herself to examine it. Why should she not take the chance to escape from a country which held as much danger for herself as for the nurses? The answer was confused, even paradoxical. She was able to accept the chaos around her as an inevitable – and temporary – result of changing a complete social order: she still had the same ideals, the same vision of a new society, which had so much excited her in Petrograd, and would be grateful for any opportunity to contribute to the task of reform. Stronger even than idealism, though, was her love for the man whom those ideals had turned into a fugitive. If she could have seen any way of taking Vladimir to safety, she would not have hesitated to do so. But this same society in which she had so much faith kept him a prisoner inside his own country; and as long as he had to stay, she would stay with him.

Perhaps it was not paradox after all, merely a double reason for a decision which had really been made by her emotions and not by her reason at all. As the long hours of the night passed and the current of the river flowed and splashed only a few feet away, she forced herself to think the decision through, to be sure that she understood all its implications.

The task was impossible. There could be no assurances in a period when history itself did not know which direction it was taking. Only uncertainty was certain. As far as consequences were concerned, she must assume the worst and decide whether she could accept them. The

215

sky was lightening now as her sleepless night came to an end. Without disturbing Vladimir she slipped out of the tent and sat down on the river bank a little way away. There was a chill in the air, and frost had touched the spiders' webs: winter would soon be here. Remembering the last two winters, she could not help shivering and for a moment or two it was difficult not to feel melancholy as in her mind she said goodbye to the past. Never again would she feel herself wrapped in the balmy air of her tropical birthplace. Her father would die, and she would have no chance to say goodbye. Would she ever visit Blaize again, to see Margaret growing old and the younger members of the family growing up? Perhaps it would be possible one day, when this time of upheaval was over; but if her choice now was to be sincere she must tell herself that no, she would never return. She gave a sharp nod of her head, a gesture to mark the promise to herself that there would be no regrets.

'Is it decided, then?'

Startled, she turned and saw Vladimir leaning against a tree. How long, she wondered, had he been watching her?

'Is what decided?'

He shrugged his shoulders. 'How should I know? But there is something, I know that. For two days I have watched you balancing arguments in your mind.' He came to sit beside her on the bank, pulling a reed and dangling it to trouble the surface of the river. Without interrupting, he listened while Kate detailed her plans.

'So your nurses will return to England. But you have not spoken of yourself.'

'I shall stay, of course.'

'All the dangers you have recognized, the dangers which you wish the others to escape, will still face you. And the ships which will take them away would have room for you.'

'But not for you. Vladimir, do you believe that there's

216

any frontier you can safely cross? Can you think of any way in which you can leave the country?'

Vladimir shook his head.

'Well then, there's no choice. I won't go without you.'

'It may be for ever,' said Vladimir. 'If you stay now, you may never see your own country again. Or your family, all the people you love in England.'

'I've been thinking about that,' said Kate. 'I've had to put my family into the balance. But I love you. However I hold the scales, the fact that I love you weighs down all the rest.'

He took hold of her shoulders and pressed her back on the ground, kissing her passionately. Then he raised himself a little, so that Kate could look up at his face, framed by the golden lattice of the willows above.

'And I love you,' he said. 'Katya, will you be my wife?'

'I'm your wife already.'

'I mean, in the old way. With a certificate.'

'Is it possible?' asked Kate.

'It's possible to try. The people in these little towns we pass are frightened, ready to run if the Germans come any nearer. Everything is unsettled, so we should be believed if we claim that we ourselves have had to abandon our home and friends. You will have to be the wife of Belinsky, I'm afraid.'

'Shall I have to show my British passport?'

'I think that would be unwise. Too unusual. You must tell them that you were in Petrograd at the time of the Revolution. Your papers were already lodged at the marriage court when it was burned down. Before we go, we will decide on a name, a Russian name, and a place of birth.'

'They may be suspicious.'

'Within an hour we shall have passed on, and they will be on the road themselves soon. If they're suspicious, they may refuse us, but they can't hurt us. I want you to marry me, Katya. I've nothing to offer you. Nothing but danger. But I want to be your husband, for ever. Will you take the risk?'

'Of course.' She stretched up her hands to grasp his head. But for a moment he resisted her efforts to pull him down so that she could kiss him again.

'There will be no going back,' he reminded her. 'You will have become a Russian. That's not a destiny to be embraced lightly.'

Kate was not interested in destiny. It was Vladimir she needed to embrace. 'I'm a Russian already,' she said.

8

The people of Hope Valley, in Jamaica, knew almost nothing of what was happening in Russia during the spring and summer and autumn of 1917. What could a revolution in a cold and far-away country have to do with their own warm and contented lives in a remote tropical village? But their pastor, Ralph Lorimer, learned of every new development with the deepest distress. As accurately as anyone in Europe he could foresee what effect it was likely to have on the course of the war. From the very outbreak of the February Revolution Germans were able to profit from the crumbling of opposition to their armies on the Eastern Front; and by facilitating Lenin's return to Petrograd from his exile in Switzerland they were actively promoting an early ending of hostilities with Russia, which would leave them free to concentrate all their forces in the west.

The gloom engendered by conclusions such as these was not peculiar to Ralph. What struck home to him personally was the conviction that his only daughter had become a victim of the terror. She would surely have escaped if she could – or at least have let it be known that she was safe – but the enquiries which Lord Glanville made through the British Ambassador in Petrograd proved fruitless. In the months between the February and the October Revolutions almost all the British subjects who had applied for repatriation had been brought safely back to England. But Kate was not amongst them and those who returned had no knowledge of her whereabouts.

Lord Glanville and Margaret both attempted to persuade Ralph in correspondence that at a time of such upheaval the absence of any message did not necessarily mean that the worst had happened: few letters of any kind were coming out of the country. But Ralph was not to be convinced. Already robbed of two of his babies, the wife he loved, the elder son he adored, he knew that God was punishing him for the wrongdoing of his youth by the destruction of everything he held dear. Kate had become a victim of revolution as yet another scapegoat for her father's sins.

The biggest sin lay like a millstone on his conscience. Ralph had never confessed to anyone – not even to his wife – the subterfuge which had resulted in the Bristow plantation becoming his personal property instead of being owned by the Hope Valley community of which he was the pastor. His claim that he was the rightful heir to what had long before been a Lorimer estate had been a lie. Almost as soon as he had spoken the words he had realized that the lie was unnecessary – but it was no more excusable for that. Later he had persuaded himself that all was for the best and that he had won God's forgiveness because of his good intentions and practical achievements. Under his control the estate had developed a prosperity which it could not possibly have attained as a collection of small holdings.

For many years Ralph had suppressed his qualms and at times he almost forgot that there had been any deception about the ownership of the rich coastal land. Now the news from Russia fanned his feelings of guilt into fear. The Russian peasants, he learned, were dividing amongst themselves the huge estates which they had worked for their landlords. Hungry for land, they killed any landowner who resisted them. The authority of the Church was under attack too. It was not Ralph's church, but what was happening meant that temporal and spiritual authority were equally at risk: and in his own community Ralph represented them both.

Common sense told him that the members of his congregation concerned themselves little with the world outside their island and did not know a great deal even of what went on in Jamaica, outside their own village. Nor could any agitator invade the valley without Ralph knowing of his presence at once. But he was unable to believe his own attempts at reassurance.

The thought obsessed him that God was intent on punishing the wicked in France and Russia – and soon in Jamaica. In the beginning, when the first news of the February Revolution arrived from Russia, it had been possible to believe that Kerensky might be capable of controlling the forces of anarchy which had been unleashed. But the October Revolution was a different matter. Lenin and Trotsky made it plain that the message they preached was for the whole world to hear, not for the people of Russia alone. Bolshevism was contagious, Ralph recognized. Once the foundations of society began to rot, wherever in the world it might be, the rottenness would spread until no form of law or decency was left uncorrupted. When he had drunk too much rum he saw himself pressed backwards by an army of black workers, falling beneath the blows of their machetes, hearing in his dying moments their triumphant cries as they staked out their own plots of land. And the times when he drank too much rum became more and more frequent.

He took the rum to control his fever. So at least he told himself and Duke, his young assistant. Both of them pretended not to notice that it was after the bottle was empty, not before, that his hands began to shake and his head to spin with dizziness. There were some moments of calmness when he realized what was happening and vowed to control both his fears and the remedy; and there were other moments, equally calm, when there seemed no point in pretending that he had anything to live for any longer. God would soon summon him to account. Although he still led the services on Sundays and paced the fields during the weekdays, exhorting his people to prayer and work, little of his time was spent in the estate office. But in his lucid moments Ralph looked clearly enough to the future of Hope Valley and considered how best to provide for what remained of his family.

As the end of 1917 approached he studied the accounts which Duke prepared and made a series of careful notes. As soon as his mind was made up, he sent for his assistant.

'We must consider what will happen when God has taken me to Himself,' he said without preamble. 'This letter is to Mr Arthur Lorimer. I'm going to tell you what is in it. You had better sit down.'

The permission caused a moment's delay, since Ralph's office contained only one chair. Duke fetched his own from the adjoining cubicle. For a while Ralph stared at the young man's intelligent brown face and was satisfied that he had made the right decision.

'If Brinsley had lived, he would have taken over the management of the plantation,' he began. 'But Brinsley is dead. Whom the gods love, die young.' He fell silent again, not concealing his bitterness at the loss of his son.

'You have another son, sir,' Duke reminded him.

'Grant is only a child. And in any case – well, there's no need for me to pretend any longer.' He laughed at the admission. 'Never did pretend very much, did I? I can't bear the thought of him taking over the work that I've built up over so many years. He's not fit to manage. He's not able even to walk over the ground. If I try to picture it, I'm revolted. That is un-Christian of me, but we must be honest now. And practical. You understand?'

'Yes, sir.'

'I recognize my duty to Grant,' Ralph continued. 'I've made due provision for him. It's all in this letter to my nephew, Mr Lorimer. I have funds in England, and they are to be managed in Grant's interest until he is twenty-one and then used to buy him a business or a partnership or an estate somewhere else – whatever his talents at the time suggest. But not in Jamaica.'

His silence this time lasted so long that Duke must have wondered whether the conversation was at an end. Then Ralph broke it abruptly.

'I have one more son,' he said. 'Has your mother never told you who your father is, Duke? Never discussed him with you at all?'

'No, sir.'

'But you must have wondered. And guessed the truth, perhaps, although we have never spoken of it.'

This time it was Duke's turn to be silent. 'I'm guessing now, sir,' he confessed at last. His eyes, unshocked, stared steadily at Ralph. Duke was accustomed to wait for instructions. It was an indication, perhaps, of the strength of the Lorimer strain, for any full-blooded Jamaican would have wept and flung himself into his father's arms.

Perhaps the restraint was imposed by Ralph's personality. He had long prepared for this interview, promising himself that it must be conducted on strictly business lines.

'You had little help from me in your childhood,' he said. 'But I shall make up for that now. You've proved that you're honest and competent. You know the work, what needs to be done. And I can trust you, can't I, to remember that the land must be used for the benefit of all the people here? They will be your people.'

'Yes, sir. But not for a long time, God willing.'

'Perhaps not for ten years. Perhaps tomorrow. God alone knows. I shall leave you the whole plantation when I die. But there's one condition. Kate.'

'Kate is my sister, then,' said Duke softly.

Ralph glanced across at the young man. Surely he could never have hoped . . . No, of course not. Duke was married to an island girl and his son, Harley, was already four years old. He had been such a close friend of Kate's when they were both children that he was bound to be pleased by his discovery of the relationship. That was all.

Ignoring the interruption, Ralph continued his exposition. In his heart he feared that Kate was dead. But it was necessary to act on the presumption that she would one day return; he must give formal recognition to hope. He had given thought to the necessary details and, although his concentration was flagging and he wanted to be alone so that he could have a drink, he forced himself to explain to Duke how a second trust fund must be created, with Arthur Lorimer as trustee, into which the profits of the plantation would be put for the next ten years. 'One third for you, as well as the salary you pay yourself. One third for the people. One third for Kate, if she is alive, or for her children if she has any. After ten years, if she cannot be traced, my nephew will divide her portion between yourself and Grant. You understand why you have to wait?'

'Yes, sir. But I don't ever want to take what's hers. If she comes back, it must all be for her. All the land.'

'No.' Ralph saw no need to mention his fear that if Kate did survive the Revolution she might prove to have been infected by its philosophy. From childhood she had been a passionate defender of the underdog and it was too easy to imagine her refusing an inheritance or accepting it only to give it away. 'No,' he insisted. 'You are the heir. The land is not to be divided, and it's for you. Kate's a doctor. To have an income would be useful to her, but she doesn't need land and she wouldn't know how to run it. I want you to have it. You have always been obedient, and you must obey me in this. Is that clear?'

'Yes, sir.' Duke rose to his feet. As always, his head was held high and his back straight. He had inherited his bearing and fine features from his mother, Chelsea Mattison, whose beauty as a young woman had proved irresistible. From his father he had inherited a powerful physique and a shrewd head for business. His body was as strong and athletic as Brinsley's had been – and he shared the same love of cricket – but his nature was more industrious and his character more serious. He was serious now as he looked at Ralph. 'Maybe you don't want I tell anyone outside about this,' he said. 'But just once I have to say it out loud. Thank you, Father.'

The emotion of the moment, unexpected because he had thought to have it under control, caused Ralph to choke and cry out. He opened his arms to embrace his son, allowing his senses to register the feel of the strong muscles and the smooth skin. It was right for him to be ashamed of his responsibility for Duke's birth, but he was proud to have such a son. He had lost his merry, hard-working wife, his golden boy, his lion-hearted daughter, but after all there was still someone to love. There had been occasions before this one when he had wept in Duke's arms, but his tears then were caused by rum and depression. Now he cried for joy.

Afterwards he made a copy of his message to Arthur, in case a U-boat should sink the ship which carried the original. The next day he travelled to Kingston and arranged for the separate dispatch of the two identical letters. Then, in his lawyer's office, he signed the will which had already been drawn up in accordance with his instructions.

The reminder that he still had family ties apart from Grant should have renewed his interest in life and restored him to cheerfulness. Instead, the assurance that he had settled his affairs on earth led his thoughts more towards the next world, as though he had not only chosen an heir but already handed over the inheritance. Knowing that it was in good hands, he no longer even pretended to interest himself in the management of the plantation. But he was still the pastor, and still every Sunday, shaved and sober, he preached to the congregation with some of the old fire and taught the Sunday School with some of the old patience. For the rest, he grew listless and slovenly.

His congregation were tolerant people. Conscious of their own transgressions and mindful, too, of the prosperity he had brought them during the thirty-five years of his pastorate, they took little notice of his bouts of drunkenness. Under the influence of rum he now became silent, not rowdy. He was waiting, they realized, for God to call him Home. In a curious way their respect for his holiness grew with this realization. Patiently and lovingly they waited with him.

9

The music room at Blaize had been preserved from the hospital's increasing demands for space. In it, Alexa spent an hour every morning practising her vocal exercises. If Piers, her husband – or anyone else – had asked her directly, she would have had to admit that she did not ever expect to return to the stage as a prima donna. The nights of triumph, the applause, the curtain calls, the bouquets – all these were gone for ever.

Were she to be honest with herself, she would admit also that this was not entirely the fault of the war. Her international career had effectively come to an end when she consented to become Lady Glanville. The interruption was intended to be no more than temporary, but the task of producing an heir had proved less simple than she anticipated. It was part of the bargain she had made with Piers that he should have a son, and a good many months had been wasted on the baby daughter who died within a week and the renewed hopes which ended in miscarriage.

After the eventual achievement of Pirry's birth there had been just one season in which, with health and voice restored, she had sung the leading parts in her own opera house; but she was as well able as anyone else to recognize that this was only a hobby, a tiny tributary of the main stream of opera. The war had robbed her of even this, but it would scarcely have been possible in any event for Lady Glanville to have stepped back into the place which Alexa Reni had vacated.

For one thing, she had already – earlier in 1917 – passed her fortieth birthday. As a young woman she had scornfully dismissed singers who spoiled the great reputations of their youth by continuing to perform after their voices passed their peak, vowing never to make the same mistake herself. If her career had not been interrupted, she now confessed to herself, that vow would have been broken. But she was realistic enough to recognize that if she were to attempt a full return to the stage she would be using her reputation only to ruin it.

To her surprise, the discovery did not depress her. With a husband who adored her, she no longer felt the need to make conquests and collect tokens of admiration: her private life was contented to the point of placidity. As for her professional life, it was enough that she had once been at the very top of the tree. She had been ambitious as a young girl and her ambitions had been fulfilled. No one could deprive her of the memory of success and so she was able to let the experience of it slip away.

Not that any of that made any difference to the perfection of her approach. The soldiers to whom she sang nowadays, whether in camps or hospitals, had little interest in opera, preferring to hear 'Keep the home fires

226

burning' or the hit songs from *Chu Chin Chow*. Either alone or in the concert party she had organized she gave them what they wanted, but with a quality of voice which would have satisfied the most meticulous critic of a performance at the Royal Opera House.

On a frosty day in November 1917, her first engagement was at a rehabilitation centre. Margaret had asked her to inspect the various training schemes in operation there, in case any of the ideas and techniques could be put to use in the convalescent wards at Blaize; and the commandant of the centre had expressed himself delighted to give her lunch and act as her personal guide before the afternoon recital began.

'Our chief problem here is one of morale,' he explained as they moved quietly from one room to another. 'All our patients have been too severely wounded ever to return to the army. In a medical sense, they've come to the end of their convalescence by the time they're sent here. They're as fit as they ever will be again, but all of them are disabled for life. We try to train them for some new career, but naturally they arrive in a state of great depression, and they're very reluctant to leave here and face the world again. We have to be rather brutal with the men who have finished their course – push them out, in point of fact. On the other hand, we sympathize with those who are just arriving and haven't yet come to terms with their disabilities. The first classes they attend are what you might call therapy rather than formal training. In the old barn, for example – ' like the hospital at Blaize, the centre was a temporary conversion from a country house – 'we're running an art class for men who've lost the use of one or both legs but still have their hands and eyes undamaged. One of our patients – the only civilian here – turned out to be a professional artist. A very talented chap. He acts as instructor – that's *his* therapy. The idea is that if one of them turns out to have any talent, he ould be more intensively trained either to teach art or to take up commercial drawing; but in any case it does them all good to feel that they're capable of producing *something*. They'll be packing up in the next few minutes ready for your concert, so they won't mind being interrupted.'

He pushed open the door. Outside, it was a bitterly cold day. But inside the barn the air was made hot and stuffy by three paraffin stoves grouped round a makeshift platform on which a model was posing. A dozen men in hospital blue sat round the platform, their chairs and easels widely spaced so that the instructor could move between them in his wheelchair. The opening of the door allowed the cold air to stab into the barn. The model was too well-trained to move, but the instructor looked round in slight irritation. Alexa gasped in a sudden shock as she recognized the man who had been her first love. She felt her arm being seized by her companion. Before she had time to understand what was happening she was outside again, with the door slamming behind her.

Dizzily, she leaned for a moment against the wall of the barn while the commandant exploded into an apology which she did not understand.

'I'm so sorry, Lady Glanville. My fault entirely – I should have warned them – you must forgive me – I do apologize.'

'What are you talking about?' Alexa asked faintly. It was clear to her that she was expected to reassure him, but since she saw nothing for which he could be blamed she found it difficult to choose the right words.

'The model,' he said. 'Mr Lorimer wasn't expecting a lady visitor, of course. I allow him a free hand in the choice of subjects. But of course if I had told him you were coming, he would have found something more suitable today.'

'Was the model naked, then?' Alexa had a vague impression of the profile of a young man, almost certainly blind; but she had been distracted before her eyes could take in the rest of his body.

'You didn't see? I was afraid – you looked so startled – and quite justifiably so.'

'Not by the model,' said Alexa. 'No, I didn't see. It was Mr Lorimer himself who startled me. He's a relation of mine, as it happens. But we'd lost touch. I didn't even know he'd been wounded. It was a shock. Is it serious?'

'I'm afraid so.' The commandant shook his head sadly. In relief that he had not after all caused offence to an influential visitor, he was willing to talk freely. 'Very considerable injuries to the spine and abdomen. Wheelchair for the rest of his life, I'm afraid, and basic nursing care. No reason, of course, why he shouldn't continue to paint. You might say he's lucky, for an artist. Blindness would have been far worse in his case. But there was no injury to his eyesight at all. Nor to his manual dexterity. Count your blessings, I tell him. But he's as downcast as any of the others. Nothing worth living for, never going to be a great artist now, all that sort of thing. It's only to be expected. He's a good teacher, though, and it's getting through to him that he's helping some of the others. With any luck, that will be a help to him in turn, given time.'

'After the concert, perhaps I could talk to him privately.' Alexa could barely bring the words to her lips. 'Is there anywhere we could meet?'

'Of course, Lady Glanville. I'll see to it.'

She felt a moment of panic at the ease with which the arrangement was made. On the day of their engagement she had promised Piers that she would never see Matthew again. But neither of them then could have envisaged the circumstances of this new encounter. A happily-married woman, mother of a four-year-old son; and a severely disabled man. What harm could a conversation between them do? And it would be unthinkable to turn her back on a member of the family. She had spoken the truth when she claimed a relationship with the instructor. Matthew, after all – in spite of being three years older than herself – was her nephew.

It was not an easy meeting. The commandant put his own office at their disposal and Alexa waited until Matthew had arrived there before she joined him. She had sung all her songs that afternoon for him – and he, meeting her gaze steadily, had known it. So there was no longer any element of shock in the encounter, but the constraints imposed by their past relationship remained. It was impossible, naturally, for Alexa to kiss him; but equally impossible, for quite different reasons, to shake hands as though they were mere acquaintances.

Twelve years had passed since they last saw each other. At the ball which Lord Glanville had given in 1905 for Alexa Reni, the star of the new season at the Royal Opera House, she and Matthew had danced together, their eyes bright with love and excitement. And then Alexa had been forced to tell him what she had only recently learned herself – that her father, the mysterious man who had had a liaison with her mother in the last years of his life, was Matthew's grandfather, John Junius Lorimer.

She had done her best to persuade Matthew then that the discovery was of little importance. It was true that they could no longer contract a valid marriage, as they had hoped, but what did that matter to an artist and a singer? Alexa had been sincere when she said that she cared nothing for convention. That had made all the greater the shock of hearing Matthew declare that she must be free to marry one day, to be respected and to lead a conventionally happy life in the class of society which her beauty and talent entitled her to enter. He had kissed her with a fervour which left no doubt of the passion he was renouncing. Then he had run from the ballroom, never to see her again. Until now.

'I don't know what to say.' Alexa felt her voice shaking. She leaned back against the door, trying to laugh at her own inadequacy.

'Well, I do,' said Matthew. 'I have to say that you're

more beautiful than ever. I wouldn't have thought it possible, but you've grown even lovelier than when you were eighteen. Lucky Lord Glanville. I was glad when you chose him to marry. He seemed a kind man. Why don't you sit down? You've been told, I suppose, what's wrong with me.'

He was talking too much for the same reason that Alexa was talking too little. Neither of them was quite certain what their relationship was or could be. She sat down and did her best to conduct an ordinary conversation.

'Not in any detail,' she said. 'How did it happen, Matthew? You weren't in the army, were you?'

'At my age? Don't be ridiculous! Well, I shouldn't say that. I gather that even old men like me are being swept into the general carnage these days. No. The really ridiculous part of the whole business is that I could have stayed safely at home if I'd wanted to. I actually chose to go up in an aeroplane. I had to beg people to let me. I must have been mad.'

'An aeroplane!'

'That's right. I was an official war artist, doing a series of battle paintings. I got it into my head that I'd like to see what the whole thing looked like from above. On the ground, it's all a mess. Dead bodies, live bodies, none of it makes any sense. There must be a pattern somewhere, I thought, and it might be possible to see it from the air. They let me go up on an observation flight, to take photographs of the enemy lines. I knew how to work a camera.'

'And was there a pattern?'

'If it counts as a pattern to see rows of ants bustling around. All keeping to their own tracks, trying to achieve some invisible goal, occasionally diverting round some invisible obstacle.' He hesitated and for the first time the note of bitterness left his voice. 'Well, as a matter of fact, it was beautiful. There was snow on the ground – you remember how late spring was. Impossible to believe that armies were killing each other down there. Little dots of people. Little puffs of smoke. Peaceful. The aeroplane was noisy, but everything else seemed to be silent. Until at last one of the puffs of smoke pointed in our direction and we fell out of the sky.'

'You were shot down? Oh, Matthew!' It was impossible to restrain her affection for him any longer. She seized his hand and pressed it against her cheek. Gently, but definitely, he took it away.

'Don't, Alexa,' he told her. 'I didn't want this meeting. I knew you were coming to sing, of course, but I hadn't meant to be at the concert.'

'But we could be friends again,' Alexa said. 'Twelve years of separation is long enough, surely. And when we're members of the same family, it's absurd. We've got nothing to be ashamed of. Nothing that happened was our fault.'

'What happened?' asked Matthew wryly. 'Nothing, alas!'

'And how much I regretted that, when you left me,' said Alexa. 'That night in Paris, after Salome – I would have stayed with you, you know, if you'd asked me.'

'And instead I asked you to marry me and we found ourselves trapped by all the Lorimer conventions of correct behaviour between a gentleman and his fiancée. But now you're married to Lord Glanville, and another set of conventions comes into play!'

'Piers couldn't possibly object – ' began Alexa. But Matthew interrupted before she could move too far away from the truth.

'In view of my condition?' he suggested, still with the same forced smile on his lips. 'It's certainly true that he'd have nothing to fear from me. Well, to be honest, I'm not much bothered about what he thinks. I'm speaking out of selfishness. *I* couldn't stand it. I'm having trouble enough in coming to terms with everything I've lost as a

232

result of the crash. To be reminded of what I lost even before that would be too much of a burden. I'm sorry, Alexa.'

Alexa was silent, recognizing her own selfishness in her reluctance to let him go. She did her best to accept his decision without letting him see what an effort it cost her.

'But where will you go when you leave here?' she asked.

Again the wry smile twisted Matthew's lips.

'I have a house – a very small house – in Leicestershire,' he said. 'Whether any of the doors will be wide enough to admit a wheelchair, I don't know. And inside the house I have a wife. Whether she'll have any use for a cripple is another thing I don't know. I even have a baby son, John. With any luck he'll get on with me for a year or two, until he feels the need of a father who can kick a football around with him.'

'A wife!' Alexa was dumbfounded. It had never occurred to her that Matthew would marry anyone else.

'A wife to whom I can never be a husband again.'

'But you can still paint.' She did not know what else to say. Her beloved Matthew reduced to this! And married.

'Oh yes,' he agreed. 'I'm a very lucky chap. I can still paint.'

Alexa realized that whatever comfort she tried to give would increase his bitterness rather than assuage it. She longed to put her arms around him, to feel his arms around her, to give him one last kiss. Instead, she said goodbye quietly and went out of the room before he should see her cry.

10

As the time of her grandchild's birth approached, late in 1917, Margaret went to Jennifer's family home in Norfolk. She felt entitled to some leave, for this was her first absence from Blaize since she had taken charge of the hospital there. By now her work was almost entirely administrative: there were plenty of doctors on the staff to deal with medical emergencies.

She found her daughter-in-law in good health, but strained and apprehensive. Margaret herself had been forced to approach the birth of her only child without a husband at her side for support, and sympathized with the young woman's fears about the coming ordeal. She did her best to be reassuring and was rewarded by Jennifer's increasing serenity of mood.

The sea was not far away from the Blakeneys' home, Castle Hall, but the flat land between was low and marshy, making it difficult to walk there easily. Its presence made itself felt mainly by the sea mists which spread inland every evening and often, at this time of the year, did not disperse until noon. They made outdoor exercise undesirable for Jennifer, who by now was in any case too big to move easily. The baby's head had dropped, making walking difficult. Mr Blakeney, Margaret's host, was elderly and frail even for his years. He too kept to the house in these cold days. Margaret, more active than either and for too long confined to her office, felt the need to spend some time each day in the open air.

She went out in the afternoons during Jennifer's rest period, using the first day to explore the Blakeneys' own grounds. The grey stone house, shabby but comfortable, had a modest garden of lawns and flower beds at the back, with a spinney at what appeared to be the boundary.

But on the far side of the trees, still within the estate, were the ruins of the old castle which gave the house its name.

Except for a single tower at one corner, little of the structure had survived, but enough of the outer wall remained to show what an extensive area it had once protected – and because the stone foundations were set in a high bank of earth, there was still a feeling of shelter inside. Outside, on the other hand, the wall was steep, an effective defence. At its highest point it was set on an outcrop of rock immediately above the marsh which twice a day filled with tidal water and twice a day drained itself back into the narrower channel of a river running out to the sea.

In the days before the war, when gardeners were easy to come by, the grass inside the walls had probably been kept neat, but now a thick growth of nettles and brambles made it impossible to cross. Round the circumference ran a well-trodden stony path, however, and as Margaret walked along it both on that first day and on later occasions she revelled in the peace of the deserted site. If she paused to look out, either inland or across the marsh to the sea, she could see birds by the hundred, but no people at all. The change from the bustling grounds of Blaize and the constant demands made on her there was so restful that for the first time she was able to appreciate how tired she had been when she arrived.

On other days she explored some of the nearby villages, marvelling at the richness of the huge churches which had been built in the centuries when the wool trade made Norfolk wealthy but which today dominated only shrunken and impoverished communities. She was returning from one of these walks when she saw approaching from the other direction the elderly village postman. He had returned to his old employment when his younger successor went off to the war. He got off his bicycle to open the gate, and recognized Margaret as the guest at the Hall.

'How's Miss Jennifer, then?' he asked.

'Very well. It won't be much longer. Can I save you the journey up to the house?'

'If you'll sign for this. Telegram. Name of Scott.'

'That must be for me.' Margaret frowned as she signed. Only that morning she had read in the paper that more than two hundred thousand British soldiers had been killed or wounded in the Third Battle of Ypres. Blaize, no doubt, like every other hospital, would be under pressure to increase its number of patients. She hoped that her deputy was not calling her back just at the moment when she could be of use to Jennifer. She opened the telegram.

'Is there any answer?' asked the postman.

Margaret shook her head, unable to speak. She stood still, leaning against the gatepost, as the old man mounted his bicycle, wobbled, and pedalled slowly away. Then, equally slowly, she walked up the long drive.

She could not face Jennifer yet. Instead of going into the house she continued to walk across the garden and into the ruins of the castle. Only when she was sure that no one could see her did she sit down on the stone wall and take the telegram out again.

It was intended for Jennifer. Margaret had forgotten that Robert's wife had the same surname as Robert's mother. It was Jennifer who had become Robert's next of kin, Jennifer to whom the War Office expressed its regrets.

She read the words again. They were not an announcement of death: not quite. Robert was missing, believed dead. Earlier in the war she would have seized on the uncertainty. It was unbelievable that Robert should have been killed and in 1915 or 1916 she would have refused to believe it. But now any attempt at optimism was crushed by the weight of probability. Too many women had been widowed, too many widows had lost their only sons. It was no longer possible to pretend that such things

236

could not happen: they happened every day. She tried to cling to the element of hope – that if he were known to be dead, certainly dead, someone would have said so. In this moment of shock, though, she could not make herself believe anything but the worst. 'Missing, believed dead' meant only that that no one had found the body.

The thought of Robert being only a body was too much for her to bear. He was all she had. His cheerful grin and mischievous eyes, his lively kindness and affection, had been everything in the world to her for twenty-three years. Without him she had nothing left. Clutching the telegram to her chest she rocked backward and forward, trying to control her emotions. Whatever she might think of the Kaiser and his advisers, she had never before hated the Germans as a race. The men in the enemy army were doubtless as puzzled and frightened as most British soldiers by what was happening to them. But at this moment she hated the man who had fired the bullet or the mortar or the shell which had killed her son. Had Robert been frightened, she wondered; had he been for long in pain? When he was a little boy she had shared his pains with him and she felt this one as well. Not exactly sobbing, not exactly screaming, she began to wail as she rocked, throwing the despairing sound out across the marsh to join the desolate cries of the water fowl.

It drew to an end at last. She had come to Castle Hall to support her daughter-in-law and it was time to consider how best to do this. The first decision was an immediate one. The news must be kept from Jennifer until after the birth of the baby and if possible until she had completely recovered her strength. Margaret knew enough about the depression which often followed childbirth to realize the danger of providing a real, rather than an imaginary, cause for it. That meant that newspapers must be destroyed, the telephone guarded and visitors interrogated and if necessary warned. But most of all it meant that Margaret herself must be as cheerful and businesslike as usual, allowing nothing in her manner to suggest that anything was wrong.

Never in her life had she found it easy to lie, even when it was kind or sensible to do so. And Jennifer naturally liked to talk about Robert. Sometimes she asked her mother-in-law to describe his boyhood, but more often she was concerned with her life with him after the war. If Margaret was to join convincingly in such conversations from now on she must first convince herself that nothing too terrible had happened. She set herself to do so.

Robert was missing. That was bad, but it was only temporary. There would be more news soon. Until it came there was nothing to mourn and when it did come, the news would surely be good. Almost certainly he had been wounded, but the lack of sure information must suggest that he had been taken prisoner. She would not believe that he was dead until someone proved it to her. There was bound to be a period of suspense and she had the power to spare her daughter-in-law that anxiety. If the news could be kept from Jennifer for a little while, she might never need to hear it at all.

Margaret brushed the stone dust off her coat as she stood up. She straightened her shoulders and walked back round the castle wall towards the house with the firm step and all the determination which had enabled her to survive earlier tragedies in her life.

She had hoped to reach her bedroom and to wash some of the strain away from her swollen face before anyone saw her; but Jennifer, restless, was waiting in the front hall. Margaret took one look at the young woman's wide, frightened eyes and gripped her hands.

'Has it started, dear?'

Jennifer nodded. 'Should I lie down?'

'Only while I examine you,' Margaret said. 'There may be still quite a long time to wait and you'll be more comfortable moving around at first. Give me a moment to wash and change my clothes. I'll come to your room.'

The monthly nurse was already in the house, so would not have heard any news from outside. Between them they could guard Jennifer from any careless word. Mr Blakeney would have to be told, but that could wait until the printed casualty lists in the newspapers began to include the victims of 30 November. For the moment, Margaret applied herself to the task of welcoming a new life into the world, and found some comfort in the familiar routines.

As she had warned Jennifer, it would be some hours before the birth could be considered imminent. Margaret prescribed a hot bath and took the opportunity to shut herself in the library and telephone Lord Glanville. Piers received the news with a groan of sympathy which revealed his personal distress. He had known Robert since babyhood and loved him almost as his own son. Anxious to complete the conversation before she was interrupted, Margaret pressed the only important question.

'What are the implications, Piers? What are the chances that he's only missing? He doesn't necessarily have to be dead, does he?'

She was asking for reassurance and Piers did his best to provide it, although the uncertainty in his voice gave the clue to his real opinion.

'No, of course not. Not necessarily. I'll find out everything I can, Margaret. The Germans are supposed to send lists of their prisoners, as we do of ours. It's bound to take a little time before details come through. I'll make enquiries – and make sure that any information which arrives reaches us at once. But Margaret – '

'Yes?'

She heard him sigh. 'I'll do what I can,' he repeated. Margaret knew what the hesitation meant. He was warning her not to hope too much, because he was already almost sure that she would be disappointed. It was a question of statistics, of probabilities. In any kind of normal society a young man of twenty-three would have an expectation of life of forty years. But a young man in France was lucky to survive twelve weeks. Robert had been lucky, in that sense. The telegram which Margaret had hidden in her drawer could have been expected at any time in the last two and a half years.

She ended the conversation with a reminder that any news should be communicated only to herself. Then for the second time that day it was necessary for her to conceal her heartache under a cloak of cheerful efficiency.

The baby was a girl, small but healthy, her downy hair suggesting that the blondeness of her mother's Danish ancestors had only slightly subdued the bright red of her father and grandmother and great-grandfather. Margaret tried to feel joyful but found it impossible. She could control her grief only by suppressing all emotion. Fortunately Jennifer was too tired and too happy on her own account to notice. Margaret waited while Mr Blakeney was shown his granddaughter, checked that mother and child were comfortable in the care of the nurse, and went back to pace up and down her own room.

The charade continued for eight days. When at last she was called to the telephone to speak to Lord Glanville her first reaction was one of hope, but the sympathetic gravity of his voice allowed the hope no encouragement. He had managed to get in touch with Robert's commanding officer and had learned the details of the German counter-attack at Cambrai – which had recaptured almost all the ground gained by the British in the Third Battle of Ypres. The number of confirmed British casualties was already over forty thousand and it was thought that almost ten thousand had been taken prisoner.

'Then if Robert's missing, surely it's most likely that he's a prisoner of war!' Margaret exclaimed.

'His name hasn't yet appeared on any of the lists, I'm afraid.'

'But if he had been killed, someone would have seen.'

'The German attack took place during a snow blizzard. It sounds as though there was little visibility. And a great deal of confusion as our men were pressed back. But in fact he was seen to fall. His sergeant and a linesman both reported it, and they were each of the opinion that he had been hit in the head.'

'But afterwards.' Margaret had to force herself to say the words. 'Afterwards, if he were dead, his body would have been found.'

'He was hit right at the beginning of the enemy attack, and the area where he fell was over-run by the Germans. Later in the day our troops made a sortie and recovered the ground temporarily, although it was lost again the next day. They brought in any wounded they could. But Robert wasn't amongst them.'

'Then surely that's good news!' exclaimed Margaret. 'The Germans must have found him first and taken him prisoner. Taken him to hospital if he was wounded. They wouldn't trouble to move the dead body of an enemy in the middle of the battle. Surely it must mean that he's still alive, Piers. What other possibility can there be?'

The silence which followed was almost as terrible as the explanation which gradually she forced out of him. Margaret had known Piers long before he married Alexa. They had been friends for twenty years and their honesty with each other was a fundamental ingredient of the friendship. Piers might try – as he was trying now – not to tell her the whole truth, but he could not bring himself to lie. Little by little, as he gave reluctant answers to her direct questions, Margaret built up a picture of a desolate countryside in which snow turned to slush and slush seeped into the pulverized soil and turned it into liquid mud. In mud like that even living men drowned. The body of a dead man would simply sink beneath the surface and never be seen again.

In more than thirty years as a doctor Margaret had seen a good many deaths, but she could not think of

Robert's death as being like any other. When she replaced the receiver at the end of the call her mind was numb but her body was retching. She needed to be alone, and it was the worst possible timing which allowed Jennifer at that moment to come slowly downstairs for the first time since her baby was born.

Jennifer was radiant with happiness. Her fears of childbirth had been forgotten, her body had recovered from its tiredness and she was delighted by her beautiful daughter. Contentment enveloped her as she came into the library.

'The vicar has just left,' she said. 'He came to arrange for my churching.'

At any other time Margaret would have registered a protest. She disapproved strongly of the service prescribed for the churching of women. On her wedding day a bride was exhorted by the church to have children and it seemed illogical that when she had obeyed that instruction she should immediately be regarded as unclean. It was a pagan ceremony which ought to be resisted. But today she was in no mood for argument, and Jennifer's happy mood allowed no opportunity for it.

'He asked at the same time about a date for the christening,' she said. 'I imagine there's no hope of Robert having leave in the near future, so I shall have to choose a time to suit the godparents. And before that I must make a final decision on a name for Baby. It's a great difficulty.'

'Did you and Robert not discuss it and have your choices ready?' To her own ears Margaret's voice sounded unfamiliar, a low expressionless mumble; but Jennifer appeared not to notice anything unusual about it.

'Oh, Robert refused to be serious. I suggested that a daughter might be called Roberta, and he wrote back to say that that would be perfectly all right as long as he was allowed to call her Bobbie or Bertie. I wasn't having that, of course, so then I asked whether he would consider

242

Florence, because I so much admired Florence Nightingale. He didn't like the name, but suggested that if I really wanted to call a daughter after a city there was plenty of other choice: Paris, for example, or Troy or Petra. Berlin, he thought, might be a little unwise in the circumstances.' Jennifer giggled at the memory of what had clearly been a long-running discussion by correspondence. 'He makes a joke of everything, doesn't he? I don't think he could really make himself believe that there was going to be a baby. He had to wait until it arrived. Well, of course, I wrote to tell him straightaway, and pointed out that we really must settle the matter and suggested three more names. So the question is, how long will it be before I get an answer? Our letters have been taking about five days each way, so I should hear by Christmas. Mother, what's the matter?'

Margaret did not answer, *could* not answer. Her voice was no longer under control. It would be unforgivable to disturb the young mother's joyful light-heartedness, but it was impossible to pretend any longer. She could not even think of any excuse to take herself out of the room, but remained frozen in silence and misery and on the verge of fainting.

'Mother! Mother, what's happened? Is it Robert? What's happened to Robert? Is he dead? Oh God, don't let him be dead.'

'Prisoner.' Margaret forced out the small lie in order to save herself from attempting the larger one.

'How do you know?'

'Telegram.'

'Where is it? I want to see it.'

'I threw it away. No, wait a moment, Jennifer. Don't go away. We must talk about it.'

'I'll come down again after Baby's next feed. I'd like to be alone till then with her. We'll talk afterwards.' Jennifer's face, always pale, was drained of all colour as she stood up; but her eyes were calm, almost blank. Still

243

moving slowly, she went out of the library, leaving Margaret to indulge the same need for solitude.

She was joined some time later by the monthly nurse.

'I'm sorry to bother you, doctor, but I'm a little disturbed. Mrs Scott's lost her milk.'

'She's had a shock,' said Margaret. 'Some bad news. The trouble may only be temporary. Have you tried making up a bottle?'

'Yes, doctor, but Baby won't take it.'

'I'll see what I can do. Will you go into the village and ask Dr Nelson whether there's anyone who could act as wet nurse if it becomes necessary?'

In the nursery the baby was crying. Jennifer had returned to bed. On the sheet in front of her was the War Office telegram.

'I may have had to steal it from your drawer,' she said. 'But it was addressed to me. And it came more than a week ago.'

'I felt – ' Margaret's explanation was interrupted by the shrugging of Jennifer's shoulders.

'Yes, I can understand what you felt. I'm grateful. Thank you very much for those few days. But now it's time to stop pretending, isn't it? This says nothing about Robert being a prisoner.'

'I've been talking to Lord Glanville. He's made enquiries. The Germans took thousands of prisoners. It may be a long time before all the names come through.'

'That's not what it says. It says that he's been killed.'

'No!' protested Margaret. 'Nothing as definite as that. That telegram was sent when nobody knew. And since then – if he were dead, he would have been found.'

'Death isn't the existence of a dead body,' said Jennifer. 'It's the absence of a live one. Absence without end. That's what's happening now. It's only just beginning. But it will go on for ever.'

For the second time since the arrival of the telegram Margaret forced herself to close a part of her mind and to

244

control the trembling of her body in order to provide comfort. In a curious way she found it easier this time. The first shock had been a general one. With no details of what had happened she had been unable to imagine Robert's death and so what little hope she had been able to pretend was based on the belief that a son could not be snatched from the world without his mother experiencing some instinctive sense of disaster. Her recent conversation with Piers had given her a second shock which provided all too many details. It was easy for her imagination, feeding on them, to build up a picture of what might have happened, but the picture was so horrifying that neither her mind nor her body could admit it. As she sat down on the edge of the bed and held Jennifer tightly in her arms, she was not pretending any longer. Her demand for optimism was sincere. Robert must, *must* have been taken prisoner when the Germans captured the territory on which he lay wounded. She had asked Piers what alternative there could possibly be, and nothing that he had suggested was acceptable.

'We must both hope for the best,' she said. 'And we mustn't believe the worst when it isn't certain. We're lucky to have been given that much uncertainty, that much hope. I think he's a prisoner, Jennifer. I *feel* it. You must feel it too. The war can't last for ever. When Robert comes back, he'll want to find you and Baby both strong and beautiful. Have a rest now, until the next feed.'

As obediently as a child Jennifer slid down beneath the sheets and closed her eyes. Neither on that day nor on those which followed was she seen to cry.

11

Once it was recognized that Jennifer's letter would never have reached Robert, there was no reason to delay the christening in the hope of an answer. Castle Hall bustled with activity as servants and family alike did their best to return, for one day at least, to peacetime standards of hospitality. A long white christening robe, finely pleated and delicately embroidered, had been taken out of its cocoon of tissue paper and ironed with the reverent care imposed by a garment already two hundred years old. Bedrooms had been prepared for the godparents who would be staying overnight and there would be a christening tea for friends of the family who lived locally. Precious sugar and jam had already been set aside over a period of several months to be squandered now in a single baking session. So much was going on that when, on the morning of the service, the wet nurse came to say that the baby was missing from her cradle, it took Margaret some time to discover that Jennifer likewise was nowhere to be found in the house.

There had been a frost in the night and, although a pale sun was shining now, the December day was still very cold. Hurrying outside without a coat, Margaret shivered as she looked quickly round the garden. The hoar frost which whitened the lawn had been flattened by footsteps leading through the spinney. Margaret followed the track and came to the castle ruins.

Jennifer was standing on the broken wall at its highest point, where it thrust out into the marsh and gave a view towards the sea. She had her back to Margaret, but the trailing end of a white shawl suggested that she was holding the baby in her arms.

The situation made Margaret uneasy. For a moment

she was tempted to dash through the tangle of nettles and brambles, taking the shortest line towards Jennifer. Or, moving faster round the circumference, to creep up from behind without a sound, giving no warning of her approach. Both these ideas she rejected, tutting to herself at the wildness of her imagination. Instead, she called across to tell Jennifer she was here and began to approach round the wall as though it were the most natural thing in the world to take a walk in her house shoes and best Sunday dress.

It had come as a welcome surprise that Jennifer had succeeded in being brave and sensible. Margaret herself had emerged from the grief of her first shock persuaded that she was right to hope and that grounds for such hope existed. Piers had agreed that there would necessarily be delays before the full list of those who had been taken prisoner was known, and this had proved to be the case. Although Robert had not been mentioned in the first batch of five thousand names released by the Germans, more were being added to the list in a steady trickle every day. Every day Margaret encouraged Jennifer to expect good news and every day Jennifer, calm and dry-eyed, nodded her head and agreed that the nightmare must soon be over. It was not a pretence on Margaret's part. She had genuinely made herself believe what she said and so she was sure that Jennifer must believe it as well. Or at least, believe that it was worth while to wait. And Jennifer would never hurt her own baby. The flash of fear at the sight of the motionless woman on the rampart had been irrational and unjustified.

Nevertheless, it would be as well if Jennifer did not stay there too long. Margaret greeted her in a normal manner but suggested almost at once that the air was too cold for the baby.

'In so many layers of wool she can hardly be conscious of temperature,' said the young mother, and it was true that the little girl, although restless for her feed, showed no sign of discomfort. 'I needed a little peace and quiet, and there isn't much to be found in the house. With the christening this afternoon, I can't put off the choice of a name any longer.'

'I thought you must have decided already and that you were going to surprise us,' Margaret said. 'Have you made your choice, then? Will you tell me?'

'Her second name will be Margaret, for you. I'm sure Robert would have wanted that. As for her first name, I shall call her Barbary.'

'Barbara, you mean.'

'No. Barbary.'

'But dearest, that's not a name.'

'It's an old form of Barbara,' said Jennifer. 'If you look in the graveyard when we go to the church this afternoon you'll see the tombstone of Barbary Anguish. She was twelve months old when she died in 1704. When I was a little girl I used to run out of the church sometimes because the sermon seemed too long. I'd sit on that grave and think about Barbary Anguish. The whole name seemed so sad, as though her parents had known even before she was born that she would bring them nothing but tears.'

'But this baby is going to bring you great happiness, Jennifer.'

'Look down there,' said Jennifer, and Margaret followed her gaze down the steep cliff of the rocky outcrop and over the marsh, half flooded now by the tidal water which forced its way through the tall reeds. Not far away, in the deeper channel of the river, the surface of the water became more turbulent as the incoming tide fought against the current surging down towards the sea. On the further side of the water stood a row of windmills. The wind had dropped, leaving them for the time being motionless, which made all the greater the contrast with the life of the river and the marsh. Tern and crested grebe cruised over the water, curlews called from the

248

meadow beyond, swans in formation flew overhead with the air screaming through their wings. A heron stood amongst the reeds as though made of stone and one by one the wooden posts which marked the river channel were occupied by sleek black cormorants which stretched their wings to dry and then crouched without moving, waiting until a fish should pass below.

'It's very beautiful,' said Margaret; but she shivered a little as she spoke, and this time with more than the crispness of the air. It was not a welcoming beauty but an alien one. Even as she watched, a low sea mist spread across the further bank of the river, swallowing the windmills one by one. If she had not seen them a moment earlier, she could not now have guessed that there was anything there. It seemed that her companion shared something of the same feeling.

'The Romans built this castle,' Jennifer said. 'Everything inside it was safe. Part of the civilized world. Everything outside was hostile. Barbary. The barbarians came from the sea and destroyed the land. My own ancestors were amongst them. The castle walls survived for a little while and kept the people inside safe, but when they decayed the barbarians were waiting. They're always waiting. In the mud of Flanders, in the mists of Norfolk. As we stand here, the guns are booming and men's bodies are shattering into pieces. And there are more ways of ending a life than with a gun. The world is full of people who can only kill and destroy. There's no refuge any longer. The whole world is barbary.'

'For you, perhaps. But not for your baby. She has her own safe place, in your heart. And certainly she's not one of the barbarians herself, to be given such a name.'

'Perhaps not,' agreed Jennifer. 'But she's the daughter of anguish. I've made up my mind. I shall call her Barbary.'

Her voice, although definite, was calm enough, but suddenly Margaret was frightened again. The wall was high and the white bundle in Jennifer's arms was tiny and helpless.

'We ought to get Baby back into a warm room,' she said. 'Let me hold her while you climb down. It's a steep path – and it's too soon, really, for you to be scrambling about like this.'

Jennifer gave no sign, as she obeyed, that she had been looking for anything more than fresh air and a quiet place in which to reflect. But that did not prevent Margaret from drawing the nurse to one side as soon as the baby had been fed and tucked up again in her cradle.

'Mrs Scott is very depressed,' she said. 'It's natural in the circumstances. You should encourage her to rest as much as possible and to eat a little more. And for the next few days, until I speak to you again, you shouldn't allow the baby to be left alone with her mother. Tell the wet nurse as much as you need to.'

She saw the woman's eyes open wide and was satisfied that her anxiety was understood. Later Margaret was to ask herself how she could have been foolish enough to channel her anxiety so narrowly. What she suspected might indeed have been in Jennifer's distracted mind as she climbed the steep slope of the earthworks, but it was only half the danger.

That afternoon the baby was christened in the little flint church to which so many members of the Blakeney family had brought their new-born and their dead. Still unhappy about the choice of name, Margaret hoped that the vicar might protest that it was not a Christian name in the literal sense: but he – presumably sharing Jennifer's familiarity with the child's name which had been carved on a tombstone two hundred years earlier – did not demur. Jennifer came calmly to the tea party which followed the service. Afterwards she claimed to be tired by all the excitement and went early to bed. The next morning her bedroom was empty.

It was three days before her body was found entangled

in the reeds on the river bank. Margaret, who did not sleep at all during that time, received the news with a numbness she could not explain. It was as though she had expended all her grief on Robert and had no tears left to shed. This did not prevent her, though, from feeling guilty at what she saw as a failure of sensitivity on her part. She had not wanted to act as a prison warder but realized now that she should have done so. Sitting with Mr Blakeney in a room which felt cold in spite of the log fire burning in the grate, she tried to express her regrets.

'Jennifer was always highly-strung,' he said. 'She never found it easy to cope with difficulties. Perhaps she led too sheltered a life here. I know that she found her hospital work very distressing when she first went to Blaize, even though she had no personal involvement.'

What he said was true. Margaret remembered her own earlier observation of the nervous strain induced in Jennifer by the need to take a difficult decision. But that was no excuse for her own shortcomings.

'There's the question of the baby,' Mr Blakeney said. 'When I die, she'll inherit everything I have. And I shall make a settlement of part of it to take effect at once. It would be a comfort to me, once she's a little older, to have her company sometimes. But I can't look after a baby. I'm an old man. And not well. If she stays here, she'll be brought up by servants. And even though she might learn to love me, she'd lose me before very long.'

Margaret made no attempt to argue, and not only because she was too tired. At their very first meeting her trained eye had identified Parkinson's disease in the trembling of Mr Blakeney's fingers, and under the strain of tiredness and bereavement his hands were now shaking uncontrollably. In years he was not yet seventy, but the greyness of his complexion suggested that his estimate of his own future might not be far from the truth.

'I'll take her back to Blaize,' she promised. 'You must come to visit her there as often as you wish. And she can come here for holidays as well.'

It could not be a permanent solution. Margaret was certainly in better health than her host, but she was not so very much younger. The war had made thoughts of retirement impossible, but she had already passed her sixtieth birthday. Like an old woman, she allowed herself a moment to remember all the other members of the family for whom she had at one time or another assumed responsibility. Robert, of course, had never been anything but a joy to her, while Kate and Brinsley had come under her roof when they were old enough to be independent to some extent. But Margaret could still recall the doubts she had felt on three other occasions when she had found herself in much the same situation as today. She had adopted Alexa without having any assurance that she could afford to support even herself, much less a child. When Alexa herself had become pregnant with no husband to support her, Margaret again had come to the rescue, relinquishing the care of little Frisca only when Alexa's marriage provided a new home for her. And then the last year had seen Grant's arrival, with Ralph's increasingly confused letters making it clear that the boy would never be welcomed back in Jamaica.

This case was different. Margaret felt sure that she would have no difficulty in loving her granddaughter, but she could not count on living to see Barbary grow up into adulthood.

It didn't matter. No better arrangement suggested itself. And one of the curious effects of the war which had been going on for so long was that it distorted the idea of the future. Like everyone else Margaret habitually used the phrase 'after the war', but this was an unreal concept as long as no date could be attached to it. It meant 'sometime' but carried the connotation of 'never'. Nothing could be less satisfactory than to live from one day to the next when every single day brought news of fresh unpleasantness; but it had become the only way to survive. All that mattered was that Barbary needed a home and a substitute mother today, and that for today and probably tomorrow, Margaret could provide her with it.

'I shan't call her Barbary, though,' she said. 'I don't like the name and I don't like the spirit in which Jennifer chose it. I can't unchristen the baby, but I suppose I can call her what I like. Would you mind if she were to become Barbara?'

'I shall leave every decision to you,' said Mr Blakeney. 'And I think that to be a good one. I'm very grateful to you. It's a comfort. Thank you very much.'

Neither of them could truly be comforted, but the decision at least served the purpose of reminding Margaret that other responsibilities were waiting for her and that it was time to pick up the threads of her own life again. Two days after Jennifer had been buried in the same graveyard where once she had sat out boring sermons on the tomb of Barbary Anguish, Margaret took her baby granddaughter back to Blaize.

1918

1

Every night Margaret dreamed that she was drowning.
Sometimes it was the reeds of the Norfolk marshes which
entwined themselves round her ankles and tugged her
under the water as she kicked and struggled. At other
times it was the liquid mud of a battlefield crater which
sucked her down, and then her body seemed not to resist
but merely to stiffen as inch by inch it was drawn below
the surface.

Whichever nightmare it was that attacked her, the
effect was the same. She awoke each morning at four or
five o'clock, drenched in sweat and unwilling to return to
the terrors of sleep. She had been tired enough before,
but now she was exhausted. Piers, concerned for her
health and knowing that she had passed her sixtieth
birthday, more than once suggested that she should retire.
But the German offensive in the spring of 1918, sweeping
again over the Somme battlefield on which Brinsley had
died, seemed about to press the British Army back into
the water. Once more the demand for hospital beds rose
as casualties flooded back from a battleground which was
no longer a place of retrenchment but of retreat. Like
everyone else in England, Margaret read with a feeling
near to despair Field Marshal Haig's grim admonition:
'With our backs to the wall and believing in the justice of
our cause, each one of us must fight to the end.' Defeat
was very close. This was no time to consider retirement.
If her nightmare had any basis in reality, it meant that
she was in danger of drowning in a bottomless sea of
work.

Yet the impression left on her waking mind by the recurrent dream was so strong that when Arthur arrived from Bristol one day in May to break the news that Ralph was dead, it hardly seemed to come as a shock. Her emotions had been numbed by too much bad news. That a man who had spent his whole working life in an unhealthy tropical climate should die at the age of fifty-eight could not be thought of as surprising. Margaret was sad, because she had loved her younger brother dearly, but she was too tired to weep.

'How did it happen?' she asked.

'There's some kind of deep pool in the Hope Valley estate, apparently,' Arthur said. 'A waterfall feeds it from above and a stream trickles out from the edge to pass through the village.'

'I've been there,' said Margaret. 'Ralph called it the Baptist Hole. He used it for baptismal services.' She remembered, though, how she had once crept towards the pool by night and had seen a very different kind of ceremony in progress, an orgy of music and movement which seemed to have come straight from the jungle, surviving the years of slavery without change. For a moment she wondered wildly whether her brother had fallen victim to some pagan rite, but it appeared that the truth was less dramatic.

'There's no doubt, I'm afraid, that he was drinking more and more heavily in this past year. My information comes from Duke Mattison. Brinsley's death must have been a terrible shock, of course, and on top of that Uncle Ralph had convinced himself that Kate must also be dead, since there's been no news of her from Russia.'

'You mean, he fell into the Baptist Hole when he was drunk, and drowned there?'

'It seems so.' Arthur hesitated. 'There are some business aspects of his death to discuss. But no doubt you'd prefer to wait until you've recovered from the main shock before I inflict any others on you.'

Margaret shook her head wearily. 'Tell me it all at once,' she said.

What Arthur had to say came as less of a surprise than he apparently expected. Margaret had never known for a fact that Ralph had had an illegitimate son in Jamaica shortly before his marriage to Lydia, but from his unhappiness at the time and the hints which he had dropped she ought to have guessed – and indeed she had wondered, but had not liked to ask. She remembered how Duke's intelligent face had impressed her on the only occasion when she had met him – and remembered, too, how Kate had praised his head for figures and willingness to work hard.

'I'm glad,' she said. 'It must have been some comfort to Ralph to have the company of one of his sons in those last days. But has he been fair to Grant, Arthur? Duke may deserve to inherit the plantation on the grounds of the work he's put into it, or even because he's the most capable person to manage it. But Grant is a legitimate son and more in need of support.'

'Grant is well enough provided for,' Arthur assured her. 'Uncle Ralph never intended to allow him a share of the plantation – the original intention was that Brinsley should inherit it all. Do you remember that in the first months of the war I invested in a shipbuilding company? Uncle Ralph had funds to spare at that time, the profits of his trading, and asked to be associated with me in the investment, on Grant's behalf. The German submarines have been making his fortune for him – every ship sunk in the Atlantic has needed immediate replacement.'

Margaret found it distasteful that anyone should have made money out of a war which had wrecked so many lives. But Grant himself had no responsibility for what had happened.

'This means that Grant will never go back to Jamaica,' said Arthur. He was warning her, presumably, that she now had no escape from her unofficial adoption, but that was something which Margaret had accepted long ago.

'Perhaps when he's older he could share in the management of this company in which you've invested,' she suggested. 'I remember you intended to make an offer of that kind to Brinsley.'

Arthur shook his head. 'Can't stand the boy. I'm sorry, Aunt Margaret. I don't know what it is about him. Uncle Ralph couldn't bear to have him around, and nor can I. I'll see that his money is well managed until he needs it, and then it can be used to buy him whatever kind of business or estate appeals to him. But not mine.'

'You saw him at his worst,' said Margaret. 'He arrived in England neglected and unhealthy – and made unhappy, naturally, by his mother's death and his father's rejection of him. But come and meet him now. He's a different boy.'

She took her nephew out into the spring sunshine. The early months of the year had been wetter than usual, but May had brought dry weather at last and all the soldiers who were well enough to leave their beds were taking advantage of the spacious grounds. They greeted Margaret as she passed them, and she did not like to move on without a friendly word, so it was a little while before she was able to discover Grant's whereabouts.

He was pushing Barbara's baby carriage up the slope from the river. Her nursemaid walked beside them, but did not need to help. Grant's arms – which he had used for many years as a means of pulling himself about – were exceptionally strong. The operation on his hip had been as successful as could have been hoped: he still walked stiffly, but the surgical boot which added a necessary two inches to his stunted leg was placed as firmly on the ground with each step as the normal boot of the other foot. Not only was he walking with ease and confidence, but he had become much thinner. In the last few months, like any thirteen-year-old boy, he had begun to shoot up in height almost visibly; he had shed the flabby fat which gave him such an unattractive appearance when he first arrived in England.

In addition to the improvement in his physique, the boy's temperament had changed in a way which must surely impress Arthur. Grant was talking to Barbara as he pushed her, pulling funny faces and jigging the baby carriage up and down in an attempt to make her smile. Whether or not the five-month-old baby was responding, Margaret could not see; but certainly Grant was laughing at his own jokes.

Barbara's arrival at Blaize at the turn of the year had gone almost unnoticed by the adults who lived there. Margaret had written in advance to Alexa to discover whether there would be any objection to the presence of another baby in the house, and had received the answer she expected. But Alexa and Piers had been as stunned as Margaret herself by Jennifer's death and the uncertainty about Robert's fate. Their embraces had been reserved for Margaret as she came wearily into the house after her stay in Norfolk; it was the wet nurse who was left to carry Barbara up to the nursery quarters.

So many young lives had been snatched away from Margaret's love and care that she had felt a need to pause before she could commit her emotions yet again. She knew that the baby would be well cared for by little Pirry's nurse. Once a day she paid a routine visit to the nursery and stared for a moment into the cradle. But she had not felt able to lift the baby and cuddle her. For the first time in her life, it seemed, she had lost the ability to show love.

Alexa had never pretended to be interested in any children except her own, and Piers spent most of each week in London. So Barbara was left to the servants – and to the other children of the family. Four-year-old Pirry saw her only as a rival who had caused his expulsion from the nursery to the more disciplined world of the schoolroom, ruled by a governess: while Frisca was too active to be interested in a baby who could not move from her cot. Barbara's first friend in the Lorimer family had been Grant.

'He was very fond of Robert, you know,' Margaret told Arthur as the nursery group moved away up the slope. 'Robert had the knack of teasing him into cheerfulness. So of course the news upset him badly. He doesn't believe that Robert is a prisoner, any more than Jennifer did. When Barbara first came here, he'd sit by her cot for hours, just staring. I suppose he doesn't understand about babies. He must have been trying to see the connection between Robert and Robert's daughter.' It occurred to Margaret even as she spoke that it was time for Grant to be given a little information on such subjects. It was unlikely that Ralph had ever had a fatherly chat with his unloved son. She made a mental note to ask Piers if he would take on that duty, and then continued with her explanation. 'So Grant was one of the familiar faces in the baby's life. When she gave her first smile it was to him, just because he was there. It was his finger she gripped when she began to play. He has a talent, I think, for all-or-nothing devotion. That may be why it took us all so long to make a good relationship with him when he first arrived. He'd been wholly devoted to his mother all his life and he wasn't going to let anyone take her place.'

'And you think he's devoted to Barbara?' Arthur's voice revealed his incredulity.

'I'm sure of it. Oh, he's very fond of me as well. But he's grabbing at Barbara just as he grabbed at Robert. Well, it will be good for both of them. When he first asked me whether he could push her out in the afternoons, I said he'd have to prove to me that he was safe with her, absolutely steady on his feet. Until then he'd been reluctant to admit that his operation had been a success. He still limped around in a very exaggerated way, and wouldn't wear his boot. But when I insisted that the baby carriage must be pushed smoothly, he taught himself to walk normally almost overnight.'

'*Almost* normally.'

'Well, when you consider his state when he arrived

here!' It seemed to Margaret – who regarded the improvement in Grant as a small miracle – that Arthur was being over-critical. 'And it's not just walking. He's become fanatical about getting himself fit. He goes to the exercise classes that we run for the men. And he's asked Piers to let him ride. He's still on a leading rein at the moment, but if he can really learn to grip with his knees he'll bring back into use all the muscles which must almost have wasted away while he was a child.'

For a moment she was cheerful. Then she remembered that she had now to break the news to Grant that his father was dead. Probably he would not care greatly, but Margaret cared on her own account. Arthur seemed to understand her sudden silence. He refused her invitation to stay the night and left her to her memories.

The wooded slope between Blaize and the river was too steep for most of the convalescent soldiers to tackle. Margaret made her way there, hoping to be undisturbed. May was the month in which the azaleas were at their best. One of the patients, shell-shocked and silent, had devoted himself all winter to the task of clearing the winding stream and the azalea walk from the mud and weeds which had threatened to choke them after the last of Lord Glanville's gardeners had been conscripted. Margaret sat down beside the water which was once again flowing cleanly along its path of flat grey stones and tried to think about Ralph.

The ipicture was too confused. There seemed no way of reconciling the golden young man, confident and handsome in the white braided blazer of a schoolboy Captain of Cricket, with Ralph as she had last seen him, thin and stooping in a shabby black suit, his eyes wrinkled against the sun. And since that time his burdens had grown even heavier. He should have died sooner, Margaret thought to herself; before Lydia's death – and certainly before Brinsley's.

Yet when Brinsley had died, it had seemed too soon.

Had they been wrong, Margaret asked herself suddenly, to feel so much sadness and regret for a life cut short? Brinsley, like his father, had been a golden boy – but Brinsley would never be tired and old and disillusioned, wondering whether his life's work had been worth while. He had always thought of himself as lucky. When Margaret considered her brother's life, and when she looked at some of her patients – alive, but facing years of pain and dependence – it was difficult not to wonder whether perhaps Brinsley's luck had held after all. Death was a disaster only for those who were left behind.

She could persuade herself, no doubt, not to mourn too much for Ralph, who in his last months had been lonely and without hope. But it was impossible to carry the thought to its logical conclusion and hope that Robert was no longer suffering: that he was dead, not sharing the pain she felt on his behalf. She had begun by feeling sad about her brother's death; but by the time she arose to walk back to the house her thoughts had returned, as they always returned, to her missing son.

Someone was calling her name. She heard it faintly while she was still in the woods, and then more loudly as she stepped out into the open. It was possible to recognize Lord Glanville's voice, although she could not see him; and the sound startled her. Piers was not a man who shouted. Nor did he ever use her Christian name in public. In private they had been close friends for many years, but in the world of the hospital she was always Dr Scott. Margaret began to hurry, fearful that some accident had occurred to Alexa or one of the children.

She saw him hurrying up the paved path from the theatre ward; he must have been to look for her there. In his hand was a card which he waved in the air as soon as he caught sight of her. That was another departure from the norm. Even in these days when formality had almost disappeared, letters were carried by servants. Margaret froze into stillness. She refused to allow her mind to think or guess; and as though in sympathy, her body ceased for a moment to breathe.

He came towards her and it seemed that he was no more able to speak than she was. Without allowing her a chance to look at the message he held, he took her into his arms, almost crushing her in the tightness of his embrace.

How could she share his emotion when she still did not know whether the tears in his eyes were of sorrow or joy? She struggled to pull his arm away, to take the card from his hand. Then it was her turn to feel the tears flooding into her eyes. The postcard – printed and formal, except for a blank space in which a name had been written in ink – was little more informative than the telegram which had arrived five months earlier. But it provided the only piece of information that mattered.

Captain Robert Charles Scott was not dead, but a prisoner of war.

2

Almost every month some new messenger arrived from Moscow; to announce a new decree, to investigate the working of an old one, to explain some aspect of Bolshevik policy, to make it clear that the blame for the poor harvest of 1918, and the consequent food shortage, must be squarely placed on the shoulders of the peasants, who had generously been given land and had responded with indolence and selfishness instead of free-handed gratitude. The orator on this occasion had been sent by the Commissar for War.

That was all Kate knew as she hurried to the September meeting, a little late because of an emergency in the operating theatre and so tired that she wanted only to sleep. But she knew that her absence would be noted by the soviet of the military hospital to which she had been attached since disbanding her own medical unit a year earlier. In any case, there had been rumours that Commissar Trotsky himself was in the area. He was known to be touring the country in his armoured train, recruiting for the Red Army. Since the assassination of Uritsky and the shots which wounded Lenin, all Trotsky's appearances were made without advance warning. But stories of the Red Terror had reached even this remote part of Russia and Kate was curious to see the man who was presumed to be responsible for the shooting of so many prisoners and hostages.

As soon as she opened the door, however, she knew that the speaker was not Comrade Trotsky. Even if the empty sleeve of his greatcoat had not given her the clue, she could not have failed to recognize the voice which had taught her to speak Russian. Sergei's pale yellow-grey complexion was even less healthy than before and his fanatically glittering eyes had sunk even more deeply into their black sockets, but his intensity of manner and shabbiness of appearance had not changed at all.

He recognized her with equal speed. His eyes, drawn by the movement of her late entry, fixed her for a moment with their hypnotic gleam. But he did not allow himself to be distracted from his theme; and that was directed to the men, not to her. He was describing the atrocities perpetrated by the White Army, the intention of its generals to restore land to the old nobility if they won, the need for all who were faithful to the spirit of the revolution to join the Red Army and fight both the enemy within the country and the invaders from outside.

When the meeting was at an end, Sergei asked a quiet question of the chairman of the soviet, who looked around and pointed out Kate. There was another brief discussion, and then an announcement that Comrade Gorbatov wished to speak to the Comrade Doctor. Kate deduced from this that Sergei had not admitted that he even knew who the doctor was, much less that they were old friends. In the current atmosphere of suspicion and betrayal, she found this disquieting; and she could see the same uneasiness in Vladimir's eyes as he watched her follow the speaker out.

At their parting, Sergei had kissed her. For two years Kate had remembered him with affection, but now she did not know how to approach him. She had seen too many personal relationships snap under the strain of divided political loyalties. She waited: and so, for a moment, did he. Then he laughed.

'So you have remained faithful to your Serbs, foolish one.'

'There are not many of them left,' Kate said. 'Those who survived the second retreat were badly treated. When the officers of the Russian divisions found that they could no longer rely on their men to obey orders without mutinying, they used the Serbs instead to take the force of the German attack – but without doing them the favour of giving them any weapons. Yet later, when the death penalty was abolished and the Russians began to desert to their home villages, the Serbs were forced to stay in the line because they had nowhere to go.'

'I'm delighted to hear you speak so fluently. I was a good teacher, was I not? But the words you use are bitter.'

'I'm speaking of the past,' said Kate. 'Like everyone else, I hope for better things in the future. Are you having success in building your new army?'

'It goes well, yes. The difficulty is in finding officers. We're having to recruit from amongst the officers of the old Imperial Army.'

'I thought most of them were in hiding.'

'This is their opportunity to emerge. Those who don't take advantage of it will proclaim themselves as enemies of the people. There will be no second chance.'

Kate was careful to keep her voice under control so

that Sergei could not guess her personal interest in the subject. 'And do you find them reliable?' she asked.

'Every unit of the army is to have its own political commissar, who will soon report any disloyalty. And of course, not all officers are equally welcome. If any of the old nobility expect to obtain an amnesty in this way, they very soon discover that they are mistaken.'

'How do you mean?' asked Kate.

'We shoot them. Except in a few cases – of men who handed over all their land and property to the people voluntarily, right at the beginning, before it became impossible for them to do anything else.'

Kate felt that her sudden pallor must be too visible for Sergei to ignore; and now that she had heard what she feared she was anxious to change the subject as quickly as possible. But it seemed that her old friend had his own anxieties.

'You shouldn't be here, you know. You should have gone long ago, while it was still possible. You could be in great danger.'

'Why?' asked Kate. 'I mean, I've been in danger almost without pause for three years now. Why should this be any worse?'

'The news isn't generally known outside Moscow and Petrograd,' Sergei said, 'but the Intervention is becoming more serious. The British have landed troops at Vladivostok and Murmansk. That's too far away for them to give any protection to you. But their presence on Russian soil is bound to stir up great anti-British feeling. In fact, hatred of foreigners has become Party policy. We have no choice.'

'I speak Russian all the time,' said Kate. 'I have a Russian name. Nobody knows that I'm British.'

'Your Serbs know.'

'They would never betray me.'

'You can never be quite sure. It only needs one. By mistake, even – mentioning the English doctor when he

265

thinks no one is listening. Would you leave if I could find a way? It may be too late already. The French and British have both sent warships to take off some of their own people: I doubt if there will be a second chance. But if I could find a route, would you go?'

'If what you say is true, you would surely be putting yourself in danger by helping a foreigner.'

Sergei smiled. 'Do you remember that I once saved your life?' he asked.

'Oh, Sergei, how could I ever forget!'

'Well then, when a man saves someone's life he's responsible for that person for ever.'

'Sergei!' They were both laughing with happiness as they embraced. 'I couldn't be sure – I didn't want to get you into trouble.'

'I'm the one who gets people into trouble,' he said. 'You may trust me not to be sentimental. But of course what makes the decision easier in this case is that I know you have never been an enemy of the people. Will you go?'

Kate needed a moment longer to think, and it was a reminder of the new barriers which had sprung up between friends that she could not afford to let Sergei know what she was thinking. She would not go without her husband, and in the eyes of a Bolshevik Vladimir would undoubtedly be an enemy of the people. They could try to deceive Sergei – but the documents which were adequate to support Vladimir's identity in a place where he was established with no reason to arouse suspicion might not stand up to the more detailed investigation which the issuing of a passport would involve.

'No,' she said. 'You are kind, as you have always been kind to me. But I believe in the new society as passionately as you do. I'm a Russian now. And soon I shall be the mother of a Russian as well.'

'Ah!' he said. He drew away and looked at her more closely. 'And I thought you were wearing three overcoats to keep out the cold. The father is Russian, then, not Serbian?'

'Yes.'

He thought again. 'It's still my opinion that you aren't safe here. You should go to some place where you aren't known. As a doctor you can make yourself useful anywhere. If I may speak without immodesty, your speech is a credit to my teaching. You can pass for Russian as long as no one has any cause to suspect that you are not. I'll give you a travel permit. No journey is safe now, I'm afraid. If the train is stopped by bandits, you'll have to hope for your pregnancy to protect you. If the line's cut by the Whites, I suppose it might be worth while to reveal your nationality. The British are supposed to be supporting them, after all. This authorization will only serve if it's the Cheka who stop you.'

'I should want my husband to travel with me,' said Kate firmly.

'Greedy, greedy.' But Sergei was smiling. He sat down and opened the briefcase he carried, taking out a selection of papers and rubber stamps. 'You'd better have an official posting to another military hospital, in order to keep your ration entitlement. What's your husband's name?'

'Vassily Petrovich Belinsky.'

'And occupation?'

'Anaesthetist.'

Sergei laughed in incredulity. 'You have been able to get anaesthetics for your hospital?'

'No,' said Kate, joining in his laughter, although with a trace of bitterness. 'Not any longer. His function now is to hold the patient down while I operate.'

'There'll be fewer problems in keeping you together if we choose something less specialized,' said Sergei. 'Medical assistant should do.' He scribbled and stamped for a few minutes before considering again. 'I'll send you to Petrograd,' he said. 'I don't recommend that you stay there too long. The food shortages are worst in the big cities. But it's the best place to establish a new identity, and it's a place where doctors are badly needed. After a year or so you could move on to somewhere smaller if you wanted to – Novgorod, perhaps – and settle down. There you are, then. I'll tell the chairman of your soviet that I've transferred you, but I won't say where you're going. You need to muddy your tracks if you're to be safe.'

'Thank you. Thank you very much. And Sergei – I am so very glad for you, that you've been able to return to your own country. I know how much it always meant to you.'

'You were kind to me when I was an exile,' he reminded her. 'I don't forget that. I only hope that you won't regret cutting yourself off from your country and your family.'

'From each according to his ability; to each according to his need,' quoted Kate. 'I believed that, you know, long before I ever came to Russia. I can see the need here, and I have the ability to help. Shall we meet again, Sergei?'

He shrugged his shoulders. 'It's a big country – even after the Brest-Litovsk Treaty. But I shall know where you are, at least to start with. And if you are in any trouble, you can write to me in Moscow. Cautiously, of course – other people will read the letter. In the meantime, I wish you all happiness.'

'And you, Sergei.' They embraced for a second time before Kate went off to find Vladimir.

'I wish it were anywhere but Petrograd,' she said, when she had told him of Sergei's fears for her safety. 'There must still be people there who know you. But I dared not risk raising difficulties, in case he should ask too many questions.'

'I doubt if I could be recognized with my beard and shabby uniform,' he said. 'And we shall hardly be moving in the same social circles as before. What worries me more is the danger of the train journey to the baby. It's difficult to believe now that there was once a time when a journey on a Russian train was the most luxurious form of travel in the world. I'm afraid we're going to find it very different now.'

3

There were people on the roof of the train and people travelling on its outside steps. Kate looked at the jostling crowd on the station platform and at the packed wagons which were drawing to a halt beside it and saw no possibility of finding a place. She felt Vladimir's strong fingers gripping her arm.

'Hold on to my shoulders and follow me,' he said. 'Don't let anyone push in between us. Now!'

He thrust forward towards the nearest wagon door. Those who were already on the train did their best to push the new passengers away, whilst those at the back of the platform pressed forward. More frightened than she had ever been in the middle of a battle – since now it was her baby that was at risk – Kate longed to use her arms to protect herself. The pressure was so great that she could hardly breathe and it was difficult not to panic. All her self-control was needed to obey Vladimir's instructions in the five-minute struggle which seemed to last for ever.

The wagon was divided into compartments and the sides of each compartment were fitted from floor to ceiling with sleeping shelves. The compartment into which Vladimir eventually forced an entrance already held at least a hundred people, instead of its official maximum of thirty. There were three or four people on each shelf and the floor between was stacked with bundles and baggage. Vladimir looked quickly round and discovered a top shelf which was occupied by only three people. Ignoring their loud protests that there was no room for more, he hauled Kate up to join them, himself standing on the edge of one of the lower shelves to make sure that she did not fall from her precarious perch. Kate, breathless and bruised, listened to the thumping of her heart and was frightened again, but her anxiety for the baby came to her rescue. She forced herself to relax, to breathe deeply and lie as still as though she were sleeping. Still grumbling, but accepting the presence of an intruder, the old woman beside her allowed her a few more inches of the shelf.

The first struggle might be over, but the discomforts of the journey had only just begun. It was impossible to move. Even after twelve hours had passed it seemed risky to produce what food they had managed to carry with them, in case it should be snatched away by their hungry fellow-passengers. The few windows of the wagon were tightly sealed against the cold outside and the atmosphere became steadily more stifling. The smell was appalling. All the travellers were dirty and a good many of them were visibly verminous. They spat, they smoked and they urinated. How long, Kate wondered, would it take to reach Petrograd?

Her defence was to retreat into what was almost a trance, removing her mind from her body so that she could feel peace instead of disgust. Occasionally she was aware of Vladimir's hand stroking her cheek or his lips softly kissing hers, but she did not speak. The train crawled on across the huge sub-continent.

From time to time it came to a halt. This might mean that it had arrived at a station, but the density of bodies within each wagon was such that it was impossible for anyone else to enter. Once – or so the rumour came down the length of the train – it was because there was no more fuel to fire the engine; all the passengers at the front had been ordered out to chop wood from the forest.

270

If Kate strained her head downward she could see out of one of the windows, but there was little variety in the view – sometimes an unbroken sheet of snow, stretching to the horizon; sometimes a dark forest, equally silent and uninhabited. Sometimes the moon was shining and sometimes there was daylight, but she made no attempt to keep track of the passage of time.

She was asleep in the middle of an afternoon when the train stopped yet again, but this time with a shuddering jolt which aroused and alarmed all the passengers. All of them were well aware of the various dangers of which Sergei had warned Kate. So many different armed bands were at large that no one could feel safe.

The door was opened from outside. Kate's first feeling was one of relief as the foetid atmosphere was disturbed at last by a shaft of air which was icy cold but so clear that its invasion of the wagon was visible. She breathed deeply through the scarf which she had pulled across her mouth, but at the same time listened with anxiety to the shouted commands coming from near the front of the train. More sinister still, there was the sound of gunfire; somebody screamed.

'Who is it? Who is it?' Everyone was calling to those nearest the door. The answer was brief and sinister.

'Cheka!'

A wave of fear swept through the passengers. The Cheka was supposed to be on the side of the peasants and proletarians and only against the bourgeoisie and what was left of the nobility, but there was no one who had not heard stories of the Red Terror, of hostages taken and executed, of innocent men shot merely as an example to others. And there were few people – even amongst the poor – who could feel sure that they were not offending against one of the new regulations which flooded out of the Bolshevik headquarters. It was generally known that anyone who denied carrying firearms and was then found in possession of a revolver would be shot immediately; but Kate detected a feeling of terror in the old lady lying beside her as someone else on the same shelf shouted a reminder that it was against the law now to possess more than two of any article of clothing.

Kate had more reason than her neighbour to be nervous. She had been told often enough that she spoke Russian with sufficient fluency to persuade anyone who had no grounds to suspect otherwise that she was indeed Russian, although he might presume that she must come from a different district from him – the huge Russian state contained so many nationalities that there was necessarily a wide variation of dialects and accents, especially amongst those for whom Russian was a second language. But it would be impossible for her to sustain a plausible identity under interrogation by somebody who was looking for irregularities, and Sergei's warning about the danger of being British had been a valid one. Nor was she anxious only on her own behalf. Vladimir, like any other aristocrat, had been brought up to speak French, with English as his second language, so he, like Kate, had learned Russian only as a foreign tongue. And he too would have difficulty in producing acceptable answers if his life before the Revolution was investigated too closely. His identity papers were those of an Estonian, and any interrogator from that area would realize immediately that he had no right to them. He and Kate were equally at risk. Their only hope was to remain inconspicuous, two anonymous and insignificant figures in a crowd.

Vladimir had scrambled towards the door when it opened, in order to look outside. Now he climbed back again and spoke quietly into her ear so that no one else could hear.

'Groan,' he said, and repeated the command urgently as Kate looked puzzled. 'Groan. As though the baby were coming. As though your labour had started.'

Kate did as she was told, moaning faintly to begin with and then panting more loudly. She was not clear what the

272

purpose of the charade was. The baby was not due for several months and she could not produce it now merely to create a diversion. She continued to groan, though, as Vladimir muttered to the old lady beside her that his wife's time was approaching, that he must go and see whether there were a doctor anywhere on the train, just in case one should be needed. Kate grabbed at his hand.

'You're not really going to leave me.'

'Listen,' he said. Once again his lips were close to her ear. 'When the Red Guards come, you groan again. You don't speak. Whatever happens, you don't say anything. The old lady will tell them what the trouble is. They won't do anything to help, but your travel papers are in order so with any luck they'll leave you alone.'

'But why won't you be here?'

'They're calling all the men of military age off the train to have their papers checked,' said Vladimir. 'You're not to worry. It will be all right, of course. But just in case anything goes wrong, you mustn't be associated with me. I'll step out from a different compartment.'

'No!' exclaimed Kate. Too frightened to be cautious, she tried to sit up, but Vladimir held her down.

'As a couple, we could make them suspicious. Separately, we can get away with it. I'll be further down the train, and I'll be watching. I shan't let them take you off. That's a promise. If there's really trouble, I'll come back to you. But there won't be trouble.'

'But suppose – oh, dearest, suppose they take *you* off, to join the Red Army. It might happen. Sergei said there was compulsory recruitment.'

'It wouldn't be the end of the world. It would give me a better set of papers when I was discharged. I'd come back to you.'

'Where? How should we ever meet again?'

'Ssh!' The warning was necessary, for Kate's voice was rising as her fear increased. She could tell, though, that Vladimir recognized the difficulty as a serious one.

'Listen, then,' he said. 'If we're both on the train when it moves off, then I shall see you at the station at Petrograd. If I'm taken off, you must go first to the hospital and take up your post there. I'll know where to find you. But when the time comes for the baby to be born, go to Tsarskoe Selo. I expect it's called something else now that the Tsar is dead, but you'll find it. It's not too far from Petrograd. We had a theatre palace there. We'll use that as a rendezvous. Not the palace itself, of course; it was looted in the February Revolution. But there's a lodge by the south gate. The lodgekeeper's wife was my wet nurse. Two years ago I would have trusted her with my life. Now, one can't be quite sure. Take it carefully. You should be able to find out whether she's loyal to the family, whether she'd help you to care for my baby. If you're doubtful, protect yourself by saying that you were seduced and deserted. Beside the gate of that lodge there's a hollow tree. I used to put messages there when I was a boy. That's where I'll look for a letter from you, to tell me where you are and who can be trusted. If I get there first, I'll leave the same information for you.'

'Vladimir, I want to stay with you. Please don't leave me.'

'I'm a danger to you,' he said. 'And to our child.' He put his hand gently on her abdomen to feel the movement of the baby. 'I love you, Katya. I'll love you till the day I die. Be brave just for a little while. We'll be together very soon, I promise. But if the baby is born before I can come, sing him the lullaby I composed for him. I shall be able to hum it in my own head and think of the two of you together. Now, remember to groan.'

Not gently, but passionately this time, he kissed her again. She clung to him, still unwilling to let him go. As he released himself from her grip he muttered something about the doctor to anyone who might be listening, and then climbed down to the floor and swung himself outside.

Kate had hardly needed the reminder to groan,

although it was fear rather than pain which caused her fists to clench and her eyes to flood with tears. But she was sufficiently in control of herself to know that at all costs she must refrain from making a fuss. It might be true that Vladimir saw himself as a danger to her, but certainly she was a danger to him. He had told her not to speak, and she must obey his instructions for his sake as well as her own.

The search of the train took several hours. When it came to the turn of Kate's wagon, all the men in it were ordered out. Kate counted that almost forty jumped down from the door. By the time the engine had begun to hiss again, and the shouting outside to take on a different note, only seven of the forty had returned. It was possible to move now, for in addition to the absence of so many travellers, much of the baggage had been hauled off the train. Stiff after the long period of immobility, Kate climbed down from her shelf and leaned out of the doorway.

The Cheka had made a good haul. A long line of men was tramping away from the train under armed guard. But a few remained behind, sprawled in the snow, the victims of execution without trial. Fighting hysteria, Kate strained her eyes in an attempt to recognize Vladimir amongst the group of living men. But the distance was too great and the unwilling conscripts were all dressed much alike.

Two of the Red Guards came running down the length of the train. Kate was pushed roughly inside in order that the door might be slammed and locked. The engine gave a piercing signal and began to move, carrying its cargo of silent or wailing passengers on towards Petrograd. Kate was one of the silent ones, dry-eyed again after the panic which had almost overwhelmed her. Even more than before she could sympathize with the helplessness which Vladimir had felt in the first weeks of the Revolution, when he found himself condemned by his birth to be an outsider in the new society. In her case it was nationality which was likely to prove more important in the eyes of strangers than all the sympathy she felt for the downtrodden people of Russia, and she was angry as well as upset at the way in which the landing of British troops at a port hundreds of miles away had forced her to keep quiet when she ought to have been able to protest, to cry, to cling to her husband.

As the train thrust steadily on, she stared out of the window at the empty countryside. The first snow had fallen in the previous week, covering the vast plains which stretched to the horizon. Its smooth surface was unbroken here, so different from the area around the train's stopping place which had been churned up and spattered with blood. She felt utterly alone in this enormous, uncaring country. How would she ever find Vladimir again? She tried to persuade herself that he was on the train, not daring to return to her under the eyes of the Cheka; but in her heart she did not believe it. What she could manage to hope was that his papers had been good enough to protect him from the fate of those who had been shot out of hand.

When the train at last reached Petrograd she was faint with hunger and anxiety and lack of fresh air. Hauling out her baggage, she sat down on it without regard to the chaotic movement and shouting all round. For an hour she waited to hear her name called or feel Vladimir's hand on her shoulder, but he did not come. It was scarcely a disappointment; only a confirmation of the fears which she had already been forced to accept.

She allowed no sign of emotion to show on her face. If anyone noticed her, it must only be as a pregnant woman, tired after a long journey, resting or waiting to be collected. But inside her head, silently, she was screaming.

At last, bringing her panic under control for the third time, she rose to her feet and picked up her bags, consoling herself with the reminder that they had had time to arrange a rendezvous. Russia had become a country of forced partings, but this parting need not be for ever. She knew what to do, and she must do it. Exhausted and unhappy though she was, Kate picked up her baggage and began to make her way towards the hospital.

4

The speed with which the war changed direction in the autumn of 1918 took almost everyone by surprise. At one moment the Allies were on the verge of defeat; almost at the next, their armies were once again pressing forward. There were rumours of a new weapon, the tank, which would transform battle tactics once its mechanical unreliability had been overcome. More certainly, there was a promise that five million American soldiers would be sent to Europe in 1919, and the advance force which arrived in time to take part in the new offensive had a value out of all proportion to its numbers, bringing healthy and bright-eyed young men to a continent whose own youth were dazed or dead.

By October the Turks had been defeated and the Bulgarians had surrendered. Even without victory on the Western Front, a way into Austria and Germany had been opened through the back door. Little by little Margaret allowed herself to hope. A hospital in a prisoner-of-war camp must be as safe a place as anywhere on the Continent. One day, and perhaps quite soon, Robert would come home.

In the meantime there was no relaxation in the pressure of work at Blaize, for a new problem had arisen. England had been invaded not by the German Army but by an enemy more difficult to fight. No cannons or machine guns could hold back the advance of the influenza epidemic. It had taken the lives of sixteen million Indians, it had swept across the Near East and had reached France earlier in the summer. Now it crossed the Channel and, on a scale comparable with that of a battle, began to claim the lives of civilians whose resistance had been lowered by the shortages of food.

The patients at Blaize, weakened by their wounds and the amputations which many of them had suffered, were especially at risk. Margaret saw the danger and did her best to divide the long ward in the converted theatre and introduce barrier nursing procedures in the hope that any infection could be contained. It was a further burden of work on someone who had been under strain for so long. Although only too well aware that the disease was a killing one, she felt almost relief when after two days of indisposition she awoke one morning to find her body heated to fever pitch and her head swimming with dizziness. Now at last she could shed all her responsibilities and lie back to sleep.

In her illness she was more fortunate than most victims of the epidemic, for there were trained nurses on hand to care for her. The time came when she was able to stare up at the ceiling, too weak to move but cool and comfortable for the first time since the attack began, and confident that the worst was over. She accepted a drink of hot milk. Within a few hours she even began to feel hungry.

'What day is it?' she asked as the tray was brought and she was propped up on pillows to receive it.

'Sunday, Doctor.' The nurse sat down to help her eat, for she hardly had the strength to lift a spoon.

'Then Lord Glanville will be at Blaize, I imagine. Will you tell him how much better I am?' No doubt he had come to sit beside her during her illness, but she had been conscious only of a confusion of comings and goings and could not recall who her visitors were. It was too soon for any of the children to be admitted to her sick room, but she looked forward to showing her brother-in-law that she was on the way to recovery, and to hearing all the news of the family and the hospital.

'Lord Glanville isn't here, I'm afraid, Doctor. He's in London.'

That was a surprise. It was true that within the last month or two, as peace came into prospect at last, Piers had spent more time at the House of Lords. Political life was beginning to revive. Lloyd George had united the country behind the single aim of winning the war, but once it was won the parties could be expected to separate again, each with its own policies. Lord Glanville had never been a member of the government, but he was politically active. The campaign to allow women the vote, which was one of his chief interests, had achieved its first great success earlier in the year, but there were other battles to be fought. Younger women were still excluded from the suffrage, and a whole range of social problems would need to be solved if peace were not to bring as much hardship as war.

So although most of the house in Park Lane had been closed for the past four years, with its staff dispersed and its furniture under dust covers, one chilly bedroom in Glanville House had been kept open for his use, with a cook to prepare any meals which he did not wish to take at his club. For some months now he had been spending only one day a week at Blaize – but that day was Sunday, so that Margaret's hope of seeing him had been a reasonable one.

'And Lady Glanville?' she asked instead.

'She's in London as well.'

That was even more of a surprise. None of the concerts which Alexa organized for soldiers in their camps or hospitals ever took place on a Sunday. The nurse, seeing her puzzlement, began to talk in an ill-concealed attempt to change the subject. The war was almost over, she said.

279

The Germans had appealed for an armistice and the terms were being negotiated at that moment.

Perhaps it was not such a change of subject after all. If events were really moving with such rapidity, Alexa might be preparing to reopen Glanville House. Margaret lay back again in the bed and tried to imagine a world at peace.

She had fallen ill in October; it was November by the time she recovered. The fog which shrouded the river valley imprisoned her in her room even when she was ready for the stimulus of fresh air and exercise. She was still confined to the house when the chief physician of the hospital brought in a letter.

'Lady Glanville asked me to give you this, but not until I considered that you were strong enough.'

Alexa's message was a brief one, written from Glanville House.

'Piers is very ill. Come if you can.'

Margaret looked at her colleague, who answered the question before it was asked.

'It's the influenza again, the same that attacked you. But unlike you – '

'Are you trying to tell me that he's dying?'

'Lady Glanville wrote to me by the same post. She's very much alarmed by his condition.'

'How long have you had the letter?'

'Two days. If you'd left the house in that fog, it would have killed you. Even as it is – '

Margaret wasted no time in arguing. Dressed in her warmest clothes, she set out at once for London.

Even before the cab which carried her from the station had come to a standstill she knew that she was too late. The curtains of Glanville House were drawn and outside in the road a boy was sweeping up the straw which had been laid in front of the house to muffle the sound of traffic. She sat without moving until the cab driver realized that his passenger was too weak to walk and rang the front door bell for a servant to help her.

Alexa came into the drawing room as she sat there, still shocked, shivering in spite of her heavy coat. For a little while neither of them could speak or move. When at last Alexa broke the spell and began to pace the room, her voice was bitter rather than brokenhearted.

'When I think of the years I wasted!' she exclaimed. 'We had such a short time together, and it could have been so much longer. I was a fool to send him away when he first asked me to marry him. And even before that, when I was singing in Italy – he may not have said in so many words what he felt for me, but I knew. I knew all the time, right from the moment his wife died. And I kept him away all that time. Eight years, Margaret, that's all we had together; only eight years, when it might have been twenty.'

Margaret's own marriage had lasted for only a few months, and the years of separation from Charles which preceded it had been made necessary by the complications of her family history rather than her own waywardness. There had been a time, too, when she had loved Piers herself and found it difficult not to resent his infatuation with the beautiful young singer who seemed not to care for him at all. But this was not the time to admit any feeling of jealousy to her heart. The man who had died had been loved by both of them; but although Margaret had lost her closest friend, only Alexa was widowed by the death. Margaret did her best to provide some kind of consolation, reminding Alexa that at least during those eight years of marriage she had brought her husband great happiness. Yet there was nothing she could say which would provide real comfort. The evening was filled with silences, until in the end they took their separate sorrows early to bed.

The next morning there were decisions to be made. Alexa was as a rule more practical and businesslike than might have been expected of a prima donna, but now she was numbed not only by the shock of bereavement but also by the sudden realization of the huge responsibilities she would have to shoulder until her son was old enough to take over the Glanville estates. It was Margaret who decided that the funeral should be held at Blaize and who made all the necessary arrangements – and for the printing of cards, the wording of newspaper announcements, the listing of friends and political allies who must be informed, the planning of a memorial service in London later. In a way it was a relief to concentrate on the mechanical decisions which were so unimportant compared with the loss of her dear friend. She was not aware of the passing of time, and it was only when she paused to shake her chilled fingers back into life that she realized how dark the afternoon had grown without the appearance of luncheon.

Alexa had been too upset to give domestic orders, no doubt, and Margaret herself had not yet recovered her appetite since her illness, so the omission was of no importance. But later she rang for a servant to post her cards, and no one came. Yet Alexa, she knew, had summoned staff from Blaize as soon as she realized that her husband was too ill to be moved to the country. Margaret rang the bell again.

It was answered at last by a young girl. She had been left behind to do anything that was needed, she explained with a trace of sulkiness, while the others were out celebrating.

'Celebrating!' For one horrified moment Margaret, unable to think of anyone but Piers, assumed that for some ghoulish reason the servants were rejoicing in the death of their master. The girl noticed her incredulity and was surprised by it in turn. Then an explanation occurred to her.

'You've heard the news, I suppose, ma'am,' she said. 'At eleven o'clock this morning it happened. The war's over.'

'No,' said Margaret. 'I hadn't heard. I see. Thank you. Post these letters straightaway, please.'

After the girl had gone she walked across to the window. Drawing the curtain slightly to one side, she looked over Park Lane to Hyde Park. It was dark by now. A bonfire was burning in the park. Round it danced a circle of people, hands linked, while others searched the ground for wood to throw on the flames. The street, too, was full of people, all pressing towards Buckingham Palace. There seemed to be a great deal of hugging and kissing going on. Not everyone in the crowd was completely sober.

Margaret allowed the curtain to drop again and tried to open her heart to happiness. This was the moment they had awaited so long. For more than four years the phrase 'after the war' had summed up every future pleasure, every future hope. And now, it seemed, the moment had come. 'After the war' had arrived. Why was it, then, that she found it impossible to feel any pleasure, any hope – impossible, in fact, to feel anything at all?

She had waited too long and lost too much. 'After the war' had been a time to enjoy with those she most loved, and where were they now? Lydia was dead, Ralph was dead, Brinsley was dead, Kate had disappeared, and now Piers was dead as well.

A series of bangs came from the direction of the park, startling Margaret by its resemblance to gunfire. She looked out again and guessed that children were throwing fire crackers on to the bonfire. It was going to be a noisy night.

Disturbed by the sound, Alexa came down from her bedroom. She had been crying. Margaret moved to one side so that she could see out of the window.

'The war's over,' she said.

'When?'

'Seven hours ago. Odd, isn't it, that it should just slip away. One had imagined something dramatic happening. But in France, I suppose – '

In France there would be silence. At eleven o'clock

that morning the guns would have ceased to spit out death; by now the ground would have stopped trembling. Tired men would fall asleep that night and expect to wake in the morning. The change was dramatic enough for them. Margaret's present sadness was in one sense a selfish one. War or no war, men in their sixties were liable to fall ill and die. That was no consolation, but she could not expect the whole world to mourn with her. The people in the streets outside were quite right to sing and dance. The years of partings had come to an end at last. Grant and Frisca and Pirry and Barbara would grow up without needing to know the anguish of saying goodbye to someone who might never return.

And Robert would come home. There was no need to be frightened for him any more. The war was over.

PART TWO
The Aftermath

1919

1

The rumour that the war was over in Europe reached
Kate early in 1919, three weeks before her baby was due.
There had been similar rumours before, but this one was
slower than the others to fade. At one time she would
have greeted the news with thankful relief, but now it
seemed more likely to increase the danger which would
face her if her nationality were discovered. Both in
Petrograd itself and in the Butyrky prison in Moscow a
number of Englishwomen were under arrest for no crime
other than that of being English. It was just conceivable
that the allied powers which had provided troops for the
Intervention might use the armistice as an excuse to
withdraw. But far more likely was the probability that
with the Germans defeated they would throw an even
stronger force into the battle against Bolshevism – and at
the same time the German surrender would increase the
bitterness of those within Russia who believed that Lenin
and the other Bolsheviks had conceded an unacceptable
amount of Russian territory in the Brest-Litovsk Treaty.
So the civil war was likely not only to continue but to
increase in bitterness.

That meant that there could be no hope yet of Vladimir's return. Because the alternative was unthinkable,
Kate had succeeded in persuading herself that he, like
most of the other male passengers on the train, had
become a conscript in the Red Army. He would have
been careful not to do anything which would single him
out from the others or suggest that he had once been a
Tsarist officer. There was no reason why he should be in

any greater danger than any other soldier; but she could not expect the western armistice to secure his release.

Once that fact was clear in her mind, Kate realized that it was time for her to leave Petrograd and establish herself at the second rendezvous which Vladimir had suggested, near the home of his old nurse. There was in any case another good reason for leaving – that if she did not make the journey soon, she might be too weak ever to embark on it. She had not yet reached the point of starvation, but like everyone else in Petrograd she was fast approaching it. The granaries of the steppes and the orchards of the Crimea had been cut off from the city by an exceptionally hard winter. Shortage of fuel meant that few trains even began the long journeys needed to bring in supplies, and bandits and Cossacks alike ambushed and plundered whatever stocks did move. The smaller estates nearer to Petrograd had suffered from the disruption caused when the peasants divided into smallholdings the land confiscated from the nobles, but proved incapable of raising more than subsistence crops.

For six weeks now, Kate had lived almost exclusively on a diet of boiled rye gruel and a thin fish soup made from herring heads – no one was able to discover where the more edible part of the herrings went. It was not a diet which she would have recommended to an expectant mother. For the sake of the baby, if for no other reason, Kate saw that it would be wise to leave. In the country at least there would be firewood to provide a little warmth, and it was bitterly assumed in the city that in defiance of orders the peasants had hoarded the cabbages and potatoes and were secretly cooking and eating them.

With the decision made, Kate applied for leave, slightly exaggerating the imminence of the expected birth. It took little time to pack up her few possessions. For weeks looters had been roaming the city, ensuring that no one any longer owned more than he could keep in his own hands. Kate possessed only two treasures. Into the waistband of her skirt she had sewn the ring which Vladimir had given her after their marriage; it was the only jewel he had dared to take with him when he fled from his palace. With less concealment she carried her bag of surgical instruments. For the rest, when the time of her departure arrived she wore every article of clothing she owned and strapped a bedding roll on to her back. Ponderously huge, she left without regret her quarter share of the icy room which had been allocated to her by the hospital soviet and climbed on to one of the trams which was still running between high walls of snow.

It was a journey into an uncertain future. As Vladimir had expected, the village of Tsarskoe Selo had changed its name after the murder of the Tsar and his family, but she had discovered where it was and ascertained that trains were still running to it. She had no idea, however, whether the Aminov palace was still standing. And an even greater doubt was whether she would be helped or denounced if she revealed any part of the truth to her husband's old nurse.

The wind when she arrived was bitterly cold and she could hardly drag herself from the station to the ridge on which the village was built. Had she not had a strong constitution she would have been dead long ago, and even as it was the weight of the baby and her under-nourished state had brought her very near to collapse. Only anxiety forced her on. She dared not enquire for the Aminov palace by name, but instead asked anyone she met on the street what building she was passing at that moment. The colonnaded square and magnificent domed church still indicated what an elegant centre the village had once provided for the noble families who used it as a healthy escape from the Petrograd swampland; but their palaces, each in its own estate, were scattered through the surrounding countryside.

At last a landmark enabled her to follow the directions which Vladimir had given her. As she trudged along the narrow track which had been beaten down through the snow, the light began to fade and she grew anxious at the possibility that she might have to retrace her steps in the dark. But the lodge, when it came into sight, was at least inhabited, even though it might prove to hold no welcome for her. The windows were obscured by frozen snow, but it was possible to see a gleam of light in the upper room.

First of all she must look to see whether there was any message. The dead tree by the gate was easily identified, but Kate stared with dismay at the blackened slit in its trunk which Vladimir must once have used as his post box. It was far too high for her to reach. He, as a boy, would have been agile, climbing the tree next in the row and dropping down to the leafless branch which stretched jaggedly out like a pointing finger. But for her, now, such a climb was impossible. Could even Vladimir have managed it in such icy conditions? Kate set down her bedding roll and moved round the tree, looking for some lower hiding place which he might have used instead.

There was nothing. Frantic with frustration, she fixed her eyes on the aperture, so near and yet so tantalizingly far. She found soft snow and carried it to pack round the trunk of the tree. She leaned her bedding against it and began to inch her way upwards. Her fingers touched the branch, searching for a hold. There was a crack in the surface and the wood was rotten; she pressed inwards, tightening her grasp, willing her arms to take the weight and allow her to pull herself upwards. But the bedding roll began to slip. She felt herself being stretched, uncertain whether to hang or to fall. Suddenly she was conscious of a violent pain, as though a horse had kicked her in the stomach; and at the same time she knew that the waters had burst and that the baby, too soon, was about to be born. She gave a single cry, of distress as much as of pain, and fell back to the ground.

It was not a long drop, but she fell awkwardly and was unable to move. Her muscles, tense with the first contraction of labour, refused to relax themselves. She remembered how Vladimir had commanded her to groan when the Cheka had stopped the train. It had been only a pretence then, but now – when the sound of pain would have been justified and might have brought help – her body seemed too tightly clenched to allow even the smallest whimper to make itself heard. Perhaps she was unconsciously defending the unborn child, endeavouring for a little longer to protect it in the safe warmth of the womb.

The black canopy of night unrolled itself above Kate's head and the snow began to fall again. As the chill of the ground penetrated her clothing she shivered for a while. Then, little by little, she relaxed in the soft warmth of the snow. From time to time her muscles tensed again, forcing her breath out in a grunt of pain: but between contractions she felt herself sinking into unconsciousness.

It was still dark when she awoke, but instead of bright stars in a wide velvet sky the blackness was broken by a spark which she recognized as the smouldering tip of a pine-bark taper. She was wrapped so tightly in blankets that she could hardly breathe, but although her skin was sweating with heat, her bones felt cold. Her head too, seemed to be frozen, so that she needed to lie for a little while without moving while she tried to remember what had happened.

As she struggled with her memory, so she absorbed the atmosphere. She was indoors, certainly, and to judge by the warmth which comforted her back she had been given the place in which any children of the house would normally sleep, on top of the big stove which served a country family for cooking and heat. There was a smell of smoke and uncured wolfskin, and the steady sound of a spinning wheel.

Cautiously, in case her head should hit the roof, Kate tried to sit up, but was at once conscious of pain. Her hand, swaddled inside the blankets, moved to feel her swollen abdomen and found instead a tender flatness.

Even then, alarmed and uncomfortable, she did not call out at once because she could not remember what language she ought to speak.

The sound of spinning stopped and a candle came near. Standing on the ledge at the side of their stove, a peasant couple looked down at her.

'I told you she was alive,' the woman said; and then, to Kate, 'He was sure you were dead, Comrade. But I said No, you were an icicle but icicles can be melted.'

'The baby,' said Kate. Her mouth was swollen, so that the words emerged indistinctly, but the woman understood.

'Yes, you have a baby. A baby girl.'

'Alive?'

'Alive, yes.' But the woman crossed herself as she spoke and Kate was afraid.

'May I see her?'

'She's not here,' said the man. He spoke more roughly than his wife. 'Do you think we could feed two extra mouths?'

'Be silent,' said his wife. 'How much food has the comrade taken from us? A spoonful of gruel, nothing more.'

'Where's my baby?' said Kate. As well as being frightened, she was unhappy. She had so much wanted to experience the birth of her child but it had happened in the end without her knowledge, as though her body were only a machine.

It was the man who answered again, in the same gruff voice. 'At the orphanage. What better place? It seemed that she was an orphan in the moment she was born.'

'Where is the orphanage? I must get her back.' For a second time Kate tried and failed to sit up.

'The orphans live in the old palace of the Aminovs,' said the woman. 'You can walk to it in ten minutes once you are strong enough. The child isn't lost.'

'But who will feed her? Who will look after her?'

'The holy saints will provide. Go back to your chair, Ivan Ivanovich, and leave me to women's work.' She fetched a bowl of water and set it down near Kate's head. But instead of washing her she leaned close and spoke in a whisper. 'You've come from *him*, haven't you? It's twenty years since he last slipped his messages into that tree, the young rascal. But no one has ever used it since. I watched you searching before you fell. You were looking for a letter. Tell me I'm right. It's *his* baby, is that right too?'

Kate did not answer immediately. Vladimir had been right to warn her that even the most devoted old servant could no longer be trusted to remain faithful. It could be a trap on the part of a clever old woman to send her surly husband away before making a show of friendship.

But she was probably not clever. And she had not yet abandoned her old faith. Now that Kate's eyes were accustomed to the lack of light, she could see the icon in the corner. Besides, if the baby was alive, her life must have been saved by the old woman's care, and who in such circumstances would harm a new-born child? If the baby was dead, Kate did not at this moment very much care what happened. 'Yes,' she whispered.

'Don't tell *him*,' said the old woman, making it clear that on this occasion the emphatic pronoun referred to her husband. 'He's afraid of the Red Guards. But he's not unkind. Truly, when he took the child away, he thought you were dead. Have you papers?'

'Yes.' Kate tried to fumble for her pocket but realized that her clothes had been taken off her. In any case, the woman gestured for her to be still.

'Not for me. How should I be able to read them? But I can tell *him* that there's no need of concealment. That will make his mind easier.' Her hand moved bonily over Kate's body, feeling her breasts. 'And you have milk. Good. Then the little one will not be a burden. Sleep now. Tomorrow, in the daylight, we will bring your baby back to you.'

2

Eight days later, with baby Ilsa in her arms, Kate stepped over the threshold of the Aminov theatre palace. Once upon a time – and not so very long ago – it had been a miniature Versailles, surrounded by terraces and fountains and by a park planted with trees in the English fashion. Inside the dignified building with its classical design and pale yellow walls, Vladimir and his brother and sister, with their Russian nurse and French and English governesses, had spent much of their childhood, surrounded by every comfort and luxury. Alexa had sung here – less than ten years ago – to an audience of Grand Dukes and Duchesses, Princes and Princesses. Kate – even in those far-off days disapproving of privilege – had stared in amazement at the diamond bracelet which represented the fee for a single evening's entertainment.

Alexa would not have recognized the palace now. The theatre itself was made of wood, although the fluted pillars which pretended to support the high painted ceilings gave the impression of being marble. They alone – perhaps for that reason – had survived undamaged. Everything else had been pillaged. The chandeliers had probably been smashed only out of spite, but the draperies must have been useful for clothing. The wooden balustrade of the tiered gallery in which the audience sat had already been chopped down for firewood, and now the elaborately patterned parquet floor was being prised up, block by block, for the same purpose.

The thickness of the atmosphere made it difficult at first to see the whole of the former auditorium. Smoke from a fire which smouldered in the middle of the hall mingled with the smells of cabbage and urine and body sweat. Stepping carefully over the bodies of children who lay alive but unmoving on the floor, Kate began to explore the building, her eyes widening in horror as her rough count of the inmates increased. The old woman, whom she had already learned to call *babushka*, had told her that the old name of Tsar's Village had been changed to that of Children's Village because as many of the parentless children of Petrograd as could be found were sent up to this higher area for their health. Kate held her baby even more tightly in her arms than before, realizing that if she had died, this would have been Ilsa's home.

Her explorations brought her in the end to what had once been a kitchen. On the only bed she had so far seen – its iron frame having presumably survived because it could not be burned – a middle-aged woman lay dead. A girl of about twelve or thirteen sprang to her feet at Kate's approach, almost attacking her in despair and agony.

'You're too late!' she cried. 'It's three days since I sent the message. How could she keep alive so long? Three days!'

'The message didn't come to me,' said Kate. 'Who is in charge here?'

'Who is there, now that *she* has gone?' The girl began to wail, as though for the first time admitting the death which must have taken place twenty-four hours earlier.

'But so many children! They can't just be abandoned. Hush now, don't cry. If I'm to help you, you must help me first. Tell me how you came to be here. And when you last had food. And how many of the children are sick. But first of all, tell me your name.'

The girl's name was Vera; between sobs she told her story. Her father had been killed at the front; her mother had died of typhus. She had been one of the first to be sent to the Aminov palace, and was amongst the oldest. There had been about eight hundred orphans in the building two months earlier, but almost all of them had had influenza. At first they had nursed each other, but by now they were all too weak. Vera did not know how many had died. Comrade Nina, the woman who lay dead on the bed, had done her best to provide rations for the children, but since she had become ill three weeks earlier they had had only what they could steal.

'Did she ever tell you who it was who allowed her the rations? Did the food come through the Red Guard or from the District Revolutionary Committee?' It was impossible for a stranger in any area to know whether the civil or military authority was locally in control, and important not to guess wrong.

Vera shook her head. But it was to the Red Guards that she had gone for help three days before. They had seemed kind enough, promising to pass on her message for a doctor to visit Comrade Nina and to arrange for a supply of food. But no doctor had arrived. They had given her a sack of frozen potatoes on the spot, but the man who offered to drag the sack back for her had stopped on the way and demanded to be paid for his trouble. When Vera had explained that she had no money, she had learned that a different kind of payment was envisaged.

At the memory she began to wail again. Kate comforted her briefly, but too much needed to be done for time to be wasted on what was past. Responsibility would provide the best distraction for Vera.

'I want you to look after my baby,' she said, putting Ilsa in the girl's arms as she spoke. 'She's very tiny and very precious to me, but I'm sure I can trust you to take good care of her while I go into the village and talk to the Revolutionary Committee. I've just fed her, so she'll be happy with you for the next three hours. And you can feel sure that I shall come back. I'm going to look after all of you here – and you will be my chief helper.'

She spoke more confidently than she felt. But the need was so great that action of any kind was bound to lead to some improvement. An hour later she was locked in argument with the chairman of the committee, a young railway engineer, as he pointed out the impossibility of finding food where no food existed and Kate reminded him of the community's responsibility to the children of their dead comrades. They both spoke with passion and the argument would have become heated had Kate not remembered how dangerous it was in these times to make enemies. Even under a self-imposed restraint, however, she could see that her arguments were having some effect. By mid-afternoon she was back at the palace, congratulating Vera on her success as a nursemaid and collecting a group of the oldest children to act as her aides.

None of them was over twelve and all of them were shabby and emaciated. Starvation had made some bright-eyed and others dull and apathetic but they all lacked energy and Kate saw few signs of intelligence. Patiently she explained to them several times how she proposed to put them into pairs and give each pair the responsibility for one room of the palace. They must bring her a report on the number of children in their room and say how many were dead, how many were ill, how many were hungry, how many were healthy.

While they were gone Kate – with Vera's help – drew a rough plan of the palace on the whitewashed wall of the kitchen, for she had no paper. She wrote in the numbers they brought her, she supervised the removal of those who were dead, she made quick plans for future organization. In the evening she went back to the committee, this time in full session.

'The children will become robbers,' she said. 'For three weeks already they've eaten only what they could steal. They've taken food which the peasants provide for their horses and they've burrowed into farm store rooms. Until now they've gone out in twos and threes, but they're becoming desperate, Comrades. If nothing is done you'll have an army of young bandits on your hands, organized and violent. If the peasants have food, it's better that they should surrender it to a legal authority.'

Kate knew well enough that this was already happening. Every town dweller in Russia believed that the countryside was full of hoarded food. Seizure was taken as a matter of course; only distribution was under debate.

The committee proved sympathetic enough in principle. Its chairman explained that one official orphanage had been established a year earlier in the palace formerly belonging to the Tsar. No one had realized how many children, drawn by the promise of shelter but failing to secure admission to the main orphanage, had established themselves in the neighbouring palaces of the old nobility. It seemed incredible to Kate – whose months in Petrograd had been regularly disturbed by official searches and checks and head-counts, with a continuing survey of papers and permits – that the men responsible for local administration should not have known the extent of the problem, but she accepted that this was the case as she saw them in turn accepting her right to speak for the inhabitants of the old palace.

In theory, at least, the battle was won. For one more night the children would have to exist on promises, but a supply of cabbage would be sent up the next morning and as soon as Comrade Katya supplied a written list naming all the living children a regular ration would be allotted.

With success in sight Kate tried to relax and found herself unable to move. She had started the day still weak from childbirth and from the hypothermia which had followed her collapse in the snow, and had committed herself to a timetable which was emotionally and physically exhausting. She was conscious of the blood draining from her face and the strength leaving her muscles as she tried, but failed, to stand.

The chairman of the committee looked at her curiously.

'You're not well, Comrade. When did you yourself last eat?'

298

Kate was reluctant to mention her stay with the old lodgekeeper's wife. So many actions these days which were innocent and even kind could cause trouble. Instead she muttered something about the recent birth of her baby.

'Then you will eat at my house before you return,' he said. 'My wife too has had a child and she assures me that every meal she takes herself keeps two people alive.'

For a moment Kate hesitated. Ilsa would be sleeping now, but would she be safe with Vera as the thirteen-year-old grew sleepy herself? And was it right to eat when the orphans were starving? The answers came quickly. Whatever food she was offered could not rob them in any way, and it was certainly true that an undernourished mother would not be able to breastfeed her baby for long. She accepted the invitation with gratitude.

The soup contained scraps of bacon fat, and there was bread on the table; it was a feast. But Kate dared not relax, for she found herself being interrogated as she ate – about the future as well as the past. It was necessary to come to a quick decision, and what she decided was that she would stay with the orphans. Their need for someone like herself was desperate. Kate knew herself to be capable of organization; and once she had obtained the basic essential of food and warmth, her medical skill would also be needed. It would be worthwhile work – and it would have the inestimable advantage of keeping her in the place which Vladimir had chosen for their reunion, without any of the suspicions which would have been aroused had she continued to visit the lodge without excuse.

But it was one thing to come to a decision and another thing to obtain permission. Since the first heady days of the Revolution Kate had had plenty of time to realize that a desire to do a particular job was often regarded as the most absolute disqualification. So when she was asked about her plans, she took care to mention her medical qualifications but replied in the properly orthodox manner.

'I shall be expected to return to Petrograd. My leave from the hospital was only granted so that I could travel to relations for my confinement. The baby came early, before I had reached them – and as a result I shall not be expected back for another three weeks. So I can afford to spend a little time here. I see the need to stay longer. But naturally my official duties as a citizen of Petrograd must come first.'

'I shall apply for your transfer,' he said abruptly. 'You are more use to us than to them. Your papers, please.'

Kate knew better than to go anywhere without them and had no doubts about handing them over to be inspected. Every move increased her security by distancing her from the time when she had been identifiable as an English doctor. Her marriage certificate had given her an official Russian name and Sergei's documentation had ensured that her qualifications and transfer to the appointment in Petrograd were thoroughly authenticated. This man, although brusque, would not be looking for discrepancies but seeking to use her medical skills for the benefit of his community. Even before he nodded and moved the dishes off his end of the table so that he could laboriously copy down details and prepare a letter, Kate recognized that – for the moment – she was safe. And Vladimir's child would be safe with her.

1920

1

Peace had come to England in drab dress. Even now, in 1920, with the second anniversary of the Armistice approaching, people in the London streets seemed shabby to Frisca's critical young eye, and the November sky was heavy with damp grey clouds. She stared down from the window of Robert's study, waiting for him to come home, depressed by what seemed a conspiracy of gloom against her.

Yet even when her spirits were low, Frisca herself illuminated the unlit room. There was a brightness about her which no temporary depression could subdue. Her golden hair and pale, clear complexion caught the eye, and an exuberance of personality, penetrated even her present sulkiness, uplifted the spirits of anyone who met her.

Frisca herself was well aware of the impression which she made even on strangers, and as a rule she traded on it shamelessly. But for the moment she was concerned to preserve the resentment she felt against her mother. She turned towards the door as she heard her cousin coming up the stairs, but did not move towards him.

A year earlier she would have rushed into his arms, demanding to be hugged and kissed. What held her back today was more than the sense of grievance which she was about to pour out. Ever since she was a baby Frisca had made it clear that Robert was her hero. Over and over again she had told him that she loved him. It had only been after her thirteenth birthday that she had begun to suspect that she *did* love him, in a manner quite different from anything which her earlier extravagance of compliment might suggest. And so – although her mother would have found the fact difficult to believe – Frisca had grown shy in Robert's presence.

Robert, it seemed, had not noticed any change. But then Robert himself had changed in the year which he spent as a prisoner of war. Frisca had been at Blaize on the day he returned there. She had found herself staring at someone who was almost a stranger, looking far older than his twenty-four years, with the skin stretched tightly over the bones of his face and his sunken eyes withdrawn and blackened with tiredness. His hair had only just begun to grow again after the shaving made necessary by a series of operations. Its bright red waves, which she had once loved to ruffle, had been replaced by a prickly stubble, with a small circle of baldness remaining to indicate the entry point of the bullet which had so nearly cost him his life.

On that day of his return, Frisca had run away to weep. And she had wept again often in the five weeks which followed when, sitting beside the bed in which he drowsed the days away, she realized that he was not exactly sure who she was.

It was her aunt who comforted her then, in a way which perhaps Margaret herself did not realize.

'He's had a bad time, Frisca, and he's very tired. You must be patient. It will take a little while before he sorts out what really happened and what he only dreamed. It's one of the effects of a wound in the head. Nightmares become more real than reality. He doesn't even remember very much about Jennifer, you know. I had to tell him she was dead. He told me how much he'd clung on to the thought of the happiness he'd had with her, and yet he wasn't absolutely sure whether it was something he'd truly enjoyed or whether he'd only dreamed it because he wanted it so much.'

It was in that moment that Frisca had realized how

302

completely her rival for Robert's affections had disappeared. Jennifer was more than dead: she had never quite existed.

By now, of course, Robert had recovered and remembered. He would always be deaf in one ear and Frisca had noticed that he was apt to become dizzy and lose his balance if he lowered his head too far – for example, to tie his bootlaces. He was more serious, as well, than before he went to fight. But he still seemed to regard Frisca only as a little cousin, to be romped with and teased. He greeted her now with a pretence of shock.

'And who is this long-legged creature? My, Frisca, how tall you're growing! Have you come up to London for Armistice Day?'

'Mother wants to spend the night at Glanville House. It's more because it's the anniversary of Poppa's death, I think.'

Frisca's real father had died before she was born. 'Poppa' was Lord Glanville, whom she had loved even before he married Alexa and became her stepfather. 'I came round to find out how your examinations are going.'

'Over,' said Robert. 'Last one today.'

'How did it go? Did you know all the answers?'

'Hope so. I'll be pretty fed up if I have to take any of them again. I can manage any practical job they set me, but all this book work gives me a headache.'

'What's the point of it, then?'

'Assuming I've passed, I'm now a qualified civil engineer. Rather different from being a military engineer. Instead of blowing bridges up or laying temporary railway tracks, I now know how to build them so that they'll last for ever; and the certificate which proves that I know should get me a job anywhere in the world.'

'But you won't *go* anywhere in the world, will you?' Frisca expected his reassurance and did not receive it. 'Robert! You're not going away?'

Robert's expression was a curious one, mingling excitement and uneasiness. 'I can't tell you anything yet, Frisca,' he said. 'I must talk to Mother first.'

'Oh do tell, Robert. I can keep a secret. I promise I won't say a word. Honour bright.'

She could see how much he wanted to share his news, and all her shyness disappeared as she took his hand and set herself to charm the secret from him.

'Well, not only must you keep quiet now, but when you hear the news from Mother you mustn't let on that you already know.'

'Promise!'

'All right, then. I was offered a job this morning – a job I applied for a few weeks ago. It depends on passing the exams, of course. But if that's all right, I shall go off to India in January.'

'India!' Frisca made no attempt to conceal her dismay, but Robert was too excited to notice.

'That's right. Down in the south. There's a big project afoot to build a series of dams. The people who live there have a terrible time. Either it rains too much and all the land floods and they get drowned. Or else it doesn't rain at all and all the crops die and they starve. The dams will help them both ways. They'll hold back the floods, and then release the water down irrigation canals when it's needed.'

'But it's so far away,' Frisca wailed, making no attempt to conceal her distress.

'I want to do something worth while, Frisca. If that bullet had killed me, I should have died without ever having been of any use to anyone. It wouldn't have been my fault then: I was too young. But if I die in ten years' time I want to leave something behind me which will make somebody grateful that Robert Scott was once alive. I spent too long killing people. Now I have the chance to help people live a little longer. Do you understand?'

'Aunt Margaret won't let you go.'

'I think she will,' said Robert. 'She won't like it. She'll be unhappy at first. That's why it's very important that you mustn't say anything to her at all. You must leave it to me. But Mother has spent the whole of her life helping other people. She'll be pleased, in her heart, that I want to do the same, even if it's in a different way and in a different place.'

Frisca was not convinced. Although in some respects she was selfish, demanding to get her own way and taking for granted the admiration she excited, she was sensitive to other people's feelings. She knew, for example, that Alexa, her own mother, had no very deep feeling for her, and she had learned this by recognizing the overwhelming love which her aunt Margaret felt for Robert. Frisca herself had been in a position to see how her aunt had changed in the two months after Robert's return. Once Margaret had survived the first shock of his appearance, all the strain and tiredness of her work at the hospital had fallen away. She looked ten years younger, and the bustle and energy with which she had organized the return to her London home while still occupied in winding down her responsibilities at Blaize had been those of a woman made happy by the presence of the one person to whom she was devoted. Frisca understood the feeling, because she shared it. Aunt Margaret would be very miserable indeed if Robert were to leave.

With such an ally, Frisca decided that she need not upset herself too much just yet. And even as she assured herself that Robert would not be allowed to go, she began to wonder whether it would after all be such a disaster if he did. In India, presumably, he would meet only Indian girls, and he would surely not want to marry one of them. He would work hard while he was out there and then at some time – when he was about thirty, perhaps – he would decide that it was time he looked for another wife. He would come home on holiday to find one – and in the meantime Frisca would have had time to grow up. It had been the only tragedy of her life that she was too young for Robert, and when he married Jennifer

305

she had thought that she must have lost him. But now she had another chance, and she was growing older all the time. Four years would be enough, or even three. If Robert went to India in January for three years she would be just seventeen when he came back. She was so intent on her calculations that she did not notice the firmness with which her cousin changed the subject.

'And now suppose you lell me why you were wearing such a face of thunder when I came into the room.'

'Was I?' Frisca had genuinely forgotten; but not for long. 'Oh yes. Robert, do you know what Mamma is going to do with me?'

'Tell me. One secret in exchange for another.'

'This isn't a secret, worse luck. It all started with my ballet teacher. Beastly old Benina. She measured my feet and my fingers and pretended she could tell from that how much I was going to grow. And she says I'm going to be too tall to be a ballet dancer. So I'm to be sent to prison instead.'

'Sounds a rather drastic solution,' agreed Robert, but he was laughing. 'I take it you mean you've got to go to school at last.'

'Yes. But why does it have to be beastly old boarding school? I agree with Mamma that Mademoiselle is useless and that we've both only put up with her because a ballet dancer doesn't need to be brainy. But there are other kinds of dancing besides ballet, and other kinds of school.'

'Not near Blaize. The village school would hardly be suitable.'

'Well, I could live in London and go somewhere every day instead of being bullied and starved and made to wear a beastly uniform.'

'I expect your mother wants to stay at Blaize, though.'

'Well, that's exactly it.' Frisca put on her most conspiratorial voice. 'She has her reasons for that, and for wanting me out of the way. She can't confess them, so she has to make up this ridiculous story about me being a giant.'

'I'm sure you're going to be an absolutely perfect height for being a beautiful woman, Frisca,' said Robert firmly. 'All that Benina means, I take it, is that it's no good if one cygnet or sugar plum fairy is waving her wrist about several inches above all the others. And you'll like boarding school. I did, tremendously. Even Grant's enjoying himself now, although at a boys' school it's difficult if you don't play games. You'll make hundreds of friends and have lots of fun. Why should Aunt Alexa want you out of the way, anyway?'

'So that I don't find out about the new man in her life. He's coming to live at Blaize. She's trying to pretend that he's family. In fact, she says he's a cousin of mine, but that's ridiculous. I've seen him. He's older than she is.'

'Who is he?'

'Matthew Lorimer, his name is.'

'Well then, he *is* your cousin,' said Robert. 'He's Arthur's elder brother. What's more, he was very badly hurt in the war. If you've seen him, you must know that he's in a wheelchair.'

'What's that got to do with anything?' Frisca demanded.

'Well, it means that he can't exactly be the new man in your mother's life in the way you seem to think.'

'Why not?' Frisca waited for an answer, but was not given one. 'I've seen the way they look at each other, Robert. *I* know when people are in love. She pretends it's all work, that he's just going to design a bit of scenery for her opera house. But that would only take a few weeks, and she's fitted up a whole new studio for him, big enough for him to move around in his wheelchair and paint people's portraits. He's moving in for good.'

'It's not easy for a man who's been badly wounded to build up his career again, Frisca,' said Robert firmly. 'You should be more tolerant. Your mother is Matthew's aunt, and if she's decided to help him, that's just generosity on her part. I'm sure she's very fond of him, but there couldn't be any question – '

Even if there had not been an interruption he would not have succeeded in convincing Frisca, but at this moment the maid knocked on Robert's door.

'If you please, sir,' she began; but she in turn was interrupted by his mother's voice calling from below.

'Robert! Robert, come quickly. There's a message from Russia. It's about Kate. She's alive!'

2

It was a new miracle, a second rising from the dead. Margaret read the message over and over again. First Robert had returned to life, and now Kate, although she had not come in person. Margaret looked at the one-armed stranger who had brought the letter. He had introduced himself in careful English as Sergei Fedorovich Gorbatov, but without explaining how he came to be acting as Kate's messenger.

'It gives no address,' she said.

'She lives as a Russian. No one at the orphanage where she works knows she is English. If the letter had been read and had provided enough details to be traced back to Katya, it would have had bad consequences for her. You must understand that the Civil War has caused harsh feelings in the country, and the support which the Whites have received from England is well known. It was the British blockade, too, which caused many deaths from starvation last winter. Katya has asked me to tell you that she dare not receive letters directly from you. If you care to give me any news of your family, I will write to her in Russian and pass it on in a way that does not reveal where you live.'

'If it's so dangerous for an Englishwoman to live there, she ought to come home,' said Robert. 'If you were

308

allowed to leave the country, sir, presumably she would be as well.'

'It's not easy to get permission,' Sergei said. 'I'm allowed to travel because I'm on a government mission. I don't think Katya's papers would stand up to the inspection needed for a passport. But the truth is that she has chosen to stay.'

'Read the letter, Robert.' Margaret passed it across. In the excitement and shock of its arrival she had kept it to herself, only exclaiming aloud over the facts it revealed. 'She's married a Russian, but apparently he's disappeared. She has to stay where he can find her if he ever turns up. She has a little girl, as well, who must be about the same age as Barbara.'

'This is not only a matter of family,' said Sergei. 'The work she is doing is of great value. If I were to tell you how many children were orphaned in our country by the years of war you would hardly be able to believe me. Katya is the doctor for two thousand of them. They are all undernourished and some of them are maimed and in winter most of them are cold. There is plenty for a doctor to do, I can tell you. I have the greatest admiration for your niece, Madame. I met her first in Serbia – it was she who taught me my first words of English. From the very first day of our friendship one thing has been clear to me; that she has no barriers of nationality in her mind. When she sees a need, she hurries to fill it. She has seen such a need in the orphanage. She told me that you yourself had undertaken the same kind of work once and that you would understand.' Sergei paused for a moment. 'My affection for your niece is very deep. You must believe that. If she had asked me to help her leave the country, I would have done everything in my power. But she made no such request. She has made the decision to stay, and I respect her for it.'

'What happened to her husband?' asked Robert.

'She married a prince. A dangerous choice in these

times. At the moment when his identity was discovered he was travelling on permits signed by myself, so for a little while it seemed that the danger might be contagious. But I was able to prove that he must have stolen them. His rank, of course, makes it impossible for Katya to enquire openly about his fate and in her own interest I have made sure that no one could connect the doctor at the orphanage with a man – one of many men – arrested by the Cheka.'

'Was he killed? Does she know what has happened to him?'

'She will not believe that he is dead. She hopes.'

'And you. Do *you* know the truth? Have you told her?'

Sergei gestured with his hand in a manner which could have meant any of several contradictory things, and Margaret felt a moment's uneasiness. They had greeted the stranger as a friend because he brought good news, but everything they knew about Russia since the revolution, and everything he was telling them now, built up a picture of a society ruled by suspicion, in which any kind of knowledge might spell danger. Could he be a government spy and not a friend at all, looking for information which might incriminate Kate in a way her English relations could not even imagine? Or could he, on the other hand, be more than a friend – in love with her, perhaps, and anxious to keep her in Russia so that he could marry her himself one day? So many horrifying stories of betrayal and death had come out of Russia in the past three years that Margaret did not know what to believe. If Kate's husband were really dead, she ought to come back to the safety of her own country. There was plenty for a doctor to do in England as well. As definitely as she could, Margaret made her opinion clear to the Russian, but once again he merely shrugged.

'Any message that you give to me, I will pass on,' he said. 'If you tell me that you have a home and a welcome waiting for her here, I promise that I will explain that to her. But I think you should not hope too much. Katya is a woman of great determination and strong loyalties. You know that for yourselves, I'm sure. She could have returned to England when she was forced to leave Serbia. When she made the decision to stay with a defeated army she was well aware that nothing but danger and discomfort lay ahead.'

Margaret was silent, knowing that this was the truth. She excused herself for a moment while she sent a message to Alexa at her house in Park Lane. By the time she returned to the drawing room she was already half reconciled to accepting what Sergei had said. She invited him to stay for the night, but was not surprised when he refused, agreeing only to dine with them. Doubtless he was no more anxious than Kate to be suspected of having friends in England. So all that remained when the meal was over was to dictate to Sergei the news of everything which had happened to the family in the past four years.

'She knows of her brother's death,' Sergei said. 'The news upset her very greatly and it was because he died, I think, that she was committed to the ideals of the Revolution even before it began. And it's because of his death that she cares so deeply for the orphans who are still alive.'

There were other deaths to report: Kate's father, Alexa's husband, Robert's wife – although Kate would not even know that Robert had ever married, or that he was the father of a daughter who was almost three years old by now.

'But there is good news as well,' Margaret said. 'Her younger brother, Grant: tell her that he lives in England now and that an operation has made it possible for him to walk much more easily. And as a result he has become a happier boy.'

'And a fitter one,' said Robert. 'I've never known such a chap for doing exercises. When I think how fat and lazy he was when he first arrived! Now he seems determined to set himself endurance tests. Where an ordinary boy would do an exercise ten times, nothing less than a hundred is good enough for Grant. He's becoming very tough indeed.'

'He will take over her father's property in Jamaica when he is old enough, I suppose,' suggested Sergei.

'No.' Margaret hesitated, wondering how far it was safe to entrust a stranger with news which would come as a shock to Kate. 'No, the land was left to one of Kate's childhood friends, Duke Mattison.'

'She has spoken of him to me. The clever black boy, with a talent both for figures and for – ' The word for 'bowling' had obviously escaped Sergei; instead he swung his one arm vigorously to indicate what he meant.

'Yes, he's a good cricketer. Kate ought to be told, perhaps, that he inherited both his talents from his father. Her father.'

By his smile Sergei showed how confident he was that Kate would not mind. He waited with patient interest for the next piece of information.

'What other good news is there?' asked Alexa, who had joined them for dinner to celebrate Kate's being alive. She had been pale when she first arrived, interrupted in a vigil of remembrance for her husband, but now her normal vivacity had returned, as though she had consciously made a decision to change her mood. 'You could tell her that her cousin Arthur has been given a baronetcy to go with his fortune – which may now be a little less than before the honour was bestowed. So when he chooses a wife, she will be Lady Lorimer. He must be the most eligible bachelor in Bristol, for he's still unmarried. Be sure to tell Kate that.'

It was unkind of them all to laugh, Margaret thought, as she saw that the family reference could only puzzle Sergei. But he added the name to the notes he was making without showing any reaction and then looked across at Frisca, who had been specially allowed to join the adults at dinner.

'And from the evidence of my own eyes I can tell her how beautiful is her young cousin,' he said, bowing slightly as he paid the compliment. Margaret, who agreed with it, noticed that Frisca glanced at Robert and flushed very slightly before laughing it off in her usual self-assured manner.

'Since it may be years before we see Kate again,' Frisca said, 'she'd better have our future news as well as what's happened in the past. You can tell her that I'm going to be a great dancer, even if I *am* a foot taller than anyone else on the stage.'

'Well, if we're to talk about the future, she may like to know what's happening at Blaize,' Alexa added. 'That's the name of my house in the country,' she explained for Sergei's benefit. 'Before Kate left for Serbia, she helped to turn it into a hospital for wounded soldiers. Now the house has been restored as a home, and the theatre will open again for opera next summer.'

She went on to give details of the productions she planned in a way which Margaret felt would be of limited interest to Kate, so far away and in such a different society. Margaret allowed her attention to wander, realizing that the significance of the conversation only indirectly related to what was being said. Alexa's emergence from her bereavement was almost complete. She was no more than forty-three years old and it was right that she should have picked up the threads of her life again and made plans for the years to come. When the enthusiastic flow of words came to an end, Margaret looked at her son.

'And what about you, Robert? What message will you send to Kate about the future?'

In the silence which followed, Margaret knew at once that something was wrong. The Russian was merely waiting politely to hear what else he should note; and Alexa's expression, too, revealed nothing more than a normal interest. But Frisca was almost literally holding her breath, while Robert's face reminded his mother of that earlier occasion when – knowing that she was bound to disapprove – he had broken the news to her that he had volunteered for the army.

'Well?' she asked.

'I have some plans, certainly,' said Robert. He made the admission with reluctance. 'But I'd like to discuss them first of all with you, Mother.'

'That means that Kate will never know. And after such an ominous hint, I shan't be able to sleep until I know what you're proposing. So you might as well confess at once.'

She tried to keep her voice light as she spoke, and with a similar effort sought to maintain an untroubled expression on her face as Robert, still reluctantly, told her of his intention to go to India. The blow fell on her like a landslide. He must have realized it, because he came across and sat on the arm of her chair, putting his hand on her shoulder.

'You have responsibilities here,' was all she allowed herself to say. 'Barbara.'

'Yes, I know.' His grip tightened for a moment. 'I can't go without your co-operation. That's why I wanted to talk about it privately with you.'

'We'll think about it tomorrow, then,' she said. Her attempt to pretend that nothing disturbing had taken place evidently did not deceive her visitor, who put away his notebook and stood up to take his leave.

'But you have to let us know where Kate is!' exclaimed Margaret. Her voice quavered under the two shocks of the evening. Just as Robert, who had earlier returned from the disappearance which might too easily have signified his death, was about to leave again, so too it seemed that Kate had only briefly come back to life and would now slip into invisibility in the blackness of a closed society. 'I understand everything you've said about the danger to her of having connections in England. But in case something really important should happen – here or there – we must have some idea of where to look for her. You've told us that because of your own affection for Kate you would never do anything to harm her. Well, you must believe that our love is at least no less than yours. We won't write to her, but we need to know where she is.'

Sergei had already taken Margaret's hand as he prepared to say goodbye to her. For a moment he stared steadily into her eyes. 'Knowledge that cannot be used is like a long fuse leading to a hidden bomb,' he said. 'The day comes when it is tempting to light the fuse, just to see where it leads.' He lifted her hand to his lips but, although his manners might be pre-revolutionary, Margaret recognized the ruthlessness with which he was rejecting her plea.

After he had gone and Frisca had been taken home to bed by Alexa, Robert lingered for a moment in the drawing room; but Margaret knew that she was too upset to be either kind or rational.

'After the service tomorrow,' she said. 'We'll think about it then.'

But the next day, Armistice Day, imposed thoughts of its own. Margaret's house in Queen Anne's Gate was so near to Westminster Abbey that the family party did not emerge until an hour before the procession bringing the body of the Unknown Warrior for burial was due to arrive at the abbey. They found the streets already packed with men and women dressed in black. Margaret had not expected that the crowd would be so great, and – because she was not tall – realized that she would see nothing of the ceremony.

She would hear it, however. Six years earlier Brinsley had left for France to the sound of a military band. Now the sound of another military band brought back memories of his departure, but it was a different sound –

not the cheerful strains of Tipperary, with fifes and piccolos disporting themselves in high-pitched mischief, but the slow, muffled drum beat of a funeral march. And it was greeted not with the cheers of a crowd which could have no conception of what lay ahead, but with the tears of a nation which had had time to count the cost. Three-quarters of a million men had gone out to fight and had not returned. Now one of them was being brought home.

The sound came nearer, masking the slow footsteps of the escort. Military orders were given: the music stopped. There was a curious stiffening as the men in the crowd straightened their shoulders and held up their heads until, without any ostentatious movement, they were standing at attention. The women, by contrast, bowed their heads as though they were in church. During the hours of waiting there had been conversation and movement, but when the slow drum beat came to an end, the crowd became quiet and still. Thousands of living people, sharing a single emotion, were together – and spontaneously – paying tribute to the silence of death.

Intense and oppressive, the absolute silence extended for what seemed a very long time. It was broken in the end not by any sound but by an almost imperceptible change in the atmosphere as the men and women in the crowd began to listen for the muffled sounds of the burial rites. Margaret's concentration, too, was broken, and she could not prevent her thoughts from returning to the bombshell which Robert had dropped on the previous evening.

In her mind the two subjects merged. There was a connection between what was happening in the abbey and Robert's plans for the future – although an hour earlier she would not have been able to recognize it. She had not been conscious of any change of heart during the long and emotional silence, but at the end of it she had accepted a new idea. The partings and losses of the war must be seen for what they were – memories, not a continuing part of everyday life. Those who had died were dead: those who were still alive must make plans for their future lives – otherwise, what point would there be in their survival?

It was right that everyone should look ahead: that Frisca should dream of dancing, that Alexa should shake off the grief of her bereavement and plan for the reopening of her theatre, that Matthew should come to terms with his injuries and refuse to let them bring his career as an artist to an end. It would not be reasonable to expect that Robert alone should stand still, frozen in the role of the only son of a widow, returning from the dead and bound to stay within her sight in order to reassure her that he was still alive. Margaret was glad that she had managed to control her first reaction of distress at Robert's news.

He would come back, after all. This would be a different kind of parting from those of the war years. Robert would build his dams and then come home again. And in the meantime he would leave Barbara behind to give her grandmother, like everyone else in the family, a window to the future.

From the door of Westminster Abbey came the clear, poignant sound of a bugle playing the Last Post. Margaret could see tears on many of the faces around her, but she lifted her own head high in a determination to be happy. Frisca still needed her love and support and for Grant and little Barbara she would for many years be the only family they could call their own.

I am a lucky woman, Margaret told herself – for what pleasure would retirement have had to offer with nothing to do? When the crowd began to disperse she put her arm round Robert's waist, hugging him gently; and as he looked down at her she accepted all his plans by her smile. The war had cast a long shadow, and perhaps she had been slow to recover from its pains and partings. But it had ended two years ago, and it was time to free herself of its fears, to step out of the gloom and into the sunshine. It was good that her son should look into the future and see only peace and happiness ahead.